Ringling

The Last Laugh

a novel
by Michael Lancaster

Published by **Ballyhoo** Publishing

First Edition May 19, 2012

ISBN - 978-0615655925
ISBN - 0615655920

Cover art: Jennifer Drumm
Cover Photos: (front) Ron McCarty
and Lancaster family archives
(back)
Courtesy of The Hertzberg Circus Collection
of the Witte Museum, San Antonio, Texas

This novel is inspired by true events. It is a fictionalized biography. Although some real historical names of the persons portrayed in these pages are used, many names have been changed. Many of the events are not factual. The intent is to convey the Ringling story.

A portion of the proceeds from sales of this book will be donated to animal welfare organizations. To find out what organizations are being supported visit www.ringlingbook.com.

In memory of my Aunt Knobby, Alice Lancaster, and my
Father, Stuart Lancaster

and

For my daughter, Amrit Ringling Lancaster

Contents

Introduction   i

All Out and All Over 1936   1

One
The Boys from Baraboo   9
(me) John
Al
Otto
Alf T.
Charley and Me
Gus
Henry
Ida
Papa and Mama

Two
Under Canvas   43
Amusement
A Big Charivari
First Steps
No Runs

Three
The Mud, the Blood, and the Shit   65
The Mud and the Blood
A Drink at Rice Station
Our Best Years

Four
The Elephant   75
Chicago
The Working Spur
I Have Seen the Elephant
The Rose Garden
The Players Club

Four (cont.)
From Moons to Elysian Fields
Excerpts from the Diary
of Armilda (Mable) Burton 1889 - 1905

Five
Big Ideas   125
Shell Beach
It Seemed Like a Good Idea at the Time
Broken Chain
My Debt
The Baraboonians
Is He dead?
The War Horse

Six
Lightning Strikes   155
Ablaze
The Thorn Garden
A Show Without Ringlings
Me, Me, Me
What I Borrowed

Seven
In My Shadow   213
Sam
The Bullman
Black Clouds
Art School
Salome and the Secret Garden
Excerpts from The Later Diary of ..
Mable Burton Ringling 1922 - 1929
The Donniker Man
High Stakes Marriage

Eight
What Goes Around   259
  The Last Laugh
  Days of Golden Memories
  The Long Ticket Line
  Requiem for a Showman

Glossary of Circus Terms   *281*
The Fifty One Rules   *305*
Acknowledgements   *309*

Introduction

The long journey of life takes us down winding and twisting routes. Sometimes it appears in front of us as such a straight and undeviating path, until we step on it, and like a dream, it rolls out before us in unimaginable directions. Some people say that circus is like that. Everything prepared, every route, every stand, every run, planned with meticulous attention to detail. Then off we go and everything unexpected happens. That's what makes it exciting. That's what makes it dangerous. Only when we get to closing day, the last stand, an empty lonely place where the reflective self can turn around and look back over the entirety of what has transpired, only then can we see the story that has happened. A story happened here. When it was over, there was so much unsettled dust, so many battles, and so many fractures that most of its characters had not seen what had happened because they had lived it – deeply.

I began writing this story from a point of view that came from my side of the family. That point of view made John Ringling a villain and my great grandfather Charles Ringling a hero. Charles was a brilliant man and was able to multitask: run a city of fourteen hundred people, a big circus family – performers and musicians, carpenters and metal smiths – that Charley would feed, house, and educate; a circus town with a post office, barber shop, church, and school; an enormous circus extravaganza that under Charley's direction would unload and reload onto a train, the entire lot in one day. On the other hand, John Ringling was not the man I thought he was. After thirty years, I am finally putting it all together. He was a visionary, and although he had shortcomings, his brilliant legacy lives on. This is not just a circus story. This is a human story.

My fascination with the family circus started around the time that my parents were divorced. I had to move all the way from Sarasota, Florida, to Albany, New York, to register the feeling I got when I stood on the back lot and spoke with some of the actors. I was just older than a toddler. My great grandmother, "Mrs. Charley," had died just two years before I was born. She had shared so many stories with my Aunt Knobby, Alice Lancaster, and my father, Stuart Lancaster. I had to receive the family stories secondhand, but always I could feel something scary and magical as they reached out and pulled me in.

My memories of family and friends associated with the circus were vague and fragmented. At age twelve my stepfather announced that the circus was being sold. When I pressed him about it, he told me it was the Ringling Brothers and Barnum and Bailey Circus, The Greatest Show On Earth.

"Sold out of the family?" I questioned him. "I didn't even know that the family was still involved!"

I remembered a bit about it, but it was distant. Oddly, it was just a few months later that my father came for a visit. He had been shooting a film titled *Born Losers*, and I thought my mother had said he was a born loser. I did not know him, a funny and overly skinny tall man, and the entire visit was quite unusual. He did talk about the circus and how he had even been a vice president at one time. He pointed to a few books in my parents' library and said our family history was there. My interest grew, however soon to be stifled when an older kid almost beat me up in school when he thought that I made up my family relationship to the circus.

The following spring my mom brought me and a friend to opening night at Madison Square Garden to see the show. I think it all hit home when she brought us to the back lot to meet the people she had once loved in Sarasota. My mother, portraitist Betty Warren, had painted at winter quarters in Sarasota, Florida, during the eight years she was married to my father Stuart Lancaster. It was a connection that reawakened something in me. She introduced me to people, such as George Henderson, the veterinarian who had worked for Ringling Bros. for decades, and Emmett Kelly, whose voice held all the silent, happy, and sad years of the greatest character clown of all time.

"Which one is this?" Emmett asked, "Johnny or Michael?"

"Oh Emmett," she said, as if he should have known by my age, "this is Michael. He's twelve now." She placed her proud hand on my head. "This is Emmett Kelly," she said, somewhat pointing my head towards him. We shook hands, and frankly I was a bit scared as he looked totally the part of the hobo character clown he was so loved for. But I will never forget the soft round voice, the absolute kindness in his self-expression. It was something I would later find exists in many a circus actor. It's as if the roughness of the road and rails, the hard work, and the family of actors who all pull together take the edge off a person, making them softer, more empathetic. Circus people "double in brass," which means they all throw in together sharing different jobs and responsibilities, in order to make the whole show work. As time goes on, this tradition has changed, but those of The Greatest Show On Earth who have lived through the majority of the first half of twentieth century, deeply understand this term.

It wasn't until 1981, just before my wedding, that I realized I had to tell the story. Throughout the year I had been getting acquainted with my father, as it seemed a good thing to do if I was going to get married. I would sit up late with Stuart, on the grounds of the former summer stock theater where not only he and my mother first met, but my wife-to-be and I met. I couldn't get enough of the stories of the circus, and I would beg him to tell me more. Stuart was an actor, and having worked with the circus, he had a feeling for it and a way of recalling what he had been told, and in circus style he could embellish, combine stories, dates and times, and recreate the feeling that was The Greatest Show On Earth.

This is the story of the five Ringling boys from Barbaoo, Wisconsin. It may not be the accurate retelling of circus route books and the hundreds of thousands of miles logged by the original shows. Against my Aunt Knobby's wishes I am telling this story from the point of view of John Ringling, "The Circus King." My great grandfather was Charles Ringling, aka "Mr. Charley." The revered four brothers, always known by Mr. and their first names, Al, Alf T., Otto, and Charley, brought an authenticity to their enterprise in a different manner than John. It is possible as John lost his grip on the family dream that he came to regret his shortcomings, the mishaps, and his myriad mistakes that made this story rags to riches and back to rags again. This is John's story, Ca' d'Zan, "The House of John," as he built it, and the pounds of flesh that it took from his soul at the end of his life: the end of the "Golden Age of Circus."

I have titled it *Ringling, The Last Laugh* because I believe there is more to this than just what the route books and history books tell. Recently a circus librarian told me that if we had an event and there were five different journalists standing right there, you would get five different versions of what actually happened. Times and dates may blend together, people and places merge, and the great theater of circus tells its own story. As I share the stories that have been passed down to me, I have followed and remain true to as much history as possible. There are many writers and circus historians to thank and acknowledge for their contributions. I am not writing a history book, but if you want history, it can be found in the many pages which can only agree on what the route books have logged. The rest of the story is what dreams are made of. This story is an American story. The five Ringling brothers believed in having a dream, formulating a way to manifest it, and then working hard to bring those dreams about. It worked because they had more than a product; they had a system of beliefs, and all of it was based in making people happy. There is a circus story in it, but I hope that as I tell this story you will hear your own calling, your own great magnanimity, and marvel at possibility, and maybe, just maybe, you too will get to work and make your dreams come true.

All Out
and All Over
1936

As a roustabout held a door open, John Ringling stepped into a dark back alley outside of Madison Square Garden. Ringling paused and leaned on his two canes. A swirling mass of paper, candy funnels, and ketchup covered litter tangled around his canes and shoes. He ignored the trash and struggled to straighten his hat, worn at its edges and just picked from the dirt and sawdust. "Good night Mr. Ringling," the roustabout muttered regretfully. Ringling turned, leaning on one cane and holding the other sideways, as the roustabout retreated back, and the light from inside disappeared as the door clenched closed. He headed toward the street accompanied by the humming of a light at the intersection of the alley and the street. The wind rushed around the corner, and it was hard to distinguish whether or not the drizzle had met his eyes – or were they tears?

"Little shit bastards," he mumbled, "think they can run my show. Pissants." As Ringling reached the sidewalk, a handful of young boys, from little to teenage, ran right into him.

"What, hey, watch where you're going you little..."

"Hey mister you watch where *yur* goin!" A main door opened and the sound of the crowd inside roared out the door. The eldest boy corralled the rest, "C'mon, it's already started," and they ran off toward the ticket office. As snow landed on Ringling's formal clothes, it became apparent that they were stained, a seam ripped open, and there was sawdust on the buttocks of his ripped pants. He looked up as snow and drizzle fell and the light blinded his eyes.

He was sixteen when they loaded their instruments into the wagon. The wagon with its three bench seats glimmered under the gas lamp, as snow fell, and John could see three of his brothers sat contemptuously waiting for the younger. As he climbed in, sitting in the third row with his brother Charles, then eighteen, Al, the eldest, turned and said, "We would have left without you, but Charley was quick to your defense." At that the driver gave a snap to the reins and the wagon started off, the back full of instruments, baggage, and trunks. Only three blocks away they came to a stop where young Ned Kimball was climbing out his second story window and shimmying down a drainpipe. Already standing by in grownup attire, too large for his small frame, was Tommy Baird, carrying instrument cases for the two of them.

Without nearly a word the two were in the wagon, which headed south toward Sauk City. Sauk City was two to three hours and the first train stop. The wagon, uncovered, made for absolute discomfort as wet November snow continued on and off for the journey. In Sauk City they were delivered almost in silence to the train station. There they stood outside a darkened train for two hours watching their breath by gaslight and returning stares to older fellows whose eyes seemed to question how such a young troupe could be traveling without parents. Al, however, was thirty and experience seemed to emanate from his dark eyes and huge mustache which adorned most men of the time. Alf too was a man but had the look of a small town boy and lacked the assurance of a man who had seen the world or some part of it as had Al. All were well dressed and sported the bowlers of the day. When the doors were opened and the lamps lit, the boys made their way into the car and took their seats.

"Best if we all get some sleep before we arrive in Mazomanie," Al half ordered and part gaped out a yawn. It was dawn and they were leaving home. They awakened to the conductor calling out "Mazomanie."

Departing the train, they clumsily gathered clutches, trunks, and instruments. From there they wandered in ungainly procession through the snow dusted streets and made their way to the Main Street Hotel, where they ate breakfast and defended curious glares and stares from locals. In the little dining room, the Ringlings got the first small town assessment of their fresh, youthful troupe of performers whose yellow "Ringling Classic Concert and Comic Co."

handbills were in every storefront window in town, including the hotel restaurant. They ate mostly in nervous silence with few interruptions.

"Pass the butter."

"Mm... more coffee please."

"Thank you ma'am."

"Otto sure did a fine job on the handbills."

"Mm-hum."

The entire time most of their attention remained fixed on the small crowd outside, although they pretended not to notice. After breakfast they held a rehearsal in the village playhouse where they were to play that evening and followed that with a parade down Main Street. The day was bitter cold, and their hands fumbled around instruments they had played so well rehearsing at home. Still, they held their parade amidst a town full of people who seemed to know that these Ringlings "come from over in Baraboo."

Less than half the seats were filled, and the performance ran together like spilled paint as every possible thing that could go wrong – did. While the sound of their musical performance was garbled, half the jokes and amusing stories went without so much as even a giggle from the audience. It culminated in sitting in the hotel and Al counting up the funds.

"Well, how'd we make out?" asked John full of inquisitive innocence.

"Nine dollars," Al answered.

"We made nine dollars! That's tremendous," said Charles.

"No, after we pay the hotel and the food and board we're *down* nine dollars," Al responded in disgust. "We have five dollars and fifty cents left. I wonder how Otto's doing? He should be almost a week ahead now."

Next morning they rose to the sound of gale force winds. Al scratched the frost from the window pane in their hotel room, revealing a whiteout of blowing snow. Worse still, the hotel keeper had informed them that the train was not running. Al turned from the menacing frosted window, "If we don't play in Black Earth tonight we're surely gonna go broke." He tried to keep his tone matter of fact. "Sure as shit Otto's booked the hall like he said he would, and we'll be out four dollars more."

After they settled the bill with the landlord, they each grabbed as many bags as they could carry at once, and another lodger held the door open, commenting on the horror that awaited them, "Since you ain't gonna see nothin' out there, turn left and go a block and a half to the livery. It's on this side of the street. Good luck fellas." He chuckled sarcastically as if he knew they hadn't a chance in hell of making the livery, let alone getting a driver to take them to Black Earth.

Feeling the walls of the various buildings in town, they began to fumble their way down the block and on into the livery. Faces wrapped in scarves, the snow and ice clung to the wool and hardened their mask-like appearance. When they finally found the livery and opened the large door, it took three youngsters to push the door closed against the wind. An hour later they were bundled in an old flat springless teamster wagon drawn by two horses, driven by the livery master who was old enough to be their grandfather. Plunging through snow drifts and a blizzard so thick it seemed they were riding a wagon of death. They had delivered their best performance and convinced the livery master that they had a huge show already sold out and that they could pay him when they arrived in town.

"We could die out here," John screamed to Al who was barely a foot away.

"Kind of old man Scott to take us," he shouted back.

"Keep on, Silty!" old man Scott shouted, using everything he had to keep his horses moving; yet one faltered, stumbled, and fell at a drift. The long hair on the horses' legs was encrusted with chunks of ice and snow, which made them a sorry sight with waving chunks of ice, against the stark white storm. "It's alright there darlin's," called Scott. He kept the horses moving under the only light, the white of snow, even though they couldn't see the road. Bang! The wagon stopped abruptly as they snagged over something, maybe a stump, solid and heavy.

"Tarn shitass! Sorry boys, this may be the end of your travels." Momentarily everything went silent as the winds let up only long enough to make the silence deafening. Then the wind and snow returned like an angry roaring beast. No one, not even old man Scott spoke. It was as if the road had run out.

Old John Ringling reached the street. Behind him was Madison Square Garden, an enterprise that John and his old pal Tex Rickard had built from its predecessor, the second Garden designed by Stanford White. The marquis read "Ringling Bros. Barnum & Bailey Greatest Show On Earth"; "Opening Night - 52nd Season." Traffic roared by, horns honking, and Ringling stood, leaning on both canes, largely unnoticed by the seemingly soulless hubbub of noise and passing fray. A limo passed close into the curb and sprayed him with slush. Motionless, he acted as if nothing had happened. Seconds later a taxi stopped in front of him and the back door opened, "Izzat you John Ringling?" a voice called from inside the cab. John said nothing but stared blankly into the darkened back seat. The man leaned forward, "It's me – Ed. Ed Strongin." John paused, speechless for a moment and then responded, "Ed Strongin. How the hell are you?"

"Never better John. Hey – why ain't you in with the show?"

"Not my show anymore, Ed."

"What the hell, I mean what..?"

Looking down and half turning away, John answered, "It's a long story, maybe too long." The taxi held up traffic and from behind, a car honked. It was John's limo, a 1922 Rolls Royce, once beautiful and new, now, like John, worn, out of fashion, yet still a sign of opulence, albeit fourteen years old.

"C'mon John, get in, I'll buy you a drink."

John signaled his driver to follow, and without a word Ringling climbed in. Strongin handed Ringling a flask, and he gladly took a swig from it. There was little conversation between the two as they passed through the Flatiron district and headed toward Union Square. John's attention was outside. He studied all the old haunts, the neighborhood of the old Madison Square Garden, the place where so much of the second half of his life had begun. Then they arrived at Luchow's. It was not unfamiliar to Ringling. Before prohibition he and Mable had spent many nights there, the gay parties, the huge garden restaurant. August Luchow had come over from Hanover, Germany, as had August Ringling, John's Father. Much of the restaurant had closed down with Prohibition, but Luchow's was the first bar in New York to get a liquor license when it all was coming back. They sat at the bar, in front of a bartender John remembered as a young busboy.

"Whiskey, Jimmy," Ed asked with familiarity. The bartender, Jimmy, eyed Ringling, his dirty clothes, worn and old. Ed saw Jimmy giving Ringling the once over.

"You know who this is Jimmy?"

"No, Mr. Strongin, I don't," Jimmy said smugly.

"This is John Ringling. *The* John Ringling!" he replied with his hand on John's shoulder.

"You don't say. Thought I recognized you Mr. Ringling." John looked at the bartender and then at Ed, "I am afraid I am without cash fellas."

"No worries Mr. Ringling," Jimmy offered, "drinks on me. You and your family have given me and mine a lifetime of fun." With that Jimmy poured the men a drink and placed a bottle of whiskey on the bar.

"Now, what's this all about, I mean, not being your show and all?" Ed asked.

"Those fucking cocksuckers, especially Sam Gumpertz shafted me right up the ass." John swore like he couldn't even hear himself.

"I'm sorry Mr. Ringling," Jimmy the bartender said, leaning in close, "this is a family joint, you gotta keep the swearing to a minimum – please."

"Sorry Mr. Jimmy, it's been a hard day and I just lost control." Ringling sipped at his drink, keeping the glass in his hand. "Mable never liked my swearing. After she died there was no one left to pull in the reins."

"No problem Mr. Ringling, you understand though?"

"I do, and again I apologize. Like I said, it's a long story." John took a slow sip.

"I got all night pal," Ed said, inviting Ringling to tell his story.

"You gotta cigar Ed?"

"Havana's finest, bud." Ed pulled out a cigar and a cutter from a his overcoat. He opened the cigar case, carefully and ceremoniously allowing the cigar to slide into his hand. He snipped the end, handed it to John, and pulled forth a match.

"Light?"

Jimmy quickly pulled out a Ronson lighter and offered it to Ringling. "If you don't mind, gentlemen, my boss don't want matches scratchin' the bar."

"Jimmy," Ed responded, "a good smoke is best lit with a wooden match."

"Let me just hold it awhile," John replied, smelling it. "I'm only allowed one a day now. Heart problems, you know."

"So I heard, John."

John studied the cigar a long while. Holding it in his right hand, long artistic fingers, he rolled it in a circle. It was obvious that his hand did not function fully. Jimmy was wiping a glass, but his attention was on John, in anticipation.

"We started small you know," John began.

"I know, I read about it, a little concert company or something – right?"

"No, smaller still. It was after we saw our first circus, a riverboat show, in McGregor, Iowa. I was four. My eldest brother Al was eighteen. At that time there were six of us, but one, Gus, at sixteen thought it was silly child's play. I guess it was. But ain't that what dreams are made of? Child's play?"

"I guess."

"I mean, me age four, Charley six, Alf seven, Otto twelve, and Al eighteen. We all got it in our blood early. We went out to the barn and made our own paint and started making sets. Those early circuses had more scenery. We painted sets and made shows – kids' shows. We got kids to come over to the barn and we charged them pins."

"Pins?"

"Pins. Like the kind your mom used for sewing. They paid us to see our little shows. When we had enough pins we'd take 'em to the mercantile and get pennies for them – by weight. Later on we made a show where we charged a penny."

"Slow down, John, you're going too fast already. I mean, like who did what?"

"Gimme a light." Ed struck the match with his thumbnail, and John puffed slowly, turning the cigar. "Good." He watched the smoke rise and then looked across at the mirror and eyed himself and the smoke. "Shit. I'm old now." He puffed some more. "We were like kids for a long time. That's what it's all about, kids. Even before you get too old, there's always a kid in every man. It's the kid in the fella that grabs his nephew and takes him to the circus. Sure he tells the parents that the kids'll love the show, but he wants to go for himself. For the kid inside. As long as we allow people to have a kid inside, there will always be a circus." John paused again to watch himself in the mirror and exhaled the smoke. "Shit, Ed, whatever happened to the kid in me?"

"We all grow older, John." Ed tried to comfort him and then threw down a shot.

"Well," John sipped his whiskey, "it's all water under the bridge now."

"Yeah, okay," Ed followed up on his shot and poured another, "what do ya mean?"

"The last laugh's on me," said John, sipping again, and continued, "that is, maybe. But they won't figure it out till long after I'm gone, anyhow."

One
The Boys from Baraboo
(Me)
John

You will have to listen to many stories about me, after I am gone, many of which will have nothing good to offer, and some of which will be downright awful. I know, because they began before Mable died and continued as I made the largest business gaffe of all my life, followed by the stock market crash in '29. But hear me out, I meant no harm, only the good I could do, especially if my brothers would right themselves from the grave and we could once again give a parade, make folks laugh, or give a grown man back his childhood, if but for a few hours under canvas, or in a great arena.

At age twelve I was the school clown. No one ever called me that. Hell, most of the kids in town barely knew what a clown was. But if I wasn't stealing the pigtails off the back of old Mr. Krowley's wagon while all the boys looked on, I would find another way to get 'em all to laugh. There was something about that moment, having all eyes on me, doing things I wasn't supposed to, or just being better than the rest, that made me a young clown. At age fourteen I stowed away in the possum belly of a wagon and pressed my luck against my brothers' will – and first toured with the Concert Company. That's all we called the first show, the "Concert Company." We were afraid to put our names on it. Wagons often had a belly underneath to stow more stuff. They made me up as a Dutch clown, and damn it I was good. I put on wood shoes, I danced, I told stories, I did hibiddy-dibiddy talk, I made grown men laugh. We went through many seasons as a concert company, first with other boys, then as The Ringling Concert and Comedy Company, and eventually as The Ringling Carnival of Fun. They were hard years, an education of sorts. We made enough money to launch our first real circus, but most of all, me and my brothers were cemented hard. We all developed our talents some. Charley in music and management, Otto in money and finance, Alf in music and public relations, and Al in production.

My acts geared me toward another stage, and maybe that's where my troubles began. Sure I loved the show good enough, and I had talents: clowning, singing, telling stories, and I could play coronet, and other brass, not so good like Charley and Alf, but I could carry a tune, and in the earliest of days we didn't need to be so good, as just to be there making a show. But even back then as a teenager and the youngest of our clan of five, I was heading down a different track. Just like my brothers I could handle the hard work, but I liked better the darkened smoke filled rooms of a private party, the gait of a gal who knew she could have any man in the club, a fine cigar, and my private label. Hell, I swore off women once I married Mable, and I was true to my vow, mostly, but there was always that knowing, when some gal would give me the wink, and I could have any woman I wanted.

I learned soon on to drive my talents to be the advance man, because the dream of our show was as big or bigger than the show itself. It seems that life is a dream, and then we make it happen. But here I am, and they are here no more; my four brothers who started this with me and the other two, Henry and Gus, all slipped away to become no more than memories. Ida my baby sister lives on, with those two impetuous circus "want to be" boys – John, my namesake, and Henry – neither one a showman, but rather gamers of sorts, who haven't the spine to make a circus the size and scale of The Greatest Show On Earth. Hell, maybe they'll get there too one day, and if John understands the hand I dealt him and plays his cards right, he might just end up running the show.

Time will tell if I did right or wrong, and I swear my brothers won't forgive me from the grave, but I'll make it right fellas; I always did. We were tight as can be. It was an odd clan, as Al the eldest was fourteen when I was born, so by the time we began making little shows he was already a full grown fellow. But I think there was a belief in each other that was given into us by Papa and a love for entertainment and art that was sewn to our souls by Mama. No one wants to hear it again, but I always said the words," Let's make a circus of our own." That's right, it came out of my mouth – first! Then again I think we each believe it started with each of us. Whatever it started with, it's ending here with me. I'm not here to drown in my woes, I just want to set the story straight, tell the world what happened. Maybe some poor soul somewhere will wake up one day to realize he has it in him. Maybe the next one will be a gal, or sisters who stand together so strong that success is never in question, but all that stands in the way of great fortune is the lack of a dream and the unwillingness to work hard.

I worked hard, not only in the early days of the circus, but earlier still, when we were just some boys in a barn giving a show. I painted sets even after the sun had set and the paint would stick the brush to my fingers. It was hard work, but we all had our fun. When I was just six, my eight year old brother Charley came home one day with a good size catfish. I wanted to show Charley up, so I went down to the river almost all day. When I came home I had a lunker that must have weighed twelve pounds. When I showed it to my brothers, Al then twenty said it was real monster. Charley got an idea, "Let's make a show with a sea monster," and so we did. We had to keep it in something so we put it in Mama's wash basin. Then we went out in the neighborhood. Charley painted signs with "Ringling Shows and Monsters." We got all the kids to come over at sunset and they had to pay us to come up in the loft. There we had painted the ocean and a boat. We used a lantern to cast the drama of the light, and we told a story of the North Sea. Some kids like Tommy Baird began to complain on account of us taking too long, "You ain't got no sea monster!" Other kids began yelling.

"You Ringlings cheated us."

"Give us our money back, you swindlers."

Just then from behind the set I was trying to hold that fish and it was thrashing in my arms. As Charley said the words, "A giant snarling black monster," it flipped out of my arms and came up between the layers of painted waves and bounced down on the floor right in front of Darcy Williams and began flopping on the floor. The light was still on the set, and no one could see much of what had just jumped out, but the screams and the flopping scared everyone to scurry down that ladder and run out into the dusk. No one ever asked for their money back again! We hadn't charged real money. We charged pins. They would steal the pins from their mothers' sewing baskets and we would charge up to ten pins a show. When we had enough pins, we could take them down to the mercantile and they would give us pennies. We always put the money back into our little shows. Mama got real mad the next day as we put the Sea Monster back in the wash bin. When she came in the next morning, it had splashed out all the water and died. It stunk.

When I was fourteen and we were in the Concert Company, I went nights without sleep and played in the street parade when it was so cold the instruments would freeze to our lips. We carried trunks and instruments when the folks we hired quit on us. Actually we ditched them, and our hands bled, and the satchels and luggage bear our marks to this date. But always, in the back of my mind, I wanted to be out front, talking up the show and staying ahead of the sawdust and shit and the mud. Surely I would meet up with my brothers and feel the endless hum of the lot, and just when I needed it the most, like a big belt of whiskey, there'd be a great charivari and my spine would tingle and then the hippodrome parade would start up and I'd remember why I did it all in the first place. I didn't stomach well the failures, however. In '29 when I bought the American Circus Corporation, I'd bought up the Hagenbeck-Wallace show. But the awful thing that had happened to that show in 1918, just before we launched the Big One, was something I could never have borne. No easier could I bear the hardship to animals, although I never had the heart of my brother Al. He died in 1916, but what did his heart in was saving animals after a fire in Cleveland set the menagerie tent ablaze two years earlier. We all loved animals. Sometimes more than people. They were performers too. They were family. Any man ever abused an animal on our show and they were out. Almost right away. We hated that shit!

It was that fall of '80, that wet morning that I snuck along in the belly of the wagon, when I knew they couldn't send me back, that I first got the show in my blood. Some folks like to say it was later, and granted it may have been, but that's where I remember it. After Lou, Al's wife Louise, found me squirming in some wraps, I was up shit's creek with the brothers, who were ready to get me on a train at Lancaster and send me back to Mama and Papa.

"What can little Johnny do that'll make our act better?" Everyone looked me up and down.

"He can bury my turds," Charley said in smirky tone. It was unlike Charles to talk me down that way. He usually defended me against Otto and Alf. I'd find a way to get right underneath 'em, Otto and Alf, poke at em, prod 'n push, until Otto couldn't take it anymore. His face would swell, his nostrils flare, and he'd explode. Then I'd run, fast as I could and he'd come after me. When he'd catch me he'd throw me to the ground, coming down on me hard. Otto was eight years older, a young man, shorter than the rest, round and stocky with arms as big as tree trunks, and his face was stern. He was different than us, not a performer, but he had the show in him. Even when I was six and he was fourteen, when we put on our first show, in the back yard, the first time we lived in Baraboo. Everyone paid a penny to see us boys, the five of us, make a little show. We'd later come to call it the One Penny.

The other brothers, Gus and Henry, didn't help. Gus wanted no part of our little game and Henry was a baby. But when Otto would be hitting me on the ground, I'd be squirming as he took my ears and twisted them. Alf would just laugh. But Charley, just two years older than me and not any bigger, would jump in. "Quit it Otto," he'd yell, "leave 'im be." Yep, Charley would jump in and he'd be swinging and kicking. Mama was usually the one who'd break it up. I'd hear the kitchen door swing shut and she'd come running with her apron – her dress made her look bigger – and she'd grab Otto, sometimes swearin' in French, but since just me and Charley spoke any French, no one knew anything she was saying. As she'd swing something from the kitchen at Otto's backside, she'd yell, "That's it! You boys is going to school." That meant something different than "going to school." Of course we all had to go to school and most of us finished early, but this was her way to get us to work together. Someone had to teach something to the others. She was always like that. Otto couldn't play music. Charley could. I couldn't dance, till Al taught me how. I knew poetry and songs. Otto knew numbers. He could do figures like nobody. That's why he always took the money and doled it out to us. She would make him teach us math or geography. Charley liked the geography. I did too. For me, it was learning about big cities, and railroad lines, the places in my dreams – my future. Charley, he was forming posters and handbills in his head. We all had to teach something to each other. Mama said to, and we did. Even after Al and Gus were grown men, she, little like she was, had power over them. If she said, "sit," we sat, "read," we read, "sing," we sang, "teach," we taught.

But Charley, he never talked down to me, except that one time on our way to Platteville. He didn't like me there. None of 'em did. I think they were afraid that when they met up with the windjammers, it'd look bad having a little boy along. In case you didn't know, a windjammer is a musician, and in the circus, we mostly play wind instruments. It got worse that morning. Charley didn't even look at me. But it was Louise, our new sister-in-law, who took to me. Lou saved me that morning. Lucky for me she was there. The other years she didn't tour with the Concert Company much, except the year we fired, well abandoned, a couple of assholes who thought they were musicians and actors but turned out to be lily sissies who couldn't handle the work.

"He can dance," she said suddenly. "He knows stories. Let's make him dance and tell stories." I didn't like the idea one bit. But I wasn't gonna say anything at that moment. I really thought they would send me back when we got east to Lancaster. See, I'd been listening for weeks as they planned their route. They set out, me hiding in the lead wagon, after the ferry crossed into Prairie du Chein, toward Lancaster. It was the only year of all the concert companies that we had our own wagons. The old Dem wagon was a piece of shit, and the only thing held it together was paint. Speaking of paint, we had two old horses, one a bay that was losing its mane and the other the old mustang we had traded Grandpa's watch for. Sometimes we got out and walked 'cause we felt sorry for them old horses. We were gonna meet up with some band members and play a little show in a storage barn in Viroqua. If the locals liked the show, we'd get a chance to play in Lancaster. Al and Otto would go ahead and paste a few posters, give some passes to the mayor. He said that's what circuses do, send advance men. I pictured myself, folks gathered round and me talking up a show. We didn't have any canvas. Heck we didn't even have any animals except the two old horses. The clothes we had were sewn by Mama and Ida. Ida was just a little girl, but she liked to help, especially 'cause Mama made her.

Because there was a good chance they could get me on a wagon back to McGregor from Lancaster, I agreed.

"I know a Greek story." I said to save myself. "It's pretty funny."

"What about those wood shoes?" Alf piped in. "He could be a Dutch clown."

"Damn good idea," Al followed. "Lou, you're gonna teach him." That was a good idea. Anything that would get me around Lou. As long as I didn't have to have a snake. Eliza Louise Morris was a snake charmer. She and Al met that spring, when Al struck out to learn circus. They told everyone they were married by the time they left the show. At least that's what they said when they returned home. It turned out they weren't married at all, but no one found that out for years. Al had gone off to learn circus and spent the summer with the Parsons Bros. Circus. They came home. Mama was so angry. Al came home saying he got married and no blessing from the folks. Showed up with a paint gallery lady, and she was "a snake charmer ta boot!" Okay, not really a paint gallery, but she had a couple tattoos. However, she knew some poetry and that quickly won Mama over. She could recite Elizabeth Barrett Browning and best of all knew some poems from Julia Ward Howe and her collection *Passion Flower*. Howe was known by many for her "Battle Hymn of the Republic," for the Union Army. Lou was pretty and she wasn't ashamed. I'd seen her in her bloomers. Her skin was pearl white, and I was just getting old enough to like seeing a woman, especially a pretty one.

Al

There was never anyone so devoted to our little enterprise as Al. In the   season of the Concert Company, when we had renamed it Ringling Bros. Carnival of Fun, Al and Lou had stayed out on tour with Van Amburgh's Shows. We telegraphed Al that the two musicians and the English showman had run off. Actually it was us went and red lighted them, what with their being so arrogant and unwilling to throw in on all the work. We never, in all our years, shorted anyone who worked for a Ringling show. They got their pay and they got what was coming to them – no more shows! Al and Lou came to our rescue within forty eight hours.

Al, my eldest brother, was a bit like our pop. Even at a young age he really liked the drink. I don't remember him much when I was real small. Maybe that's because even then I thought he was Papa. Being fourteen years older than me he was, in my eyes, a man. He knew a little German, although Mama would stop him, and for that matter she'd stop Papa from speaking German.

"You're American now," she'd say to Papa, "stop with the German speak." To Al she'd just say "Unh!" and raise her hand quick in front of his face, and he'd stop. In later years we all let out a little German and French. France and Germany were our heritage, along with America. See, Al looked a lot like Papa. He had that skinny head and big high cheeks. His eyes were dark like Pop and when he'd talk, we'd all gather round and listen.

"Get over here," he'd say, and we'd get on the ground in front of him, all four of us. "Here's what I learned this season. I'm a 'funambulist.' Means I walk the wire." Al had first walked it back there in the One Penny, our little show in the backyard at the old house in Baraboo. I was little, but I remember. It wasn't really a rope at all. It was a board. I guess we call it a rafter board. He and Papa nailed it between two trees. It went sort of uphill and it bent a little, in the middle like a slack wire. He was about eighteen. When he got halfway and was above head high, he almost fell off. The whole crowd, maybe forty five or fifty people, let out a big gasp. We learned something that day. It made sense later and we incorporated it into our acts. We learned to shake 'em up. Don't make it look too easy. Just the same, he almost fell, maybe about seven feet. He actually did walk a wire at The Parsons Show. Back then tents were small, and aerial acts were often outside, on top of the canvas. To this day people tell made up stories about Al walking a wire between two buildings in Brodhead or someplace. He was never that good. Then, when we were mulling the word "funambulist," he'd throw us another.

"Otto can be a 'ducat grabber.'"

"Ha," I shouted, "he is a grabber. Fat man." Al raised a fist like he'd hit me.

"Shut it," Otto said, and Otto had a way of just looking angry and bothered that could make me stop.

"He's not got an act, but a ducat is the ticket," Al continued. "Otto can do the money; he can do something we can't – math! So, early on, he can sell the ducats right off. When our show gets bigger, we'll hire a ducat taker. Otto'll know when we can afford to 'paper the house.'"

"What's tha.." Charley started.

"That's when we want it to look like we sold out, so we give away the ducats, by way of an advance man – like Charley."

"What's a advance...?"

"He goes a day, a week, whatever we need, ahead and with a bill poster or tack spitter, he talks up the show."

"What's a spitter...?"

"Spitter or poster puts up posters on poles, trees, where folks'll see 'em. Advance man talks to people, sets up the place for the lot an' tells 'em their cut, gets townsfolk all set up to come, gives out some ducats, so we get all the seats filled up."

"Aw, c'mon Al, we ain't even got a wagon yet," Alf whined, a familiar complaint.

"Alf," he went on, "Alf, he's gonna be our public man in the advance. But first, we can put on a small show here."

"Wait a minute Al," said Alf, annoyed with his big brother. "Billy Rainbow is just a one horned goat." It was true, but a few years earlier at the One Penny, we got Alf to get Rustler, our rat dog, to jump on the back of Billy, who seemed to like it. He ran around, and the dog jumped off and then back again, and everyone cheered.

"Lookit Alf, all of you. We ain't gonna make it unless we start with what we got. We'll get a wagon. We'll get some horses. Maybe early on we use the team in the act. Maybe we have a rat dog to get the rats out an' later we get a team of dogs. Maybe we get some ponies an'..."

I had to say it, "It'll be a Dog an' Pony..." Without a word Al hauled off and slapped the back of my head.

"You ain't even gonna come with us Johnny."

That's how it was, early on with me an Al. He didn't like me much and he didn't want me messing up his show. But I knew it was for me. The One Penny was my idea – sort of. It was around 1870. I was just starting to wear real clothes. We were all in town, McGregor, Iowa. Mama had us kids along, and we were helping her carry some goods home. Ida wasn't even born yet, but Mama had Henry in her arms. He was one fat baby. He was so big she couldn't hardly carry anything else. That's why we were there. To carry the goods. We saw Papa over by the landing, and he was talking to a fancy looking fellow. The fellow was handing something to Papa. Mama drew a deep breath and sort of under her breath she said "Shyster."   I thought it was something German, and Mama would occasionally speak German or French when she was angry. What I didn't know was that a year earlier there had been a small mud show in town. They had paid Papa with tickets to repair some harness. No cash – just tickets. Al, Otto, Alf, and Papa went to the show. That's what got Al started in juggling. This day, we finished shopping early and went home, us boys playing in the yard, well Charley, Otto, and Alf. Me, I tried, but they'd leave me out, so I just doodled in some mud. Mama called dinner late. When we sat, Papa's place was set but no Papa.

"Where's Papa?" Al asked, after blessings.

"Eat jur dinner," Mama answered and muttered something else. In hindsight I couldn't blame her. Papa had gone broke more than once. He came home halfway through dinner. I could smell it and you know Mama could smell it. Stronger than beer, rye was a whiskey that was made locally. He was all smiles and had a twinkle in his eyes.

"I got work." Long pause, while we all sat in Mama's anger.

"Harnesses."

"Harness what? Rye? Down at Arthur's?" Mama hated it when Papa drank. I once saw him try to kiss her when he was drunk, and she made a fist as big as his head and knocked him on his ass.

"No, a circus is coming to our little town." He was smiling, proud. He could be so proud when he was in the money. Of course Mama and the older boys already knew on account of all the paper all over town.

"And?" she asked.

"And I got work making up some new harness." The table was silent. I didn't know what a circus was. Now I know that the silence was because everyone was waiting to hear if we were going.

"I got paid with tickets to the show and some money to boot!" Mama dropped her fork, full of potato, which bounced off and landed on Al's hand. She got up, apron still on, rubbed her face clean with the apron and went to the sink. She just started pumping water and washing up. Not a word. My older brothers were smiling, and Papa's face was red. Through the thick dense cloud of Mama's silence and clanging pots, they all looked at each other and smiled. I looked up and could see my Mama's fanny shake back and forth as she scrubbed pots – hard. I had no idea why she was mad. It was those tickets. We were poor. Most of the time we didn't have meat on the table. We were poor as dirt farmers, maybe worse even. The McGregor house was so small that we had only three rooms, and all of us boys shared one room.

"What's a circus?" I asked.

"You little... why, Johnny, it's where clowns and horses and pretty girls and music and..." Charley, just six, was trying to explain it to me.

"He's not going," Al said.

"Everyone is going," Papa said and turned toward Mama who washed with a fury, "even Mama and the baby." He turned smiling and looked at her backside as she was scrubbing louder. Mama was silent.

"Do I have to sit with these children?" Al asked.

"We all sit together," Papa answered.

That night I awoke to the sound of Al and Alf talking about it. They were saying something about how the girls would be dressed.

"You can see their legs," Al exclaimed.

"How much? I mean there were no girls in that other show."

"Almost all."

"Ohh," Alf rolled back in his bunk. Alf had a top bunk, and Al had a bed all his own. He was standing up leaning against the end frame talking to Alf, who had grown too big for the same bunks we had. Otto was down below and snored some of the time. We were used to that. Mama said it was his belly made him snore. They had been looking at a book Mama gave them after dinner, that had some drawings of circus. It was old and French and had some pictures of the Louvre. I liked the Louvre and thought that was where the circus would be. Then, as I fell asleep, I remember thinking, "Where was our Louvre in McGregor?"

Just before first light I woke up. I wasn't sure why but figured it'd be the steam whistle. Boats would blow as they came round the bend toward Prairie du Chien. Then I heard it. A whistle never sounded like that. The first time I ever heard the calliope it was magic to my ears. I looked out and could see those last few stars still mingling with the morning gray, and instead of the steam whistle it was steam music. Just a few notes as they rounded the bend: "Doooo, jaaa, whoom Daaa Jaaa!" Somehow it conjured up pictures I'd seen in that book: clowns and lions and people hanging from the bar and spiraling somersault like through the air. My blood prickled and I remember feeling like I was gonna float off the bed.

"Charley, Charley, you awake?" I called down below and leaned over and saw him laying there. His eyes were open and he had a look. "What is it Charley?" At age six he could already play a bugle. I don't know if this was what really got him going about music, but one day he'd write music for that steam organ we called a "Kally-ope."

"I don't know what it is, but I want one of them," Charley answered. There was no more sound, and we fell back to sleep for a little while till Al woke us up with that usual slap to the side of our heads. I never knew if he woke everyone else up that way, 'cause he'd wake me last. Slap!

"Chores – get up! Now." And I did and Charley was sitting there half out of bed, feet on the floor, ready to stand, and I'd see how he always had his long unders half down from the top. I didn't like how Al did that. Every morning, same thing. It got me up and we all had chores. Except Al. He had work. He'd help Papa and Gus, almost right before breakfast. Papa made harness. Some people called it tack. As a boy I figured it was because they hung it on walls on things called tacks. Tack it up. Later I came to find that it had some older English history. You can spend a lifetime believing little odd facts and then later come to find it was something different.

We all had chores. Usually before breakfast. Charley gathered the eggs from the henhouse. Otto set out the plates and tableware. Alf would milk the cow, when we had one. Sometimes we did and sometimes Papa had to sell it off. Sometimes we ate what was left after he slaughtered it and sold most of it off. Sometimes we didn't have chickens either. Those times we ate cereal. That's what Mama called it. It was whatever grain and flour she could cook up in the morning and put in some molasses or sugar, if we had molasses or sugar. She made believe it was better than eggs. She didn't want to let on that we were poor. I was to grab the split wood that Al left on the porch, and bring that into Mama to make the fire in the stove. Sometimes we had no wood, and they'd have us go down by the river and pick up dry drift scraps we could find in piles. When everything was just about right and the fire hot and some coffee or chicory was ready, Mama would make sure everyone was at the table before anyone but Papa could eat or drink. I got milk. She'd put out all the food, like she was proud that we'd start all over again, and she'd mutter a little blessing. Papa did not like prayer. For some odd reason he and the Lutheran church weren't on good terms. Later I'd find out it was because he was a Mason. Then she'd say "Eat, now!" Then the day would start and everyone just set out talking about what was ahead that day.

This day was different. She didn't say anything. Mama was still angry over Papa and the tickets. We'd heard them around lights out, arguing about him drinking and being had by an American showman and not thinking about food on the table.

"Who can eat paper tickets anyhow?" She scolded him.

Then in that morning's silence, we heard it again. That beautiful sound. Steam music. Al jumped up, having barely eaten.

"Can we go down to the river Papa?" Papa looked at Mama through sheepish eyes. She smiled, trying not to. He turned back to Al.

"Go, but be back before noon. You and I got work to be done." Then he turned to Otto, "You be a fine harness maker soon too son."

As I jumped up to go, Al flat out stated, "You aren't going little man."

Mama looked at Al with those do-it-or-never-survive-my-wrath eyes and said, "You'll take Johnny with you." There was no argument, just a disappointed look. Al never liked being ordered around. Not at his age, but Mama said so, and Mama was law.

The landing was less than a mile off, and we all started out walking, except me. I had to run to keep up, and they weren't waiting for me. Every time we heard that calliope we went a little faster. We passed by the smaller houses – hell, they were shacks like ours – then the houses got prettier and then by the school. By the time we could see the landing off over the bluff we were walking in a veritable parade.

It was a weekday and no one was in school. In fact, I spied that gray dress up ahead that Ms. Elsberg, our teacher, always wore at school. Boys were running and girls were trying to be ladylike, holding their dresses above the mud and making it look like they weren't running. The main part of McGregor was six blocks long. To me it was the city, and next to Baraboo, the biggest town I'd ever seen. The mud streets were wet with wagon wheel ruts. There were some shops, the wholesale, Arthur's rye joint, some whores, and too many Scotsmen. There was the ferry over to Prairie du Chien. By the ferry landing there would always be commotion when a steam wheeler came up, but today was busier than usual.

I couldn't see over the crowds, but Charley, just two years bigger than me, put me up on his shoulders. I still couldn't see, but I heard it. Finally we all found our purchase and stood where we could see something. They were off loading horses and some kind of animals none of us had ever seen before. Turned out later they were llamas and some kind of little yaks.

Then – there it was – that calliope. It was up on a wagon and a man with a huge mustache and a bowler played the keys, like a piano, but steam blew out. We all looked at each other like it was from the Gods. Turns out Calliope was the one of the nine Greek Muses. Although a mud show circus had once come to McGregor, this one was a boat show. Not just any boat show, but Spaulding, Rice and Pritchard's Great Animal Monster Show and Clown Fantasmagorical Acts, or something like that. I heard later that it folded just a few months after we saw it. But Dan Rice, the Equestrian Director, sure could talk! There he was, slight, tails and top hat, one leg up on the rail and spouting off a mile a minute about the show, the acts, and in words that I'm sure he was inventing as they came out his mouth.

There weren't many boat shows, because there weren't many rivers, and sooner or later they all had to get off the river and go over land. This was my first circus parade and I never saw anything like it. They paraded the gangplank and onto the main street of McGregor, which was really the only street I remember, and headed uphill with everything. They had all the actors on a wagon and all the animals out front and horses like I never saw before. There was even a big cat wagon, and well, none of us ever saw a lion before. The calliope wagon was pulled by a six horse team. That in itself was a miracle, in my eyes. Behind the calliope was a bandwagon and the music would fast change from calliope to windjammers. They all headed straight up to the other side of town and headed right toward the field between Main Street and Ann Street.

After they passed us boys, Al Called out, "C'mon" and turned in between the whorehouse and Findlay's, shouting, "they're goin' up toward the Ann Street field." We ran after, and Charley didn't take me off his shoulders till we were past the row of buildings and passing the main houses that most of the merchants lived in and past the livery and we could see the fields beyond. Somehow Al always managed to stay in front. He was "Papa" out there, and later he was Papa on the road.

This little show didn't have many roustabouts or riggers. It seemed that everybody doubled for something. Right there on the spot they were hiring young men, and before we knew it, Al was right there pulling some funny wires and helping to get that big top up. It was only a "three pole," and some of it looked like they were making it up as they went. Later on we'd call this kind of tent a "baby top." Al helped out for about two and a half hours, while most of us just watched. When Al realized how late it was, he ordered us all to leave. As Al began walking away, Mr. Rice came up, all of about five feet and an inch or two. Al was taller than most of us, and yet when Rice put his hand on Al's shoulder he was able to sort of spin him around.

"Where in heaven's name ya think yur going, young fellow?"

"I've got to get home, sir," he replied nervously, sort of leaning away as if he thought Dan Rice was gonna hit him one right in the face.

"If you leave now, young man, you won't be getting your pay."

"I don't need any pay, sir. Anyway, I'm going to help my father finish the harness your man ordered from him." Rice stopped for a moment and paused.

"Well then, son, do as you may, and hurry back before one-thirty p.m. with those harnesses." There was an almost apologetic nature about Dan Rice, as he changed his grasp to a patting motion on Al's shoulder. We later came to find out there were few showmen considered more important than Dan Rice, outside of New York and the big cities of the East.

As if the band struck up, Al started walking. and we all fell in line behind him.

"All home," he commanded as our little parade began, eldest and tallest all the way to me, the smallest. By the time we were home, Mama was already putting the noon meal on the table. Everyone had something to talk about, but Papa wanted only to hear from Al.

"Now, tell us son, how did you get that pole to stand up? What type of wagons were they? Ya know your cousin Henry Moeller is a wagon maker over in Baraboo? Did 'ja know that Al? And he's made a wagon for some kinda circus outfit."

"I saw a cat that wanted to eat me!" I exclaimed.

"Oh Johnny," Papa laughed.

"Al, how much tether'd that driver have for the six horse team?"

So finally, we all just submitted, and let Al tell everything.

Otto

Back in the early days of the Ringling Classic Concert and Comedy Company, Otto was likely the better advance man between him and me. Although I was too young then, I am really thinking of how level minded he was. Much like a workhorse, once he started a thing, he just kept up with steadfast regularity. He could run clear out of money, not even a cent in his pockets, and still he'd have a room or a place to stay and a promissory note in the landlord's hands, who'd believe a total stranger, all of eighteen years, would be good for the money later.

There came a moment when we had to operate without an advance man and Otto allotted himself back into our troupe. After we had abandoned William Gooseby, Ned Kimball, and the other young brass player, whose name never seems to have had much weight in my memory, we headed north with plans to play in Minnesota. While still in Wisconsin, but closing on the northern river towns in Iowa, we managed a telegraph to Otto. By the time we met up with him, we exited the train lines at Trempealeau and then arranged and traveled by wagon to Galesville. During this time we decided we would have to pool our resources and manage our troupe more expeditiously.

It was at Galesville that we changed our tactics, and we were ready to transcribe handbills and a manuscript of a dodger program. This meant we would expedite the advance work by setting out first thing in the morning to the local press, which was always the newspaper office. We printed as fast as possible our needed advertisement so that we could travel house to house to personally deliver the word. With the ink still drying, we were often able to accomplish our tasks by the dinner hour, just past noon, and only left our paper in the hands of those we could coax to the front doors. This also gave us the unique opportunity of offering a personal invitation to our evening performance. While Charles, Alf, and I would make our rounds, Otto would procure the performance hall and Al would make our hotel arrangements. Rather than settle into our hotel, we would launch our parade as soon as we had finished invitations and pasting of posters. There would be time only for a quick meal at the hotel, after our parade, and then off to the performance.

I have a hard time placing the town, as it was dominated by Irish folks, but had its share of Swedes as well. It could have been Galesville, Wisconsin, but my recollection is Winona, Minnesota. They are both in the region of the river, and both towns had their share of Irish and Swedes. We had packed the house and the show came off without hitch, or so it seemed. No sooner than it ended and we had taken a bow, then leaving the stage, we heard some sort of ruckus from in the hall. There, a group of town ruffians, and the largest log-moving lumber types of men, had Otto pinned against the stage and were about to take their pound of flesh from our brother.

"You'll be strapped to get your band of brothers out of here in one piece, fat man!" yelled the largest, while holding Otto round the neck.

"I say we kick this one out the door on his ass and then find the others." Then more of a mob of unruly men appeared.

"There's the rest of them brigands," another cried out as we entered from the stage, in time to snatch Otto away and pull him up. That's when I heard a crash and noticed a chair had sailed across the head of Al and knocked him to the floor. Soon came another and another, and as the chairs were flying and men were jumping to the stage, Charley blew the most awful sound from the trombone, which brought everything to a standstill, just for long enough for him to begin a speech.

"Gentlemen," he began, "it is only by chance that such ill will is brought against such a kindly group of performers from a little town to your south." Crash! Another chair, then four more almost at once and Charley made the same awful sound from the trombone again. This time it merely added to the insanity of the moment. Then Otto raised the stage pistol from our props, which should any man have looked in the barrel would have seen that it was poured full of plumber's lead and never could have fired a single shot.

"Gentleman!" shouted Otto, "it is to your peril to continue this anarchy." Now we all knew Otto was taking a risk greater than life itself, for had any man there produced a weapon, Otto would have been the first to fall. It was at that moment that I felt a tug on my shoulder. To my surprise, two of the fairest young maidens, yet several years my elder, repaired my very self to the back door. Since it was me the townsfolk were after, I hastily explained it was because of my jocular story about a fellow in town and some of my inventions of fancy regarding his propensity for red haired maidens. Taking offense was a fellow named Tom, in the center audience, who was engaged to red haired gal. Further I think it may have been the line, "I wonder where else her hair is so fair?" that got the fellow so fired up! They escorted me to the hotel where I'd for a moment lost my wits, surely believing something romantic would arise between myself and the young women, and there they told me to hide in the closet. After they left I opened the front door to the quarters and then returned to the closet and sat patiently awaiting my brothers' arrival. I figured that if any of those ruffians came looking for me they would surely see that the door was open and no one could hide in a room with an open door.

What I had not witnessed was my brother Otto, who passionately defended my honor and outwitted the attackers, finally and diplomatically convincing them that my intentions, albeit impetuous, were indeed light hearted. The mob backed down, and my brothers with blackened eyes and bloodied noses were able to leave the hall, instruments and props (the important things) undamaged. When they returned to our quarters they found me hiding amidst our soiled clothes in the closet.

Otto was a different kind of animal. I mean here we were, four brothers who could dance, who could make music, juggle, walk a slack wire, stand on the powder-back horse. And Otto, well he didn't do any of it, until that summer where we needed him to fill in, and the best he could do was play a small role or bang on a drum. However, he was the glue. He made us rich. I remember back when I was six. It was Otto that got us all lined up.

"How much you got to put in?" he asked, back in our first five minutes of cooking up the One Penny.

"I got a three pennies," I said.

"Go get it," he said faster than I could spit the words out.

"Ain't got to."

"You ain't part of the show less you buy in."

"I'm buyin' in with my words," I told him.

"Your words! Ha. You're six years old. Your word ain't no better than Rustler's," he replied, making me feel no more important than Alf's dog.

"My words more'n a dog's!"

"Prove who you are." Now the other boys were smiling as I ran off to my room and got my pennies. By the time I returned they were already formulating a show.

"I can hitch a board 'tween them trees and walk on it like a wire," Al said, "and I'll get better at the juggling."

"I can blow the bugle and make an entrance for Alf when he might come in on the mare. Maybe he can get Rustler up there with him." Charley was all excited like, as I came running up with my pennies.

"Here it is," I showed my pennies to Otto, and everyone laughed.

"We got us a clown," Alf said and pushed me into the middle and everyone laughed some more.

"Leave off!" Charley yelled, defending me, "He's just a kid."

"Am not, I'm a clown," I said, and everyone laughed again.

"Alright then," said Otto taking charge of the bank, "put your money where your mouth is. All in? Let's get a till going, and then we'll figure out how we're going to make this proper."

It was that very week that Al developed an act that would come to make even our smallest shows loved by the farm folks. He could take a plow and hold it in the air, set the blade on his chin and balance it. It took strength, but it wasn't really that talented. But the farmers – well they just about fell out of their seats! Yet, still, it was Otto who insisted we put that on a poster: "Farmer juggles balls and balances a plow on his chin." Charley made the poster. I miss Otto; he was the first of us to die, in my apartment in New York, in 1913. He never got to see the Big One, all the while it was his doing, his money management that landed us the deal to buy the show from Bailey's widow and shareholders.

Alf T.

Alf T., who we all called Alf but everyone else formally called Mr. Alf T., was almost as good a musician as Charley. French horn, coronet, violin – hell, when he died he had a place in the country in Jersey with a pipe organ that made Charley jealous. But music wasn't his real love. He loved the show. All of us loved the show. What Alf loved more than anything in the show were the animals. First horses but then everything from the dogs right up to the bulls. He had more respect for animals than for half the actors. One time a new handler, a bullman was poking the rubber cow. That's what some circus folks lovingly call an elephant. He was poking him with the bull hook, right behind the front leg, in the chest like they all did, but with anger and force. Now this was early on, might have been one of the first two Indian cows I bargained for back in '89, Fannie or Tillie. He was poking so hard the elephant was bleeding and starting to cry, in a kind of sad droning. The handler was trying to prove himself, the way a horseman overpowers the horse. But this was wrong, and before Charley and I could say anything, Alf was upon him and the bull hook was in Alf's hand, Alf holding it smack in the middle. He began poking the fellow, half with the stick, half with his fist, right in the chest.

"Is this how you do it?" he yelled angrily.

"No Mr. Alf T., I didn't mean nothing."

"Mean? Mean is right. I ought to throw you right out on your keister, you cheap excuse for a bullman."

"Honest, I didn't..." The hook hit the bullman in the head and drew a little blood above his eye.

"Get outa my sight for now, or I swear I'll..."

"Yes sir Mr. Alf T. I'm sorry. I didn't mean to hurt it."

"When you come back you apologize to her. Am I clear? Do you hear what I'm saying?"

"Yes sir, yes Mr. Alf T." He walked off and as he did, you could hear him make amends – over and over. "Sorry, didn't mean it – no way – sorry." That's when we adopted a credo: any handler or trainer on a Ringling show so much as hurts an animal, and they're out – forever. I don't remember what happened to that fellow. He didn't finish out the season. In fact that was the year we hired a mahout, an Indian elephant man. Alf was respected, especially the way he could be with animals. I suppose that was found from Papa. Papa, stern as he was, always taught us to respect and treat animals proper. But that anger that Alf had when he saw abuse started back at Dan Rice's show. That's when Papa nearly killed a fellow. Least ways, that's how we thought it.

Rice's show ended after the evening show. Most of the actors would go back to the boat, though they had a dress tent. The menagerie and the equestrian acts would stay put till the tent and all the rigging was packed and ready to be hauled off. Papa and Al had arrived before the first show with harness and they didn't get paid, so after they came back with all of us for the evening show, they pursued their pay, after the show was over, when they were contracted for settlement. Mama, Gus, and baby Henry went home. We all stayed with Papa, and Mr. Rice referred Papa to a fellow named Evans who had the main office back on the boat. I guess he was the Boss Hostler. By the time we got there they were already loading up, and Papa, taking Al with him, wasted no time getting on board in pursuit of his funds. He was paid promptly and headed back toward the gangway where we boys were waiting on shore.

Before he got to the gangway, an equestrian handler was pushing a timid horse up the way. The horse spooked, and the handler with his whip began lashing the horse right across the flanks. There was a good moon and a clear sky combined with the oil lamps, and we could see blood. You could see something in Papa's eyes and it was like fire. The handler got the horse up and past Papa, and as he got himself alongside Papa, the whip seemed to just jump out of his hand and into Papa's. All of a sudden Papa just did what the man did. He started thrashing the handler, right across his neck. Once, twice, then the fellow's hand was up, and Papa did it again on his arm and there was blood. Papa reared back with the whip, and Al grabbed it and brought it to a stop.

"Pop!" Al was trying his best to make him stop.

"You are a scoundrel, mister, and should be punished." Al pulled Papa back, unable to really stop the arm with the whip. But Papa came to his senses.

"You're a fool, Ringling," the man said, taking advantage of his moment to squirm by. "You Ringlings'll never work for any circus."

Papa spat at him, and the man slithered into the dark following the horse.

"I'll never work for *your* circus, miserable excuse for a human." Al moved Papa toward the plank and they headed toward us. That's when I saw it. The look in Alf's face. He so admired Papa for that. In a way we all did. But Alf had a special way with animals. It was like when he spoke English they heard horse, or dog, or whatever animal they were. I suppose that's what got under his skin and caused the anger that day in 1914. That day that burdened him so bad right up to his death. What happened that day in 1914 also caused both Al and Alf to take heavy to the drink, even in the daytime.

Charley and Me

Charley, Karl Edward Ringling, was my brother. Oh, I had six brothers, but Charley was my brother. I suppose when he died, back in 1926, after rushing home to Sarasota from Evanston, we weren't the best of friends anymore. A lot of things happen in life, bad things. Things we think we can't control, but it's water under the bridge, and by God you can drown in that water.

He was a take charge kind of guy. He could do everything. Even as a boy, he could play bugle, coronet, piano, and a little violin. Why, back when Al was first wanting to sneak off with his friend Ned and start a little concert and juggling act, Charley was already practicing. I think it was Ned's doing. See, Al, bossy and stubborn as he was, actually wanted all of us in a company. Papa wanted us to become a big harness making company, "Ringling and Sons." But Al, he was ready to run off when I was still wet behind the ears. He got Alf and Charley to get together with Ned and Ned's teacher and learn music. I never took much to music, but Charley, well almost right up through 1925, he'd play opening night with the band at the Garden. They were playing his compositions. On opening night the band would pause and then a fellow (Charley) would walk out and join in, anonymous you know, and then start playing horn. Some years he would replace the band leader, Merle Evans – we called him Merley. Charles Ringling's music is standard for circus all over the country today. So, by about age ten Charley could outplay any kid in school. By the time we moved back to Baraboo, Charley was head of the city band. He was fifteen. There he was, in a uniform, waving that stick and windjammers older than Papa would play music on Charley's count. He was a born leader.

Back there at that first circus, Dan Rice's show that came up the river, I was watching the animals – especially the lion. Al was helping the riggers, but Charley, he'd already started with a love of music. No one's gonna fight me about the facts, that I was the first to say, "Let's make our own circus." Naïve and all, I was just a little boy.

But Charley jumped right in, "Yes, our own circus show." He stood up straight and marched, like he could hear the band.

"I'll be the band leader," he said as he picked up a little stick and conducted his make believe band, marching in place. It seemed like we all could hear the music. Alf immediately got Rustler to roll over and over and over. He could teach 'em tricks faster than you could say "steak bone." Both Alf and Al could do that with anyone's dog. Alf said it was all a matter of commanding the animal's attention. Even then, Al as a young man already picked up two rocks and tried to juggle. A spell came over us boys. Otto was smitten by the spell too.

"What'ya think we can take for a show?" Already a teenager, he allowed he could do the math on Papa's books.

Charley answered, as if it was really gonna happen, "Let's start cheap at a penny." Now a penny was real money, and Otto began to divide up the neighborhood.

"If we can get someplace to put a hundred people..." Gus was listening in, and he was always as cynical as Papa.

"You ain't gonna get no hundred." Al was on top of it and being two years older than Gus, he had his way of staring Gus down.

"Oh stick a cork in it, rock face. If the boys want a show, let 'em try it. How come you always have to come around and piss on their fire anyhow?"

Gus defended his position. "Look, you don't know a thing about circuses. Just because we saw a show, and Papa got paid for the harness, don't make you no showmen."

"There it is again, just like a turd in a punchbowl." Al continued softly, to fall into the dream web that held us all, "I kind of like the whole idea of a circus myself." Gus just walked off mad, sort of muttering under his breath. Yep, I started that whole thing, but Charley was right there, right after, always holding me up. He was my brother. He was my shield from the older boys, and he was my rock. Never mind that we were always gaming each other. I guess that was on account of us being so close in age. He'd catch a big old catfish, and I'd stay out till dark trying to catch a bigger one. He would carry a bucket of paint up in the loft for us to paint the background of a show, and I'd come up with two buckets. Later in life I outdid him with real estate, hotels, oil wells, even train lines. My brother Charley had one thing I never had – feet on the ground!

In 1882 a minister named Conway from the little town of Zumbrota, Minnesota, moved next door. He was a stern fellow, with a big Scottish brow and a clumsy gait. He had two daughters and the elder, Edith, was always looking over the fence at Charley. Now we had just moved back to Baraboo ourselves, and none of us knew too many folks, and the kids around the streets were referred to as "urchins" by Papa and Mama and Reverend Conway as well. We had stopped going to the Lutheran church. I didn't know why, but Al explained it to us boys.

"It's on account of Pop being a Mason and all," he told us one day.

"He ain't a mason," Alf corrected his brother, "he's a harness maker."

"Not that kind of mason, silly. They're called Freemasons, and I've been invited to join in, now that I'm a man and all."

"Well, what do these Freemasons do?" Charley asked.

"I don't fully know, but I think they kind of help people in need, and stuff like that."

"I think we should all go and ask Papa if we can be Masons," I offered.

"It's a secret order," Alf interrupted and lowered his voice, "that's why the church don't like it so much. They don't want people helped in secret none. When the church helps, they want everyone to know, so more people will join."

Well, I think that did it for all of us. It set the stage. One day we were all going to become Masons. We could actually do good, and we didn't need the minister's approval. As for the Reverend Conway, well, he was an Irish Baptist. It seemed they had no problem with Masons, so we started to attend his church.

So in the first years back in Baraboo we held mostly to our own boundaries, and kids would come to our home and play in our barn. Charley was a teenager and already versed in every kind of music, and Al was off working circuses part time, and having already started the Concert Company, we had a season under our belts with Ned Kimball as band leader. Charley, however, was all the more daring a band leader and would soon replace Ned. Reverend Conway didn't respect us boys too much, and with two little girls he was quite protective.

However, as Charley could play any instrument and the reverend had a piano, he was amiable to the idea of young Charles Ringling teaching his daughter Edith to play music, especially as she was too young to be of interest to a boy five years her senior. What no one had realized was that Charles liked her as a child, and as she became older he grew more fond of his young pupil. It was more of a friendship than a boy-girl bit. In that first show in '84 when we opened in our hometown of Baraboo, Charley had reserved a front row seat for "Deedee," a name he coined for her, and even though the Reverend and Mrs. Conway, as well as Deedee's sister, had to sit there, you could see that Charley paid too much attention to her while he led the band. The remainder of us brothers were well aware that he was already smitten with Edith.

It wasn't until the 1890 season, the year we took the show to the rails and became a respected name, as shows go, that the reverend would give his blessing for his daughter, age twenty, to marry a showman like Charley, age twenty five. I had tried in the early years to engage Charley with some of the girls in the cities that were what we deemed entertaining, but Charley's heart had always been with his childhood sweetheart, the little girl from next door, Deedee.

Still, it didn't come that easy. In the early years we would open in Baraboo for our hometown folks. Deedee was teaching school and brought her children to the opening matinee. We had bought our first two elephants the autumn before, and they had proven important to help the baggage stock, as well as become a major draw. Like any show, we ran a show outside before the "all in," and it was big entertainment. We weren't ready yet to give kids elephant rides, but we did sell them bags of peanuts to feed the elephants, and Edith's school children were eager to spend their money on those peanuts. As she turned to get her children to put their hands out with the peanuts, one of the elephants slipped its trunk under her dress and lifted it clear up to her shoulders and exposed her bloomers. Everyone, and I mean everyone, roared, except Charley, who walked right up and gently pulled her dress down, offering her dignity back. That moment was clearly the moment when the two knew they were in love. I think as love goes, every true love has that moment.

It didn't hurt any either that by 1890 we had gone from ruffian circus boys to over twenty five railcars and a show that made the larger shows take notice. This, along with the fact that we were already considered important businessmen in Baraboo, earned us the respect of Reverend Conway.

Deedee – most often referred to as "Mrs. Charley" on the lot, and even after Charley is many years departed – was not your average girl, especially as a teenager. Why, when the reverend would go off in his carriage during his monthly journey to meet with those in the parish that seemed to have forsaken Sundays, or maybe God himself, and Mrs. Conway would leave to do errands, Deedee would jump the fence, and she'd either be playing music and any kind of instrument, or she might go right down to the river with some of us younger boys and try her wits at catching a big old catfish. She was half girl, half musician, and already one hundred percent Ringling. There were girls, including her sister, that weren't considered to be comfortable in our boyish everyday dealings, but Deedee was more than welcome, as we just expected that she would be there.

I know I missed so much of my brothers' lives when I took to be advance man after the '85 season, and I missed out on the sense of family that Al and Lou, Charley and Deedee, and Alf and Della must have known in those early days. Charley and Deedee played music every night when work was done, right up until those last days in Evanston just before he died. By 1893, only Al and Otto were full time on the lot, along with Henry. The rest of us, and even Gus, all worked advance. After Charley died in '26, Deedee stopped traveling with the show, but by 1928 she was right back there at every show and as much a part of the spirit as was my brother. I miss him more than terrible, but I delight in knowing that a part of Charley is always on the lot as Mrs. Charley, even if we do have the utmost contempt for each other these days.

Charley was quick witted, even as a youngster. Back when we put on little shows in the barn, he could come up with ideas, posters, and acts that would bring the whole neighborhood. One time Charley looked at two of the newborn kittens in the barn and he got an idea.

"Supposing we had gone over to Black Holler and stole these kittens from the Beastly Lion of Black Holler?"

"I like it – go on," Alf egged him on, "you always come up with good ideas, Charley."

"We get all the kids lined up and tell 'em a story – just like we did with that catfish," he said, grinning. He cooked up quite an act. We got about fifteen kids to come over, and this act too was after sunset on a summer night. We played music and worked slowly through several acts and made them wait to see the Beast of Black Holler. Finally with Alf hiding in the back, we told the story of how we led an expedition into the dark and terrifying place. Thereafter Charley drew the short straw, and he had to crawl into the lion's den and steal the cubs of the dreaded lion, which stood almost six feet at its withers. Just at that moment I held up the two kittens which appeared under lamplight to have unusually large heads, especially because we had torn the filling out of a pillow and gave them each a mane, which we had painted brown. Charley went on with the story: "We had run across two swamps and the Wisconsin River, all the while being trailed by the Beast of Black Holler. To this very hour we think the very beast stalks us!" Then suddenly – wrapped in a brown blanket, Alf roared and jumped from behind our Black Holler scenery, and by the way that Otto was shaking the light Alf appeared to be a huge beast. Screaming kids were climbing over each other to get down that ladder. Charley had a showman's knack for how to word the story. He made all the wording up for our posters for over three decades.

Many will debate how many concert tours we had, and that'll be fine, but truth is, in my recollection, a couple years are blended together better than the finest scotch. There was a year when Al did not come with us. I believe it was back in '82, and Al was already with Louise. That year they had signed on with a bigger show, and I recollect it being Van Amburgh's Combined Shows, a fine rail show, which we fellows would one day merge into ours. We needed a sixth for the troupe, and Ned and another youngster had joined in, but we felt we should have someone older, more like Al, to take his place.

A musician and Shakespearean actor named William R. Gooseby had chance traveled to town that summer, and when he heard Charley leading the band on the town central, he had asked to join in. Seeing that he seemed all the part of the performer we were seeking, Alf and Charley proposed to him that he join us for our autumn tour. It took more than a farmer's tale of persuasion to convince him that we had taken a profit in prior years, and Otto joined in by showing him certain pages from our books, especially those that verified profitable stands. He agreed to join in but had numerous questions regarding our experience and knowledge of business, and often, after band practice, he would engage Ned and the other youngster in agreement on us not being the businessmen needed to attain success.

By the time we left home that autumn, we three Ringlings, who would be the heart of the performers, felt less than secure around the fellow and the little troupe of outsider actors. As Otto took to the road to be the advance man, Alf was left as the eldest at only nineteen, Charley then eighteen, and myself sixteen. We now really were the Ringling Boys, and we three reveled in our strength but wore our concern in our lack of ability to manage the rest of our show. The first several towns might as well have been washouts because almost everything possible went wrong. Fortunately we were plumb with funds as we had each worked all summer and saved up for the trip. However, it was clear that if this was our education, the semester would soon end, as we would eventually run out of reserves. Worse even was the fact that Gooseby had completely taken charge of the others, and they had decided they were better than us boys, and Gooseby himself would no longer carry any other trunks or equipment.

"Not up to the bloody task of being a servant," he would say emphatically and then order the others, "Not you either Ned, let the Ringling boys do their share."

We three began a mutiny of our own, and it was completely by Charley's design. We were planning to head farther north and the trip would be two days. So, it would be perfect timing to leave our other performers and get off without concern that they might follow. After a dismal night at the theater in Black River Falls, we went back to our rooms, us Ringling boys in one and the other three in theirs. We drank ourselves a pot of tea ordered up from the hotel restaurant, and after it was late enough for the others to be asleep, we set out with our trunks and instruments. This alarmed the landlord, who thought we were about to take a powder. We not only paid all our debts but those of the other three. Charley had scheduled us onto a midnight freight, and after we convinced the landlord to not tell the others where we had run off to, we made haste across the way to the station and boarded an empty car. We paid extra to the baggage handler to seal his lips and headed north to Osseo, where we would then head east toward the river.

This was an honorable desertion as we left no financial obligations and yet were able to rid ourselves of performers who were unruly and lazy and had no future with us. The entire plan was orchestrated by Charley, and to this day such an honorable desertion is called "a Charley" in circuses all across the country. Less honorable was called a "red light," a move never taken by a Ringling show as long as we ran the lot. Red lighting is when you tell the feller to meet up with you, for his pay, at a designated place and time, and when he arrives he just sees the red lights of the train going down the tracks.

Gus

Now there's a man who took a shine to be like Pop. At first he refused to get involved with our "wild goose chase," him quoting Papa. And though he called it a "wild goose chase," in time he did join up with us. Like all my family, I had to admire Gus. Second eldest, he looked like Papa. In fact he took to harness making and schemed along with Papa to make a great harness company. He worked long hours, followed Papa's word to the letter and law, and he was always trying to keep a lead on me. When he was older and the work in the harness shop became slim, he left home to find work in northern towns, returning to Baraboo and McGregor on occasion to work for Papa.

In the season of 1879 Al, Alf, and some boys from town were off to try and make a concert company. Some of the fellows, like Ned Kimball and Dan Ryan, had to sneak away as their parents wouldn't have it, their boys running off to be performers. Papa wouldn't let me or Charley go, but Charley snuck off with Al and Alf anyhow. Otto wasn't terribly interested and was beginning to work for Papa and help with his books.

That was the summer I ran off. When school ended and summer came about, Papa wanted me to work in the shop. Not me. No way I was going to hang around a boring shop and make harness. I had other plans. Big plans. I had been reading up on how soap was made.

I knew it was easy enough, and I had found a handbook that told all about the founding of Larkin Soap and Products of Chicago. It seemed to me that half the battle was selling the stuff, so I figured I could barter for lithographed labels, a room in a city, and even the equipment I needed. I was twelve, but when I peered in the mirror I thought myself to be quite the handsome young man.

So off I went in the middle of the night and down to the ferry at McGregor Landing. I could save my funds if I snuck on board the ferry, so I swam out and climbed on board, hiding in the dark under some tarped down goods. Morning came, and the sound of folks talking woke me up as we went across to Prairie du Chien. I made for Madison, and the first teamster came along gave me a ride. He was all farm boy, and I knew he must have come from a dairy farm because he stunk like cow shit.

"You can ride with me, young fellow, long as you ain't running away from home or nothing like that!" He couldn't have been much older than sixteen himself, and I answered him with such sincerity.

"Oh no sir," I said, "why I have to get to Madison because my aunt took sick and Ma and Pa sent a telegram saying I better come quick before she dies." It was enough to convince him, so off we went to Madison.

River towns at that time were boom towns, and I was used to lots of people, but this was different. There was every kind of person, and the streets were lined with stone. There were women with full fashion dresses that required to be held above the dirt of the road, and hats of fashion with feathers, and men in vests and full suit coats, some in top hats and others in bowlers. There were teamsters who looked liked they smelled like shit and coaches fit for royalty. There were wagons with teams of six pulling huge loads and folks on the street selling wares without storefronts. At one point I am certain I looked up and saw a whorehouse with women showing their parts to men with wanting gazes below. This was the most excitement I had ever had. My driver let me out at a mercantile and asked if I was close enough to my aunt's home.

"Oh, well this couldn't be more perfect," I said. "Her home is practically around the corner." From there I set out on my mission to barter work for a room, find my supplies, and invest the $1.12 I had brought with me. It didn't take me long to find a room on Franklin Street. The landlord was busy cleaning the steps when I came across the fellow and inquired.

"Excuse me sir, but do you know where I can find the landlord of this establishment?"

"Tell me," he replied, "why would a fellow your age be looking for the landlord?"

"Well, sir, it seems I have very important business to conduct with him."

"Sonny," he turned toward me, took off his hat and scratched his head, "I doubt that a boy of your age could have business of any importance with the landlord of this establishment."

"I wouldn't expect a working class fellow like yourself to understand," I went on. "My business matters are quite important and could bring the landlord quite a reasonable sum." Taken by my manner he began to laugh.

"You've got my attention young man, now explain your business. You see, young fellow, I am the landlord!" Momentarily embarrassed, and I am sure red behind the ears, I explained that I was The Mr. John Ringling and that I had come to Madison to make my fortune in the soap business and that if I could work for a modest room, I could have a place large enough to start my endeavor.

"Well, Mr. John Ringling, I am afraid I have no work for you, and even if I had a room available, it would be beyond any work you could provide."

"No work, sir, indeed! Then tell me, what does your family think when you have to clean the stairs and the hallway? Furthermore," I went on, "couldn't a man of your stature be making more income by focusing on less menial tasks?" Once again, he stopped, took the boater cap from his head and scratched. I could see this was how he reacted when perplexed.

"Alrighty then," he replaced his straw hat, "what kind of work can you provide?"

"Well, sir, I can clean the halls, clean your own apartment, and by the looks of it, you could use my sign painting talents to paint a better 'Rooms to Let' sign. I think if you made better use of your time, we could both benefit."

"My name's Bill Parkes." He reached out and shook my hand and then said, "I don't know where this kind of thought comes from, but I get the honest to God feeling that you are going to be very famous one day, Mr. John Ringling! But do tell me, you are over fourteen, aren't you?"

"Why yes sir, I am sixteen," I replied, and I could tell, first, he didn't believe me, but second, my say so was good enough.

"I have a one room downstairs. It shares the bath with the larger flat, and it has a two burner stove. There's not a stick of furniture to go with it, and it's colder than a schoolmarm's ass in winter."

"Mr. Parkes, it sounds like what I have been looking for. When can I move in?"

"Just as soon as you get these steps cleaned and polish the railing." He handed me the broom, and no sooner than I got to work did I feel the freedom of being in business for myself. I bartered what I could for shares in my business, and with recipes from the library I began making soap from oil, lye, animal tallow, and herbs which I bought from the apothecary. My first labels read, "Ringling's Great Soap Company," and captioned, "no finer soap in the Midwest." I produced and wrapped my first fifty bars and went out on the town to sell them. It was easy work, and at five cents a bar I soon had money to reinvest. By week's end I had pocketed over eight dollars and owned enough equipment and materials to double my take for week two. I had not only repainted old man Parkes' sign but had also made a nice little sign for my downstairs door which read "Ringling's Great Soap Company." Unfortunately that was rather an untimely error on my part because no sooner had I placed it on the door than there came a loud knock. Thinking that I had already lured customers to come to my place of business, I opened the door. There at my face was Gus, and behind him, Papa.

"How'd you find me?" I asked Gus, trying to avoid looking into Papa's eyes.

"Easy job, little brother, your posters are all up and down the street."

"And with the family name, no less!" Papa said angrily. "Pack your things, we leave now."

"But Pop," I said, "I am a success here." He grabbed me by the collar and tie, pulled me close, almost up against his face, and said, "Mama is worried sick, out of her mind." He let go my tie and continued, "Pack now, we leave immediately and can get home before morning." That was the end of my first business venture. But, you know, I always felt it was a success, and had Papa and Gus not come and found me, I would be the baron of modern soap. It was Gus who somehow figured out where I went, and it was Gus I have to forever be thankful to for saving me from being the king of soaps.

Gus did not take to the circus at first. He was certain it was a "wild goose chase." But after so many years of success, he joined us, and in fact with Pop's blessing, as Pop's biggest clients were his own kids, the Ringling Brothers World's Greatest Show. Like Henry, Gus was never a partner, but he proved to be a good advance man, and the year we first bought the Barnes Circus, we gave it to Gus to manage and promised him that if he could make a profit with it, he could own it as his own. Gus died that year and we sold that show.

Henry

Out of the five of us that started the circus, I turned out to be the biggest. Henry was bigger! Almost six foot four, he outweighed me by fifty pounds. As a boy he was separate from us, as he was three years younger than me. He was shy and quiet and didn't seem interested in much, other than eating. Papa had taught him the old German saying, "Better belly busts than good vittles go to waste." Unfortunately all the vittles went to his waist! Mama would say, "My big boy, such a big boy, if he keeps eating he is going to burst!" The big boy with the soft voice who could see over the crowd eventually joined our show.

He was so kind and made a great diplomat, so we made him our ducat man. He took the tickets, what we would later call Annie Oakleys, as they had a punch hole in them, like the playing cards Miss Oakley would shoot in mid air. They were given out to mayors, city officials, Masons, and religious leaders. These people were important, and it took a kind person to greet them and get them situated. These free ticket holders got all their friends, parishioners, and other folks to fill our stands. Henry was the best of all at this job and trained others at it. Because he had such a kind and giving nature, he became a high level Mason. He loved Baraboo, likely more than any of us, and the townsfolk loved him back.

I actually didn't get to know my brother Henry all that well until 1913, when Otto died. Henry was still in Baraboo when Otto died in New York. When I got to Baraboo for the service, Henry sobbed in my arms. We had already lost Gus, but Henry loved Otto more than any of us. He didn't even know, but Otto had left him all his shares. Henry took differently to the show after that. It was like a showman awoke in him. He actually became a partner and in the absence of Otto, we were glad to have another brother as a full partner.

Ida

Ida was ten when we launched the first tent show with Yankee Robinson in 1884. We never give her enough credit for some of what she did for us. After Mama gave birth to seven boys, Henry being the youngest, she had a girl. That was the "stop" to baby making. I was eight years her senior, and being that she was a girl, I never had to much watch over her. After our first season with Yankee, and seeing how other outfits let their people dress rag-tag and shabby, we brothers made a decision. It was late October 1884 and we were putting the show in the barn. Back then the barn really was just a barn! We were getting ready for another season of the Concert Company. Al, Charley, and I were rolling the canvas and tying it off inside another canvas that was rubbed down with camphor. That helped to keep the mice and pests out of it.

"What would you fellas think if we made part of our reputation on being clean?" Charley asked out of the blue.

"What are you talking about?" I asked as we all three lifted the heavy canvas up onto the hay mow. We had placed three ladders, and all of us rolled it upward as we climbed. After we got it up with a huge dusty thud, we continued the discussion on the ladder.

"What I mean," Charley said, "is why don't we make a pact to always be clean and neat, always have the brightest uniforms, never let any of our performers get sloppy?" We descended the ladder to get more of our props.

"I think Charley has a solid idea," Al piped in, "God knows I've seen some sad operations over the past few years." We made a pact. All five of us. Never would a show with the name Ringling be sloppy or threadbare.

That's where Ida came in, that very winter. We talked it over with Mama and Papa, and while we hit the road for the Concert Company, Mama and Ida worked on making up first class uniforms for our band for the '85 season. Papa, Lou, and Al worked out a higher grade of harnesses. Some of us went off and performed in November and December, while Ida and Mama worked through Christmas and even through March. When we bought new canvas that season and the next, Ida was there helping stitch it together. Although by age fourteen she no longer played a role in our preparations, she certainly was there helping, like every part of the family. Like Henry, there were so many years between us that I missed out on her childhood. Especially because we were off performing and building our shows. Still one day, after she and her husband would join us in Sarasota, I would come to love my little sister. I just hope she and her boys will figure out what I've done, and get the signal, and straighten it all out.

Papa & Mama

There's never been an unkind word any one of us eight Ringlings could say about the folks. Sure Papa would occasionally take to the drink, but I'd be calling the kettle black if I made a fuss about that. They both came from good stock. Grandpa Frederich Runglinge and Grandpa Nicholas Juliar had once fought each other, one under Wellington and Von Blucher and the other under Napoleon. In the end, however, our families ended up here, Grandpa Juliar a pioneer and Papa the short lived "King of Hops," when hops was king. That lasted until every smart German in Wisconsin and Iowa plied their hands at hops, so we German Americans could drink our beer.

Then the market crashed in the late '60s, and Papa became poor like everyone else. College educated, he also had allotted himself a trade, made upon him by his father: saddlery. He became the chief harness maker in the boom town of McGregor and later in Baraboo. All towns along the river were boom towns back then, as everything from fur to lumber and ore came down the Mississippi and had to have a place to leave off. So wherever there was a landing became a town, and they grew as fast as rain fell. Papa had his own dreams. He had dreamt "Ringling & Sons" would one day become a great enterprise for harness making and outfitting every horse and wagon in the Midwest.

We boys heard a different calling, however. He didn't try to stop us any. In fact, he cheered us on, laughed and clapped along with Mama, and even lent us materials to build our little shows, especially the One Penny and the Five Penny. But when he thought we took it all too serious, he'd scold us saying, "Time you boys put some feet to the ground, and made a future, and end the wild gooses chase." His English was nearly perfect as he had studied English in college in Hanover, Germany, but he always called it "gooses." It made us all laugh, and I think, if not for that, we might of taken him more seriously.

The stern looks would wear down quickly when Charley would lead the band in the center of town, and you'd see the look in Papa's eyes, so proud of his boys. At times we would all play, but Alf and Charley were the best and most serious, and along with our neighbor, Ned, they made a real band with some of the adults older than Papa. For Papa to see his son lead a serious enterprise made pride well up inside him. When we asked permission to leave off and take to the muddy autumn roads of Wisconsin in order to ply our hands at the entertainment business as the Concert Company, he wholeheartedly gave his blessing.

Mama had a temper. Oh I don't suppose it was much more than any other mother of eight children, but when she was angry and looked your way, why you felt like the whole skies were about to come down hard. Like Papa, she was proud, and she wanted her boys to have success. By the time I was eight, her English was as good as any. They prided themselves on being American. Why, at age sixty four Grandpa Juliar wanted to join the Union Army. They wouldn't allow for that, being he was over sixty and all, but everyone rumored what a great American to be so determined. He passed his love of art to her, as he was a weaver, a vintner, and a great reader of the classics.

So Mama would read to us, and as the older brothers, Al, then Gus, and then Alf were able to read – well enough – then she would make selections and have them read to us younger boys. In time I would even read to Henry and Ida. That didn't last long, as by twelve I sneaked off with the Concert Company, by myself in the belly of the wagon, and by thirteen was part of the Ringling Classic Concert Company. But later that fall, even after Mama and I had exchanged several letters from the road, she slapped me hard across the face at first return, before she hugged me, and then said, "Next time you're going to be a performer, you'd better have your parents' blessing." That was a softer finish than earlier that same year when I'd run off to Madison to start the Ringling's Great Soap Company. I'd say over time I had just worn Mama down, the way boys do with their mothers and misbehaving.

But Mama would hush Papa at times, when he'd tell us we'd have to "plant our feet firmly and give up the wild gooses chase."

"Stop now, August," she'd say, "the boys have special talents," and he'd yield awhile and listen to our jokes, or watch Al juggle. I think the farmer in Papa also a had an eye for business, and the day that Al balanced a plow on his chin while juggling three balls, Papa stood up and turned around to us boys and said, "You boys'll be famous one day." Papa almost took a bow for his son! He was right about the plow. If anything got farmers all excited it certainly was that. So when Al at age twenty four wanted to leave town and go off and work in a show, he'd already had Pop's blessing. It was hard for Papa because it meant that Al, the eldest of all of us and in many ways our caretaker, would leave the harness shop and go off to ply himself at another trade, so as to come home and teach us all how we maybe could, one day, have our dream – separate from Papa's. But that's the crux of it: Papa, reluctantly, was giving his blessing. Same time, he could see the future was changing. The big harness factories made it hard for Papa to compete. It was 1876, and trains were all across the country, while the end days of the horse and buggy were on the horizon, and like the smell of autumn moves in, you could sort of smell the big change, almost sour-like. I could see it in Papa's face, a tear held back, for pride, while one let go.

Each and every time us boys needed a bolt or a handful of nails, Pop handed 'em over willingly. When we wanted to make a trade for that old mustang, it was Papa that gave us the old skiff and a few tools he no longer regarded as useful. Mama threw in Grandpa Juliar's watch, which had been water damaged after Grandpa had hid it in an old tree stump, for fear that someone would steal what few valuables he had carried over from Europe. When we came home, not only with the mustang and a box of whistles, we had also traded for an old and rotting Democrat wagon that had one seat. Papa looked over at the wagon, full knowing that it was rotten, but no less so than the mustang, which was as run down an old nag as any, and after a long pause and trying to look serious he said, "You boys struck a fine deal."

Mama smiled and tilted her head, while wiping her hard working hands on her apron, in both pride and in the satisfaction of knowing that her husband gave his blessing to the children, their dealings, and their dreams. It was as if she bore witness to something special that only a parent can experience. I'll never forget that moment.

"Our children are smart like their Papa," she said, wiping her hands on the apron, "and I know one day, if they stick together like glue, they'll be a great success." In hindsight I know Mama, in her pride, was just doling it out, in a good way, the way that parents do when they know it'll build the kids' character.

Two
Under Canvas

Amusement

The years, the routes, the rails all blend together. My God, I wish they were all one. It only took us five years to go from mud to rails. Five years of mud and blood and shit up to our elbows. I left most of it to my brothers; I mean all that foot soldier stuff. Sure, well enough I went out with the show the first couple seasons in 1884 and '85. We didn't have much, but to Papa's great surprise the Concert Company made money in '82, '83, and '84 despite how bad the first year was. Between Otto and Al, they made certain we had money to put back in the pot for canvas, lithos, any equipment we could scrape together. Al thought like a farmer: save a little seed, put some by, plant a new field, hold some back. Otto, what a bastard! I mean when it came to money. We called him the "Iron Fist," and when he got it into his clutches you couldn't pry it loose while he was alive. So, when we went out that first season and we played ninety three stands as Old Yankee Robinson and Ringling Brothers' Great Double Show, in 1884, almost entirely in Wisconsin and some in Iowa, we went with rented wagons and rented horses, but we owned our canvas. We used our stock horses as ring horses, with the exception of one ring horse, a beautiful large bay, that was Al and Lou's special. I was still a clown and not very happy about it. I doubled in the band and we were all riggers too. Come to think of it, we all did everything we could. It was only part way through that season that we discovered our advance team was stealing us blind. So over time I had to become the head of the advance, and I must admit that my tricks and antics might well have been part of what made us so big. But we all learned, every inch of the way, every time we fell we pulled ourselves up from the grave and stumbled ahead, each time being the best teacher and the best student we could be.

As soon as the '83 season of the Concert Company ended, Al and Lou went east toward the Ohio Valley to meet up with Fayette "Yankee" Robinson. Robinson had a number of small shows over the span of his career, but we had heard he had a difficult season and might be willing to take on us boys if he thought we would work hard. He wanted his name first. He was a great showman and a fine teacher, but he was as old and weary as our first nags, and from the moment I laid eyes on him I wondered who would last the longer, him or the nags? We still only owned the two wagons from the Concert Company, but we had been storing away what we could in the barn, including canvas from three bad tents which, with help from Mama and Ida and Gus, we would make one large tent. Gus only worked on the tent because Mama and Papa made him. He was begrudging the work, but we were always a family that held out for the other's dreams, even when we didn't agree. Music was still the centerpiece, but Ned and the others in the band doubled up work, including clowning. When it was time to perform and we had been sufficiently practiced at our lot in Baraboo, we began to plan the route.

Charley had sent Henry, all of sixteen, ahead to be the advance. Henry really wanted nothing to do with the show yet, but Papa made him go. "I'll not have my boys go out as failures because the youngster wouldn't be interested in the whims of the elders," Papa declared. It was only two weeks of travel, and we thought he was up to the task, being sixteen. This would give us time to continue to prepare, as he was not going to be the real advance man, but just there to lend a start up hand. As I recall he was going ahead a little over a week, which would have carried him almost to Broadhead. Al had worked there as a performer sharing the spot with a puppet show, so we figured the locals would respond well to our circus. Somewhere just past Sauk City, Henry met up with a couple of young women who'd given him more beer than he knew what to do with, and after picking his pockets, sent him off in the wrong direction. He was way off course in Waunakee when Papa received a wire.

"Mr August Ringling stop Have lost way and money is gone stop Need help and must return home stop Your son Henry"

Al and Gus rode all night to meet up with him and bring him back by way of Lodi. In the '90s he would rejoin us, this time by his own choosing, and he became the superintendent of special seating, as well as head of security. I suppose he learned a valuable lesson about the nature of people, because he was perfect at the job, a real charming man. We all gained some knowledge. The five of us pondered a new chapter: never give a man a job he doesn't cater to. In fact all the opposite; find out what a fellow wants to do and send him in that direction. No one was angry, and Papa, maybe a little saddened, put Henry to work at the harness shop, while Yankee helped us find a man to do the advance work. It was our plan to have John Hunter hire on as advance man anyhow, but he wasn't supposed to be available until opening night in Baraboo. We had lost valuable time and had lost two days without our production manager, Al.

Al came by it naturally. From the day we could walk, it was Al who could keep us walking in lockstep, and at whatever speed he commanded. There were only a dozen performers or so, a few ponies, a ring horse, and some stock horses. It was Al and Yankee's decision to mend the situation by getting a wire to Hunter and pressing his palm a bit to start earlier than was originally planned.

When Hunter showed up early, he acted like he owned the show. Papa was at the door to the barn and watching as Al performed his wire act and Lou prepared an equestrian piece on the one and only bay stallion we owned, which would simultaneously take place below Al. It was a daring feat as for what they lacked in skill they made up for in bravery. Hunter strolled up behind Papa and, with his hand on his back, confronted him as if there had been wrongdoing.

" You Ringling." Papa turned, startled as I headed toward him, myself already aware that this would be the new man.

"I am August Ringling," he answered slowly and somewhat irritated with the lack of respect of this man touching him without a proper introduction. I approached to relieve the situation.

"I am John Ringling," I began with complete civility.

"I'll talk with the grown up, junior," he replied.

"You'll do nothing of the sort," Papa snapped, "this 'boy' is one of the Ringlings in charge."

"As I said, I am John Ringling, and with my brothers we comprise half the management of the show." It was apparent from the start that Hunter did not like me, or any of us young upstarts. At that moment Yankee approached from behind.

"That you John Hunter?"

"Fayette, you ol' curmudgeon!" Hunter seemed relieved. As they began, Yankee shook his hand and placed his arm around his shoulder and began to walk him toward the river.

"Listen here now, I have no designs upon working under the direction of a bunch of boys no older than any 'first of May.'" He continued insinuating that we were too young and without any performer's sense and season.

"No, now you listen here, John, these boys may be young, but you will never, in ten lifetimes, find the kind of talent and horizons ahead that these five boys have." As they walked off toward the river, I realized at that moment that, one day, we were going to have to be the managers and the advance.

"You're here only for a short while," I thought, as I returned to my work in the barn. I saw clearly, for the first time, that one day it would be me who would go ahead of the show and beat the drum. I would see to it that all the world ahead of us was waiting for our grand enterprise to come to the aid of their boring little lives and bring the delight that everyman's child inside has been dreaming of. I even began imagining myself with the rare beauties that one could find in the real cities, like Madison, or even Chicago, and in the company of such women, I already could feel older, stronger, and respected. Meantime, I shoveled shit. My brothers liked the straw and sawdust, the hard day's work, and while we all could sit together and make musical melodies which conjured up fame, fortune, and future, there was the endless toil of shovels and pitchforks and shit. To them it made sweet smelling future, especially Alf, who so loved animals. But for me, I longed for city lights and knew how I'd get there, but first, work hard, keep my mouth shut, and wait. As a youngster I had not yet imagined that all of us would one day manage the show, that Charley, Alf, and Gus would be the advance and that my advance work would be the routing of a mighty enterprise. It was these kinds of moments when you just see the straw and shit and the end of the pitchfork and the future seems lifetimes off.

We had less than two weeks till our first show and opening in our home town where everyone knew us, and that timing was unnerving. In the Concert Company we always liked to get far enough from our home so that no one would think us as "local boys." But having such a famed circus legend as Fayette Yankee Robinson in our pocket, to open the show, gave us a confidence and shine we had never before felt. The tickets were sold ahead at Lyon's Apothecary for twenty five cents each, and we checked in every day as the sales mounted. It was most exciting to find, with less than a week to go, that farmers from around Baraboo, and farther away yet, were providing us with advance sales way beyond what we had figured. This was no "one penny" show, and as the day grew closer we realized we might not have planned for enough seating.

There were tricks of the trade we had already placed under our belts, and one was a way of expanding needed seats, by using barrels and planks, and another was a way of giving away seating to attract a wider audience. We had given the Reverend Conway tickets for the family, and Charley wanted them in the front center of the grandstand, especially Deedee. But we gave out some free seats for them to give to parishioners of importance, as well as giving some to the mayor of Baraboo, some to the town council members, and a few to George Merton of The Bank of Baraboo. Papa gave a few out to his lodge members who were higher degree Masons. There would never be enough free tickets to include everyone, so this always improved upon existing sales. The Reverend Conway had grown fond of us boys as we were already developing our "Sunday School Circus" reputation by never performing on Sundays, and we'd established a few rules which were right admirable to churchgoing folks.

A Big Charivari

It was all so easy for the boys from Baraboo. It all started with a big "charivari." If you're not familiar with the word, it's a big loud musical, drumming, hawing entry. Everything went according to plan – better yet. There were less than eighteen of us including the two gals. That included Jim Testor, who was the "candy butcher" and ran his own stand, paying us from his take. Back then a candy butcher sold pretzels, followed by pink lemonade, and in the end chewy candy. Besides the five Ringling boys, there were a few more windjammers, including Ned Kimball, George La Rosa, and George Hall. Frank Sparks and Al could walk the wire. Everyone doubled in brass. G.P. Putnam was an acrobat, and along with me, he was a clown and not bad at the stilts. Louise was an excellent equestrian, and although we used a Friesian trotter, she rode sidesaddle and did some trotting and back-walking that was damn good. Later on, with rosin on its back, Frank Sparks could do a somersault and a vault, although normally one might use a more broad-backed horse like a Percheron.

It was an amazing hour and a half. Folks cheered like they were seeing the big time, but it was more likely just hometown pride. Just the same we were a real show, not just five boys from Baraboo.

First Steps

Off and running, there they were with half a dozen farm boys as teamsters and across the roads of Wisconsin to their first real stand, away from home. They all felt a sense of victory, all the while reluctantly holding a little bit of fear and trepidation. After all, that was home town. Those were their people. Their parents and brothers and sisters, the Reverend Conway, his family, especially Deedee who cheered and gushed with unabashed glory, not just for Charley, but for all the boys and a kinship for Lou. There was not a stranger in the crowd to the Ringlings, but also known were half the performers, and all the while rumor ran around town about what a famous old fellow Yankee Robinson was. That was Saturday, May 19th, 1884. That was Ringlings' first circus show.

They set out on Monday. It should have been Sunday, but tearing down and packing took far more time than they ever expected. Yankee said nothing as they would later find out he'd let the boys fall flat on their faces before he'd try to teach them anything.

"A fellow is more receptive after a good wallop than when he thinks he knows something," he'd say. Yankee slept all the way to Prairie du Sac, just a ways north of Sauk City. Nothing went according to schedule, and the boys, especially Charley and John, wanted to wake him from his snoring which whistled so loud you could hear it two wagons forward and two wagons back. There were nine wagons, all told, and Ringlings owned only two, while Yankee's wagon, a covered Democrat no bigger than about five feet wide and eight feet long, was sort of on loan to the boys. They hoped to tally it as property of the show as they'd put so much time into painting and fixing it to look red and bold. One hour out of Baraboo, two of the tent poles fell out of a farm boy's wagon. The set of them had been precariously balanced off the back of the wagon so that every time they hit a pothole they'd sway up and down until finally, off they went. That cost about half an hour to reset and tie all of them down so it wouldn't happen again.

Sauk City was less than twenty miles off, but still with so many wagons, horses, and people to coordinate, it made for a long journey. Later that morning a wheel began screeching and turning crooked, and they had to stop and fix the wheel and axle. It was late morning when they were off again and finally past the road to Devil's Lake and had left Sauk Point behind. At midday they were near the road to Merrimac and high on the bluffs where they could see the river.

"Dinner breaks here," Al shouted out, leaning out from the lead wagon and waving his hand back and forth. The old wagon they had bartered for back in the early seventies served as the dining car, and they brought out planks and laid them across some saw squares and set up kitchen and dining all on one long table. Everyone fell in line and seemed to know what to do, as if this had all been done before. It was a simple meal and required no cooking as everything had been prepared on the Sunday after that first show. They had only taken small steps toward what would one day be called "The Sunday School Circus," but that first step was to never perform on Sundays. Some of this was Charley's attempt at impressing the Reverend Conway, because Charley was already scheming to ask for his daughter Edith's hand in marriage. Later on, the five brothers would make moral rules a marketing tool that would earn them the respect and patronage of every family in the Midwest, and eventually would give them a "clean" image that set them apart from every other circus in the world.

They had set several planks atop the food and water barrels and made a large circular social for dinner. Setting up makeshift seating was a tool learned on tour from The Carnival of Fun, when they played some stops that had only a few limited chairs, and they had to improvise creating their own theater. It was quiet up on the bluffs, and through the slight breeze, an anxious silence fell over everyone. Occasional snores and gasps came from Yankee's modest covered wagon.

"He gonna sleep the whole season?" asked George Hall.

"Don't fret over Yankee none," Al commanded. "He knows more about the road than you'll ever..."

"Ya, but he's old, an' he don't smell so good," George interrupted.

"Like I said, George, it doesn't matter, Yankee is the Boss Hostler, and if we want to learn anything about circus and how to be showmen, he's the one."

George was a windjammer and played coronet. He was as tall as Al but skinny. He was strong enough and was a great rigger.

Dinner was quick and Al kept the pace up. Conversation was light, and there was little time on their hands. Sauk City would be their longest stretch on the first week out, at just over seventeen miles. It was less than half an hour that all the tins were washed and the planks loaded up. The little band of wagons moved on. This would be one of only a few times this tour that they would stop for a midday meal. It seemed to get dark a little early, and then a light rain began to fall. About an hour north of Prairie du Sac it began to pour. The soggy little band of actors and teamsters were hunched over as they passed through the small village before dusk. The rain was falling hard enough that most all the townsfolk were under cover, and the troupe passed unnoticed. A loud crack of thunder and lightning woke Yankee; he popped his head in between Charley and John who were hunched forward, both at the reins.

"Well boys, how do you like life on the road?" Yankee cracked off a huge laugh. "Yes sir, this sure is the life well lived. Are we there yet?" Laughing again he slipped back into the drier place inside. The Ringling boys, soaked to the bone, said nothing.

The plan called for the troupe to arrive in Sauk City late afternoon, before most folks would be sitting to supper. However, it was dusk, or so it seemed with the rain and clouds in Prairie du Sac. This meant no parade, no grand entry, no charivari. As they approached Sauk City, small signs with red arrows, painted wide and quickly, appeared on trees and poles, especially at forks and turns in the road. These had been placed by Hunter and his small advance team of two tack spitters. They had worked closely with the bill posters and the advance man, pasting posters and arrows for directives. These small signs led the way for the troupe and teamsters to the lot, which in the driving rain was a relief for everyone, although it signaled upcoming work. The lot was just past the center of town, sandwiched between a lumber yard and a mercantile, and the setting was park-like, with several trees on one side. As fast as they could get the wagons in place, the rain let up, and a patch of sky opened, illuminating the site. It was almost magical. Al was off his wagon and signaling the positions for each wagon to deliver its parcel. Yankee was afoot before Charley could bring the wagon to a halt.

"Move my wagon over yonder, Charley, so as to set up the ducat box right off." He yelled across the small field, taking charge of his end. "Back right up here, now, so as we can get the front right in the crowd." Charley was quick off the box and was already moving the team of the two old nags, their first acquisition and probably their greatest lesson in bad logistics that the boys ever made.

It seemed they had been finishing their tour of last year's Concert Company, in Portage, when they came across a bargain on two horses. The horses were being liveried by a teamster, and Alf overheard the fellow say, "If only I could part with these ol' horses, I could get back to Madison and see my poor, sick Mama." Thinking on his feet, Alf saw a bargain and made a strike at it.

"Say mister, what if I could give you a fair price, and you could be helpin' me as well?"

"I'm all ears, young feller," the teamster responded as he smelled a sweet deal coming his way.

"Well," Alf leaned in, so that folks around the livery couldn't hear his offer, "how much would you be needin' to get you back to Madison?" The teamster rubbed his palm up and down the side of his face, then stopped, looked at Alf and rubbed his index finger under his eye.

"I reckon fifty ought to get me there just fine."

"Fifty." Alf rocked back, feeling almost tipsy. Now it was Alf's turn to rub his face and take his time. "Why, those ol' nags ain't worth twenty dollars." Although he had not realized what he had just said, but they really were old, with harness sores and had been far overworked, Alf was merely thinking with his pocket and the amount of cash he had on hand. "But I'll tell you what," he really thought himself clever, "seeing as your mother's ill, and I am a generous man, I'll give you the twenty, and you start on your journey tonight." The teamster hesitated, knowing he had the upper hand, and then went for the deal.

"Tell you what, mister, make it twenty five and I will be on my way." No sooner had he made the offer, and Alf reached out and shook his hand. "Done." Alf was grinning, ear to ear, as he had not bought any livestock since he and his brothers had traded for the old mustang, years ago. That horse was long gone, but they still had the wagon and intended to put it to use in their first circus, and now he had a team to pull it. These two old Percheron mares had long leg hair that looked like it had never been trimmed and likely was hiding more sores.

Minutes later, Charley and John caught up with him and nearly froze dead in the street when they saw Alf leading the two old nags.

"You gotta plan there Mr. Alf?" Charley asked sarcastically.

"Our first team!" Alf responded with pride.

"I'm no teamster, Alf, but judging by these two, I don't think they'll last till next spring." John placed a hand on one which wearily winced and backed away as if he'd hit a sore spot. It was getting dark out and their true condition was not even apparent.

"Listen up little brothers," Alf defended himself, "these are teamster horses, and they just need a little break and some rest over the winter. Besides, I got these for only twenty dollars, and that's a bargain." In circus style he was already learning the art of ballyhoo. Tell your cronies you got a bargain, but when it came to the public, tell him you paid double, so as to make them all the more important.

Ringlings didn't argue much once a decision had been made. It was something they had evolved into over all the years of working quickly to resolve problems and surpass obstacles. They all agreed these old nags could work fine but now had to find a place to winter them over. After inquiring in the livery, they were directed to a farm about a mile up the road, and into the night they went, leading their bounty to what should be a fine respite for the winter months. The farmer, a fellow named Larsen, spoke little English, but agreed to take the horses for ten dollars, as long as the boys returned before April and took them from his care. "Ya, make fat and happy by planting season, ya," he said, and with that the Ringlings headed back toward Baraboo, knowing they had their first team, already deciding that when the time came they would draw straws for who would make the trip back to bring these horses home.

It was Alf who drew the odd straw, and he was pleased to be relieved of all the work that was shaping up that March of 1884, which ranged from painting to sewing canvas and even sewing uniforms. He headed east toward Portage and found one of several ferries which made landing across at Portage. By the time he made landfall, the light was getting dim, and he quickly made his way through the little town and headed toward the farm to proudly pick up his horses. The sun had nearly set as he approached the farm.

There in the barnyard he looked for his horses but only saw two run-down and sickly old nags. The farmer's wife approached, recognizing the young man.

"Thurs yur horses n faten and ya takem now yung mann."
Somewhat dazed and in a sweat, Alf turned to the large figure of a woman, her head wrapped in a bonnet, wearing a long dress, with boots and her hands, which looked like carved wood, a size larger than his.

"Where's your husband ma'am," he asked her nervously.

"Me husbund, he tooken him sick abut a mont aback. Please taken yur horses, as we've no mur fodd ta givem." He eyed the sickly horses, noticing how the hair on their legs and manes hung off in patches.

Alf, struck with the graveness of the situation, tied off the horses and began down the road, leading, almost pulling the two sick and weary creatures on their nearly thirty mile journey back to Baraboo. As he left the farm a light rain began falling and the temperature dropped to that foggy point where it feels like snow but is wet like rain. The reluctant animals followed, one with a leg hobbled by a wound Alf couldn't make out in the dark. He made the ferry for the evening trip across. The ferry master said nothing of the condition of the poor creatures but stared frequently with an agonizing and judgmental scowl on his face. The long journey home would change Alf's life and lead him to be deeply compassionate about animals and their welfare.

After the first hour, the roads were so muddy that the horses' hooves occasionally made a slurping sound in the muck as the pair swayed up and down, moaning in pain and protest. Every step, every several yards, Alf felt more and more for their suffering. Somewhere after midnight, Alf broke into a sweat and began to shiver uncontrollably with chills. At one point his left boot stuck in the mud and pulled clear off his foot and he fell forward and landed on his knees. He pulled himself up and wiped the mud from his sock, balancing to replace the boot, and he saw a light from a farmhouse a couple hundred yards across a field. He made his way to the back door where a farmer and his wife were rising for chores. The farmer, hearing the sound of the weary animals, greeted him before he had a chance to knock.

"I was about to question your presence, but seeing that you, mister, look nearly dead, and those horses look like they died yesterday, I'd say you best get in here. The wife will take care of you with some nourishment while I take them poor unfortunate critters to the barn for healing."

Some time later it would be a split between Alf and Al on who would be the more caring when it came to animals, and Al being the

Equestrian Director filled the bill. But as Alf, taken to fever and chills, lay recovering in a stranger's house for three days, he had time to think on the welfare of animals. He would later make a pact with his brothers that any show with the name Ringling would respect animals as much as any other performers, and that any handler caught mistreating animals would be immediately removed from the Ringling lot.

The two sickly old nags were treated with absolute care by the stranger, and after the horses were fed well and their wounds tended to, Alf hardly recognized them. The three of them were somehow bonded for life, albeit a short life for the horses. The remainder of Alf's journey was short and fortunately all in daylight. His brothers, who had been worried enough to consider sending someone to look for him, were glad to see he was well, and even welcoming of the aged beasts. After hearing the story and feeling Alf's bond and respect with the horses, they were fed extra, a Ringling trademark, and treated with honor.

Setting up for their first performance away from home was hurried and hectic. Somehow, from what seemed to be a worrisome state of sleep and lethargy, old Yankee shook from his stupor and took command of the troupe. With all the mud and the arrival behind schedule, everyone, including Al, seemed to lose their grip. But Yankee was like a ship's captain awakened in the storm and taking command when all others were torn from their duty. He shouted commands, occasionally inaudible yet somehow understood, and immediately caused action.

"Bob, you, Meltz, and Jimmy guy up that king pole and then get them four shorter ones and arrange them with eight yard steps 'tween 'em and face 'em all the same direction. Then pace out the six side poles each side facing opposites, just like we practiced." The tent was a three pole and could seat four hundred proper, but they would make seats for more if needed.

"Charley, Lou, Hayes, and John, roll that canvas and move right behind them." Yankee was in his element. He was suddenly not the elderly and tired fellow, but a younger man, as if middle aged and still in his prime and very much in charge and very much the Boss Hostler. All at one moment he could direct the riggers, then get the horses and wagons under the control of the teamsters and direct John and Otto to begin to entice the onlookers with proper ballyhoo, all the while lighting lamps and setting up the ducat wagon. He even managed to get some gilly help from the onlookers. Gillies were outsiders who helped when needed, and right then they needed every bit of help they could get. Yankee was aware, as far back as the dinner stop, that there would be no parade, and the best way to get a crowd that was expecting their arrival was to entice folks of all ages to get involved. Dark was settling in and the clouds made nightfall seem imminent. There was no wind, so while John, Otto, and several townie boys strung and lit lanterns, as a makeshift chandelier crew, the whole area came alive and outshone the lanterns on the street. The center poles and rigging were up in minutes and the stakes were driven hard. As fast as the canvas rose, the interior was lit and several boys laid a ring and then set the stand. Yankee settled back from command, and he made sure John changed to costume quickly. Others followed suit while several arranged the stands. It seemed a show was about to happen.

Al, feeling more confident, assumed his role of Equestrian Director and began setting an entry of canvas, called a "back door," behind which the band was assembling. By the time the band struck up a tune, Yankee was calling a crowd. There was rarely ever an orator as good as Fayette Yankee Robinson. While John juggled out front, Otto took the ducats. This was the "ballyhoo." Folks were filling the streets and in some cases running to the promised show. Prominent members of the community had arrived with their free ducats given them by Hunter and his crew. There wasn't time for Jimmy, the candy butcher, to make a concession stand, so Lou and Emmy Hanson passed hard candies in paper, which parents readily bought for anxious children's mouths. The seats filled and several new benches had to be set. Straw was laid in front of the grandstand to make ground seating, and children filled it quickly. Although not capacity, they sold over three hundred seventy five tickets and figured another fifty had been given out. Still another dozen children peered in from under the side sheets.

It wasn't much of a show. That didn't matter, however. The boys were seasoned, and Al already had a knack for showmanship and direction. He knew how to keep a pace and to always have something moving. Never a silence was allowed. Charley led the band and it was a real windjammer's act with eight performers. John clowned and tried some mime for the first time, although much of the mime was too difficult for farmers and lumbermen to comprehend. But when Al balanced that plow on his chin and juggled three balls, some folks began stomping their feet and almost brought down the stands. Lou had what was one of the show's first menagerie and sideshow acts, a boa constrictor, and for small-town folks to see a gal with a snake and tattoos on her arms was totally captivating. Jimmy Pearson and three others did tumbling, a small pyramid act balanced and sprang off a large teeterboard. The show was small; even the one horse act was humble, but still, what it lacked in content it made up in show-manship.

It ended with a small parade, just as it had begun with a small spec, but the people of Sauk City were elated. The only hitch was that the band stopped for too long as Al blew his whistle and the show ended. It was an "all out" move where the band actually left, and on Al's command they played outside which signaled the crowd to go. The performers left and only a few riggers remained. When the "all out" signal was given, Yankee summoned the troupe back in. They were proud and elated and sat in the ring, as if they had just won the war.

"So, this is a circus!" Yankee was half smiling, and the band of twelve performers and a few teamsters laughed nervously. "And to think, I foolishly put my name on this sniveling excuse for a sideshow!" The group fell still, but he had their attention. "Somehow the show was rather good." Nervous laughs. "But if you think for one moment that a circus, a good circus, relies on a one and one half hour show as a testament to its quality, you are gravely mistaken. Bring me a seat." A teamster boy grabbed Yankee a stool and he pulled it close, stayed standing and balanced one knee on the stool. "Now listen here," he softened his voice to almost an intimate level. "I wouldn't waste my time, nor my good name on a show if I didn't think this troupe had what it takes, no way. Especially these five brothers. And I put my name right alongside theirs. But today was a test. Saturday was easy cause we were in hometown territory. But what happened on route today was abysmal. Why, in my fifty some years of show-manship I never stopped for supper. That cost us a packed house."

"But we sold over," Charley stammered.

"Shit sold!" Yankee yelled. "If we'd been in town midday we could have had all the canvas up, could of had a parade, could have cooked and sold them cakes, could have filled six hundred seats. Could have had a matinee and an evening performance, could have, could have, could have! Hunter and his crew postered the whole damn town and every farm road to the west. The mayor, the best merchants, the pastor, and their families were all there in free seats and we could have done better. A circus is more than a show. It's a dance from May through September and we never stop." Yankee stood upright and began to pace. "Al, you are the Equestrian Director and from now on you are the Boss Hostler. You ride ahead and check the roads and you ride the length of our caravan and watch the wagons. I am the general manager of this little rag-tag enterprise. Lou, you and Emmy and Bertrand see that everyone has a roll or two and some dried beef for the ride to keep 'em fed. Amongst you we need someone to oversee the rigging and the arrival at each stop. Charley, John, and Alf, you see that the performers are ready, soon as we are fed and just before the parade. Otto, you got bills to pay, now, and business to keep track of, soon as we arrive. Most of the time we are going to leave for the next stand at three or four in the morning. Smiling sarcastically, John turned to Yankee and asked, "And what are you gonna do, Fayette Yankee Robinson?"

"Sure as shit I'll watch over you and be sure you don't fuck it all up!" Everyone laughed except John. "Listen up all: Let's strike this show, load up and get some rest. We move at four o'clock sharp. Tomorrow we'll give a parade in Black Earth, and if we leave on time we can follow the parade with a matinee, then we have a night show and leave again at four a.m. – Get it?"

No Runs

We learned just about everything we really know about circus that season. Yankee is the reason. We have almost as much gratitude for that man as we do Ma and Pop. Sorry he didn't live out the season, but I guess he wasn't meant to. We learned that circus makes as much dough from all the other vendors and activities, like food sales from butchers. We learned to sell dry salty food first, and drinks second, then hard candy and chewy foods last. We got young boys on the horse with a pretty gal cause that's what we had that was special, but later on it would be on a giraffe, an elephant, or what have you, and that brought more dough. By mid-season we made Iowa, and Hunter and Yankee had us playing little towns, no "runs" – stands with more than one day – but he had us win the hearts of small town folks.

"Stay clear of big towns and big cities till you're ready. Those folks are used to top shows, like Van Amburgh, Dan Rice, and James Bailey, or Coup and Barnum. There's plenty of seasoned shows out there too, not a whole bunch bigger'n yours, but they got years on you boys, and once you play and play poorly you'll not show in that town for a while, no way, no sir!"

Yankee was pretty matter of fact and spoke like he was the law, so we took his words for gospel. Good thing too, cause he was right. We learned about morals, long before we started the circus. We had some ideas even during the earlier Concert Company tours. True, these were business decisions, before all else, but I do reckon me and my brothers were moral fellows. Even in our first years as a circus, there were always grafters trying to muscle their way in. Otto ran the ducat wagon, also known as the Red Wagon, which doubled as the "everything in the office car." Since it looked the most official and had "Yankee Robinson and Ringling Brothers" across it, every grafting son-of-a-bitch along the route would come there first. Yankee'd sit back and let us learn – the hard way. By the time Otto would be shaking the hand of some fellow who proposed to short our clientele, and he'd realize he'd been had, Otto, all five foot six and stocky as he was with them coal black eyes would say, "No sir, not in our show, no one is going to do such trickery to the patronage of this fine show," and he'd send 'em packing. They'd laugh and scoff at us.

"You Ringling kids belong in a Sunday school. You'll never make your share if you're so honest and so high an' mighty, nope." This always just made us stronger in our convictions. We figured money would come to those that did right by others, and so it did.

We played one-show towns and often had Hunter and his helpers in the advance turn back and be everything from the two week advance to the twenty four hour man. We learned, each and every one of us, who we wanted to be, who we would become and what our strongest points were.

I developed a love of routes and planning so that I knew every little road and fork in Wisconsin, and one day it would be trains. I would come to know every train, every arrival, every departure in the United States and Canada.

Charley, he came to be wanting to adjust the language and color of the posters, how they were pasted, and how they were handed out. Charley could mix words in such a way that he could get people talking about the show every day for weeks before we arrived.

Otto developed a knack for finding money, honest money, in every minute of the show. We'd have a ducat wagon downtown before the parade, and once the parade came and folks saw their neighbors buying tickets or cheering, they'd line up by the dozens, each wanting to get tickets for their families. There was money to be had from candy, crackers, corn, and drinks. Like everything we learned, it all started small, with what we could dig up from our funds, what we could wrap in paper, and what we could entice folks to buy. Why even after the show was over and the folks were out, they'd still be spending and they'd want something to take along.

Alf, who everyone else called "Alf T.," became the best talker in the business. He knew every editor and their families, what restaurants they liked and what dishes to order for them. He got ahead of the show and got the newspapermen literally eating out of his hands. He loved them and they loved him.

Al learned how to manage everyone, whether it was a windjammer, a bull handler, or a canvas man. Everyone followed Al's every command, and I'm guessing it was 'cause every one of us that first season did everything that gave him a handle on how to manage folks. Hell, there were barely more than twelve of us and the comings and goings of about ten farm boys as teamsters. We were close and Al learned to keep on our every move. Most of all, Al, our eldest brother, learned something that would make Ringling Brothers the strongest show in the world. As Equestrian director, he could direct the whole show, captivate the audience, and no matter what went right or what went wrong, he always kept the move on. Never a dull moment, so to speak. Never a silence, never a slip, except when one was needed to keep folks on their toes.

Our mission was to give the most spectacular show that started when all would come in, and finally when all were out and folks were home in their little beds at night, all they could think about was the show they saw and dream about the show that might come back – next year.

We learned what was taught us most from the great teacher: the route. But Yankee, bless his soul, was like a teacher and a father to us boys. He let us learn by failing, and when he knew we were ready to get the lesson, he'd sit us all down and pure gospel'd come right out his mouth. He didn't just teach us the tricks of the trade that he'd learned along the way, the hard knocks, the cirky lingo, the way of the route; he taught us to keep digging, to keep learning and never stop. For that, and that alone, we'll never forget him, but more so, never was there a more kind fellow. Even when he'd have words with us, stern like, there was more love in his heart than Mama's, and for me to even have a thought like that says plenty.

We were most of the way through the season when he'd got a telegram from his son in Ohio. September, I believe it was, late. He had to go to Ohio and see his son. He didn't say why, just that it was important. He caught the train from Clarion, Iowa. A week and a half later we were in Rockwell, Iowa, when we got a telegram. It seems along the way, while switching trains in Jefferson, Old Yankee Robinson suffered a heart attack and died on a train platform. Several years later while playing that town, we would give funds to erect a memorial to Yankee. Until that day I never saw my brother Al cry. I think we all let loose a few tears. We held a special actors' ceremony for him. He had left his mark on every one of us. Here it is fifty two years later and my eyes still well up.

All tallied, we played over one hundred small towns that first year as Old Yankee Robinson & Ringling Brothers Double Show. We were just over a dozen actors. We were actors, band leaders, security, canvas men, concessions, marching parades, roustabouts, agents, riggers, managers, stock managers; you put a label on it and we did it. We live for the show, not for some false pride, but for the success of all. So the best most seasoned performers will get right down in the mud and push alongside a roustabout. We set that precedent then, and everyone has always lived it thus. A handful of actors and nine farm boys and one fellow who was too old to farm but too broke to sit home, all set out on May 19th, 1884. Only three of those farm boys finished out October, but still we went home with nine teamsters and God knows where they all came from, but we all ended up home in Baraboo. Before the first of May, we went under the tutelage of one the great circus men of our time, and before the frost of the harvest season we would offer a eulogy to his honor. Although every one of us Ringlings was seasoned in show and trials of the road, only Al and his good wife Lou had the spice and familiarity of circus under their wings when we started out, while the rest of us were still just wide eyed boys.

By the time we made the barn in Baraboo, every one us was a seasoned circus man with more knowledge under our belts than most any veteran on the road, and more hunger and thirst for knowledge and success than most men. Stronger still was the bond amongst us. We had yet experienced what we thought was the worst that could be, from night hauls where we'd fall asleep in the middle of a brotherly chat and run smack upside a tree, to a blowdown late season where we thought we might have lost our grip on the entire show.

It was late September and we played La Motte, Iowa, on a Saturday. Everything we had learned that season had come into our hands. We arrived in the morning after a short haul and set up perfect like in what they called the town square. Very few towns had such a field where we could play right in the center. The lot was cheap and there were no city fees. It seemed Otto had to give a little extra to the man who called himself mayor and was also our landlord at the smallest hotel we saw all season. Everything went better than a show in heaven, and the canvas was tight by mid-morning. We had a ducat wagon (the Red Wagon) two blocks over by the mercantile, which made our presence bigger, and by dinner time when folks were milling around, we gave a noon hour parade, maybe the best of the season. The sky was crisp and not a cloud shown forth as our little troupe and our few wagons passed through. We were able to give both a "band wagon" and a "fife and drum," and Al rode through twice on our one and only ring stock, a horse smaller in stature than a parade horse but able to perform more tricks than most folks in farm and river country were used to. This was further exemplified by Al in his equestrian top hat and formidable tails. I have to tell that he was downright elegant!

All was as if in a picture – perfection. The girls gave children rides on the working stock and sold peanuts and salt cakes, and the band made a stupendous effort at entertaining the parents. By the time we had come in, we had sold out the afternoon show and were selling evening tickets as well. Both shows were exquisite, and we had numerous opportunities to exhibit the tricks and acts we had polished over a long season. We had a slack wire act with Lou on the wire and simultaneous with Al juggling and balancing the plow. W.H. Pearson and three other boys performed acts of balanced pyramids, and no faster than they had finished, Al had that horse performing at liberty. No shows all season had come off the likes, and to have an evening show sell out as well made us all feel the top of our play. By God, when teardown came we were all humming and aglow. So moved by the success that we woke the landlord early and demanded breakfast at one in the morning.

"Do you folks have any idea what time it is?" All we could do was laugh in unison.

"Time," Charley roared, "why there's no time like the moment at hand!"

"Why I ought to send the bunch of yous packing." We all roared, laughing all the harder at how ridiculous we were, and drunk with happiness.

"Listen up Mr. Warren, we'll make it worth your while to get up early and serve us breakfast," I said and slapped him on his back. Old man Warren, in his long gray nightshirt and the silliest nightcap I'd ever seen, leaned forward.

"Suppose you tell me what 'worth my while' is." With that the whole bunch of us broke into uncontrollable laughter.

I never remembered what we settled on, but I do remember that he and the misses started right in cooking as fast as they could light a fire in that stove. Before three in the morning we were riding a moonlight haul to Bellevue, all the while not even figuring that it was Sunday.

Bellevue was a long haul, and we planned all Sunday hauls that way. Being a moral company we never played Sundays and always tried to plan the route accordingly. We arrived and parked ourselves near the lot, and several made their way to the church. This was customary. Although only a few of us ever really had religion, it was good business to show our faces in church. Most of these farm towns were full of what they called "God fearing folks," and we best bide by their ways; it made for good ticket sales. "Why, I do hear so much good about you Ringling boys being men of God" was common speak for the reputation already preceding us.

We played for the people of the land, not for grafters and urchin making trash that made fun of us. Every move was always calculated. We not only talked about it, I mean amongst us brothers, but did so behind closed doors. No one should be able to cipher whether or not we were moral for business or we were moral cause we were. After service we made our way back to the lot, talking long enough for proper and polite introductions and informing parishioners that we would never consider selling any tickets until late afternoon on a Sunday, but really would avail ourselves to the hardworking folks of Bellevue on Monday. As the years went on, we even developed a baseball team and played the locals, after church and after Sunday socials. In some places Al, Alf, and some actors would go fishing, usually allowing local folks to take them to favorite fishing holes.

Sunday afternoon was more bucolic than Saturday, and we took more time than usual for setting the canvas. Life was good and we were appreciative. By afternoon there were twenty five youngsters pulling the rigging with us, and fathers rolling up sleeves and driving poles. We scarcely needed the working stock as we had enough men and boys with us combined to set a fine lot.

Sunday supper was social, as most were in those first years, I mean with the town folks. We were few enough in number that social was acceptable, and Lou wore a dress that was provincial and covered her paint. This was years before we established our own dining cars, tents, and "hotels" wherein we would feed our own and live like a great family. The meal was provided by Mr. and Mrs. Ackerson who ran the Town Central Hotel. This had been set in advance and Hunter and his crew had struck the deal. As always Otto was not happy with the price, but we are always men of our word and never went back on it. The mayor, the parish minister, and their families joined us. The youngsters were all excited about circus performers and could scarcely contain themselves.

"Can you really walk on wire, ma'am?"

"Do you have any wild animals?" We worked our way around that question, knowing full well we would one day have some sort of animal actors, and maybe a menagerie with strange and exotic creatures, but we had what we had, and we made a show of it.

The night ended early for everyone. Sundays were the one opportunity we had to catch up on sleep. Ever since Yankee had scolded us for our lax attitudes, we ran our show on our toes and slept less than three hours most nights. The lack of sleep pushed our mental condition to a place of restlessness and right best thought. We had no choice, lest we fall apart. Monday morning we rose to skies so magnificent we had to take a second notice. The oranges, reds, and purples on clouds spread across the plains like scales on a fish shimmering aglow.

"I don't like it," Al remarked as we walked a fast pace to the hotel for breakfast.

"What don'tcha like brother?" I asked him, stopping in the street and forcing him to stop.

"We'd better keep an eye out for bad weather." He lowered his voice. "We need some kind of signal during the show, if something should come about." Alf had stopped, and Otto saw the three of us in the middle of the street. Before we knew it, Charley was in on it. "Listen now," Al continued, talking to all of us, "if someone gives me the signal during the show that there's weather coming, I'll blow the whistle three times fast. Charley, change a tune then – on the band."

"To what?" Charley demanded.

"I don't know. Maybe whatever was gonna be your finale. Alf, you spread the word and spread it so that it'll stay amongst us. We don't want no people stampeding, and no one should catch wind that we are expecting something."

The morning continued on beautiful, and the menacing clouds broke up as we held our parade. It was September, but you'd reckon it was the fourth of July, as the whole of the townsfolk were with us and all happy as pigs in shit! As our parade wound onto the lot, so did a parade of excited folks who readily bought food from our stand while children rode the pony and the horse with Lou and Emmy. By the time the folks came in, the excitement was rich in the air. This was better than Saturday's show and most of us had forgotten our woes of ill weather that might be coming from the south and west.

I was at the Red Wagon, which Otto and I had moved back toward the entry. Otto was organizing the proceeds as we had a straw house, meaning we had a packed house and had to place straw in front of the stand for folks who would sit on the ground. The show was mid-way when I noticed that the sky, which had been darkening the entire time, was now black as night.

I made a decision about two thirty in the afternoon to give word to Al that it didn't look so good. He was nearly ready to perform the ring stock piece where the horse dances backwards at liberty. Just as he saw me heading his way a gust of wind sucked hard at the back door, and the canvas curtain picked up and whacked W.H. in the face, where the fife and drum band stood ready to play. Al looked back at me and no word needed to be exchanged. He blew the whistle three times, and Charley immediately began playing a C.L. Barnhouse march that I had never heard before.

This gave the "all out," and actors and teamsters began escorting folks from the tent. The sides were lifting and you could feel the panic. Still we kept most of the folks from fleeing. It took all of two minutes before everyone was out. Minutes after the signal was given, every hand was atop of it, and everyone was driving loose poles and pulling the sides. The entire big top leaned east and then went slack. For a moment there was a sense of relief. Then there was a roar, as if a train was passing, and the center-pole leaned so far east I was afraid we'd lose the whole canvas. This was followed by a series of ripping and groaning sounds, only made worse by the sounds of the twenty of us in exasperating gasps. The whole ordeal lasted less than a minute, but it seemed like an hour. When it was over our big top was in thirty pieces, and seams were waving like circus flags in the wind. No one was hurt.

We learned something of foresight that day. Always be on the lookout for the worst, all the while expecting the best. We cancelled the evening show and refunded money, and although we had only a bit more than half a show that day, those who came were more than impressed, and those who would miss the evening show were sorely disappointed, all the while asking if we would return next season.

We played Hanover, Illinois, the next day, open air, under threatening skies. We filled only half the seats but at least made our expenses. And by not having a night show we had all hands on the canvas making repairs for the last four stands on our route before we headed back to the barn. The last stand was Benton, Wisconsin, and being close to home we played our hearts out. Still every one of us was shaken by how close we'd come to catastrophe, just days earlier.

Look here. Most people never dare to make so much as a start. With Yankee as the real Boss Hostler, we played plenty of hard starts that season. Some lots weren't more than a mud hole. We started calling 'em frog ponds, mostly because they were full of frogs. Hell the horses sunk so deep they'd get lame just by being stuck in the mud. W.H. would put on them stilt legs and sink clear up to his feet in the mud. We had shows we had to cancel because there was no place to show. Yankee taught us to keep on walking.

"Put one foot in front of the other," he'd say, while demonstrating with his own feet, "walk, head straight for your dreams and don't look back."

We played towns where tragedy had struck the day before. We came into Waukon, Iowa, in late June, and before we knew what had hit us, we realized half the town had been knocked flat by a tornado just the day before. We didn't try to mount a show. We pitched in to help the folks there, and before we left they were begging us to juggle, tell stories, and clown a bit. They wanted to feel good again. They fed us and tried to put cash in our hands, but we wouldn't take none. We left in good standing and generous spirits and told them one day we would play there again, and to expect us back. We never played Waukon again, but when we played neighboring towns, the folks from Waukon would come by the wagonloads.

Three
The Mud, the Blood, and the Shit

The Mud and the Blood

Each year had its trials and each year offered its rewards. Eighteen eighty five was grand and '86 grander, while each year we strove to add more, be more independent, and always put back more than we took out. If ever there was a year where we let self pride and avarice get the most of us, it was 1888. At first, like any year, we had our share of big water coming down and filling our dates with no shows and ponds for lots. This year was particularly bad.

There were many years where we were made fortunate by the misfortunes of others. Shows went down and they sometimes went down hard. When times were good for us, some had it bad. Why, during the early years before we had a tent show, when Al would go off and work in circuses, small shows, he would return with tales of blowdowns and floods. Some of the equipment of those shows ended up in our show. Sometimes we'd buy the whole show, acts and all. It was hard to see seasoned performers and grown businessmen take a fall. But then, we know what it was like. We almost lost our show in our fifth season.

It was the spring of '88. I was the head of advance. We had made tracks and reserved performances in three weeks procession before the show opened in Baraboo. The whole time the skies let loose rivers of water wherever we went. The posters went up wet and the inks ran bad. We had to treat the sheets with paraffin so that the ink wouldn't run. It was tedious and made for less coverage. I left Minnesota and made opening night in Baraboo. The good news seemed to be that the rains had relented and the show could now look ahead toward brighter days.

Our little show was bigger than it had ever been. For me to be at the opener was good for my heart, and I could allow for such excitement to be carried back to my advance team. Our 148 foot big top could now seat over a thousand, and with standing and straw seating we could handle twelve hundred. We had a real menagerie, with a giraffe, birds, snakes, three lions, monkeys, a zebra, emu, performing dogs, eighty horses, and by my forceful push we had our first two elephants.

We had over two hundred persons in our show. Joe Parsons, who had just years earlier employed my brother Al, now was an aerialist in our show, while his brother Al (we called him Butch on account of his being a candy butcher), joined our troupe as well. It was a splendid show. It was real circus. We had a separate concert, just like the big shows. Parsons walked an outside wire over the canvas as a free act. We had a fife and drum band. Both Alf and Charley played with the band. As a master Equestrian Director, Al had several Normans that could dance at liberty, and Lou was an amazing actor on horseback and dazzled the best horsemen in the audience. Besides the main show we had a real sideshow with twelve performers, and yes, I do say performers. In our show the sideshow people are regular people and treated as such. Fat lady, midget, dwarf, bearded lady, tattooed man: it really doesn't matter what they are; they are part of the show.

We left Baraboo with money in the til and excitement in our hearts. I headed toward Caledonia by rail, and the boys struck out for Wisconsin towns like Reedsburg and Cazenovia. No sooner had the show headed out than the rains began to fall. It rained day and night. The roads turned into rivers of mud, and at times they had to stop as the rain fell so hard they feared they would drive right off the roads. Some days they missed entire stands because a half day drive could take a day and a half. In Reedsburg the lot was under half a foot of water by the time they got some canvas up. The only spectacle in the show was that all the wardrobe trunks were floating around like boats. It was worse in Cazenovia.

Three wagons were ripped from their axles by hired farmers' teams pulling them out of the mud. I received a telegram from my brothers, and they asked me to join with them to ask our banker, George Merton at the Bank of Baraboo, to intervene and loan us one thousand dollars. It was in those few days of awaiting a response, as the rains continued to pour, that as a band of brothers, we were in despair. We had made a decision to reduce our show and spend the money to ship wagons and personnel back to Baraboo. Worse yet, we made a painful decision to reduce our admission ticket to twenty five cents. This, after all the quarreling and convincing over prior seasons to become a fifty cent show. We made a decision, and even by telegram, I laid in big on it. We would transcend victorious. No matter how, we would make it through and be better than before. But before we could ever arrive at such a decision, we had looked through the darkness and absorbed every dire consequence of the experience of failure. There, meeting failure face to face, we vowed never to succumb.

No sooner had we received the funds did all fortune roll out before us. It began with the sun, which burned away the clouds and shone like God's countenance upon us. What had been the beginning of the worst of seasons transformed into the best of years. That year, 1888, would mold us into more than just showmen; it would elevate us to circus men. We never spent the one thousand dollar loan. The money had been wired to us in Caledonia. Caledonia would become our symbol for transcendence. In a week's time we had paid all expenses. I had bought new paper and we were printing sheets faster than ever, and we had two thousand dollars in our till, after we repaid the bank. Most of the rest of the season was profitable. However, there was more knowledge to be gained and more decisions to be made.

In Webster City, Iowa, one of our canvas men, Tom Bassett, shot and killed a roustabout, James Richardson. Worse yet, it was over a stupid argument while drinking. Although we had rules already, this was cause for us to expand our rules and begin the list, which would eventually become "The Fifty One Rules." We were to become "The Sunday School Circus." We had rules for behavior, dress, ethics, drinking, socializing, and a special list for the girls. It started small but we enhanced it every year, and as we did, we enhanced our reputation. As hard as other shows laughed at us, our reputation amongst families and churchgoing people grew.

We grew further by mistakes in that year than any year prior. But as mistakes had always been a fair teacher, we were, therefore, well schooled. We learned more about the welfare of animals. Sadly, some died while in our care. And people. People were a lot to care for and we had to be prepared. There were accidents. Riggers would miss and hit the foot of a canvas man with the sledge and break toes or sometimes knock toes clear off. People fell. Performers fell. In the grand entry in one town, some little urchin of a child slingshot Lou's horse, and she was thrown from her horse and landed on her head. The crowd thought she was dead. The more we had, the greater our responsibility. We agreed to come forward and meet the challenge and do everything in our power to foresee the potential risk and tragedy before it happened, and therefore be always prepared. We experienced something else that year: fights. We called a fight a "clem." The shout out to the show was "Hey Rube!" That meant get your ass in gear, as one of ours is taking a thrashing!

That very year in a small town in Missouri, Bolivar I believe, it was hot and muggy. The air was so thick you could see it, like a cloud, and it made your ears ring. Some fellow thought one of our men had picked his pockets. Likely it was a grafter had followed along and worked the crowd. We caught them at almost every show and turned them over to the local authorities. Within a couple years we would have a crew of Pinkerton detectives to work with us on every show. I guess this grafter got by us. Before our boys knew what had transpired, a local ruffian had smashed open the head of Jimmy Stillman, one of our canvas men. Within minutes there were a couple hundred locals, and they were knocking down menagerie cages, pulling stakes for clubs, and Butch Parson's stand was trampled.

By the time the "Hey Rube" went up, a force of most of our show was up against it. No one was seriously injured, but some heads were bloodied, and some farmers broke their fists up against some of our boys' noses. We gave no evening performance and never played Bolivar again. When I talk mud and blood and shit, that's the blood I hate the most. Sure, I never hesitated to come to the aid of my brothers or any of our people. They were family. But I knew, we all knew, every time it happened, it hurt our image. Every time something hurt our image, we stood up to it, defended our reputation, and always sought to expand our image as good people who run a clean show. We never shied away from it.

"Closing stand." Those words send chills through my heart. Two lonely words. Even in the mud show days, I would always be on the lot for the closing stand. When all was done for the season and the winds of winter were blowing dry leaves around the wheels of the ticket office and the business was over, it was an all out time for the great family of performers who had lived so close, had divined one purpose, had fought for each other, had struggled through the mud, and had buried man and beasts along the route, a journey which had seemed like a lifetime. We would all be in different places by Thanksgiving. Me and my brothers and a crew of twenty or so would be back at the barn in Baraboo, where lonely animals far from their homes of origin would be cared for and kept warm against a Wisconsin winter. A place where we would design the next stupendous year, a year which must far surpass the prior year. Where blacksmiths and wagon builders, costume makers, and designers would quietly work through the dark hours of winter and begin to bring forth the wonders of the future.

It is beyond melancholy to play the closing stand. It's as if the party's over and favorite cousins, best friends, aunts and uncles are all going home and we have to say goodbye. At that moment it isn't the loneliness yet, it is the mere idea of it. We know it's coming. We expect it. We have experienced it before. We know we'll experience it again. So back to Baraboo. Our closing stand was Sauk City where we played to nearly two thousand, and the afternoon show was full to the ring banks. The night show was packed as well. The local paper wrote that we were "as good a show as any of the big shows," though not nearly as big. Still, I had to look back at our company of more than two hundred and remember that first stand in '84, when we were just a company of less than twenty. Yankee would've been proud. So long, 1888.

We returned home, all debts paid, and placed nearly fifteen thousand dollars in the Bank of Baraboo. This did not account for the first time me and my brothers loaded up our own goods with fistfuls of dollars. In personhood we were each well stocked. Within the month we built a new sixty foot square ring barn and several other buildings on the Bassett property we had purchased at season's close the previous year. Success was in our pockets, our hearts, and our outlook. Never mind that this had started as the worst year in our history. Our victory was never to be questioned, but moreover to be acknowledged and nurtured. Good things were coming to us, and by God we had our hands out, arms spread wide and greeted every inch of it.

Eighteen eighty nine would be our last year as a mud show and we knew it long before the decision was made. We stood on the shoulders of '88. We quit going out in the fall for Carnival of Fun shows. We began our plan of how to get the show on the rails, and although it took a whole year, we did it! We added something special to the show and it took all year.

A Drink at Rice Station

Jim Langer was a track inspector. It was eleven p.m. May 16th, 1892, when he left Concordia, Kansas, and headed toward Rice Station. The clouds were thick as he walked along the track carrying his lantern. A waning half moon drifted in and out of the clouds occasionally making his journey easier and friendlier. There were several trestles in the first mile and he checked them over as usual: "Banner Creek, top, okay, under, check cross members, look for wear, cracks, anything out of place – okay." On to the next. He walked along the track like any other night, checking the rail, loose fill, anything out of the ordinary. About a mile out the tracks, he made over a series of fill and spillway as it crossed part of Cloud Lake. There's where Jim saw it. He needn't go any further and there was no trestle to go under. A rail, left bent upward a good half a foot or more.

"This is a problem," he thought to himself, rubbing the scruff on his chin. "Gotta give warning. Where to go?" He turned back looking toward Concordia and knew it was a mile back. Rice Station, three miles. "Rice Station, home, not far, I can get there soon enough."

Langer thought about the new bottle of whiskey he'd left outside in the wood pile. Martha didn't allow drink in the house. He bet he could hurry on to Rice Station, finish out the inspection along the way, make it home and have a drink before any train came this way at this late hour. He hurried through the night checking the rest of the track the best he could. As he strolled into Rice Station he reported to his boss, Bert Hollerick.

"Bert, we got a bender out on the pass over Cloud Lake."

"Jimmy, you ain't got no business comin' all the way up here to tell us that. You should of turned back and reported into Concordia." Bert in his anger grabbed Jimmy by his collar and tie, while Jimmy tried pulling away.

"Listen Bert, I made good time and finished the rest of the inspection."

"Oh hell, what time is it?" Bert looked over at the station clock. Two forty. "Shit Jimmy, we got a train coming through any minute out of Beloit for Washington." The two men ran for the telegraph office.

Our Best Years

Our best years were sometimes our worst. After '90 and '91 we were unstoppable. Two years now on rails and me and my brothers were riding high. There was a separation on some fronts between us and the core of the show. We were still there, especially Al and Otto always on the lot. But in the close of the '91 season we commissioned our own car. Sure, we'd had a car the two years prior, but this was special. We named her the "Caledonia." It was a beauty. It glistened like green gold, all of eighty four feet. In 1888, the year we almost lost our show, the year we wrote to George Merton to borrow one thousand dollars, it was the bank of Caledonia where he had wired the money. Within hours of Otto signing for the money, the sun shone through the clouds and the earth began to dry out. We brothers made a pact before taking that money. We decided that the worse things got, the stronger we would get. If you knock us down, we would become twice the men we were before. The sun breaking and ending the weeks of nasty storms felt like providence that can only come from making such a declaration. I rode with the show when I fell back from the advance. The advance had four cars, but sometimes we split 'em off two and two, and broke away by a week or more. The Concordia had several private rooms, a parlor, servants' quarters, and cook station. Della and Alf, Charley and his new bride Deedee, and Al and Lou would get the larger rooms, and me and Otto would share the fourth.

Like every May there was plenty of water come down out of the sky and many a lake and mud hole where we played. Still, no year was ever so good as '92. Then again, that's what we said about '91 and that's what we said about '90. There were days when money came in so fast at a show that Otto couldn't get out of the ticket office as he was sitting in a sea of money. Henry had started working tickets and security that year, and we had Pinkerton men with the show. Otto would have to signal Henry to get the Pinkertons over to help him get the money out and get it over to the safe in the Red Car. We had new canvas all perfect and white. I can recall it just as good as I know every rail line and every train schedule in the United States:

Big Top, length 380 feet. Round Top, 180 feet. Four fifty-foot middle pieces.

Oblong, length 280 feet. Round Top, 80 feet. Five forty-foot middle pieces.

Dressing Room Top, length 100 feet. Round Top, 70 feet. One thirty-foot middle piece.

Connections, Oblong, 15 feet; Dressing Room, 30 feet; Main Entrance, 25 feet; Oblong guy ropes, 15 feet; Dressing Room guy ropes, 15 feet. Total of triple tent measurements, front to back door, 860 feet.

Sideshow, length, 120 feet. Round Top, 80 feet. One forty-foot middle piece. Added to above, 980 feet.

Horse Tents, six seven-pole pavilions, each 70 x 40 feet. Combined length 420 feet.

Dining Pavilions, two seven-pole, each 70 x 40 feet. Aggregate length 140 feet.

Wardrobe Tent, Round Top, 30 feet.

Grand Total Length of the great white City of Tents, 1,570 feet, or nearly one-third of a mile. Miles of rope are used to seam and uphold this canvas!

Since the season the year before, the importance of our canvas and our stake and chain cars could never have been more aptly expressed than by "Bismark," the stake and chain guard dog. We had over sixty ring stock, and fine horses they were, a menagerie too big and too odd to recount, and even four elephants, but no better known creature was there than Bismark. He was known and beloved by everyone on the lot and never an outsider did he trust. But when Ben Bismark, manager of stakes and chains, strayed away from the car, old Bismark, no more than twenty pounds of terrier, would guard that car with his life. In fact he would also guard the ring stock if his master was nearby, or when the big top was being hauled up, he would guard the working stock. That night of May 17th, Bismark was there, every step of the way, doing, as a dog, what he could.

Sixty ring stock were amongst the finest show horses me and my brothers ever saw, and over forty working stock - we called 'em baggage stock. We treated horses as the prized beauties they were. It was tough to get them all in the cars, so tight, up against the padding in the railcar stalls. We put the horses first behind the engine and fuel so as to get the smoothest ride. And so they were that night of May 17th, when the show set out from Beloit toward Washington, Kansas.

I was in Chicago and it was Al who recounted the whole of the horror to me. I don't know if I could have had the stomach for it. "Black Tuesday," we called it. Al began telling it like this: "It was some thirty miles out and just a mile east of Concordia." And he would half well up each time he'd tell it.

"It was two forty five a.m. and most everyone had settled down and sleep had set in. The first train had seventeen cars, and the Caledonia was the number eleven car. I was settled in my sleeper and Lou had dimmed the light just a moment earlier. There was an awful sound, slamming and sharp, and I was on the floor, and you could hear metal shriek. I heard Della scream and then footsteps running through our car. The sounds I heard next, I'll never forget. Ghostlike screaming and whinnying from horses up ahead. In an instant there were calls from the men's sleeper: 'Horses over the side.' Alf lit a lantern and we were all out the side, fast as we could. Up in front I could hear the terrible sound of the horses, now coming from down below, in the water.

"Alf and I were running toward the front, Alf yelling, 'Get some lights up here, get some light on it.' Actors and roustabouts were scrambling from the train, in the dark. We were running smack into each other, in a panic, as we could hear the horses scream in pain. By the time I got close enough to see what had happened, John Hamilton, Tom Murphy, and Charlie Wingate were already over the embankment. A rail had sprung so high that when the weight of the engine hit it, it stuck up like a brake and smacked clear through the horse cars, throwing some sixty or more horses over the side. Some were dead right on the spot. Men were in the water with knives, cutting free harnesses and pulling the horses' heads up out of the water. Horses lay next to the track, sliding down the embankment with their insides hanging out. Behind the stock cars were the razorback and working cars, and they didn't look so good either. Men were falling out, some right on the ground. One fellow had a piece of shattered board straight through his thigh. Lou and Edith got some of the gals together and began setting up an infirmary right on the spot. Della went up and down the cars comforting the injured and guided some to the makeshift infirmary. Some dozen fellows were hurt bad. This went on for a couple of hours, but as the light came up it got worse. We found two fellows dead on the spot. Robert O'Donnell had a footlong wooden shank drove through his head, pinning what was left of his skull against another piece of timber, and sixteen year old Adam Dietzler's head was smashed clear off."

Al recounted how the train was mangled and cars were smashed into indistinguishable little bits. Just as sad and shocking as the deaths of O'Donnell and Dietzler were the twenty six working stock. Percherons, Clyde stallions, and Normans were strewn about, some floating dead. As the sun rose men were shooting and killing those with broken legs and ripped out guts. Al cried when he spoke of it, even years later. The engine was stuck pointing up in the air, clear on the other side of the trestle. The two sleeper cars behind had narrowly missed serious damage, or there could have been fifty or sixty performers killed. Still there were eight men with serious injuries and two dead. Later, at an inquest, the train company would be found culpable for negligence. It seemed some fellow wanted to get home instead of turning back to Concordia. The report read, "He had made a miscalculation."

Sad as it was, it caused us Ringlings to jump to. While good times made for celebration and repetition, bad times made us work harder, and disasters made us rise to our best.

I awoke to a loud and unyielding pounding on my door that morning in Chicago.

"Sorry Mr. Ringling, but I'm told to give this to you right away." I was given as long a telegraph as ever I'd get describing the incident in great detail. We made no bones about the costs of a telegraph. If the show and the advance could talk to one another, from afar, then we made the best of it at any cost. Al, Alf, and Otto would make the necessary reparations to get the show rolling again. Handbills were printed on site, as well as circulated by me, Charley, and the team in Chicago. The news spread and it seemed that farmers, livery, and help from every kind of personage came forth. By morning, folks showed with draft horses in response to the flyers and telegrams. That day the show played Concordia, high on a bluff, a mile out of town. We gave a half price show, but news had spread fast and the locals would have no part of it. We said twenty five cents and they gave us fifty cents! By show's end we had almost thirty new working stock. According to Al, the winds blew so hard that we showed with sides only. Just the same, the spirit of kindness filled everyone's hearts, and the show moved on like it couldn't be stopped, made all the stronger, no matter what nature or God had thrown at our feet.

The show continued on through Marion and Wichita, each stand making good on our promise and giving our best shows. By Wichita we had regained all the stock, and in some celebratory heroism picked up eight new men to replace the roustabouts and three razorbacks no longer able to travel with us. The show was better than before, but I do say that even the slightest lurch of a train car causes many a performer to hold tight, even today, especially for those who were there.

Four
The Elephant

Chicago

It's likely we grew more as businessmen and as a show in the first half of the '90s than any other time as The Ringling Brothers. Competition was our great teacher. It was a circus war and it was show eat show. Old Phineas T. Barnum died in '91, and that made for a monster of a show, especially without the old man to get in its way. At that time Barnum and Cooper's Greatest Show on Earth was a force to reckon with. We sometimes referred to the show as "Old Elephant Bones" or the "Old Stuffed Elephant," as they toured with the sad remains of Jumbo as a feature attraction. We had other woes than just Barnum. Any show that traveled on rail was likely capable of speed and stealth, and some had advance teams that had taught our guys. Advance teams for bigger shows had two, three, or four cars. They could hitch tandem or all separate and travel one, two, and four weeks out. As was so with the best, we carried much of our own sheets and posters in the lead car. We traveled with ad men, relations men – Alf was the best ever – who we sometimes called talkers or programmers, and poster bosses who were unstoppable. The posters knew the towns as well as everybody and knew the time of day to strike. Sometimes the car would come into town late at night, quietly, without notice. After hours when things were quiet, they would go to the best spots and assess the possibilities. If the timing was right, they would arrive after a competing show, wait for their team to roll out of town, and then go and paste right over their posters. From factories to grain elevators, they knew every spot and claimed the territory as ours. Of course many buildings and sites were contracted, and we paid cash and tickets for those spots. Sometimes some shows made believe they were us and told the business owners that they were merely traveling with a different name for the same show. We had names for our advance cars, War Eagle, Thunderbird, Cannonball, and Battle Bolt. We were warriors and we were at war.

We learned early on about the battle for territory. It actually started in the mud show days. We learned because some shows were mean and unscrupulous. In '86 we played a stand in Nashua, Iowa, where we met up with the Parsons Bros. Great Shows. We gave a big parade with everything we could throw into it. We had a band wagon pulled by a six horse team, which was all we could muster in our third season. We had equestrians, a clown show on a baggage wagon, our few caged wild animals, and every teamster's wagon dressed for show, but somewhere unseen by us was a wagon from Butch Parson's Show with a banner that read "This Show is darling, but wait for the big show – PARSON Bros. – next week!" And even as we finished the parade they were pasting over our posters. Butch was Al's former employer and mentor, and we all respected him. It was just another opportunity for us to learn and grow. After a horrendous blowdown in '86, Parsons lost everything. In '87 Joe and his brothers Arthur and Butch worked for Ringling Brothers. We bought the remains of their show. Those kinds of tactics ran into the '90s, and we learned to act defensively more often than to take the offense.

That same year we rolled into Rockwell, Iowa, and noticed that our show was backed up against a little show – I think it was called The Burr Robins. They were asleep and we made good time arriving before sunrise. They had papered over us, and we could see it as we arrived. So too were the rails and markers in the road moved, but one of the acrobats in our show was from that town and guided us through the dawn. It was light enough as we passed through the town toward our lot to see the new paper, so we had our boys quietly paste as much as possible over the top of their posters. After we off loaded we set for an early parade, and by the time they were finishing breakfast we had the whole town in our hands and heading for our show. We were very small, but so were they. The choice of shows was already made by the townsfolk, and we were filled to the ring banks.

The news of the competition by the Sunday school boys from Baraboo spread, and in the season of '88 it reached a crescendo. Our advance team had a few boys who were only a day or two ahead. They often traveled separate from the main team and used the rail, as our show was still a mud show.

In one town in Minnesota another show's advance was going to pull the "wait" trick and slip a wagon into our parade. Charley was part of the resistance and hired a wagon and a paint cannon with several local boys, two of which had told him of the plot. They figured out exactly where the offending team and wagon was coming from. It was all tricky timing, as they had to get between them and our parade and wait under a bridge with the paint, all the while keeping out of sight. As the wagon approached with the banners "wait for the Big Show – next week," Charley and the boys stood under a bridge in almost knee deep water. Charley moved into the bushes on the banks and at the last moment, while the two fellows pumped furiously back and forth, Charley aimed the cannon and covered the banner on one side with paint, also covering the two men in the coach. The coach was followed by other wagons carrying locals who were rushing to get down the street and see the parade. This aided in keeping those paint soaked fellows from starting a brawl with Charley and the sprayers.

We tried lots of tactics to stop other teams. The best was to try to enlist the locals, which we always did, as we learned that our best allies were the folks we played to. If we had a team of locals who were paid and on the lookout, they might go so far as to unbolt an axle from the attacker's wagon. These tactics went on into the early rail years. As we went on the rails, our territory and velocity enlarged and so did the tactics. It reached an unintended peak in 1893, the year of the depression. It was also the year of The Columbian Exposition in Chicago.

There were bank runs as the national economy was changing. While banks had been loaning out folks' money so other folks could buy homes, bankers made stupid ass investments. Hell, whoever meets a banker that doesn't fuck around with another fellow's money has probably met a minister or smart farmer. Bankers could be such assholes and politicians let it all happen. By changing the laws, congress made it possible for the sons of bitches to take unimaginable risks with other people's money. Who am I to talk? After all I had my own bank at one point, and I risked it all at one point, and I got shafted right up the ass. Anyhow, we were in a bad depression.

Even though we were riding the rails, we still kept to the suburbs. We did play a few mid sized cities, but we were certain that the money was in places where people couldn't get to an opera house, a real museum, or a big show. That year The Columbian Exposition opened, and we figured it was going to kill the business around Chicago. Just the same we had to give it a go. We opened in the traditional manner in Baraboo on Saturday, April 29th. Then came the risk that proved us to be five of the best smart ass showmen in the world. We played Sterling, Illinois, about one hundred miles out of Chicago, May 1, the opening day of The Columbian Exposition. Even our bankers thought we had gone nuts. Well, you know how I feel about bankers. We left Baraboo with thirty five railcars and three advance cars, over seven hundred employees, over two hundred horses, nearly two dozen wild animal cages, seven elephants, and what we billed as the largest giraffe in the world! It wasn't, but who cared? It was a giraffe, and this was the largest Ringling show to date.

We were well aware of what we were up against. Farmers were getting the lowest pay in years for their crops, banks closing, and twenty percent of every employable man was out of work. Then, there was the biggest, greatest, most highly billed exposition, the never before seen enormity of The Columbian Exposition. And us. We had clowns, acrobats, three bands, tightrope walkers and even Charles Fish, an equestrian acrobat who back-somersaulted from one horse to the one behind it. Needless to say we paid big bucks and took big risks. And we won! That's right, we filled the show to the ring banks.

And it didn't stop there. In fact, a week or two later when we played Milwaukee, there had been a run on the Plankton Bank. The news was grim. You'd think we would've had an empty tent. We were so full up that we actually thought about seating folks on the ring banks. It seemed that, bad as things were, people needed to forget. That's what we worked for anyhow. We just wanted to make people happy. What more could a fellow ask for?

Sometimes it seemed when things were at their best, terrible things could happen. Our shows had gone well and average takes were up, after The Columbian Exposition. The news traveled faster than us that we were running a first class show. We sold out many matinees, and evening shows were good. Rarely did we fill evening shows like a matinee, especially in smaller towns, because farmers did not like to travel by wagon at night.

On May 20th we pulled into Arkansas City, Kansas. We were met by a series of armed guards, deputized citizens, and police officers. They explained that rumor had it that the Starr Gang was nearby and that they feared for a bank robbery or a circus holdup. Our show was not as well attended because of the fear shown by the locals, and after the evening show, we had a group of nearly twenty mounted armed men escort our take from the Red Wagon to the local bank. But an unusual highlight of the evening, also a source of dismay for our performers, was that over two hundred local boys from the territorial Indian School showed up in school uniforms. Circus was all about expressing different cultures, and besides, Indians were often great attendees in our audiences and most appreciative of equestrian performance. Two hundred of anyone in uniform always looks good in the audience, but it upset us brothers and the performers because we liked the Indians in their native dress. The Starr Gang scare turned out to be nothing at all, and we went on toward Pittsburgh, Kansas, a long haul over a Sunday that brought us through Independence, Kansas, and an unexpected stop.

All five of us and Henry were on the Concordia. As we passed through Independence, we came to a halt for a switchyard. That's when we saw it. Within eyeshot of the tracks, we could see the saddest sight in the circus world. We signaled ahead to keep our two trains stopped. This demanded our attention. It was a blowdown in massive proportion. Further, it was a great show, The Great Adam Forepaugh, run by James A. Bailey and Joseph McCaddon.

We brothers went to the show, leaving the gals behind. Some of our best performers got off and joined us. The round top was crushed and ripped through the oblong. The poles were snapped in half, and canvas men and roustabouts were working to pull it apart. Pieces of canvas twenty feet long waved in the wind as fellows tried to wrestle them under control. The menagerie tent was half standing but in shreds. Charley and I ran into Bailey who was feverishly giving orders and trying to get things under control. Superintendents were giving orders and rounding people up. It seemed it had happened the night before, but the winds stayed so strong they were unable to work with anything until daylight. Horses had been killed by flying debris, wood, splinters, poles. Three performers were also killed, and several children in the audience had died, while dozens more were injured.

The saddest thing I ever saw was that they were determined to give a show and were trying. The winds were still high, and the dust was filling our eyes. They had set up a small stand, and there were a few spectators, likely better dressed than the performers, as the entire wardrobe tent had just blown away. To the right of the ring they had set up an area for the sideshow – no tent, a few stages, and the sideshow performers looked like dirt farmers, in rags and tattered clothes. There was only one tent that had survived, the Red Tent. The outer stage had "coochie dancers" in makeshift dirty ripped dresses. There were two orators calling ballyhoo to fill the tent. The women and the orators were filthy with dust, made worse as occasional sprays of rain would wet them down, and then the dust would blow up and stick to them again. There was a line of men, maybe sixty or seventy long, to get in. It sent shivers down my spine. The Adam Forepaugh Show had been reduced to nothing more than a filthy ten cent strip show. It felt like whoring.

James explained that a tornado had struck during the show the night before. He really didn't have to describe much, it was evident.

"Jimmy," I asked, "is there anything we can do?"

"Thanks John," he responded sadly, looking down, "We'll get through this. It's been a pretty good season and we got funds coming and some canvas too." Then he looked at me apologetically, "Our vet got hit in the head and is out of commission for a few days. Could your man take a look at some injured animals, just for a little while?"

"Not a problem, I actually see that George is already on your lot."

"I'll go have a talk with him," Charley added and headed toward the animals where the vet George Hendershott was standing. Charley turned back and called out, "We're here to help in any way we can." We spent a little over an hour. Some of our performers and roustabouts helped out too. We had to move on, however, and left Bailey and McCaddon to the elements. It turned out that the blowdown nearly busted his show. Yet within a few years he would end up buying up the Barnum show. One day we would own all these shows.

As our trains pulled out I'll never forget the un-uniformed, dirty, and dismal sight of a show that had been nearly ruined and was making do by running a dime burlesque with grubby looking women who were dancing to music that was missing half its band. Some people would have found it nauseating. I just felt deeply saddened.

We went on arriving in Pittsburgh on Sunday, May 21st. It was a good show and a fair night show. On the 23rd we played Lamar, Missouri, and then the 24th in Butler, Missouri. It started with some dangerous winds, but they faded and both shows were better than average. We moved on, the next day, for Sedalia, Missouri. Charley, Alf, and I had planned to move out and catch up with some of the advance teams over the coming week, so Sedalia was our last show where all of us would be together for a while. Kansas was the home of the wind, and after the Forepaugh blowdown and some of the winds we had been through, we were pretty sure we had left all that mess behind. The afternoon show was above average, and although not sold out, it was a good take. Our folks usually finish eating by about four thirty and the public begins to arrive around five thirty. We usually offer some kind of concert by seven, but the ballyhoo starts by five thirty. As it did, it began to rain.

At first it was modest and not too windy, but by six thirty everyone was either in the sideshow, the menagerie, or the big top as the rain was falling pretty hard and the winds were making the show folks nervous. At around seven fifteen, we had about two thousand people under the big top, and there was a sound outside like a train rumbling and it was only getting louder. Al blew the whistle and we changed the music like we always had. It was still years before we would play *Stars and Stripes Forever* to alert the show to an emergency. The entire audience was ushered out of the tent, as the windward side was not only listing but lifting. Most folks fled to the menagerie, which was on the other side of the big top. Most of the performers were either in the wardrobe tent or under the wardrobe wagons. Other workers ran for wagons and got underneath. Al and a few roustabouts were still in the big top when it lifted ten or fifteen feet off the ground, poles splintering, ropes snapping; some of the stands exploded with boards flying in every direction. The tent came down, most of it laying flat and trapping Al and a few others inside. The entire event lasted only about three minutes, but we feared for the worst. Several wagons had turned on their sides, panicked patrons were screaming for children or husbands or wives, and three performers were injured by flying debris. The menagerie tent stood strong, and as awful as it was, we were fortunate beyond belief.

As we helped reunite families and search for injured persons, of which were only Okeo, Zano, and Charlie Miller, we directed the public to the Red Wagon, where we refunded all their money for the show. The remaining sideshow and menagerie take was slim. We went on to Boonville, where we cancelled the show and spent the day and night repairing canvas and replacing poles. We left at 2:00 a.m. for Marshall, shaken but strengthened and maybe more united than ever.

We had started a practice in '93 of signing "non compete" agreements with some of the big shows. It was a smart move and when it hit the news that Ringlings had instigated it, which I am not certain we did, it was great publicity. Just the same, the Ol' Stuffed Elephant show would play Pennsylvania, while we were in Iowa, or the Forepaugh show would play west while we were east. We would even agree to play separate cities. We added huge fines, sometimes as much as twenty thousand if anyone broke the agreement. But it didn't always work, and we didn't always sign on.

We were set to play Des Moines on May 28th, 1884. The Columbian Exposition had come and gone, but the depression, especially in farm country, was worse than ever. Tempers ran high. War Eagle was in town on May 1st and was the number one advance, headed up by my big brother Gus. The advance boys called him "Mr. Gus." He had three lithographers and two programmers. But the trouble came when W.H. "Bill" Haskins, boss poster, may have let the heat get to his head. You see, a poster and a tack spitter get the lithos pasted and tacked on every possible corner, grain elevator, open wall space, you name it. We mixed our own supplies of paste right on the cars. It was hot like summer that day in May, too hot for May 1st. Most of us knew the fellows from other shows, and when it came to bosses like Haskins, he had worked other shows. Pasters on the other hand were hired on, and only the best would stay year after year. Pay wasn't that good that it warranted loyalty, and these fellows were either going to move up or move out. It was Gus' job to see that we had supplies, that the litho men made the paper up, and that the boss had a route laid out so he could get in, paper the town, and get out and on to the next place.

The heat and humidity were making the job impossible, and the sweat was burning the boys' eyes. They were finishing a wall at the corner of 12th and Thompsen when they came across a group of pasters from the Sells Brothers Show who had been doing the other side of the same building. It was simultaneous and they all just stood there a while, and then some bastard from Sells yelled out, "Hey fellas, it's the little Ting-a-ling boys from Baraboo." Haskins lost control of his wits and began calling some of the Sells boys worse names. "Looks to me," he yelled, "like some Sells pasters been stickin' up paper with elephant shit! I don't know what smells worse, the elephant dung or the pasters." He then grabbed a paste stick and held it in front like a weapon. "Smells like these boys been eating the shit, if you ask me."

One of the boys from the Sells show took his paste bucket and threw straight at Haskins, hitting him across the shoulder and practically knocking him to the ground. From behind Haskins came Ringling paster John Curtain, who swung hard and smacked his brush across the fellow's head. Mayhem broke out and the dozen or more posters were exchanging blows, first with pasting brushes, and when they broke, they used fists. A crowd appeared and Haskins, knowing full well that they had already overstepped their Ringling code of ethics, pulled his boys out. As they turned and went around the corner, they passed the first fellow that Curtain had struck in the head. If he wasn't dead, he sure looked miserably bad laying in a pool of blood, which flowed out across the underside of his head and covered a Sells Brothers poster.

The eight men and their boss Bill Haskins headed fast for the train yard. When they got there, Mr. Gus was just returning from dinner and had a good stiff smell of whiskey about him.

"We got a bad problem, Mr. Gus," Haskins said as he followed Gus onto the railcar.

"What kind of problem could be bad enough that you're going start me a case of indigestion, Bill?" Gus asked, as he stopped on the back of the car and took a cigar from his coat pocket, savoring the very look of it and obviously not too terribly concerned about Haskins.

"Well sir, Mr. Ringling sir, it's Johnny Curtain," he paused for a moment and watched while Gus lit the cigar. "See, we come to a corner downtown, and we come face to face with the posters from Sells Brothers Show."

"You don't say," Gus responded, still not expressing much concern, "and now I suppose you're gonna tell me that Johnny had a little fight, did he?"

"Worse yet Mr. Gus, you see..." Haskins paused and leaned back on the railing, looking down. "You see, we all had a fight sir." Gus took a big puff and seemed to be enjoying the entire bit.

"And so, did you all make up and buy yourselves a beer or something?"

"Well, no sir, that's just it, I think Johnny Curtain might of killed one of their guys." Gus threw the cigar down on the track.

"Oh... oh, shit!" He turned to Haskins and grabbed him by the collar and tie. Gus is tall, about six foot two, and Haskins plump and short, but Gus had him in the air. "Is the guy dead or do you just think he's dead?" Gus barked. Choking, Haskins replied, "I don't know sir, I mean there was a lot a blood coming out of his head and we just left kind of quick like."

"That's what we're gonna do Bill, leave kind of quick like. I'll get us a hitch and we'll move to the next town. You're gonna pay off Curtain, in full, then we will drop him off in another town. From there I gotta telegraph my brother and see what plan we can make. We also need to get word to number four car. Cleanup is really their job."

Each advance car had a specific job. The only real printing going on rail was for handbills, while the huge lithos that were pasted sectional were made in Baraboo, Madison, or Chicago. Car one carried the advance men, which usually traveled by themselves and included Alf and Charley. Alf met with newspaper folks, placed ads, gave out the copy which had been written in March by the time we were sure of every act. He gave the editors a handful of tickets and took 'em out to lunch or dinner and spared no expense. Alf was the best at this, while Charley was a master at advertising. For example, when Charley printed a litho about our giraffe he made it sound like it was the last one in the world. It should have cost a million dollars and he could make people think so. Then Alf would stretch a little truth and tell the editor we were lucky enough to get it for twenty thousand dollars. Now, it was really about two thousand, and we had our pick of giraffes spread across the Serengeti as far as the eye could see. This was a depression, so if folks felt they could see a rare animal that the circus had paid twenty grand for, well, hell, what was going to stop them from spending fifty cents to go? Then another ten cents to get into the menagerie. It was the same with our human performers. We'd say that it was an act that had cost a hundred thousand dollars. Call me a liar, but no one wants to go to a show if you tell 'em you made a deal and got a hyena for the cost of taking it off the hands of a circus that just went under.

We Ringlings and John Curtain were lucky. The fellow didn't die, only suffered a cracked head and good bit of blood. In fact it wasn't more than a week that we were at the table, first with Sells Brothers and then eventually every big and mid size show in the country. We weren't going to have this kind of stuff ruin us or them. As far as me and my brothers were concerned, if a show couldn't make it on its best merits, then it didn't belong in the game. Everyone deserved a fair playing field, and we Ringlings were going to see to it that we got one. We were never for or against unions; after all, everyone deserved their fair share. Any asshole that's going to tell you that workers shouldn't organize or shouldn't have the right to bargain, is just a selfish spineless piece of shit who can't see past their own bottom dollar.

Running a big show was dangerous. I know half the circus world will tell you that I wasn't on the lot as much as my brothers, and that'd have to be true, but I witnessed bad things happen and people that worked for us died or lost their limbs. But we not only passed the hat, but all of us brothers put serious amounts of money in to help folks out. I remember being on the lot in North Dakota in June of '97, and the canvas crew was right in the middle of putting up the tents. Lightning struck the king pole and instantly killed two men: Walters and Smith, I believe. In fact it was so bad that about twenty fellows were laying around unconscious like they were dead.

Al, me, and Charley were right there and Al called out, "Charley, John, get over there and see if any of them are still alive." Lightning was flashing with monstrous thunder. It had barely started to rain, but Charley, me, and Bob Wills, a canvas man, started checking to see if they had a pulse or not. Within minutes the vet and the doc were on the scene and checking for life too. That's when I went over to C.E. Walters, and when I went to reach down and check his pulse, he stunk like burned meat. There was gook coming out of his eye sockets, and his hands looked burned around the king pole, kind of like inseparable.

"I'm afraid this one's dead," I shouted out and saw Charley run to the other fellow just next to him. Before he could reach out and check his pulse, he gagged.

"This fellow's dead too," Charley called out. Everyone else recovered. That night we passed the hat for the two fellows' burials and for their families. I felt sick about it. I put what I could from my pocket, I guess a hundred or so, but we asked Otto to take two thousand from the Red Car and put it in there. Sure, we didn't have any unions, yet. This was all new to us. But we believed in taking care of folks and we did our best to.

We Ringlings were Masons anyhow, and if that wasn't a kind of union, then what was it? That's one of the reasons why we never liked the IRS and Wisconsin for setting an income tax. See, we believed in helping our fellow man. We did well, so we gave back. We paid property tax and we imported plenty and paid tariffs and felt good about it, as if we were helping our people. If a new school was needed, we helped get a bond and then we would get every lodge brother we could to buy that bond. I know I'm not supposed to talk about this stuff; it's supposed to be secret, but hell, I'm gonna die soon. I know it and so do you, so who gives a shit? We would of given more through the Lutheran Church, but even when we were kids and just Pop and Al were Masons, we were more than frowned on. That's why we ended up at Reverend Conway's church. Baptist. Brought over from Ireland, and I guess the Freemasons and the Church of England had some

good blood between them, because as I grew up and became a Mason, there was the Reverend Conway, sitting in some of the more
important seats.

Now, I can't say for sure when our battles with other shows
became more balanced and the bloody fisticuffs seemed to end. In
fact I know bad blood continued even up to when we bought out The
Greatest Show On Earth in 1907. But by the mid '90s everything
changed for us. We had one good year after another and better after
that. When we closed the 1894 season, we had made more money
than ever before. We had averaged over $2400 a stand and had about
170 stands that year. We had expanded our little rail show to forty
two cars and were about to enter a new age.

The depression was deep, and by '95 it reached far across the
country, no longer was just confined to the heartland. All seven of us
brothers were working together. Henry and Gus did not own any
stock in the show, but that went back to their not being willing to
share in the original risk. Still, we worked as a team, a huge machine.
However, when it came to decisions that would affect the major
operation, it was the five of us who made them. We still had our
original office over Horstman's Meat Market, but the whole of
Ringlingville was growing. We had over seven hundred employees
traveling with the show in '84 and it was about to get bigger. As each
season closed, there was no rest whatsoever. That's when the real
work began. It was November 1894 and we had found enough time to
enjoy Thanksgiving. Papa, Mama, and Ida had moved back to
Baraboo from Rice Lake, and we were a huge family again. Although
I loved to get the hell out of Baraboo and scour New York and Europe
for new acts, and being that I was well off, I could have plenty of good
times with the ladies – and did! But that time period, close of season
and holidays, was not just a festive time for us Ringlings. This was
where we formulated the next year's show. It was December 4th and
just after Charley's birthday when he called a meeting. As usual we
locked the door.

"I have an idea, brothers, that's going to take us to the top,"
Charley announced. I was quick to jump in, "Don't you think we are
already on the top, Charley?" He leaned back in his chair and rubbed
the back of his head, making us all wait painfully long. Then, after
deep sigh, he placed his chin in his hands and leaned forward.

"As long as there is a show called The Greatest Show On Earth,"
he leaned back again, rubbing his mustache, and then came forward
and continued, "we will always be second best."

"Oh come now, Charley, Ringling Bros. World's Greatest Shows
are giving them a run for their money. We are right on their heels,"

Alf piped in, "besides, we all know, if we keep on the pace, we will surpass them one day."

"That's the problem, Alf," Charley said, "how long are we going to wait to get to 'one day?'"

"I'm all for the 'one day' bit if we don't have to spend new money," said Otto; he took out a cigar, snipped the tip, and then held it up. "It's a little like this smoke. You light it," which he then did, he began puffing and turning, "then you get it just right." He smoked it some more and held it out in front of everyone. "Then you savor it for a time, knowing all the while it will keep getting better. What's the hurry?"

Charley had his back to Otto the whole time and had been looking out the window. Then he turned quickly, "What if I had an idea where we could expand and save money?"

"What if I could make a hippopotamus fly?" Otto said, sarcastically.

"No, really, I have an idea, but I need you all to hear me all the way through. I mean it, no fights, no interruptions, just hear my whole plan." We all agreed to give him the floor for five minutes. Then we figured someone would have to beat the crap out of him, and we all laughed at that idea. We had a strange way of making decisions. We would go behind closed doors, present ideas, sometimes fight – even real fights, like the time Al gave Charley a black eye – although fisticuffs were rare, and then we would strike a deal. We sometimes would come to an agreement to try one brother's cockamamie idea and then give it a real go, maybe even for a whole season. If it worked, we would do it again. If it failed, then that would be the end of it. No one would chide the other over it. It was done, over. Finished.

So Charley presented us with his idea. At first I thought he had lost his mind.

"Ringling Brothers has made its mark by playing small to mid-sized cities all across our nation, up until now," he began. "We are even reaching west and south to Oklahoma. It seems that most of these cities are less than twenty thousand in population and many less than ten. Well, I suggest we prepare to open in a real city, say like Chicago." At this point the room, now full of cigar smoke, was also full of moaning. "Wait now, brothers, I have the floor. Look at it this way. Our competition opens every year in that huge indoor arena known as "The Monster Hippodrome." I knew he was talking about Madison Square Garden, but I had no idea what role it would play in my future.

"I believe we can open our show, bigger and better, in Chicago at Tattersall's, the biggest indoor horse arena in the Midwest." More moans, especially Otto who followed with, "Charley, that'll cost a fortune, and we don't have those kinds of funds."

"Wait wait boys, you promised you'd hear me out." He had this look, like he knew something big and was about to unleash it upon us. "I have it on good authority that if we lease it for more than two weeks, we can get a great price. Further, there's no canvas men needed for three weeks, less work, less labor, and we can start the season early."

"Okay Charley, you are making some sense, but there's a problem here," I challenged him. Then Alf added, "Charley, we never worked a big city. And for two weeks or more?"

Then I said, "Chicago's a pretty sophisticated city."

"I know, I know, but..." Charley tried to stop me, but I continued, "I mean they had The Columbian Exposition just last year and they have museums and they have opera houses." I went on talking over him, "How do we even know they're gonna cater to a circus or not?" Somehow I felt like I had just capped the matter and put my older brother in his place. But that's when he did it. That's when he posed the question that all of us knew had to be, if not inspected, completely respected, and answered, and there would only be one way.

"How are we ever going to know, if we don't give it a try?" That was that. The question was answered at least for the time being. We had to do it. Otherwise we would never know.

His point, well made, is owned by all of us now. When Otto spoke up, we all had to listen: "There is, after all, only one way to find out."

So we set our sights on opening our season in 1895 in April, in Tatersall's of Chicago. An arena show, our first stand, more than one day, would be our first crack at a truly big city.

The Working Spur

It had taken a few years and much of it was still under construction, but the rail moved to Ringlingville. Even after twelve seasons and six years on the rail, it still wasn't possible to switch everything to the barn. Winter quarters was complicated, and the brothers and their superintendents kept adding structures. None of it had a master plan, but little by little it was beginning to show forth, like a proud city, a village with a purpose. As big as it had become, there were still less than fifty winter employees. But there was a special spur built, two blocks away, just for the advance cars. There had been three, but now there were four, and they kept the Caledonia right there so that the brothers, the advance staff, and entire press and advertising team headed up by Alf and Charley could be always ready to go. This was separate from all the other offices that were appearing on the lot, Water Street, and other parts of town. This was five railcars, sitting still, and acting at high speed. The energy never left, with one exception. From time to time they might hitch the Caledonia and take all or some of the five brothers plus an operating staff and head to Chicago for negotiations. Rare, but manageable and especially important that year.

The deal with Tatersall's had been handshakes and talk, so far, and would require a great deal of negotiation to pull it off, if it was really to take place. January was the month and it had to happen. This was Charley's incubation, and he needed to make it happen. When it came to new ideas and manifestation, Ringlings created ideas first and then figured out how to pull it off – second. Dreams, ideas, construct. It was their way. Charles Ringling was committed to this, and he would show his brothers that not only could it be done but would be done with a level of excellence never before seen by the Ringling Brothers, Chicagoans, or the circus world at large.

After the five brothers had agreed to this new approach, a letter was immediately dashed to Chicago to the current but outgoing Mayor, J.P. Hopkins, the first Irish American mayor of Chicago. The boys were reluctant to work with Hopkins as he was a Democrat and highly conservative. He had despised The Columbian Exposition and its assassinated founder, former Mayor Carter Harrison, the five times elected mayor who would have gladly welcomed the brothers with open arms. Harrison had been assassinated just two days before the end of The Columbian Exposition.

His pro tem replacement, George Bell Swift, who had been Commissioner of Public Works and was again temporarily appointed as such, was now also the mayor-elect and would be inaugurated on April 8th, 1895. This would be just two days after The Ringling Brothers World's Greatest Shows was scheduled to open. This seemingly complicated political mire would actually work to the benefit of the show if they played their hand correctly. A letter was returned on behalf of the office of Mayor J.P. Hopkins and written by George Bell Swift. It appeared that as the outgoing mayor, Hopkins had finished much of his business and that, out respect for the mayor-elect and current head of Public Works, he would defer many of the decisions to George Bell Swift. This was more than a stroke of good luck; it was providence.

Mayor-elect Swift called for a meeting with the Ringlings, who agreed to send Alf T. and Charley by way of the Caladonia arriving on Friday, January 4th. Chicago by train on the Ringling private car was less than four hours. However, because it was the last week of holidays and with the New Year's celebration falling on a Monday and Tuesday, time was of the essence in order to prepare such a grand show. Charley and Alf made a study of likes and dislikes of Mr. George Bell Swift, his background, his church, and most important, his lodge. The fact that he was a Mason was important because they knew that the Roman Catholic Church, of which acting mayor J.P. Hopkins was a member, frowned on Masons, while Mayor-elect Swift was a Methodist, and the church took little opinion in the matter. In their research they found that he was a brother and of high degree, and that certainly could not hurt. Alf, Charley, and John researched all that they could: his six children, his background, and his former special appointment by President Arthur to the Treasury. But even a small detail such as the fact that he and his wife Lucy liked to fish was especially important to Alf. Alf had two great loves in life, the show and fishing. Perhaps it could be narrowed down to music and fishing.

What was needed most of all was a plan of presentation. It was widely known that Ringlings were now considered the "Sunday School Circus," but it would not hurt to bring along the rule book to further enhance the idea. The guarantee of there never being a "red tent," also known as a "cooch tent," on a Ringling show would be important. They would also document their practice of catching and handcuffing pickpockets, and chaining them to the rigging up front, which exemplified their honest and upright show. The theme for the '95 show was still in the works, but was to be decided before week's end and before the meeting.

First of all, the event to be proposed was to begin at Tattersall's on April 6th and end on April 28th. Such an engagement would take an entire extra week and a half to execute. But this was to be Tattersall's Arena, the pride of Chicago, modeled after Tattersall's in London, the greatest horse trading arena of Europe. Even now, after the great "white" buildings of The Columbian Exposition were losing their draw, their exciting attractions had not faded in the memories of millions who had attended – the huge Ferris wheel, the great water chutes, the magnificent palace-like museums – and these marvels were already inspiring Luna Park in Coney Island. Still, Tattersall's was a world unto itself. Unassuming on the outside, this mission style building with its peculiar arrangement of arched windows had been the home to the greatest horse sales of the midwest. The Arabian horse had never been heard of in America until sold at Tattersall's, just following The Columbian Exposition. And when the Exposition itself did not host William F. Cody and his Buffalo Bill's Wild West Show, only one season following a command performance for Queen Victoria, Buffalo Bill performed at none other than Tattersall's on its outdoor lot.

So the Ringling Brothers started with a concept based around that which they were already known for: equestrian feats extraordinaire. Having had almost three hundred baggage and ring stock in the 1894 show, they decided to expand. They had long since left the days when they needed to borrow from the bank, yet their banker, when called upon for the various drafts to add so many horses to an already amazing show, left the bank and headed for the show office, calling ahead for a meeting. Ringlings relied little on telephones, as they were limited, and besides, the other fellow had to have one. But between George Merton and the Ringlings there were regular phone calls. Within ten minutes of his garbled phone call, Merton was standing at the Caledonia where Alf and Otto were inside preparing some of the costs for the proposed budget.

"Come in George," Otto said as he reached out shaking his hand and helped bring the fellow up a step. Otto went on, "What's all this chatter about a letter and a draft that has to be a forgery?"

George pulled the letter and the note from his chest pocket and went to hand it to Otto, but Alf snatched it from his hands before he had a chance to finish the action. Opening the letter and the draft, he folded it immediately and said, "George Merton, have you no trust in us anymore?"

"Alf, that letter," George stammered, "it calls for the expense of over thirty thousand dollars, and for horses!"

"And that's just the beginning George. Have a seat." He handed the two pieces of paper back. Merton sat nervously looking over the lavish Caledonia and looking to find something to do with his hands. Unlike the Ringlings, or the fashion of the time, he did not smoke, so he often fidgeted with paper or rubbed his hands together.

"Gentlemen," George began with authority, "are you aware that this is an economic depression? That the people who attend your shows are busted broke?" Alf sat down, lit a cigar, and began to puff. He took his time and Merton was growing anxious.

"George, when times are bad, we Ringlings believe more will be needed from us. And we have yet to be proven wrong on this theory," said Alf. George was sweating now and he turned to Otto, who after all, ran the money with the "iron fist" as they called it.

"Otto, talk some sense into him," George pleaded. He almost stood then sat again. "You can't spend all your reserves at a time like..."

"We are going to procure Tattersall's in Chicago for an engage-ment of over three weeks, George," Otto interrupted, and it was plain to see that George was about to jump out of his skin, "and we intend to invest more in the show than ever in our twelve year history."

"You've completely lost your minds!" he said, jumping up. At that moment Charley climbed the stairs and entered the back of the car. Seeing George in a state of absolute panic, he too became upset.

"George, George, what on earth is the matter? Have we gone broke?"

"You're well on your way." Charley turned to Otto, almost yelling, "Otto, what the hell is going on?"

"Relax little brother, we are going to be fine," he answered and turned toward George, "it's Merton who is losing his wits."

"I don't understand. I walk in the office, our banker is going berserk and telling me something terrible is about to happen, and you're telling me it's okay! Would someone please explain what the fu..." He stopped himself from swearing, remembering they were on the grounds and bookkeeper Warren Patrick was on board the Caledonia. "I mean what on earth is going on?"

Alf started laughing, "Sit down Charley," he ordered his little brother, "George is distraught about how much money we are spending on horses and has the letter which instructs and allows Delevan to spend over thirty thousand on new ring stock."

"Oh," Charley responded and gave out a laugh. "Wait till he gets the draft for Hagenbeck and the money we are going to spend on the rhinoceros!" Then all three Ringlings began chuckling, each one's laughter goading more from the others.

"Rhinocerous?" George screamed, "Have you gone mad – all of you?!"

"What about Speedy?" Alf choked out with a hacking cigar smoke filled laugh, "That's going to cost a fortune, and that's only one of the new acts John's found!" They were all laughing hysterically, all except George Merton.

"What the hell is a speedy?" George asked. Alf doubled over and almost fell on the floor, red in the face and answered, "He's a fellow that jumps 130 feet and lands in just over three feet of water." Merton jumped up again, frowning, and began pacing through the car. The three Ringlings were laughing so hard that tears were streaming down Otto's cheeks, Alf almost gagging, as he was laughing and coughing so much. Finally, unable to resist the infectious humor, George just broke into laughter, and they all roared for another minute, during which time even Warren Patrick began to laugh out of control.

Eventually the moment calmed, and Otto explained it as only Otto could. "George, you know me," Otto said soberly. He stood and paced. "I don't spend money needlessly or foolishly."

"It's always been your nature to be tight fisted, Otto."

"We also have learned that the worse it is, the more we need to put into it. I know this is a depression and I know we are not out of the woods yet." He turned and leaned in towards George, "There is one thing we know. If things are bad and you give something affordable to people that'll make 'em happy, then by God – give it, and give your all. They'll spend and they'll spend big. We know it, and it's going to be good. This is the year we make it happen George. Happy New Year."

The men all had a glass of whiskey and included Warren in the toast. They did, however, request that he keep it secret as drinking was not allowed on the lot. Warren promised as they all did, as lodge brothers, to keep their secret safe.

Delevan's orders to purchase over one hundred new ring stock was a horseman's dream come true. The best of Noble trotters, who would dance at liberty, and there would be the largest and brightest of Normans selected for the chariot races, and more beautiful white Percherons with their broad backs. Their backs treated with rosin, the Percherons would be used by Mike Rooney, who was perfecting an act where he could flip backwards six horses in a row. There were additions to the baggage stock, as well, which in themselves would be part of the parade, as some of the smaller wagons which were drawn by less than six horses would be drawn by bays, with their stunning black manes and black tails.

Delevan worked all year and had a home in Baraboo. This year was extra special, as he would require additional trainers that usually did not arrive until March. Work on the lot was always quietly intense throughout the winter, but this year would ask more. More of the town, more of H. Moeller and Sons in wagon making, and more preparation to come. The brothers would follow Chicago with a larger canvas than any other time as they anticipated business beyond the past. There would be cities where they would show under canvas, including St. Louis and Boston, and the pace would be set from Chicago. Although they would bring riggers and some of the canvas men to study and be prepared for what would follow Chicago, the teams of canvas makers and riggers who would wait behind, by three weeks, would work night and day in preparation. A larger show would need more railcars, and new sleepers were added. These pullman sleepers were the finest on any show and could sleep up to seventy in a car. All together the new show had over forty five cars and four advance cars. It traveled as four separate monstrous trains, each pulled by its own locomotive. The route being planned by John would get them into Chicago over a week ahead of the opening night.

The two brothers headed out on the Caledonia early in the morning of January 4th, 1895. The meeting with George Swift had some unusual preparations, never before employed by the Ringlings or any circus. First, rather than meet at city hall, they agreed to meet in the Caledonia, at the spur behind Tattersall's. Further, they invited Mrs. Swift and their six children. The small train brought one advance car, War Eagle, somewhat as an expression of force and an expression of stability. Charley regretted not bringing John, who had a way with youngsters. However, John had already left for New york, where he was to meet with several new acts that were the top Japanese aerialists in the world. John Ringling, who had the ability to hobnob with the social elite, carry on farm talk with a sod farmer, get his boots in the mud with a roustabout and push a wagon, most of all, could befriend children. Charley would hope that the kids liked to fish and they could talk about that with Swift's six boys. They had brought along a chef and a servant to make lunch and include the whole Swift family.

As the locomotive slowed its way into the huge stockyard behind Tattersall's, it huffed and hissed, slowly stopping within twenty yards of the coach where George and Lucy Bell Swift and the six boys were already waiting. Fortunately their wait had not been long. The boys leapt from the wagon, running excitedly across the snow covered yards. Their father had to get them under control.

"Hold up now there, young men," he yelled, "at least give the train a chance to stop!" Then came the real voice of authority, "Boys!" Lucy ordered, "slow down, this is a formal meeting, not the circus." The six boys had it in their heads that the circus was coming to town just to meet with their pop.

"But Mother," complained Jason, the eldest, "Papa told us we were going to get a preview of the circus."

"Take your time boys," George ordered sternly, "and act like men of civility." The parents got in front, first George, then Lucy, then the boys, eldest to youngest all in a row. The rear door of the Caledonia opened and Alf T. with his grand smile stepped out. It was cold enough that, as he spoke, he could see his breath. He was dressed in tweed and a bowler style hat known later as a pork pie. He had no overcoat, and you could tell he was cold, but his elegant smile was warming in the January cold winter sunlight.

"Welcome Swift family," he said reaching out and shaking George's hand as they all ascended the steps. "Let's get inside where it's warm." They all followed and immediately were given grand treatment. Their coats were hung and hot chocolate served all around.

What followed was the show of shows. The children, it turned out, loved to fish with their parents. George was open to the participation with his lodge brothers, the sketches and pictures of the acts to come were thrilling the boys, and Lucy gave one hundred percent consent to the Fifty One Rules and the exemplification of the Sunday School Circus. The climax came when they showed the drawings of Speedy and his dive into a pool of water no deeper than the height of their own pop's belly button.

After a splendid lunch of prime rib, potatoes, and green beans, followed by cake, the three men sat together, while Lucy kept her children in dreamlike conversation of the show that their father was going to help bring to town. Smoking their cigars and sipping brandy with Swift, the two Ringlings waited to hear the offer that might be coming to make their show and their dreams come to fruition.

"Fellows, I'm gonna let you have Tatersall's for the unbelievably low price of $100 a day. Further, because it is city property, I will see to it that you get a team of more than fifty of our best public service employees to help with the preparations. There will of course be the usual permits and city costs, but I believe that I can convince the local businesses that Ringling Brothers will bring nothing but the best business to our neighborhoods."

"I am beyond words, but offer my gratitude sir," Alf responded. And Charley, so taken back, stuttered out, "I too... I mean thank you sir." Once again it was no less than providence had rolled forth and met the boys from Baraboo with a blessing of unparalleled opportunity.

I Have Seen The Elephant

There are moments in life when everything pivotal happens, and it isn't that one moment, but the time. This was that time. We have a saying in the circus and amongst those who have traveled the world: "I have seen the elephant." It means that I have traveled the world, seen the greatest of wonders, the most magnificent of seas, but at last I have seen the greatest thing of all and we call that wonder – the elephant. Now, if you think I am going to give you some kind of talk about elephants you've got another fucking thing coming! I am talking about 1895. That was the year Charley helped us all see the future. There are people who are telling us today "circus is over." It's been railroaded by talking movies, phonographs, and radio, and from what some of the inventors I have met tell me, there's plenty more coming. There are those who will tell you that there has been a golden age of circus and that it ended by the war. Hell, by 1914 we were ready to launch the Big One and would have by 1916 if it wasn't for the war. We wanted to launch it in 1915, but Al was growing steadily ill. I can't tell you when there was or wasn't a golden age of circus. When we stopped The Greatest Show On Earth parades, something changed. But I can tell you when it was golden for us, when all that glittered was gold, and that day came in April 1895. I don't want to start just with the show which opened on the 6th at Tattersall's in Chicago, but on the 4th, at night, in Chicago, we gave the greatest damn parade in circus history. Sure there were others and there were some bigger, but the first of its kind, well it's the first, and no matter how many times in life you do something, there will never be anything like that first one. Well, except for getting laid, and that seems to get better over time. Anyway, nothing like that first parade can ever occur again. After a week and a half of trains arriving, in four sections, we were ready for the parade of parades. Now, we had given some big ones. In Madison a year earlier we had as many eighty thousand show up. This was a night parade, so we set the chandelier boys to work with the city and the lighting, and we made a parade like no other. But as the saying goes, "No parade is complete without spectators." Some say that nearly half a million folks showed up for that parade. It was the spec of specs. We had over four hundred equine beauties; three hundred were ring stock. We had fifteen elephants, eight camels, two reindeer, six sacred cattle, water buffalo, two elk, a hairless horse, Prince Chaldean the long-maned horse. And we had twenty four cages of wild beasts, including the giraffe, lions and cubs, hippopotamus, rhinoceros, Bengal tigers, silver lions, monkeys, exotic birds, antelope, albino deer, and the list goes on. We had the bell wagon, a mounted military band, clown band, fife and drum band, the sideshow band, clowns and performers, and some of this was just the stuff between the stuff, and then there were the teams. Delevan could run a team with twenty four horses pulling the bell wagon. This was long before Jake Posey and the forty horse hitch. It took Delevan and Dave McGraw behind him to sort the reins. Charley and Deedee, Alf and Della, Al and Lou, and me were all in our carriages, but sometimes I was so excited I would forget that I was part of the show. It sure is special to be a spectator in your own show. Even after it ended, all you could hear in your heart was the calliope, windjammers, and the bells.

It was April 4th, and we weren't opening the show until matinee on the 6th. However, as all parades are followed by a parade of spectators, we opened the menagerie, the sideshow with the sideshow band, and we had various acts and performers: jugglers, clowns, and vaudeville all about the great surround that was under the seats of the great arena. We held much the same the next day and began passing out handbills about the final ten days of performance when we would launch an act with "Speedy," Kearney Speedy, the fearless high diving act who would jump from the highest eighty feet of the arena into a pool no more than three feet eight inches in depth. Of course these handbills were given only to those who had already purchased tickets to entice them to pay for a second show. We had moved the Red Wagon to the front of the building where the streets were closed off and the circus spilled over into its own magical world. By noon on the 5th the shows were already sold out for the opening matinee and evening performances, and the remaining tickets were standing room only. Sunday was a predicament, and me and the boys had many a go round over how we would handle Sunday. Ringling shows were renowned for not operating on Sundays. Here we had a show that would open on a Saturday for a three week run. Momentum before, during, and all about the show was what made for success. It was Otto who first proposed it: "I think we should play Sunday in Chicago!" He had said it at one our meetings, leaning forward in his working bowler, chewing a cigar. It came out of the blue.

"Sunday!" I roared, "What, have you flipped your fancy? That's the craziest thing I ever..."

"Just hear me out, boys." He leaned into the work table. "Every day is a big nut – right?"

"Yeah, biggest nut we ever had to carry," Charley piped in.

"Well listen," Otto continued, "most of the time we travel on Sundays, don't pay for the lot, and sometimes play baseball with the locals, right?" We all agreed. Otto went on, "That costs nothing. It's just good relations with the public. – right?" We all agreed some more; he had our attention. "Look, why don't we open the show early for a service, like the kind we give our folks? Have a 10:00 a.m. service, let some public attend, let 'em know it represents over fifteen religions, Christianity being the most important, and let 'em know we Ringlings are moral."

"Lookit, Otto, we already have a problem with how many lodge brothers'll show up, and you know a good many churches don't go for that," Alf said, getting to the bottom of the press problems. "Suddenly we are going to have Masons, Catholics, Lutherans, Baptists, Jews, Muslims, Punjabis, and some names I can't even pronounce in the same ceremony? I think the whole idea is insane."

"Gentlemen," Charley began a speech. He was really good at figuring people, but he also could calm us down. "If we hold all the non-Christian ceremony early, get the chaplain to hold the Christian ceremony at ten, it'll go over better. That's four Sundays of good press." Charley rubbed his mustache for awhile as he tallied in his head; then he leaned back in his chair a minute and went into more soul searching. Somehow it made us all the more still as we waited. "Besides, I betcha there won't be all that many who'll come. It's just good sense, it's good advertising, and it's good relations with the churchgoing crowd." Al had been silent the whole time and finally spoke.

"In a form, this is just business. Remember that Swede, the year Lou and I had to rescue you boys when you walked out on your musicians? I mean the guy who kept saying, 'Thees is not beezness.' He kept trying to tell us we didn't know what we were doing?" We all chuckled and remembered. "Well he was wrong." Sometimes we have to make changes. Some are big and some are little." No one knew this better than Al. He was a master of the quick change. "Now, I would never suggest we change our policy. But Tattersall's is a big nut, and we have to pay, every single day. We might as well make it pay and pay good." Al was still the rock. If Otto was the fist, Al was the thing that kept us rock solid and tied to our principles. "Boys, we can have it all, this time – on this one."

We all agreed that we would not lose our Sunday School Circus reputation, but rather, enhance it. We were going to use this to get more out of our show. In my stupid, get-in-the-last-word fashion, I added my two cents' worth.

"Besides, these are Chicagoans, and city folks are different, more sophisticated." Of course, that had nothing to do with church, religion, or our Sunday School Circus reputation, but I had to act like I had an opinion on the subject, even if it was a dumbass opinion.

Friday was a collaboration as our folks were still working side by side with the teams of city workers. They had hung over five hundred flags from the ceiling, representing over twenty eight nations. The opera seats had been placed, and all the seating, if not new, was newly refurbished. It glistened like a jewel.

We Ringlings often made our rounds separately. Alf liked to tell folks that I never did (make my rounds), but what started out as a joke ended up being perceived as the truth. On Saturday Alf, Charley, and I all made the rounds together. The show would open at noon, but the ballyhoo outside had already begun. Henry was helping Otto with the Red Wagon, but his job was to oversee special seating. We had more dignitaries than ever, and with the mayor's inauguration on Monday, we had an entire section for George and Lucy Bell Swift, their six children, and a dozen city officials and their families, not to mention the archbishop and his entourage. Things were remarkably ahead of schedule and everything in place. This normally would have made us all a bit uneasy, but just as we were becoming alarmed about it, we ran into Al, who was checking the function of the back door and posting the Advise, which is the schedule of the acts. The back door led directly to the center room of the dressing tent. In this case we had only sidewalls of the tent. There were three rooms: one for the women, one for the men, and one that was an entry hall where the animal actors would line up and be met by their trainers and handlers.

"It's remarkably well put together today, isn't it boys?" Al shouted as he greeted us.

"I think it's too good to be true," answered Charley, "are we overlooking something?"

"It's rare that everything ever feels this right, this close to opening," I said. Al laughed a bit and then, releasing the back door, which is just a large sheet of canvas, he said, "My brothers, we have been here for ten days. We have set everything to perfection." Then he looked quite seriously at us, in a way that only an eldest brother could. "Did we not declare victory already?" he asked. We nodded a pre-victory nod, laughed nervously, and all went on with our inspection.

The cook house and dining tent had been moved to one side of the great halls that made the outer ring of Tattersall's, and food was set for all. Lunch was the sit down meal of the day. Although we usually had a workingman's tent and a smaller, performers' tent, there was only a separation by a sheet of canvas. The atmosphere was subdued but not overly nervous. With the exception of Al and Otto, we other Ringlings had a practice of not eating before first performances. Besides, breakfast at our hotel had been ample. This show was going to start and start early.

For the price of fifty cents, we added an extra performance by Signor A. Liberati, the World-Famous Bandmaster and Cornet Virtuoso, assisted by a corps of high class soloists. The concert would last one hour. All the while, those who had not been interested in more classical pursuit could take in the sideshow, see the menagerie, or pay the ten cents for the elephant ride. By the time the Red Wagon was open, they were selling tickets for the first Sunday show we Ringlings had ever offered. Gumpertz would one day have other ideas. Sunday was selling out. Speaking of Gumpertz, whom I had not yet met, me and my brothers visited the sideshow, which we titled the "Grand Musee and Theatre." Not only did it sound better than "sideshow," but we had as much respect for the folks in that show as we did for every other actor, right down to the hippopotamus. A show is a show, and it's made of every person and creature in it, around it, and about it, including the thousands who lined up to see the performances. It took five men to run the sideshow tent including two men outside as orators. Their ballyhoo could bring in the most timid of people. One thing never on a Ringling show was a red tent. That's another kind of "sideshow," and its curiosities and contortions are not snake charmers or dog faced boys. A red tent is a full burlesque, and as the years went on, the women wore less and less. We never had such a show and never would. If men want to go and see a woman shake her ass or spin tassels on her titties, then every town and city in America has such a show place, or at least a whorehouse. Let 'em go spend their money there. We don't want that kind of money; we want families and that's what we got. If you included the two horses, Chaldean the long mane horse, which was a Percheron with not only the longest mane in history but I think the most beautiful, and Bird, the hairless horse, which to me is probably the ugliest equine wonder, plus our Punch and Judy show and the Royal Marionettes, we had over a dozen acts in the sideshow.

"Read my mind," I requested of Mrs. Charles Andres, mind reader and wife of Professor Andres, who performed with his acting monkey, Daisy. She flipped a card and then another.

"You are seeing a lot of 'alfalfa,' a veritable sea of green." That made Charley laugh.

"There's none better than you Mademoiselle," I said as I laughed. She continued, "Hmm, I see also that you speak the truth." We all laughed and continued our rounds. The show was opening, and there was a fever pitch unlike any we had ever seen. We went on to the menagerie, which like the rest of the lot made use of the great ring of space that surrounded the oval of Tattersall's great arena. The elephants had just been given a complete scrub down, and the floors were being spread with new sawdust. Before entering the show, the handlers would give a command, and mountains of elephant shit would fall. Charley and Alf liked the smell of elephant dung, but I could never get used to it. We cleaned it up as fast as it fell. Our elephants were treated like royalty, and we had fourteen in this show. Then the ring stock, from Percherons and Normans to beautifully groomed bays. We had a pony show that would make you want to kiss their little horse lips, but you'd better not: ponies bite! The dogs were groomed almost as often as the horses, which was daily. However, dog skin is very sensitive, so you can only wash them once a week. Still, rubbing, grooming, and loving was at every section, and I think that the crowds who paid their ten cents to come round the menagerie could feel it. When we got past the oddities, like the albino deer and yak, and came to the temperamental beasts, it was always questionable to every one of us. We did it for years, because in order to compete, we had to have wild animals and eventually had wild animal acts. But it rubbed us Ringlings the wrong way. One day we would begin a discussion to bring an end to such displays, at least me and Charley, but then Sam Gumpertz would change that too.

It was noon, now, and time for us to meet up with Henry and begin to greet the guests of honor. The first five shows we would give out some six hundred ducats (free seats) to folks of importance. From the acting Mayor Hopkins and his family to the mayor-elect George Bell Swift. We gave tickets to ministers, priests, and Master Masons, aldermen, council members, and of course extras for their friends and families. Henry was in charge of special seating, and his huge size and presence made him the perfect fellow for the job. He could walk through a crowd and part the "Red Sea" of patrons, making room for anyone we wanted to give a special seat to. We joined him outside, by the Red Wagon, where he was already meeting up with the dignitary guests of the show. Besides his huge size, he had a gentle, soft but strong voice, and there was something about Henry that made everyone trust him.

"Never seen the crowds like this before," he said as we approached, "it's like a sea of bowlers out there, and somewhere buried in that sea are the sweetest little excited youngsters I've ever seen!" He was wearing his finest, all dressed in black, a good quality bowler, and a wool vest tailored Chicago style. He turned and motioned to a tall fellow with red hair and a charming wife holding three little kids in succession. "This is alderman George McManus and his family. These are my brothers Alf T., John, and Charles Ringling."

"A pleasure to meet three of the great Ringling brothers," McManus commented, "I and my family are looking forward to your outstanding enterprise." As we all shook hands, Mrs. McManus, also red haired, blushed a bit as she met me. I pretended not to notice and averted my eyes. She was gorgeous, fair skinned, and red headed, and those were the days when I could imagine taking off her corset and screwing her till she screamed for mercy. But I remained professional and leaned to the tallest of the three freckle faced boys and asked, "What's your name young fellow?" I reached out and shook his hand. He didn't say a word – at first – and then finally squeezed out his name, "Sean, Sir."

"Well Sean Sir," I said, "how would you and your brothers like a ride on an elephant?"

"You mean it, sir – an elephant?" I patted his orange head and said to Henry, "Get all these boys a ride on Tilly." Henry was quick to keep it moving and grabbed Al Sanders and made sure they were taken care of. With less than an hour to go before the opening concert, there were tides of people with special seats that needed to be seated, and half their children wanted more fun than a boring concert. But boring it was not.

Signor Liberati played a concert performance that would have won the hearts of Europe. The most novel and artistic musical entertainment ever given in a circus. He offered impressive overtures, selections from grand opera, a variety of popular airs, and instrumental solos by many of the world's greatest artists. This had never happened in any circus, in any part of the world. Unlike Weldon's music still to come, this was more classically styled, less quick change, more designed for the discerning ear. If ever we were to capture the attention of Chicago's sophisticates, we were doing it – in style.

Al blew the whistle and announced the opening of the Ringling Brothers World's Greatest Shows, and then the great circus music of W.M.F. Weldon, the greatest of Ringling Brothers Circus Bands, began to play. A display of such pageantry opened the spectacle of a hippodrome of magic and splendor, of chariots of equine dance, and finishing with the magical rotating human statuary in mid-air of Charles and Marie Neville. Timing was stupendous, as the rings were immediately occupied by ladder acts, pyramid acts, and feats of daring by Akimoto and Son, who could climb over forty feet on ladders held by no one, followed by a Japanese perch act, where an acrobat stands on his head atop a twenty five foot pole, and then there was the beautiful Okeo, who upon swords on a pyramid, placed her feet in such daring that you feared for her beautiful life. The rings were filled as Kikamonte and Oudora balanced on foot ladders in the middle of the air, suspended high above the breathless crowd of thousands. The tension broke as Yosomite began the slide for life on the great spiral coming down from the dome of the arena. Great diversions were added as Miaco, West, Adair, and Tournour came along the hippodrome track in stilts towering above the crowd. If there was tension there would be clowns, and so one followed the other in perfect timing.

As the great stilted clowns had the attention of the crowd, the aerialists were assembling. Between the flying brothers Murilla, the great English acrobats The Eddy Family, and the revolving act of Miss Adair, the excitement in the crowd was now at a high pitch, every breath held on the moves that defied death itself. Lamothe and Maynard flew bar to bar, somersault to catch. And whose eyes could keep from focussing on such a great feat? It was breathtaking. All the while the rings were being prepared, for in came the equine acts, and since the show had grown so large as to have three rings and two stages, we needed more ringmasters than just Al as Equestrian Director. Mademoiselle Elena rode bareback standing, sitting, pirouetting in one ring, while in the other the great Spanish equestrian Senora Julia Lowande danced from the ground to steed then rode sidesaddle on a beautiful Frisian stallion. The clowns Miaco and company showed in another ring, falling off bays and being chased by ponies. As the equine acts disappeared, all attention would remain on the clowns as the set was changed again. Then came the almost impossible but graceful contortion of the Nelson sisters, while in Ring Two Human Enigma Joe Lewis posed almost serpentine, and in Ring Three, George Zamert and Ida Miaco offered clown contortions that were both funny and amazing.

Next appeared elephants, camels, and even the yak, and the best of acrobats and the silliest of clowns leapt over or snuck under the beasts, creating tension between laughter and fear. Acrobats who could teeterboard over four elephants, or free jump and somersault over two camels. Clowns who made you think they would follow suit and then slyly crept under the elephants' bellies. This was followed by the master equestrian Mike Rooney who had the most beautiful Norman stallions dance at liberty, coordinated as if in a ballet, while in another ring, Monsieur Natalie had his beautiful porcine dance: pigs, in unison, dance, leap, roll, and even sing.

The acts went on, with more liberty dances by other masters. Later, Mike Rooney somersaulted backwards six times onto six circling horses, The Great Dacaomas did the most frightening and skilled arial feats ever performed, and Kikamonte walked on the edge of knives in mid-air. There were pyramid acts, floating wire acts, and oriental posturing. There were whirlwind riding and jumping acts, trained dogs, and there was Achille Phillian who ascended on foot on a rolling globe which came down a spiral from the great dome of the arena.

But the grand pinnacle was a throwback to the great Roman Empire. Chariots raced with teams of one, teams of two, teams of four, and Dan Leon rode a chariot with twenty one horses, a near impossible feat. There were clown chariot races and an Icelandic pony who outpaced a thoroughbred. This was followed by a race of horse and chariot against two men who were given a quarter track head start, and they almost won. It ranged from the absurd to the highly skilled and nearly deadly serious. Those who attended the first shows were given a handbill announcing Kearney Speedy, who would in the last week of the show, make his death defying dive. This would ensure thousands more who would return for a second or third visit to the show.

The news was unrelenting in its praise of our Ringling show. "The first performance of Ringling Brothers' great show is a success," said the Inter-Ocean. "It is the best circus ever seen in Chicago," said the Times-Herald. "The most satisfactory and complete ever seen in Chicago," declared the Tribune. To the brothers and the huge family of seven hundred seventy eight people who made the entire operation work, it was a show that came off without a flaw. After the show and the "All Out" was complete, Al called his brothers and the performers to the center arena. The roustabouts, trainers, and others were all there, and in his greatest Equestrian Director voice, he said, "Miracles do happen. This show is one of them." A thunderous roar went up, and then he said, "All right then, let's get to work and make this thing even better this evening."

The Rose Garden

Everybody's got a story about when I met Mable. "He met her in Chicago..."; "She was a show girl..."; "She was a dancer in the spec!" Ha! Some folks said I met her in Coney Island. Some folks said I met her in Atlantic City, and that's a fair bet. Before he died, Alf told everyone that she was a show girl in our show. Mable told him that as a joke, although she had been in an Atlantic City show before we first met.

Actually I was on route to an Atlantic City poker game. I had visited New York earlier in the season when we had played Troy, NY, and then Albany on Decoration Day. New York was my favorite city, and though I did not yet have a home in the city, I certainly longed for one. Alf had a place in Gramercy Park, and I would stay there. After playing some town in Arkansas, we finished out the season in Malden, Missouri. There had never been a season like 1903. Every show came off without a hitch. With direction under Al, the ballet under the supervision of Signor Marquetti depicted Jerusalem and the crusades, and all the chivalry of knighthood. As advance, I took extra days to go to New York, even though we would not play there. There is no town like New York. It gets in your blood. The show went on into Canada, then back west, and eventually even Spokane. We were everywhere. We had started some discussions that year about joint ownership of The Forepaugh-Sells Show, with James A. Bailey, and although the show's winter quarters were in Ohio, and the Barnum in Bridgeport, Connecticut, Bailey had a home in Harlem and enjoyed New York. That gave me another reason to be there. I headed for New York while the show made a home run for Baraboo and back to the barn for November.

In New York I ran into you, Mr. Ed Strongin, and you informed me of some goings on in Atlantic City. I liked poker and I liked Atlantic City. Why, a good whiskey, a card game, a pretty gal, and a fine cigar; what more could a man ask for?   Outside of circus there was nothing finer! So from New York, I took the B & O down to Atlantic City. The line changes at West Belmar to the CNJ, and a fellow can get the train into Trenton or take the 1070 down to Atlantic City.

I was waiting for the 1070 to arrive, watching passengers come and go, people saying goodbye to loved ones, characters pretending to read the newspaper, slyly watching women on the platform. It was as if a great play was taking place. A very beautiful woman approached in a gray wool dress and short jacket. Her hat, which covered the top third of her face, was straw and indicated to me that she was a laborer. Her figure and the almost athletic manner in which she walked was more like a dancer. Although slender, she was a fairly large gal. She looked down the track for the train and then went back into the station. She did this three times, and I found it somewhat unusual. The train arrived. I boarded, and taking my seat I looked around and wondered what had happened to that gal. Just as the train was leaving, she ran out of the station and boarded as it was moving and took a seat opposite me. She was looking around nervously as I studied her face. She was attractive, and even as she glanced about, trying not to make eye contact, our eyes met. "Afternoon ma'am," I said. She smiled in a way that was suddenly familiar to me. It was bright, warm, and I felt it inside. Later I would think about that moment, how it was as if a light came over her face. She looked down, smiling, and said nothing.

"I'm John Ringling."   I reached across the aisle and shook her hand. Through her gloves I could tell her fingers were like mine, long and slender, but likely more delicate.

"I'm Armilda Burton. Glad to make your acquaintance, Mr. Ringling." At that moment the conductor entered the car on the other end and began collecting tickets. She quickly retracted her hand and acted nervous again.

"Is everything alright Miss Burton?"

"Not exactly," she answered looking across the car at the conductor. "I haven't a ticket and can't really pay for the fare."

"I see."   She began to get up as she would flee to the next car. Gently I took her arm and motioned for her to stay seated.

"Miss Burton please don't go. I'll see to it that your fare is taken care of." She sat, still looking uneasy as the conductor approached.

"Tickets, please." He stood in the aisle facing Miss Burton.

"She's with me, George, I'll take care of her fare."

"Oh, alright Mr. Ringling." He went on collecting tickets. I had ridden the 1070 so many times that I knew many of the conductors.

"Armilda." I contemplated her name.

"Yes." She answered although I was only trying to recall my French and figure out the meaning of her name.

"It means 'armored maiden,'" I finally said.

"Oh, no one ever told me. She looked surprised, "My friends call me Mable."

"May I call you Mable?"

"Why, yes, Mr. Ringling, call me Mable."

"You do know what Mable means – don't you?" She drew a deep breath, looked down a moment and then back at me.

"I'm afraid I don't."

"Mable means 'loveable.'" She turned a bit red and then smiled at me. Again I felt something in her smile. It was so familiar I had to question the feeling. "May I sit with you? I'm afraid turning like this is a bit awkward."

"Well, I guess you can Mr. Ringling, well, yes, I'll sit by the window."

That was the most momentous train ride of my life. For the first time in my thirty eight years I was comfortable talking with a woman, other than my mother or sister. All the affairs I'd ever had, all the women in clubs, parties, and the various cities had merely been leading me toward this. The others, well, they were just so lacking in dimension. I was completely at ease. Mable said she was looking forward to a new job in Hoboken and explained that she'd just quit a job at the Belmar Station Cafe, and her boss refused to pay her. She had been sharing a room with another gal in Belmar and because the place was so small had left many of her belongings in Atlantic City, where she'd worked as a dancer. That day, Mable was bound for Atlantic City to retrieve her belongings.

Well Ed, I never made that card game in Atlantic City you told me about. But I definitely have you to thank just the same, I mean for telling me about it. Had I not headed toward Atlantic City, I would never have met the love of my life. I accompanied her to her former apartment which she had shared with three other dancers. I certainly was familiar with dancers from the show; however, as management I stayed clear of women in our employ. Her cases were canvas covered, round top, wicker steamers and too large to carry.

"Mable, did you have a plan as to how you were going to get these back to Belmar?" These trunks were enormous. One trunk alone was more than I could handle.

"No – not exactly?"

"Did you think about how you were going to get them to the station?"

"No, I just knew that if I am going to move from Belmar to Hoboken, that if I left my things behind in Atlantic City, I would never see them again. You see, all I have in Belmar fits in a small cabin trunk."

"Well, what's so important that you have to drag around in these two monstrous trunks?" She seemed a bit embarrassed, and I hadn't yet seen the brashness of my question. After all, what a woman keeps in her steamer trunks would of course include her personal garments.

"One has my garments," she said softly, somewhat nervously, and the other has bedding, family photos, and fourteen pairs of shoes."

"Shoes! Mable, why so many shoes?"

"I worked in a shoe factory here in Atlantic City, and they gave me great bargains on shoes. I love shoes."

I hired a coach; we took the large trunks to the station, and I accompanied her on the train back to Belmar. During the trip, I learned about Mable's life in New Jersey. It seemed a hard life, and I tried to comfort her. All the while I was totally captivated by her. She also talked about the boss at the Belmar Station Cafe, how he mistreated her, dropped things in order to make her bend over, and repeatedly patted her on the behind when she would pass by. In Belmar we hired a coach, and as the coachman loaded the trunks, I looked across at the Belmar Station Cafe. I paid the driver to wait and then I took Mable's arm.

"Come on."

"What are we..." she noticed right off I was heading straight for the cafe, "oh wait, I don't think we should..."

"The fellow wronged you, didn't he? In more ways than one – it sounds like."

"Yes, but John, I don't want trouble." Mable was clearly afraid. "I don't want to trouble you."

"Mable, you shared the story with me. I don't like this fellow, and I plan to see to it he comes straight and settles up – for your sake." We continued on and then Mable walked upright more intentionally. I held the door open and she walked in first.

He was behind the counter. A small fellow, bald with a small white cap. He looked like he smelled, and the whole place had an odor of old food. He seemed surprised to see Mable walk through the door and just stood there, agape, mouth open, and you could tell he was speechless. There was a table of three, but otherwise the place was empty. We walked right up to the counter, but I stood a step behind Mable.

"Bill, I've come for my pay." Bill shook himself from his surprised stupor.

"Look here missy, I don't know what gives you the nerve to come around here again, but I told you you weren't gonna get no pay." His voice was raspy and annoying. I waited to see how Mable would handle herself.

"You owe me six dollars and thirty five cents, and I intend to get paid." I liked that; she was stubborn and strong.

"You quit and quitters don't get nothing," he said in that disgusting raspy voice. From behind the counter I could see a waitress watching, and she seemed to be smiling, perhaps happy for Mable, and the three folks at the table were watching. My fists were clenched, and I could feel myself edging toward the counter.

Then the words just popped out of my mouth, "Listen you little weasel, either you pay Miss Mable or I'll bash your little bald head in."

"Who the hell's Mable?" He asked and apparently was serious.

"I'm Mable, Bill, and maybe it's about time you begin treating your help like real people, instead of like slaves, isn't that right Clara?" Mable addressed the waitress in the back of the kitchen who nodded her head.

"I'm only paying you because you brought that thug in here to threaten me," Bill wheezed. Mable smiled smugly and looked towards me, "This man happens to be John Ringling – of the circus."

Mable got her pay, and I think she got some of her dignity back. The money was nothing, but dignity is priceless. I took her arm, and as we walked out the door, I left behind a lonely period of my life, and together we both walked into a new life.

We hired a carriage and spent the evening in a park overlooking an ocean inlet in Belmar. It was cold and we shared a lap robe. We talked all night. She told me of growing up on a farm in Moons, Ohio, and I told her of growing up in a little town in Wisconsin.

"My father was a farmer," she told me. "We had dairy cattle, and me and all my sisters and one brother had to work all the time. The only garden I ever had was for food on the table. All my life I wanted a rose garden. A place of my own, kind of like a sanctuary, where I could get to know each flower." The moon was coming in and out of the clouds, and as it illuminated her face I could see the sincerity in her wish. I wanted to kiss her, but moreover, I wanted her forever, so I held back. Now and then I could see some stars.

"As a boy I remember looking up at stars and making wishes," I told her. I wanted to let her know what made our dream come true, me and my brothers. "Mable, when I was a little boy, a circus came up the river. My papa was poor, but he made harnesses for the show and they gave him tickets. He took us all, me and my brothers, to the show. We were children, but we had a dream. Our dream was that one day we would own the best show in the world. Nowadays some people say we own the best show in the world."

"I've heard people say it's the best, John," she responded almost in a whisper.

"Mable, you will have your rose garden, one day," I told her as I held her hand. Even as we both wore gloves, I could feel the tenderness in her fingers.

"Do you think so John? I mean life has been... well it hasn't gone the way I thought."

"I know so, Mable." I looked into her eyes and the moonlight opened on her face again, and I knew she could see my eyes. "You see, Mable, dreams really do come true – sometimes, especially if you believe. Dreams come true." I squeezed her hand. "Ringling Brothers Circus went from child's play in the barn to The World's Greatest Shows."

We sat in silence, and I held her hands and then pulled her close, and we stared out over the sea. I took her home making no advances, but when I shook her hand, she held fast, and we stared into each other's eyes holding that moment, knowing this goodbye was just for awhile. I returned to New York, but before I headed west toward Chicago, and eventually Baraboo, I would send her flowers half a dozen times and telegrams proclaiming the strength of my feelings for her. We planned for New York for New Year's evening and to bring about 1904.

This was tough for me. I mean, I was what they called a lady's man. But there was more to the story. From that point on, I could not get my mind off Mable. I met a gal that December in Chicago named Hellen Langley. She was gorgeous. We danced all night, and it was all leading up to something. At one point I reached to place my hand through the ruffles in her gown and feel her ass. Then I thought about Mable and everything went dry. I took her home. That was that. Over all my years with Mable people inferred that I had other women. People say all kinds of shit about you when you have money and a reputation. I did like to flirt. It made me the center of it all and felt good. Mable was gorgeous, and I knew she thought me pretty good looking too. But it was refreshing to have another woman look at you like you would tear each other's clothes off. I don't see anything wrong with it. I knew when to curtail it too. I mean sometimes you could feel it was going to build into something where it could happen, or just as bad, I would have to turn a gal down. When I felt that coming on, I would just avert my eyes and make believe she didn't exist. Just walk away.

Mable was it for me. I knew from that first night I was gonna marry her. But I didn't know when. Furthermore I knew she was struggling with money, and I didn't want to make her feel less by helping her out. She could feel cheap, and Mable was way above that.

So I devised a scheme, where she wouldn't think it was about her. I rented a nice little flat in Hoboken. It was off of Willow Avenue in a good neighborhood, across from a park. I had it decorated and made it a little gentleman like, so as she wouldn't think it was done for her. I had to come to New York in January to meet some new acts, so I left Baraboo in late December. Some years I would go to Europe and look at acts, but not 1904. The show would open in Chicago. The difference this year was that we would run the show in St. Louis through the very day the World's Fair was to open. We actually ran the same spec as the year before, based on the Crusades, but we enlarged it and made the new focus on the grandeur. So we didn't have to add many new acts, just more dancers, more scenery, and more sizzle. I promised I would see Mable just after Christmas, as she wanted to spend Christmas with a couple of her sisters.

We met for lunch at a little place in Jersey City called Tamwin's. It was quaint. Our first moments together were awkward. I was nervous that maybe the love and excitement that had filled our letters and the night we met had disappeared, and I imagined she felt the same. The nervousness wore off quickly. I don't remember a thing about eating, unusual for me. I just recall her eyes and the way I felt. I was whole, I was myself, and I was happy, happier than I'd ever been.

It was unusually warm for December 28th, and we went for a stroll. She wore a broad brimmed hat with her hair tucked under and a motoring jacket which was several inches shorter than her gown. Her gown was checked and wool, not fanciful, and had a stiffened collar. Her neck was covered, and her pale white skin above it tempted me to want to kiss her neckline. I wore a brown three piece suit. I detested black suits and wore what we used to call a Homburg hat, so as not to be just another man in a bowler cluttering up the street. I wore a knee length overcoat, my collar was properly stiffened, and I had a white tie and stickpin. I think we were well dressed but not too showy. After we walked and chatted, I stopped at a hansom cab which I had waiting. The driver saw us coming and dismounted and opened the door.

""Mr. Ringling. Ma'am," he said, motioning and helping Mable up the step. She turned and looked at me like something out of the ordinary was going to happen, and her expression was one of questioning and concern.

"I assure you, my darling, that where I am taking you is only a step away from your rose garden." She didn't say a word but allowed the driver to help her into the cab. I followed.

"John," she said and paused leaning toward me, "you know how I feel toward you?"

"I believe, Mable," I answered, "if in anyway it is like the way I feel about you, then it is the truest and deepest feeling I could ever have."

"Yes," she responded, but then her tone changed. "I hope you don't have any expectations of me, I mean at this moment, this time."

"Mable, I do have an expectation, and that is for you to have a happy and fulfilled life."

"Where are we going?" she asked, "I mean this is so sudden."

"I have a surprise place I want to show you." I smiled and turned away as I knew we were close. Minutes later we arrived at a small three story building, rather new. The street was tree lined with young maples. The driver opened the door and we stepped out. As I took her arm, we headed for the stairs which were gray granite with simple iron railings. The building was a narrow brick townhouse as were most of the new buildings on the block. The doors were double and white. As I unlocked the door, I said, "It's on the second story." Mable, now blushing, turned and said, "I think you've the wrong idea."

"No, my dear, I have no ideas. I want to show you a home I have that I don't use." We climbed the stairs and the combination of the silence and my own anxiety was making my ears burn. I knew she thought I was expecting to take her upstairs and have a sexual encounter. That was not my intention. As we approached the apartment door I could feel that she was walking slower.

"Please Mable, know that my intentions are honest and with utmost integrity." She seemed to relax. I opened the door and we entered. It was modest, but I knew it had to be far superior to what she had been living in. It had curtains with valences and a parlor area and pocket doors. The parlor was furnished with a dark horsehair couch and a wing chair. The kitchen and dining area were separated by pocket doors. I let her find the bedroom by herself. The bed was simple, with a walnut headboard, but aptly appointed.

"It's yours," I blurted out. I hadn't really planned on how I was going to tell her, and if I had planned, I certainly would not have blurted it out like that!

"John," she turned to me, "I can't. I mean what did you?" She looked down at the floor and collected her thoughts, then back at me. "I mean I'm not that kind of girl. I can't be a kept woman."

"Kept woman!" I almost shouted. "Oh God Mable. I have this unused place. I want you, I mean, I am not going to propose today." I was really flustered. "Oh damn. I planned on proposing on New Year's – I mean... I feel so clumsy. This isn't at all going to plan." I started to sweat, but then as I looked at Mable she was radiant. I had never seen such a light come from anyone. It was as if the room got brighter. "Look, in a few days, I plan on asking you to be my wife – forever. I just knew you could use a better place to live and I thought..." Tears began running down her cheeks, and she took a handkerchief from her sleeve and dabbed them.

"Oh don't cry, my darling, I didn't mean to upset you."

"Upset. John," she smiled, "you have made me the happiest... I never... oh God." She threw her arms around me and we just held each other. It could have been forever. It was probably less than a minute. I had never felt this from a woman. I guess it was love. I never wanted to let go. Little by little we let our embrace pull away. Then I looked her in the eyes and said, "Please know that I will propose, but it will be a bit more formal – soon." She just nodded. We stood there holding each other's hands. I had taken my gloves off, but her white gloves only accentuated the beautiful feeling in her hands. We stood in silence for a bit. As I gazed into her eyes, it was as if I could see her whole life, a child in Moons, Ohio, a waitress in Jersey, a circus man's wife, a socialite. I could see time passages that I had never seen before. Then I said, "Let's make preparations for your move. I am going to have to get back to New York, but we will celebrate the new year unlike ever before."

The Players Club

John met Mable at Grand Central Station, as it was being renamed. Portions of the old terminal were being torn down and new ones built. The coming year of 1904 was to be momentous for New York, and for John and Mable, as the energy in the city was mounting. You could feel it in the excitement, especially as it was December 31, 1903, and the whole of the city was awash with expectation. Longmeadow was being rebuilt and would soon be called Times Square. The subways were about to be completed all across the city; while the uptown tubes and tunnels connected to Hoboken, the downtown tunnel would soon be finished. Grand Central Depot was being turned into Grand Central Station where all subways, trains, and every means of accessing the thriving city would meet. Forty Second Street was becoming a hub of entertainment, and one could simply walk from the great station to an opera house or a show. New

York was alive with change, and it was the kind of change that made men walk faster and women lift their skirts above the road.

The couple went first to the Waldorf Astoria, where they ate a light but artful supper. John Ringling was already well known at the Waldorf but had gone ahead and given the maitre d' forty dollars, twenty for himself and some to spread around. He asked for the finest table and the best of service.

"For you Mr. Ringling, it is always the best, but tonight you will receive the finest!"

They were greeted as royalty, given the best table in the house; they drank champagne. Mable was modest in all her eating, and John made up for it. He had an appetite for the times and never hid it, although he was never gluttonous in front of Mable. There was not a moment missed by the staff, and no more perfect meal had ever been served in the restaurant of the famous hotel Waldorf Astoria.

From there they traveled by coach to 7th Avenue and 42nd Street to the Victoria Theater. The theater was changing from light plays to vaudeville and music, and this night would bring a special performance. They were greeted by Willie Hammerstein, who owned and operated the establishment.

"Good Evening Mr. Ringling," Willie greeted him with great familiarity. Willie's father, Oscar, had given him the Victoria that fall. Oscar, most noted for his numerous opera houses, was also known to John for his many inventions which included cigar rolling machines that made a more perfect gentleman's cigar. Willie's son Oscar Hammerstein II would go on to become one of the most successful librettists and theatrical producers in American history.

"Willie, my friend," Ringling led Mable's hands towards Hammerstein's, "this is Miss Mable Burton."

"Not only a pleasure," he responded, gently taking her hand, but as he held her hand he looked at Ringling, "and might I add, the most beautiful woman in the house tonight." Mable blushed and said nothing. Indeed she was beautiful, and dressed fashionably as John had sent her to the finest dress shop in Hoboken. Hammerstein motioned for an usher who took them to their seats. They had a box for four all to themselves. The music, extremely modern, was led by James Reese Europe. A colored man, which was new but festive for Mable. He played orchestral music that was considered by many – ahead of its time. Princess Raja danced on the stage with her "all too short" dress, which when she twirled would show her legs and colorful bloomers. Her full figure shook in a belly dance, tasseled top swaying as her breasts shook. Her finale included picking up a chair with her teeth and dancing, swirling round and round with the chair high above her head. The last piece was a theatrical sketch by John Barrymore and Alyson Coyne. It was comical and light.

From there the couple headed toward Gramercy Park. In the coach, while sitting under a fur lined coach robe, John turned to Mable. He reached over and took both her hands. She was nervous that he was going to propose, and thinking about her infertility, she wasn't certain she would say yes. She questioned every thought. How could she say no? She loved him so deeply. How could she say yes? She might hurt him by not being able to give him a child. They had never once discussed children. Only "rose gardens" and "art" and "culture."

"Mable," John began, I am thirty eight years of age. I have in my past had no romance, only affairs. I have not loved, nor have I ever lived, until now." Her heart was pounding; he was going to ask her, and she just had no idea. If she said no, she thought to herself, then she'd have to tell him, tonight. John continued, "It is clear to me, God, my whole life is now clear. You are all I have ever wanted. Mable, will you marry me?" Her eyes welled up and she looked deep into his, and answered, "Yes!" She leaned over and hugged him. "Yes, Yes Yes!" She sobbed with joy. John then took from his pocket a small box and opened it. It was a ring with a beautiful yellow diamond. She removed her left glove and he placed it on her finger. Then he said," Forever."

"Forever," she whispered.

The carriage soon arrived at the Players Club at Gramercy Park for the New Year's Eve Ball. Mable had to take a moment by coach light and fix her makeup. John escorted her to the ball, where actors, musicians, writers, the rich, and the entertainers of the rich, danced into the evening. She met many, most of whom she could not hear nor remember their names. But one, the very designer of the Players Club, the famous Stanford White, was most memorable, as he was with a young girl, questionable in age, and her blouse cut very low, like that of a show girl.

"I want you to meet the great architect and designer of this establishment," John said, leading Mable toward the man, "Mr. Stanford White." White took Mable's hand, raised it to his lips and kissed it.

"This is one hundred percent my pleasure," he said with a twinkle in his eye, as he made all about Mable, examining her with a lustful gaze.

"Careful Mable, he devours the gals," said Ringling, smiling, but sincere. His young escort moved into the crowd to speak with John Barrymore, who they had seen just moments earlier in the show. "Oh, and you recognize Mr. Barrymore from the Victoria?" He introduced the two.

"My pleasure," Barrymore responded and then disappeared quickly. John noticed despondent looks from Stanny White and allowed the matter to drop. John and Mable would find out later that both Stanny and John Barrymore had relations with a certain young chorus girl that would some day figure into the demise of Stanford White.

Mable later asked John, whispering in his ear, "Was that Mr. White's daughter?" John laughed and replied, "You have to forgive Ol' Stanny; he has a propensity for young show girls!" When the countdown came and started at "ten, nine," John leaned over and whispered, "You have made me the happiest man in the world." Mable responded, "You have made me the happiest woman in the world."

"Three, Two, One!" The screams went up: "Happy new Year." They hugged, then kissed in public, and after one more dance found themselves heading down the block to the Ringling apartment. It was Alf's apartment and John stayed there frequently.

When they arrived at the apartment, John offered another champagne, but Mable just pulled him close and kissed him. There was only an entry light and the apartment was dim. There was a frenzied moment where they seemed to tug wildly at each other's clothes, but then John, remembering all the dissatisfying sex, the hurried pace and the unresolved and unfulfilled encounters said, "Let's take our time; we have all night." Mable was not a virgin and had been married for less than a year in Chicago at age sixteen. Based on her infertility, the marriage was soon annulled. John, having had many women over the past decade, had never had a moment of satisfaction. He had never felt like any of it had made any one woman happy. Here, they enjoyed each other and took their time. When it was over, they held each other. Mable cried light tears of joy, not sobbing, and John never knew. Their intimacy was bliss and would set the tone for a lifetime of romance.

John returned to Baraboo for necessary interactions with his brothers. It was time for lengthy meetings and decisions that would make or break the 1904 season. Although the show would run the same theme as 1903, the '04 show would need to be bigger and better. St. Louis would open the World's Fair Exposition on the closing day of the World's Greatest Show, and it was more than a one day competition. The show, as it had been in the past, would be a full week run, and the question was whether or not the public would hold back and wait for what would be the big show, or embrace the circus as well. Given their previous history, a week in St. Louis could be worth over twenty thousand, and that was a whole sack of alfalfa.

John was more than in love. After his night with Mable, he discovered something new about himself. Certainly it was romantic, intimate, but more so, it was a discovery that he could truly adore someone. This was nuanced as a feeling that there was more to life than success, money, and notoriety. He questioned himself, "Can this be real?" He found himself bursting out in laughter, unprompted, wishing he could just go and grab someone and tell them that he was madly in love. That it was more than just infatuation but was something eternal, something that only God could have given him. By the time his train got to Buffalo, he took the time to send Mable a telegram. He had struggled since Albany to write it, trying to say something poetic, something special, expressive. He scribbled poems and notes over and over. Finally with several choices as he stood at the station's telegraph office, he sent two words," Love - John." It had seemed the final, most romantic, uncomplicated thing he could send.

In Hoboken, at the new apartment, Mable received the telegram in the morning as she was departing for work. She was on her way to the door when the bell rang. Through the tube she could make out a garbled voice that it was a "telegram for Miss Mable Burton." She was late for work, so she grabbed her satchel and ran down the stairs. As she opened the envelope and read the two words, she understood immediately. There was nothing else that could be said. No poetry, no wordsmithing, not formal follow through for what had transpired between them; it was just love. Pure.

Mable continued to work in the millenary shop. She had made a promise to herself and to John that until they were to be wed, she was not going to be a kept woman. Still John showered her with gifts from the finest stores in New York. They wrote each other almost daily, and at times the letters spoke of hearts that ached and longed for each other. John promised he would return before the first of March so they could have time together before the show opened in Chicago.

On January 22nd she unlocked the front door at the millenary shop as she did every day. She drew the curtains as usual and turned on the three electric lights. Her employer Mrs. Parker arrived in her daily routine at 11:00. The store was open and everything set up, but there was no sign of Mable. Mrs. Parker made her way to the main hat counter, and there on the floor was Mable, just as she had fallen, on her side, legs bent. She bent over Mable and tapped her face several times, and her eyes opened. "Where, what happened?" Mable asked, in a daze.

"Are you alright dear?" Mrs. Parker asked. "I think you have fainted."

I don't know," Mable answered, righting herself, "I don't remember anything."

"Can you stand?" Mrs. Parker took her hands and helped pull her up.

"I don't feel anything," she answered, "I mean, I feel fine now."

"Dr. Petersen is three doors down," Mrs. Parker said, still holding Mable's hands. "I'm taking you there now."

"Oh please, I think I'll be fine," Mable protested.

"No arguing," Mrs. Parker commanded, "we're going." Mrs. Parker wrapped Mable in her coat, turned the sign to "Closed," and they went out, locking the shop door.

It was still early, and Dr. Petersen's waiting room was near empty. He was able to see Mable right away. As they spoke, Mable suggested that she could be pregnant; however, she explained that her first marriage had been annulled because she could not conceive. Just the same, after hearing her history of a six month marriage, the doctor included a pregnancy test in a series of tests. He suggested other tests, drew blood, and spent over an hour. He had to get her blood to the hospital lab and suggested that they meet again in a week. Meanwhile he suggested a couple days of bed rest.

Mable continued to write to John, as he did to her, but did not mention the incident. A week later she met with Dr. Petersen. His demeanor was serious. After a few moments of polite small talk, Mable interrupted and said, "I want to know everything."

"The first thing, Miss Burton, will take some more tests, but we think you may have a fertility problem."

"Well, as you know, that's not a surprise."

"We don't have enough information, but there is an indication of a blockage." He continued, "I would like you to see a specialist, Dr. Jacobs. Sometimes people change as they get older, and your chances of childbearing can improve."

"I was under the assumption from my first diagnosis that the blockage was likely permanent," Mable responded. Then Dr. Petersen went on, "There were some abnormalities in your blood sugar levels."

"What does that mean?" Mable interrupted.

"Well, I don't think you have diabetes, but maybe you have a tendency toward the illness."

"Forgive me doctor, I've heard of it, but I don't know what it is."

"Well, the word comes from the Greek," he explained, "dia, as in your kidneys or urine, and betes which means honey or sugar."

"All right, so what does that mean to me, I have sweet urine?" she asked, trying to joke about it.

"What it means is that your body might have a hard time making use of sugar. In your case, if diabetes is present, it's minor, in the early stages. The sugar level was abnormal but not that high. All food that we eat, other than protein, must change into a kind of sugar in your body to give you energy. For now, I want you to keep your sugar and alcohol consumption modest, and eat a little more meat."

"I can do that," she responded. "Is there more I should watch out for?"

"Let me know if you are excessively tired, or extremely thirsty. Really, let me know if anything abnormal should happen."

"Should it get worse," she paused, "I mean, if I get the diabetes, is there a cure?"

"I am sorry my dear; there is no cure for this disease, at this time." After a long pause Mable asked, "Doctor, what do I owe you?"

"My dear, you owe me nothing; your employer has taken care of everything. But please, I want you to see Dr. Jacobs as soon as possible. I have already sent your test results to him."

John returned to New York in mid-February. After stopping briefly at the apartment at Gramercy Park, he took the ferry across the Hudson for Hoboken. The Gramercy apartment was fine, and John frequently stayed there before he and Mable found their home on Fifth Avenue. Gramercy Park was a small community, filled with writers, actors, industrialists, and those who wanted to step back two blocks from the mill of constant movement of trolleys, people, wagons, and small, seemingly useless automobiles. It was in every way a park-like haven in the middle of the massive growing metropolis. There was always a hansom waiting to take a wealthy patron from the park.

Mable knew he would arrive soon but was not certain of the day. Today would be a surprise. At Hoboken he took a short line to Fayette Station, and from there he walked down Clinton Street to 7th Street. He enjoyed walking, today. The air was crisp, cold, but the late February sun made it full of hints of spring. By the time he reached 7th Street, it was an overwhelming mass of frenetic movement. Traffic officers tried to direct wagons, trolleys followed one behind the other, horses pulled wagons ranging from hansoms to teamsters with loads, and then there was the sea of people, mostly men in black or gray, and women with long and full dresses that scuffled along the cobblestones and concealed all but their pointed boots. The ebb and flow of hats was astounding. Men wore boaters of straw, bowlers, top hats, Homburg hats, and pork pies. Women wore every conceivable fashion of hat which dominated as much space as the women themselves. They ranged from great woven shapes, some with wings, to others with exotic feathers or gatherings of fur; still simpler were those of felt and straw, out of season, that encircled women's heads like globes and overhung great brims which added to their modesty as the hats could conceal not only hair but some of the face. The pace on Broadway was every bit as exciting as anything John knew in New York or Chicago, and he became more excited as he approached the corner of 7th and Clinton where he would find Mable at Parker's Millenary.

He stopped at the door for a moment looking in and noticing that it was busy. There were several customers, and Mable and Mrs. Parker were helping with hats on and hats off. Mable's back was to John, and her slender figure and full bustle captivated him. He watched as she reached up to a rack replacing one hat with another; her waist would stretch and move and her buttocks were so inviting. Finally he couldn't stand it any longer and opened the door and entered. The bell rang and everyone turned and looked. First, there was a look of surprise from all six women, as a man in a millenary was somewhat out of place. Then Mable lost all control. "John!" She practically screamed, as she ran and threw herself into his arms. "You're early. I thought, well, it wouldn't be until the weekend."

"Life is more exciting when filled with surprise my darling," he responded and then they held each other again.

"What about my hat?" asked the older woman Mable had been assisting. She was not happy about this interruption and had a nasty scowl.

"I'm sorry Mrs. Morgan," Mable apologized, "I'll be right with you."

"You'll do no such thing," Mrs. Parker interjected, "I'll take over from here." She looked back at Mrs. Morgan, with a victorious smile, and then turned toward the couple, "You and your Mr. Ringling take the afternoon off."

"That's John Ringling," one woman whispered to another.

"Are you certain?" Mable asked. "I mean you're so busy already."

"My dear I have been doing this for eighteen years, and I think I can manage." She began reaching for a hat that Mrs. Morgan had wanted to try on, and turned back to John and Mable, "Now hurry up before I change my mind."

The two were out the door, arm in arm, walking down Broadway in the mass of people, a sea of activity. Because it was after lunch hour, they stopped at a bakery, and John had coffee and pie while Mable had tea. They nervously caught up on small talk, the show, Baraboo, the scenery for the circus, new acts, Mable's job, and life in the little apartment and the park across the street. Mable was nervous. She didn't want to tell John a thing about the diabetes. Doctor Jacobs had told her that if she kept her weight down and avoided sweets, she would be fine. He said they would monitor her blood sugar, and he gave her signs to watch for. At that moment, she could feel only the excitement about John. Deeper in her mind was the infertility. Although the doctor told her it was a blessing in disguise, as complications with pregnancy and diabetes could be fatal, she worried that John would not want a wife that could not bear a child. She was thirty and he thirty nine, so it was late already for a woman her age to give birth. Still, her heart was rushing. There was a magnetism between them. Other people in the bakery could feel it. They paid the bill and went walking. After a while John noticed that Mable seemed a bit cold. He hired a cab and they rode to her apartment. He acted as if he would call again.

"You mean, you are not coming up?" she asked him in dismay.

"Oh my darling Mable, there is no place I'd rather be. I was just... I mean I am being polite."

"To hell with polite," she whispered in his ear, "and to heaven with love." They paid the cab driver, and by the time they reached the stairs, they were moving quite fast. Before even opening the door, she was in his arms and they kissed, the kind of kiss that made her breathe hard. She opened the door, and they almost fell inside, where he not only began undressing her but she too was removing his clothes. Their intimacy and familiarity had grown to a new level. They made love until well after dark and then just held each other. They spent the better part of the week together, mostly making love and going out for small meals. They talked of their dreams, things outside of circus. But John was also preoccupied with the show. He had to finish the routing, and it took a great deal of travel. Soon he would return to being the circus man he was and would only see Mable in between shows that were on the east coast. Still, John and Mable were now and forever a couple, and it seemed that nothing could break them apart.

From Moons to Elysian Fields
Excerpts from the Diary of Armilda (Mable) Burton
1889 -1905

June 11, 1889 – we were visited today by Alice Hartnan, a teacher from Galludette College in Washinton, DC. She is a teacher of English Studies and American History. It is a school for deaf people. She is here to see Clara and Amanda. It was good that Amanda,

Mama, Clara and I all know some sign language. It always makes Father nervous when we sign.

Thursday June 13 -Reverend Mahoney for dinner again this week. He talked about Steven Clearey over on the other side of Fayette and how he expressed an interest in me. If I stay here in Moons there won't be anything left of me.

Friday June 21 – I fear that Reverend Mahoney is going to introduce me to young Mr. Cleary at the social on Sunday after church. I have to leave home. I let Clara know. She cried and screamed. She couldn't hear herself and I worried Papa was going to come in from the barn and find out. Mama seems to know something. I have saved my money for two years now. Amanda called me "Mim." She has been speaking a little – a few sounds. Now everyone is calling me Mim.

Saturday July 6 – Father shot his gun in the sky at night on Thursday. I think he was drinking. Friday morning the big cow, Yancy, calved and papa slaughtered the calves and hung them in the barn over the mama. It made me sick and I protested. He said as a farm girl I had to learn the ways. I cried. How could he? I have to get away.

Sunday August 4 – It's Alma's birthday. After church we had a party and when we sang "happy Birthday," Clara and Amanda tried to sang. They couldn't hear themselves, but I heard their hearts. They are such beautiful sisters. Who cares if they can hear? Why do people call them dumb? They are the smartest people I know. I am going to leave soon – maybe before school starts. Father doesn't want me to go back to school. He thinks I should stay here and teach my sisters – especially Clara and Amanda. Dulcey is growing up fast too. Im glad she can hear – unlike the other two and Alma can hear fine. Bill is still such a baby – we hope his ears are fine.

September 7– I think it's Saturday. I am on the train – outside of Champaign. I overslept. I think we stopped in LeRoy, Illinois. There is a circus not far from the tracks. I can see the tent. I never saw a circus. I can hear the music. I wish I could see more. Headed for Chicago.

Wednesday – December 4 – 1889. I am with Larry Fischer. He wants me to marry him. I am cold. It has been a long time on the street. Chicago can be so heartless. I love the library. It is the one place I feel in control of my life. I am going to marry him. He has a job.

Tuesday March 11 – 1890. Larry, I don't think he intends to hurt me. He forces himself on me every night. He smells. Like plumbing. He works for the city – underground. Maybe he wants to love me. I so want someone to love me. I miss my sisters. I miss the farm.

Tuesday May 6 – My only solace is the library. There I can read about far away places, art, and history, I can read books and in my mind and my heart I can turn the pages and stand before the great masterpieces in the Louvre. Larry and I had another fight. I bled today and he is upset. He wants a baby. He wants me to see a doctor. I told him it just takes time.

Tuesday May 13 – Doctor Adrian told us the results of the tests. I can't have children. Larry won't look at me. He is drunk and I am writing in front of him. His eyes are closed.

Monday May 19 – The judge agreed with Larry that we married under false pretenses. Larry has packed my belongings. He kept the silver that I took from Grandpa's chest and said it was a dowry. I am to leave at once or he will have the authorities take me. I remember Father slaughtering the calves. It's raining outside. Maybe I can sleep by day at the library.

Thursday June 4 – 1891 – Atlantic City. I have been dancing in three different shows. Men look up our dresses and we wear no bloomers. I feel like I died.

Saturday September 26 – I met a man I liked. He seems friendly. His name is Henry Mathesson. He wants to take me to dinner. Maybe he is a gentleman. Next week he will call. Meanwhile the library has much to offer here. It is my sanctuary. Today I read excerpts from "Passion Flower," by Julia Ward Howell. I feel better.

Friday October 2 – Henry is a monster. After dinner he took me to a hotel. He forced himself on me. It hurt. Not just my heart but it hurt – down there. I wanted to throw up – especially when he said he couldn't be seen in public with me for fear his wife might see us together. What a shit.

Sunday April 22 – 1894 – It seems like I have worked in this awful shoe factory forever. I used to like Atlantic City. The smell of leather and glue is sickening.

Wednesday March 16 1898 – My birthday. I am alone. The job at the clothier here in Hoboken is good. I am saving my funds. I heard from Dulcey and the girls are looking forward to coming east. I can't wait to see them. Bill is thirteen. Clara has found a man who loves her in spite of her impairment. I went to the old site of the Elysian Fields where the first baseball games were played. It's a park now – Elysian Park. I feel good there. I ate an apple and watched children play. I smiled at a little boy. He is smiling back now.

Tuesday July 22 – 1902 – I hate Atlantic City. My job is agony. I have to clear tables while drunk men fall all over chorus girls and wet their pants. If only their wives could see them. The one thing that helps is working at the Berg Shelter – the ASPCA. The animals need me. I love them. Their longing stares, they miss the one thing they were so denied – a mother. I can help.

Wednesday December 24 – Belmar is too small. I don't know why I moved back here. Nothing ever happens here. I am cleaning houses and working for Celia T. She is a witch. Maybe I should call her something more wretched. She makes me get on my hands and knees even when there is no dirt. The little library in Belmar is only open on Thursdays, Fridays and Saturdays. Not much time and very few books.

Wednesday October 28– 1903. I am working by the train station at the Belmar Cafe. My boss, Bill is a shit. He deliberately spills things so that I have to bend over and clean them. I can feel him looking at my fanny. The Library is still my church. The other day I fell asleep reading about Italy. It wasn't boring. I just felt so comfortable. It was like being at home. Home. I could go back, if they would have me. My baby brother Bill is going to leave home. Father and Mother will be alone soon. Maybe I should have stayed and married Steven Cleary. I don't know. Thirty – that's old. I don't have any prospects. Dulcey, my little baby sister is getting married. Why is life like this? I won't have a child of my own. Maybe my sisters will share their babies with me. Have I lost my faculties? I am a spinster in New Jersey. I like the ocean. It's different than Ohio. I miss the animal shelter.

Thursday November 4– It has been raining for a week. I miss going to the shore to look at the sea. There is supposed to be a full moon tomorrow. I doubt I'll get to see it.

Sunday November 7 – I quit my job. Enough of Bastard Bill. I couldn't take it any more. Besides Rebecca helped me find a new job in Hoboken. I went to Atlantic City to get my things from the old apartment. Something wonderful happened. I met someone special on the train – John Ringling – of the Big circus! I felt like I'd known him all my life. He helped me with my trunks and then we went back to the Belmar Cafe and I got Bill to pay me the $6.35 he owed me. John stood by. I can hardly believe I am calling him John. It just feels right. We went toward the sea in a carriage. The moon came out. I feel good again – like I haven't felt this way in a long time. I can't remember when. John did not try to take advantage of me. He held my hands and we watched the sun come up over the sea.

Friday November 20 – I telegrammed John and let him know where I was moving to in Hoboken. I start the new job on Monday – Thanksgiving week. John keeps sending telegrams and flowers. I am not sure if this is a dream and if it is will I awake to the nightmare again? I have to be stable. So many times men have hurt me. I don't want to be hurt agin.

Tuesday December 29 – John came yesterday. He is letting me stay in a Hoboken apartment he doesn't use anymore. I know he is lying. It is not a bad lie, he just doesn't want me to think I am being kept. I don't want to be kept. I love him – I think. When I picture him I feel something inside. I can't stand not being with him. He has set up an account at Reilly's so I can buy a fancy dress for Thursday night. He is taking me to dinner and a show in New York. I think he wants to ask me to marry him. I have not told him that I can't give him a child. I don't know what to do.

Sunday January 3, 1904 – It is quiet here. I can look out the window at the park. I miss John. He went back to Baraboo. He has asked me to marry him and I said yes. Everything still seems like a dream. We haven't said when we would get married. He has to work on the show all winter – it seems.

May 19 – I am on the train to Albany to see John. I can hardly breath. The Hudson River is beautiful. Little towns, Garrison, Rhinecliff, Albany soon. I am going to travel with John and the show.

November 1 – We are in Corsicana, Texas. I never knew I could love strange animals so. Elephants are sweet and huge and remind me of cows on the farm. They seem to have such a bond to each other. I know they recognize me every different time they see me. John and I are more in love. He bought me beautiful things in Dallas. I have seen more of the world in just a few months than in my whole life. The season ends in two weeks. Then we are going to Chicago. I have mixed feelings about Chicago.

Sunday November 20 – I hardly write about my life anymore. I am more alive. John is right. Chicago is much more exciting when one has money. He wants me to go to Baraboo for Thanksgiving and meet his mother. I think we will get married soon. I have to tell him.

Wednesday November 23 – I am going back to Hoboken. We had a terrible fight. I told him. I can't even recall what we said to each other. He put me on the train to New York. I don't know if we'll ever be right again. I hurt so bad.

Tuesday January 24 – I have gone back to work at the millinery shop. I have not heard from John in two months. When it's warm enough I like to go to Elysian park and watch the children. It is snowing today.

Friday February 17 – John wrote! He sent a post from Germany three weeks ago. He misses me and is cold and wishes I was there. I wish I was there.

Thursday November 9 – on route to Charleston where at last I am going to see John. Mrs Parker finally found a replacement for me whom may stay with the job. John's talking about going to Europe.

Saturday November 11 – We had a fight and we just couldn't seem to talk to each other. I am going home. I am sick about this.

Thursday December 28 – John was at my door – We went for a long walk. It was warm and we went to Elysian Park. There were children and they sleighed down the hill in the wet snow. He told me he never wanted children – just me. We are getting married tomorrow – in Hoboken. Then we are going to France and Italy. A new year's celebration on ship board. I am going to start a new chapter of my life. I am going to be happy. I don't need a diary anymore.

Five
Big Ideas

Shell Beach

We were good to Baraboo. After Mama died, things got kind of messy in Wisconsin. Taxes. Now we had always done good by the people, in the town that reared us up, and the state itself. Winter quarters was growing. In 1906, by the time of Mama's passing, we were already well into talks with James Bailey's widow and attorney about the acquisition of The Greatest Show On Earth. Otto could foresee the difficulty of owning two major shows with two separate winter quarters. Hell, as far back as '91 rumors went far and wide that we were going to move winter quarters to Madison. Even though it had been brought amongst us for discussion, it was never to happen. Otto had a grip on our monies and why it would be necessary to keep to what we owned, stay in a small town like Baraboo where goods were cheap. Papa had been our harness maker; cousin Henry was our wagon maker. Our cousins, the founders and managers of the Golmar Bros. Circus, shared in the employ of the many artisans needed to make the goods and costumes for the two shows.

Mable and I did not go to Florida until 1910. Our arrival in Sarasota was awkward. We were to follow the likes of Bertha Palmer, widow of hotel magnate Potter Palmer. Although we only met Bertha on rare occasions, she was most kind to Mable. She was encouraging to us, and especially Mable, to be involved in civic and social callings in Sarasota. I had already come to criticize the locale as there was no real train route to the town. The train line was an abysmal, wobbly piece of junk and was designed for hauling fish from Sarasota to Tampa. However, work was well under way to upgrade, and Ralph Caples was working hard on a new line which would be completed in the next year. We had to take the rail to Tampa where we were to be met by limo and taken as guests of Charlie Thompson, general manager of our third and smallest show, Adam Forepaugh's Great Circus. Next to the World's Greatest Shows and The Greatest Show On Earth, it was probably the biggest show in the country. Like everyone who had put in their time, he had worked for many shows, including Ringling. His other pals Ralph Caples and W.H. Burkett were more than familiar to me. Caples, a railroad man and an advertising tycoon, was already a working associate, and being invited with Mable to "come see the paradise" was an invitation that we had to follow. It seemed that Florida, Ponce de Leon's fountain of youth, was a magnet for anyone with money who might want to engage in the sport of real estate investment, while avoiding the harsh, unrelenting winter in the north. I was well aware of the problems of a lack of rail lines and having to travel by car or steamer from Tampa, but the stories of tropical splendor, winters without coal stoves and wet feet, was allure enough to make us try.

In the 1910 season we added Tampa to our southern states stands, and Mable and I visited the show. It was November and the weather was crisp, like September in Wisconsin, clear and comfortable. We made our rounds, trying the various haunts of the wealthy and the travel savvy. We went to Tarpon Springs, a sport fishing mecca, where the skippers and local business people were less than warm. When folks were never gracious enough to give Mable the reception I thought she was deserving, it usually drove me to do something drastic. Mable was distraught that we were treated like commoners when we tried to charter a local sport fisher, and spend a day with Edith and Charley, trying for the great tarpon. Neither Mable or I were big fans of fishing, but Charley and Edith both derived great pleasure from the strange act.

"You can't let him talk to you like that," Mable demanded, "like you're just some commoner."

"I'll take care of it dear." I had no idea what I would do. I went back to the wharf to speak to the captain, ready to let him know that I was John Ringling and that I was the owner of three of the greatest amusements in the world. In an odd way, we had chosen both a common life and the life extraordinaire. The place on Fifth Avenue was generous in proportion but not particularly grand. But our lives were the circus, great travel, and I think we lived more lavishly away from home than in New York or Chicago. When I arrived, the charter boat captain was having some kind of haggle with a local businessman and made me wait, in the background, ignoring me for some five minutes. Finally I walked away, angry enough to want to bloody his stupid cranium. That's when I saw something. A fellow, standing on a small yacht named Louise II, next to a "for sale" sign. One hour later Mable and I owned our first yacht. The next day we took Charley and Edith fishing. Everything in Florida happened fast. See it – buy it – take it. I did.

Getting to Shell Beach took some extra travels, often as the show was in Tampa, but in time I grew to love Sarasota. When Ralph Caples and Charlie Thompson invited me to Sarasota in 1911, Mable and I arrived in the cold. It was December, and it felt like December in Wisconsin, except the sun was shining. We visited at Ralph's rustic log home. I didn't feel out of place without a tie, stickpin, or bowler. The house was sort of ordinary, dark, and not real tropical. Unlike my brothers, Mable and I had been content without a house. Everyone was in a buying frenzy, and it seemed that Owen Burns had got there first and bought up the best properties. Still, there were vast tracks of land that I could buy and own as if like a king! This was not Palm Beach, or Miami, which to Mable and I seemed spoiled.

We dressed warm, as if for autumn, and dined with our new friends and their wives. After dinner we men sat in the parlor and smoked cigars, while the women donned their overcoats and walked outside at twilight.

"John," Ralph began, "there's a huge opportunity here, in and around Sarasota, in real estate."

"Well," I teased him, "if we were to push tourism for ice fishing and winter sports, we might all strike it rich."

"This little cold snap will pass in another day or so," he responded quickly, missing my joke. Ralph never had a great sense of humor. "Listen," he went on, "I have some land for sale. It's about thirty acres, but it's right next door here in the Shell Beach area."

"I'll buy it," I snapped.

"Don't you want to know how much?" Ralph questioned.

"I am sure if you are selling it, to me, then your price will be fair."

"Well, I have a house in between my place and the land," Ralph injected hastily.

"I'll buy it," I told him. "It's the Thompson place, right?"

"Yes," he answered and tried not to smile. "You've seen it?"

"Of course, Ralph," I said, then let him have it: "You're pretty sneaky – aren't you?"

"What do you mean John?"

"Listen here, you are a show man, I know you. You thought you'd sneak the house in and let me think buying it was my idea, all the while it was yours."

"You are pretty clever, Mr. Ringling," he complimented me, and that was all I really wanted. "Come by the land office tomorrow and we'll settle up."

It wasn't long after that night it all began. Even before the war, Charley and I were flush with Florida opportunities. I outdid my brother, but he was sly. He'd wait for me to move and then he'd move. It was like chess and checkers all in one. But in the early years we were what we always were – family. Charley built his first home right next door to the Palms Elysian. That's what we named our first home. Other than the Wisconsin, our railcar, it was the first real home Mable and I owned. Ralph and I had gone in on one hundred thirty acres in the Shell Beach Colony, and we paved driveways, and some lots had real gates, not as flush as ours, but real formal entries, designed and influenced by Mediterranean architecture. We advertised in New York and Chicago and used our Ringling name along with Admiral Phillips, actually his widow, and others to impress that this was the new place to be. Otto had died that year, and it made all of us Ringlings tighter, and so I encouraged everyone to come – which they did. But not all my siblings had the love affair with Florida that Mable and I had. The war years paraded by fast – too fast! Al and Louise came and rented, but they were more clearly married to the show than any of us. Then Al died. Henry and his wife Ida liked the lakes better and bought a place inland at Eustis. They kept their launch, The Salome, named after Mama, at our property on Shell Beach. Mable loved it more than they did, so they practically gave it to her. We built an eighteen hundred foot dock to clear the shallows so she could keep it there. Mable was closer to the Shell Beach property than I was, as she had made her rose garden there. It was bigger than our house. In fact it was over twenty five thousand square feet. By the end of 1913 she had finished it. She modeled it after traditional Italian circular gardens.

Shell Beach eventually became more than just home to us Ringlings; it was the center of family. Certainly we always loved Baraboo, and Henry, Alf T., and Al, more than Charley and I, were devoted to the place. Ida loved Sarasota and also loved Baraboo. Her husband Henry Whitestone North always liked Baraboo, and so Ida and Henry maintained two homes, even after brother Henry died. After the war and after all my other brothers were gone, Charley and I took after Sarasota. He had given over his first yacht the Zumbrota to the war effort and built a second Zumbrota – named after the place where Deedee had grown up in Minnesota before her family moved to Baraboo. We enjoyed our yachts, if for different reasons. Charley and Deedee liked to fish and spend time on the water. They even had smaller boats just for fishing. I liked to be able to show off my goods and show prospective buyers the Ringling Isles, while I toured them around the waters off Sarasota, in style. It was a boom for us Ringling boys, and Charley and I went in on over sixty thousand acres. We portioned off the land and set up developments. I had this idea that if we had one architect design the master plan, the roads, the houses and the entries, and it all had a Mediterranean feel, people from the big cities in the north would buy up land like crazy. Meanwhile, we both loved Sarasota, and we were willing to sink everything we could into the place.   During this time period my first Zalophus yacht exploded in Tampa, and a fellow was killed. Charley built a beautiful craft, the Symphonia. It exuded stealth, was sleek, graceful, and steam powered at one hundred thirty feet. I didn't want my brother to out perform me, so I built the second Zalophus but didn't call it the Zalophus II. It was one hundred thirty five feet. It was designed for entertaining, and that's what I did with it. Unfortunately for me I couldn't get the thing into my Shell Beach property where we had already built huge sea walls. Charley and I also floated a bond for the Sarasota Pier. We ended up paying for most of it. There were a couple times when Charley's skipper brought the Symphonia in behind his home. The skipper could have really made a mess of it. He had once tried to show it off in St. Petersburg at the Yacht Club and snapped off the stern jack staff of the yacht Presque Isle. It was in the St. Petersburg Times and made a laughing stock out of Charley. But my big brother was unscathed by the criticism. I would have been burned up mad and gone and done some other fool thing to try to right my reputation.

Sarasota doesn't seem to like me these days. It all goes back to the fever we all had for the place. When there's a lot of ballyhoo and something goes wrong, everyone will blame the last guy standing. In the end, it seems like it was me, the orator, the caller. I teamed up with Ralph Caples and Owen Burns. By 1923 the whole plan was in full swing. The center of the plan was St. Armand's, and it was going to be a beautiful place. We used every ounce of our skills to show off. We made beauty where we could, and every time we sold to a millionaire, we'd hold that fellow up for all the other possible investors to see. The causeway I was going to build was going to tie together all the isles from St. Armand's to Lido and Longboat Key. That's where we were going to build the Ritz-Carlton. By late '23 and early '24, I had bought up boatloads of statuary from Italy, and we placed pieces conspicuously throughout the landscape. I didn't really know it yet, but my buying was leading Mable and I to something different, more artistically important. At the same time we started building our own place, Ca' d'Zan, which was "House of John" in a Venetian slang. I didn't like the sound of pure Italian "Casa de Giovanni," so I changed it. It turns out Zan is closely related to the Italian for tusk. We enlisted architect Dwight James Baum for our home, and Owen Burns was our contractor. Because the Ritz was so promising, Owen decided to start into the hotel business, and Baum designed the El Verona, named after Owen's wife. I set Owen up with my friend, hotel man Harry Griswold. I really thought the guy was good. Turned out he was a swindler. Owen and the El Verona went bankrupt. Everyone blamed me. Then Sam stepped in with his bankers, the Prudence Bond Company. Next thing I know they tossed Owen Burns, the man behind Sarasota, right out on his ear. It seemed everything good and bad was coming all at once. Here we had a town of just over five thousand people, and almost twenty million dollars in land investment came in that year. Owen opened his hotel and went bust. In March of 1926 Florida bank loans failed and the banks crashed. We had been selling Sarasota in circus style in New York, Chicago, St. Louis, and every major city we could hang paper. That's what it turned out we were selling, paper! When the market crashed, the first crash of 1926, everyone was selling their paper and taking down the price. Owen's wife died. Charley had a small stroke. I finished the causeway, but I ran out of money and switched the cypress planks to pine. Mable and I were finishing Mable's dream home. Charley finished his. The land boom died. The Ritz-Carlton went idle. I wasn't going to give up. I couldn't. I had come too far, and it had taken a big bite out of my soul.

It Seemed Like A Good Idea At The Time

I did a lot of crazy stuff all by myself. Mable was strong in my defense, and I guess it's because she really loved me. You don't get that more than once in life. I almost screwed it up several times. I mean by screwing. I never told Mable about my outside affairs. That's what guilt ridden cowards did. They'd tell their wives, "Oh Darling I'm so sorry, I didn't mean to..." Of course they meant to! Did they think someone else took their rod out of their pants? Then they'd ruin their marriage and hurt the one they really loved. If I screwed up, that was my doing, and I had to live with it. I couldn't put that kind of hurt on Mable. I think some of my colleagues believe I screwed around more than I did. The biggest affairs I had were business relationships. Now that I look back at my portfolio, I realize those were affairs. In hindsight I see what I was doing – who I was trying to impress. I was a showman, and I wanted to be seen as something more. Over time, I became more. Mable and I sat down and talked about it, as far back as 1906, right after we were married. We wanted to make something greater of our lives. I never told anyone else, but we weren't ashamed, even though I think some of the very rich, very affluent folks thought less of us. We made a decision to enrich ourselves, become the best we could. Some of the people we knew who pulled themselves up by their bootstraps, educated themselves, and elevated their status were Jews. We wanted that. Unfortunately so many Jews were persecuted. That's where we came from a background in the show that made us more accepting. I am well aware of how many bad things I said about Jews, lately, but that's because I was angry with Sam. I wanted to lash out and hurt him. If you want to hurt a Jew, say something bad about them being a Jew. Frankly I don't think there is anything bad.

Before Mable and I really began our quest for culture, we struck out in business. Between living in Chicago and New York, and traveling with the show on our own car, the Wisconsin, we began to see the power in rail lines. Long rail and short. It was too late to really move into long rail, unless that would be my full time avocation, but the short lines were ready for the taking. Many were just asking to be built. I wanted rail lines, and that's what I bought. By 1907, the year we bought the "Old Elephant Bones" show, we, me and Mable, were alive with electricity. Hell, if Otto could arrange for New York bankers to loan us $350,000 to buy a show, then we figured the world was ours for the taking, and now let's go get it. We had our first railcar, and it was a Pullman, made back when cars were still wood. We named it the Wisconsin. It was a sweat car, but never what the Jomar would be. It was green, like so many cars. Pullman had a formula for how to hide soot. It was a range of palettes called Pullman Green. Inside, it had painted ceilings, kind of like frescos, gilded work, stained glass. The wood was mahogany, and it would have made Stanny White proud. We had our quarters, guest quarters, servants' quarters, full baths, a kitchen, and a parlor, and it was seventy eight feet long. We traveled all over in it, but Mable, when we'd be in Chicago, she'd rather be in our apartment or for the sake of being pampered be in the Blackstone. She got so tired of the bumpity bump and reminded me that railcars, luxurious as ours was, never seemed still when they stopped. I know she longed for a real home and a rose garden, but we were on the go. There was another Wisconsin, in the show, and it was the car used by us brothers, before the Caledonia. Mable and I owned our Wisconsin right through 1916, right up until the Jomar was finished.

In 1913, I left Mable in Sarasota at the Palms Elysian. She was raising up her sister Darcy's daughter. The girl was deaf, and some folks would say she was "deaf and dumb," but I never liked the use of the word dumb. She was a sweet girl and bright too. Never mind that God gave her another world to live in. She was special to us. We loved children and maybe on account of the fact that we couldn't have our own, but I always thought we had thousands of children. The circus. Those kids were ours.

I had hooked up with a prospector in Oklahoma named Jake Hamon. Jake had been after me for over a year. In fact he'd practically attacked me at the Waldorf Astoria, in New York, to get me to invest in his schemes. I don't want anyone to ever misunderstand me, because me and my brothers had a dream and made it big. It takes more than a dream to make it big. Sure, the five of us were dreamers, but we worked bare knuckle hard, night and day, to fulfill our dreams. Yeah, I invested in Hamon's scheme, and we struck it rich. But what was underneath that, what my brother Charley understood, was the mud and blood and shit. Everyone'll remember that we made money, like in the early days, when we had the Concert Company, but they may not realize how hard it was. What we did, in order to save up enough green to buy that first canvas and the few other paltry bits that made that first circus, was none other than death defying. In many a town we arrived after sleeping the late night on a train, because we didn't make enough money for a hotel stay, only to stop and eat some biscuits and coffee at the local hotel, then go out and make a little parade. The weather would be so cold that the brass mouth pieces would freeze to our lips, but we would go on for as long as we could, in order to drum up the business, literally. Then we would put on a show, and when we didn't have enough money for a hotel, we would take the late train, sleep through the night for a few hours, and do it all over again in the next town. Day after day after day. So folks should never get the wrong idea that just because some guy like me might come along and throw some money at your idea, that you don't have to work your fingers clear to the bone to have your dreams come true. That's exactly what you have to do.

So there he was, Jake Hamon, sort of a showman, after me like a fly on shit; he wouldn't stop. He was talking up a storm about minerals and short rail lines and moving beef and the Oklahoma Territory. Frankly I couldn't make a shit's worth of sense out of half of what he was saying. But he had two things that grabbed me: perseverance and passion. If there's anything that drives a fellow's character to success, it's perseverance and passion, and I saw it almost right off. So I had to go there and find out for myself if it was true.

When I arrived in Ardmore, I inquired about who knew the land the best and was directed to the local newspaper office of The Ardmoreite. There I met a fellow named John Easeley. He was a skinny and tall fellow built like a stick. What made it worse was that he liked top hats and seemed a dozen years out of place, like New York at the turn of the century. Not that folks didn't wear top hats anymore, but along with his grey suit and long vest, he just seemed out of place in a little Oklahoma town. He knew who I was before I even closed the door.

"Come in Mr. Ringling," he said as the bell on the door rang. "I heard you were in town. Love your show; we can't wait for it to come back again."

"And you are?" I asked somewhat irritated that he hadn't introduced himself.

"I am John Easeley," he said, "the editor and proprietor of this little enterprise and several other profitable ventures in these parts." I knew I didn't like him right off as I could feel he was inching his way toward my money, and I never liked it when smalltown people made believe they knew me before an introduction. We shook hands and I got right to the point.

"I am here to look into a mineral called grahamite," I stated in a businesslike fashion, "and I am told there are people here with great knowledge of where I can find it."

"Well," he answered, "I am not certain about people who can help you, but there is one person, Mr. Jake Hamon, who has an office across the street and down a ways. He is the expert on land and minerals." Of course I was here to see Hamon, but I wanted to see if there were others, or if anyone should have inside knowledge of the character of Hamon.

"Is there anyone else I should see and inquire with who could be an equal to Mr. Hamon on such matters?" I asked, knowing full well that Hamon was likely the man.

"Oh no, Mr. Ringling," Easeley went on, "Jake is well versed in law, the land, real estate, and geology." This was what I had needed to hear.

"Well then, I'll be off to speak with Mr. Hamon. Oh and Mr. Easeley..."

"Yes Mr. Ringling."

"I will trust you to complete secrecy regarding our conversation."

"You can count on me sir." I knew of course him being a newspaperman I couldn't count on him, but I had to establish a future as I did with all press people. I figured if things went a certain way I might need Mr. Easeley for newspaper relations, whether I liked him or not.

"Well sir," I said opening the door, "I look forward to some sort of business relationship in the future."

"I do hope so Mr. Ringling."

I made my way down the street and to Jake's land office. It was small and informal, and the sign outside read "Jake Hamon, esq." As I entered I realized it too had a bell, and it made the experience of Ardmore seem quaint. Still the whole of the place had an air of excitement, from the rail, to cattle in corrals right off the main street, wagons full of ranchers, and noisy motor cars with showy men and banging and popping that scared horses, cattle, and passing onlookers. For the first time I understood the excitement of a wild west show. I wanted to stand up and shoot my rifle in midair! I didn't have a rifle at that moment or I would have.

The office was small and had few appointments, a couple chairs, a map on the wall, and a small reception desk with a phone. I was glad to see a phone. In hindsight, the phones of that time were pretty unsightly and had as much a feel as a toy than as an important device. Jake heard me come in and came from the back office.

"John," he greeted me with exuberance, "I was wondering how long it would take you to find your way here." Jake was a big fellow, about as tall as I, but with a frame like a muscle man in the circus, wavy blond hair, blue eyes, and a smile that wouldn't quit. I am certain the gals just fell all over him.

"Hello Jake," I greeted him, shaking his hand, and noticed a very pretty young woman coming from behind him in the office.

"Oh, this is Clara Hamon," he said turning to introduce me, "my niece," he said, as I greeted her.

"Miss Hamon," I shook her hand, noticing that she was blushing. My thoughts went to suspicion as I thought there may have been something going on in that office.

"Married to my nephew," Hamon sputtered nervously, "she's my secretary."

"Well, then, Mrs. Hamon it is" I corrected myself, smiling. Then I turned to Jake: "It seems we have business to discuss."

"Since I received your telegram, I made preparations and set various meetings with people in town." He led me into the office, which although better dressed than the reception room was still modest, stark, unimpressive. He had maps on two walls, recently pinned up and with demarcations of parcels of land and rights of way.

"Jake," I addressed him pointedly, "I think a man of your ability can do better than this for an office."

"John, you'll find that my office is the rolling hills, the open sky, and the geological formations. I take little pride in trying to impress here in the office, but out there, I think you'll be every bit as excited as I am."

Hamon was right. His real office was the Oklahoma countryside. This was a raw visceral picture that I could see myself in. He brought me chunks of grahamite, the future of America's roads, an odd bituminous material. He sat me down with rural bankers, guys I understood, and showed me maps and land and railroad rights of way. It was a picture made clear for me. In hindsight he was trying to diddle me as fast as he was that niece of his. Just the same, I was as ready as a little kid in a candy store. I bought up parcels of land, rights of way, and made tracks as fast as I could across the Oklahoma territory. The bankers took me at my word for the thousands of dollars of promissory notes I wrote. I liked that feeling of having a reputation lay out before me and relished the idea that bankers would fall all over themselves to place trust in me. I was ready, and I hoped the world was ready for me. I started my first short rail line, the Oklahoma, New Mexico, & Pacific. I was suddenly a rail man. This meant that wherever I was, I could hitch the Wisconsin and go wherever I wanted. It was the gift allowed me by being in a new class of American citizens.

Mable and I had been married just over five years. We now enjoyed a freedom we had only dreamed of. Not only had we traveled to Paris, seen the glory of Florence, but we enjoyed a life afforded only to the few who we had once aspired to live like. It all happened faster than a blink of the eye. Jake and I made regular journeys to oversee my holdings. We prepared to have this new rail move cattle, grahamite, and whatever other glorious findings we would encounter, ahead from Ardmore all the way to Lawton and perhaps off to the Pacific and God knows where. We never made it there. Instead, as small encampments sprang up, and the excitement of little gatherings of horses, cattle, roads, and rail moved on, we had an unexpected find. Right there on my land, my holdings, we struck oil. It was near the town of Healdton. I called in my attorneys, John Kelley from New York and Eugene Garey from Chicago. We started my first oil company, the Cardinal Oil Company. Later I made two distinct companies, Rockland Oil and Sarasota Oil, which are one hundred percent mine, and the oil flows even this very minute. The money, however, is all tied up in court, and the fucking IRS has got its grip on it. When it came to business, I was the luckier of Jake and me. He did okay, but the big money was flowing to me. I think Jake was upset as I basked in the glory of it.

"I should have owned it," he complained, both happy for me and expressing a sense of loss and misstep. "I mean, those were my parcels once, John." We gazed off a train platform, looking across oil derricks and a mess of twisted immediate township that we would one day call Ringling. "I'm happy for you John." I knew he was, in a melancholy way. After all, he made his fortune selling it to me, all the while knowing that he might have done better had he not.

"Mr. Jake Hamon," I addressed him, "you and I have done well." I did better. Not only was I an owner of my first rail line, but I was an oil man. It turned in money like Mable and I couldn't believe. It would last well past her death, until the IRS put a hold on my funds, later on, when so much went dry. By 1913 you couldn't slow the money down. It was beyond my dreams, and now Mable and I had freedom we had scarcely ever even dreamt about. I think that's when things changed for us. Had it not been for the coming war, we would have spent even more time in Europe and begun putting our designs on even further cultured lifestyle at an earlier period in our lives.

It didn't take but a matter of weeks until we gave my name to the little town of Ringling. It was Jake's idea to name it after me. I was moving crude like I could compete with East Texas, and the rail line never made it to where it was headed. My first business dealings were nearly complete in Oklahoma, and I was turning my attention back to the show and the next season. Jake was vice president of my new rail line. I stopped by the office looking for Jake, but it seems he was off in the field doing something. I walked in, the bell ringing, and Clara was up at the door greeting me.

"Well, how do, Mr. Ringling," she said softly. Clara was enticingly beautiful, about age thirty and fifteen years younger than I.

"Why Mrs. Clara," I responded taken aback by the way she moved in so close, "where's Jake?"

"Well, Mr. Ringling," she leaned in closer, "Uncle Jake's gone out on the rail, and I'm feeling a little bit lonely." Out in Oklahoma, in farm dress, the gals wore dresses a bit more utilitarian, meaning they wore less and were less formal. She pressed up against me, and I could feel her breasts. My hands naturally fell around her buttocks, and my fingers found purchase – only for a moment. Then I confronted her.

"Mrs. Clara," I spoke softly and directly, "you're married."

"Marriage isn't all it's made to be," she responded.

"I'm married," I went on, "I'm not going any further with this." She pushed away and that was that. Not another word. I left town the next day. I never returned. When the town of Ringling had its dedication three weeks later, I sent my emissary, Charlie Wilson. I didn't relish the idea of standing up in front of a bunch of working folks, making a speech or cutting a ribbon. It seemed so unimportant. I let Charlie do that. He was a talker. That was his profession. A month later Jake announced to Mrs. Clara that he was going to Europe – with his wife. Within minutes after the two argued about it, she pulled his revolver from the desk and shot him three times in the belly. Before he died, he claimed it was an accident, but too many people on the street had witnessed her screaming, "You cheap bastard, you ruined my life." After a long legal battle, Clara Hamon was acquitted. She had claimed that he had beaten her into sub- mission. It took down Jake's reputation and destroyed her marriage. I guess it crushed the whole family. He was a good man, but he never should have screwed his nephew's wife. Ringling, Oklahoma, bears my name today. It's not the only town with my name.

During the run up to when the United States became involved in the war, we could see the changes coming. The demand for certain goods was going to change. Our two enormous shows were almost out of control. Ringling Bros. World's Greatest Shows had three rings and five stages, and The Greatest Show On Earth had three and four. In the last year of Otto's life, we had all fought intensely over expanding their great sizes. Under canvas these shows could seat more than fourteen thousand. Alf and Al would create the great themes and the spectacle of nearly a thousand performers in each show. At one time the Ringling show had over fifty aerialists performing at the same time. It took every bit of our energy we could throw at it to manage the two shows, and at the time of Otto's death we had the third show, the Sells Bros. Circus. Nineteen twelve had closed without any of our most exotic animals in the menageries as the U.S. government banned us from having any cloven foot animals travel on rail, due to the hoof and mouth disease. That was the beginning of Alf wanting to give animals to zoos. The shows did fine without these creatures, and he argued against a future of exotic animals, pointing out the complexity of caring for them. The vast numbers of animals were in his care on his farm near Baraboo that season.

The war actually broke out in July 1914 in Europe. Even though it would take years for the United States to enter the war with armed forces, we were immediately involved in the supply chain. It didn't take long for me, with my routing ability and relations with both short rails and trunk lines, to see a business opportunity. Before I was ever born, legend had it that a fellow from Troy, New York, started packing meat and selling it to the U.S. government in the War of 1812. They called him Uncle Sam. I looked at it thusly: if I could help the war effort in Europe, and place a bit of gratitude in my bank account, then it would be a fair deal. The Transcontinental Railroad ran through Montana near White Sulphur Springs. We called it the Milwaukee Road. It was actually the Chicago, Milwaukee, St. Paul, and Pacific Railroad. I had bought bonds in it although I never owned any trunk lines. That lead me to privileged information about enormous cattle ranches, and from there I could smell the money trail. Never mind that Tex Rickard was my crony and business colleague. Tex had made a fortune in cattle ranching, and I thought I might try my hand at it. I had a secondary idea for cattle and horses. It occurred to me that after the war was over, Europeans would need cattle and horses. I could be ready to sell.

Alf had asked me to keep an eye on his son Richard, whom everyone liked, but most of us feared for his well being. He suffered from the excesses of an older fellow and had started drinking and smoking cigars at age twelve. By the time the war was in full swing, he was almost eighteen and had the appearance of an older man. Near the close of the 1914 season, Mable left Chicago for Sarasota, and Richard and I headed west to Montana. When we arrived, we discovered vast tracks of leased land with cattle ranches as far as the eye could see. The cost of land was pennies an acre, and we had plenty of funds. Richard, who was not yet eighteen, could not buy land in Montana. I began buying land and had my ranch manager set some aside in trust for Richard. I never let him know. Later, when he turned eighteen, I sold him adjacent land and padded his parcels with the trust property. Meanwhile, I bought over eighty thousand acres. This was the second place they named Ringling. It was odd to have my name strung out in such lonely lands, one in Oklahoma and the other in Montana. I had hoped to build a hotel and spa resort. I was told that the hot springs water could heal many ills. Not everything went according to plan. It seems that some of the land was reservation land, and the deeds were not clear. There were other problems with title, and I found the whole thing annoying.

Over the course of the war and even after, the ranch became a sort of amusement and a place to bring friends and family. In 1919 after the war ended, it seemed that life blossomed and collapsed all at once. Alf was ill most of the time, but he was able to see the Big One launch at Madison Square Garden. He loved his home in New Jersey and missed his farm in Baraboo. He had wanted Richard to become a showman, but no one becomes successful if it is all just handed to him on a silver platter. During the war, Alf had set Richard up with a small road show. It was a smart move. Alf had this idea that circuses would one day get off the rails and travel by truck. He bought up acts and small shows and built Richard the R.T. Richards Circus. The problem was that even though Richard had qualities of a showman, he lacked the discipline to pull it off. He missed show dates, shorted the actors, and made a terrible mess of the whole thing. A rift formed between Richard and Alf. After Alf died, Richard confided in me that he regretted his attitude towards his pop. Alf had tried to give his son everything, and no matter what he did for Richard, he ended up angry and belligerent toward Alf. He never changed his bad habits, heavy drinking and smoking, and I think in part he was trying to cover up his regrets about never letting his pop know how much he really loved him. He moved out to White Sulphur Springs, Montana, and lived on a ranch near Ringling. He raised his family there and died in 1931. Even though he inherited his father's share of the show, Charley and I disregarded his input as he didn't know shit about circus. I loved him just the same. His life of excess got the best of him. Then he left me saddled with his wife Aubrey, who teamed up with Edith and Sam. It ended up being them against me.

Nineteen nineteen was not only the year we launched the Big One but also the year we bought the house and one hundred acres in Alpine, New Jersey. Alpine was a charming place. That was a damn good idea. It was close to the city and closer to Hoboken. Mable and I always loved Hoboken; after all, that's where we got married. It gave us a chance to escape the bustle of New York and feel far away in the countryside. Gray Crag, we called it. So many beautiful memories, the Hudson river, parties with top circus performers, and Mable, in her rose garden. After she took sick the last time, I had hoped to take her home to Gray Crag. She never made it.

I had so many business ventures brewing they were popping out my ass! That's probably where a lot of them belonged, but then I was making money, even more money than came from the shows. Tex and I were already scheming to build a better Garden in New York, but it seemed like there were too many obstacles. Maybe my dealings in Sarasota were pulling me away. Tex was involved in Miami's boxing scene. He loved the fights more than anything. It didn't help in 1922 that Tex was indicted for statutory rape. He was acquitted, but that messed up 1922 for getting the place started. We finally settled in on plans in late 1923. It took the better part of the next year for Tex to assemble the investors. I was one of the top twenty. There were over five hundred investors, and it cost almost five million. It was far more functional than the Garden number two, designed by Stanford White. There would be no rooftop club. This was a large box that could seat over sixteen thousand for boxing and almost fifteen thousand for the circus. The only ornate thing about it was the marquis. I worked close on that and envisioned the "Ringling Bros. Barnum & Bailey Greatest Show On Earth" on the arched entry. We were very utilitarian in the design. It was Tom Lamb who was the chief architect, and his designs were more modern and down to business. I remained on the board as long as I could, until that day in 1929. They would of thrown me off anyhow. Better that I quit them first. Tex died unexpectedly in Miami while promoting boxing in January 1929. He had an appendectomy, and some doctor screwed up. He was a good friend and a real sports promoter, maybe the best.

Between 1911 and 1924, I couldn't be stopped. Otto was gone; otherwise he might have put a stop to what I was up to. I bought up, built up, or even founded from scratch a number of short rails, such as the Eastland, Wichita Falls, and Gulf Railroad, and the Kansas City, Mexico, and Orient Railroad, of which I was director. With Jake Hamon I founded the Oklahoma, New Mexico, and Pacific Railroad and eventually sold that to the AT & SF. They used to call it the Ringling Railroad. In Montana I founded the White Sulphur Springs Railroad, and we could shuttle people and animals from the Montana line down to Yellowstone. That one went right through Ringling, Montana. Its real purpose was to move cattle and head them east to Chicago and beyond. As with so many ventures, I kind of lost interest. I was founder, director, or chair of a few banks too, including the Chatham and Phenix National Bank of New York. As a director and major shareholder, it put me right where I wanted to be – alongside J.P. Morgan, whose father had helped start the Phenix, and when they merged in 1911, there I was, a director alongside Morgan. Of course there was the Garden, both of them. I was president of the

Madison Square Garden Sporting Club, after Tex got arrested, and was vice president and later chairman of the board of Madison Square Garden Corporation. That's a shitass story! There were the oil companies, which my nephew tried to get me to sell, and the IRS was sucking the money out of. Being an oil man gave me status, and combining that with ownership of railroads made me feel like a big man. But there was nothing greater than Sarasota.

Some people think what I did in Sarasota was downright stupid. The verdict's not in. Like any business venture one gets in his blood – a yearning – and can't be stopped. You can judge me now, but Sarasota is more than just a small town. I know I screwed up something awful, but like a tree or Mable's rose garden, it'll be here a long time. Right now it's getting pruned, like so much of America. Things grew too fast and had to be cut back. Maybe it's not my season to witness. Maybe I went too fast. History will bear me out. I guess I'll have to see it from another place in time, after my body is gone. This body is nothing more than an old overcoat anyhow. One day I'll take it off, hang it up, and walk away to another place. I hope that someone I love is waiting for me there.

Broken Chain

At the Friday night show, Otto left before the opening performance, leaving Alf on the lot as the managing Ringling. He returned to John's apartment, where the nurse administered laudanum for the pain he felt in his lower back. His kidneys were failing. He telephoned Alf on Saturday morning and said that he was going to need the weekend to rest. Early in the morning of April 2nd, in his sleep, Otto Ringling died.

It was the morning before the matinee on day two in the Chicago opener for the World's Greatest Shows. John and Charley were making their morning rounds when Delevan approached them.

"What brings you out so early, Delevan?" John asked, with a smile.

"I have this telegram boys," he said and then handed it to neither but held it out. Charley reached out and took the telegram, unfolded it and read it. John could see from where he stood that it was short, but

Charley kept looking at it a long time.

"Charley, what is it?" John asked

"Otto died."

John did not react, at first. He stood, stupefied, for a long while. Tears ran down Charley's cheeks, and Delevan interjected, "I'm sorry fellas." John seemed to be drifting, not reacting. Finally he spoke.

"We've got to find Al." The two brothers went quickly to deliver the news to their eldest brother. When Alf T. was given the news at the Garden, he wept openly.He left immediately for John's apartment, in shock and disbelief. When he arrived at the apartment, the doctor was gone but had already signed a certificate of death. Nurse Woosic was sitting in the room and had an envelope in her hands. Written across the front was "Alf T."

"He left this for you," she said, handing him the envelope. "I acted as a witness. He had this drawn up over the last week." Alf took the envelope and said nothing. He walked to the bed and stroked the side of his brother's face. Feeling the cold lifelessness of his cheek, he fought back more tears and then left the bedroom and walked to the parlor. There he opened the letter and read it by the light of the window above Fifth Avenue.

"My Dear Brothers," it began, "this letter will instruct you as to how I wish to be buried, and my last modest requests. My last will and testament is a legal document that I have left in John's hands and I know you will honor my decisions. I am sick and likely will die soon. You have been my rod and my staff, and you have been my closest friends. My wishes are simple: for the sake of the show people, the shows can hold a service. Bury me in Baraboo, next to Mama, Papa, and, Gus. Please make my stone small, perhaps no more than a couple feet in length and a foot tall. And for my burial, I don't want anyone there but family and a few closest friends. You know that I have always been a simple man and that's how I want to be remembered."

Alf understood. It was how Otto had lived. Otto derived pleasure from being modest and not from acquiring goods. The front page of the Monday, April 3, New York Times had a small notice: "Owing to the death of Otto Ringling and the funeral today at Baraboo, Wisconsin, of the circus proprietor, there will be no performances of the Barnum and Bailey Greatest Show on Earth, owned by the Ringling Brothers." The obituary was equally modest: "Otto Ringling, Circus Man Dies."

There was no service in Baraboo until April 7. However, both shows held circus funerals. In the center rings, surrounded by the thousand persons per show, performers gave eulogies and honored the great leader. Of all the brothers, it was Otto who was thought of as the kindest. He was shorter, rounder, and had a soft voice. Never was an actor, a roustabout, a razorback, or any person owed a cent by the Ringlings left unpaid or in debt. Otto had been the binding element of the shows. It was his dream to combine the two great shows. William Henry "Otto" Ringling was the first of the five to fall. The family service was small and included some of the workers from winter quarters, the Norths, the Moller family, a few business people from Baraboo, and the remaining four brothers. He was buried alongside his father and mother in Walnut Hill Cemetery. His wishes for a small stone were kept. The band of five brothers had been broken. Gus had died the year they bought The Greatest Show On Earth, and now there were the four brothers, plus Henry, who would inherit all of Otto's shares. Still, the five were not "the five" any longer. The great watchdog who had kept their money in order, made certain they were always stable, the one they called "The Iron Fist" was gone. The great brotherhood was weakened and would never be the same.

My Debt

I can never forget that moment when Charley said those words, "Otto died." It was the strangest sensation. For a moment I thought it was a joke. Like the kind of joke a brother would play on April Fool's Day. It was April 2nd. We had played many pranks on each other over the years. Brothers do that. The thought of it being a joke lasted only a short moment as I watched Charley's face change and then tears ran down his cheeks. It was suddenly real. I had had that same feeling for a moment when Hester came down the stairs and said, "Grandma's dead." I thought I would burst out laughing, and then it became so real. Otto. He was the show. In all our endeavors the only musical performance he ever gave was to bang away at the drum. He wasn't very good at it. He was a genius when it came to money. When we bought the Barnum show, it was Otto who went before the bankers in New York and was able to get them to loan us over $350,000. Everyone trusted him. He exuded integrity. Back when we were kids, and he had me produce my pennies, just to prove I was in, that there was something to it. From that point on he and I began building a trust.

I don't fully understand it, but he sent his will to me, only about one year before he died. He said he trusted I would take every step to carry out his will. His will had an accompanying letter:

Dear Brothers,
Rather than have any contest over this will, in case it should be

attacked, I believe you will have no trouble in fixing it up, by a reasonable settlement, as I believe there are only four who would dream of trying and I hardly think they would, and they have not been ignored. We have labored together successfully for a long time. Good Bye, Otto

We owned three shows, Ringling Bros. World's Greatest Shows, Barnum and Bailey's Greatest Show on Earth, and The Forepaugh-Sells, which was still in winter quarters. We had moved the Forepaugh show to Baraboo, and this just made the whole town a sad place that day. There were over two thousand people in our employ, and everyone had some kind of relationship with Otto. So, on April 3, 1911, the entire enterprise of shows came to a moment of silence. I know everyone always accused me of trying to be the big man on the lot. Truth is, the smallest of us, the simplest of us, Otto, was the big man on the lot. If there was a single leader, and there wasn't, it'd be him.

Then came the will. He left his share of the show to Henry. This made Henry an equal partner. In a way it was kind. Just like the year Gus died, we were going to give him the Forepaugh-Sells as his own show. Sadly, Gus died too soon, and that never got to happen. But maybe, when he was dying, it gave him some peace. Otto was more than generous to everyone. He felt most of us had more than we needed, but he did leave his holdings in the Orient Railway Company, and bonds in Smith Valley Land Company, to me, and some books and furniture and jointly owned land to Alf T. It seemed he left money in trusts and bequeaths to all the children, of those siblings who had them, and a good bit of money to our sister Ida. He also left some money to some of our managers who were his good buddies. But his largest trust was to Alf's son, Richard, whom he was very fond of. After his estate was totaled, there was a problem. He had more cash than he left, and the courts were perplexed. Before they could decide how to manage the remainder, Gus' three daughters challenged his estate saying they were left out. In the end they got more, and the arguing stopped. Life went on and so did the three great shows.

But Otto had made a strange request of us, and we couldn't exactly follow it. He asked that we take his picture out of the grouping of the five of us in our advertisements.

"That's just wrong," Charley said at the reading of the will, "his picture belongs there."

Then Al came out with the oddest thing: "It's not like he's gone or anything!"

"Al," I corrected him, "Otto's dead." my voice quivered and I got choked up on the word "dead."

Al said it again, "Yeah, but it's not like he's gone." We all looked at each other like Al had lost his mind. He was so much older and his hair white. It would have made sense to think his mind was going. After a long silence he spoke again, "As I see it, he's here, all around us now." That's the kind of thing the eldest brother would say.

"Let's let it rest a while, boys," Alf said, "sit with it for the season."

And so we did, sat with the loss of our staff and rod. The man who stuck us all together like glue. It was like a link had broken. That year of 1911 held another tragedy for us brothers, and this too was almost like family. At his hotel room in Fort Smith, Arkansas, Delevan died suddenly of a heart attack. Spencer "Delevan" Alexander was loved throughout Baraboo. He was the best Boss Hostler we'd ever had, and no man understood horses like Delevan. It sent shock waves through an already shaken circus family.

When we returned to the barn in Baraboo that fall, we decided that three big shows were too much to handle without Otto, and we put the Forepaugh up for sale. A fellow in Lancaster, Missouri, was set to buy it for two hundred thousand, but that deal fell through, so we sold it off in parts and incorporated some into the other two shows. Somehow, that all added up to the lonely feeling of not having Otto there to tell us what he thought was best.

The Baraboonians

The two great shows moved on in separate towns, often not far from each other. This was smart planning on the part of John for routing and Charley and Alf for public relations. The advance teams could travel ahead of both shows, working in tandem in locations that overlapped. In May of 1914 The Greatest Show On Earth played from Newburgh, NY, to Buffalo, while the Worlds' Greatest Shows played from Wilkes-Barre, PA, and other northern Pennsylvania towns to Binghamton and Elmira, NY, and west as far as Toledo, Ohio, all simultaneous as if one great show. It was more difficult since Otto's passing, but the remaining brothers managed to pull it off. The "machine" set in place by the five of them still operated in harmony.

Rumblings of a coming war were soon to come into play, but something else would happen, something far closer to home.

While The Greatest Show On Earth played Buffalo, the World's Greatest Show arrived in Cleveland for a two day stand. They had just played Elmira and then Olean, NY, which were almost earshot to Buffalo, capitalizing on May circus fever for residents of western New York. While one show played small towns, the other played larger cities. The great Ringling Brother's World's Greatest Shows trains rumbled into Cleveland at 6:00 a.m. on May 25th.   The two impressive trains with over forty four cars was a spectacle on its own. The cars off loaded that morning and everything went according to schedule.   After the parade, the set up was smooth and free of any trouble or incidents. Al Ringling was the only brother on the lot in Cleveland. The matinee was nearly full to the ring banks, and the performance was one hour in when Al received word that the lumberyard only two blocks away was consumed by fire. Outside the big top, embers rained down like a fury from hell.

"Ladies and gentlemen," Al announced with his commanding voice, "May I have your utmost attention. It seems we will have to close the show early." Sighs and moans of disappointment filled the tent of over twelve thousand spectators. "Upon your exit you will be given a ticket for tomorrow's matinee. However, due to forces beyond our control, we will close today's show, effective immediately. Please calmly exit the stands and exit the big top. Ushers will help to escort you to the exit."

The band played *Stars and Stripes Forever*. The audience moved out quickly. There was little panic with just a few mishaps inside the big tent. However, outside in the crowd, an elephant ran in fright, knocking over a mother and two children, breaking a child's wrist. The blaze was now consuming the Ringling railcars which were parked next to the lumberyard. A decision had to be made and the canvas needed to come down. Before Al could summon Tom Milbank, the Boss Hostler, Milbank was in the center ring at Al's beck and call.

"Tom, we need all the canvas men for each tent on the go now! The razorbacks need to get to the railcars and throw every spare piece of equipment over the side. Tell each and every one of them that their lives are more important than any piece of equipment. Do you hear?"

"Yes sir Mr. Al." Tom was turning to go on the run when Al stopped him by grabbing his shoulder. "And Tom, go even, don't panic, lest everyone else panics. You get everyone on double duty. We need all the canvas down, folded, and watered down. You hear?"

"Yes Mr. Al, clear as a bell."

The menagerie was vacated quickly so as to get the animals to safety. Horses, elephants, and the other creatures were terrified.

Teams of razorbacks rushed down the street to the train, but they were unable to do anything as the paint on the sides of the railcars burst into flame, and forty railcars were engulfed. Al's main focus was on the animals. As the menagerie tent came down, several embers ignited it. The animals were out, but the mayhem was unstoppable. Hundreds of spectators were still on the grounds, and performers had to guard that they not be trampled or kicked by horses or trampled by elephants. The fire raged on, burning the entire lumberyard and three warehouses. The bulk of the flames was not extinguished until nearly midnight. It took until three in the morning to get the lot under control. Al Ringling worked nonstop, even though countless performers and his wife Louise begged him to rest. Not only was he working the lot, but he was working with train men, renting cars, and trying everything possible to retrofit rented cars to carry the show to the next town.

The Catriani brothers went to Louise and pleaded for Al to stop. "Please Mrs. Al, Mr. Al can't go on like this. He's worn out and pale." Al was nearly as white as his hair, but for being covered in soot from the burned menagerie tent, he would have appeared a ghost.

"Al, please," Louise pleaded, "take a moment!"

"Lou, should I stop now, I won't have the strength to start again. I have to be sure that all the stock is safe and the elephants under control." Every time the animals seemed tethered and safe, some would break free. Others were injured by running into wagons. He and the veterinarian and several assistants spent hours tending to superficial wounds, gashes, and bruises on baggage stock and ring stock. At four in the morning Louise ordered a chair be brought for Al. At dawn he sat in the chair in the middle of where the center ring had stood half a day earlier and immediately fell asleep, all the while still trying to give orders and care for the show. Louise placed a blanket over him. As the sun came up, those who were blocks away could see the damage. Nearly all the train cars had been destroyed before the fire had been extinguished. No animals were seriously injured. One tent gone. Al awoke at nine and jumped to his feet.

"We can't stop now!" he yelled, "everyone get to work." The weary Ringling city of over one thousand persons had been spared. Without trains to travel on, Al ordered the downtrodden crews to get to work. The city of tents was resurrected while Tom Milbank sent telegrams ahead to John. The show played a matinee and an evening performance to nearly eight thousand on May 26th. The people of Cleveland, Ohio, were genuinely impressed by the Ringlings' perseverance. The headline read: "Ringling Bros. Unstoppable." Al Ringling however was absent from his usual job of Equestrian Director. He had suffered a mild heart attack. What most of the show, perhaps none but Al and Louise, knew was that Al had filed for divorce only ten days earlier.

The show set out late on the 27th for Marion, Ohio, a one hundred fifteen mile run. It left with rented cars, makeshift stalls for the animals, and a tired and traumatized Ringling show. The only Ringling on the lot was seriously ill, resting in fatigue, his condition widely unknown to all. It was thought that Al, age sixty-one, was merely exhausted. They would arrive in Marion, skip the parade and matinee, and play only an evening show. Al did not direct the show that day.

As for the divorce, perhaps it was never more than a bad spat between the couple. It began a year prior, on May 12th, outside Atlantic City. All the brothers were on the lot for the Atlantic City show, and it was a packed house with over thirteen thousand in attendance. The next stand was in Camden, just outside Philadelphia, a fifty eight mile run. John convinced his brothers to join him for a poker game after the show, sending the show ahead with the wives. The game was set up by Sam Gumpertz and his business associate George Hamid. It was a typical private Atlantic City game and was hosted in a suite at the Chalfonte Hotel. Hamid was in everything from amusements to Lucy the Elephant, the elephant shaped novelty building, in South Atlantic City. He was also involved in many private dealings with Sam Gumpertz. Some people think it was Hamid's idea to put a cigar store inside Lucy the elephant. Gambling was not allowed on the Ringling lot, but they all enjoyed an occasional game. John had convinced them that since Otto had died they were drifting apart, and a good game would be a fun get together – away from work.

"We don't get to spend much time together as just brothers," he explained to Mable, "besides, we can travel by auto to Camden and be in by morning. This is important, I mean since Otto died; time is precious, right Mable?" It seems Charley had to do similar convincing with Edith and Al to Louise, but Alf and Della weren't speaking and in fact were in the midst of a separation. Alf had taken heavy to the drink, right along with his son Richard. John enjoyed gambling the most, and it gave him a sense of glee, win or lose. They all lost money that night, but the game was less important than what was to come. It was the drive across New Jersey that became a memorable affair.

After midnight they set out with a driver in a rented Duesenberg. The car was more luxurious than their own, which traveled with the show. The driver was able to travel in complete cover, which was good, as within the first half hour it began to rain. The night wore on, and they talked about things they had not spoken of in years. This was the best meeting they had on tour in some while. Otto was a subject and they reminisced.

"Remember that fight during the Concert Company, when Otto brandished the prop pistol?" John recalled.

"He was saving your ass, little brother," Al recounted. "It seems to me those folks were throwing chairs on account of some dookie that came out of your mouth."

"Hell," John exclaimed, "it was two young Irish gals that got me out of there."

"It was your dumbass anecdote about 'where else was her red hair so fair' that got them boys so riled up in the first place!" Al reminded John.

"Don't expect anyone to believe that something exciting happened between you and those two," Alf jumped in.

"Yeah, but don't ya ever wonder if their hair, down there, is red?" John grinned.

"It is red!" Alf replied.

"What makes you sure?" John asked.

"Ah me lads," Alf responded, in Irish brogue, "I've tasted the sweet thing meself!" They all laughed and then after a silence Charley reminded everyone, "We know where Johnny was, hiding in the hotel closet – alone." Everyone laughed again. The night went on and they talked about the show and combining the two great shows. There was a bit of tension over some of the ideas of how to do it and when to do it, as most thought in silence, "too bad Otto's not here to get us through this thing."

"We should be able to launch the Big One by 1916," Charley said, lobbying again. "I mean, it's too bad that Otto won't be around to see it." They fell silent. The road was paved in some areas, and in others it was dirt, turning rapidly to mud. The rain fell harder and harder. The drive should have taken about two hours in good weather, but it was after 4:00 a.m. when the car went silent, with the exception of some snoring from John. Alf was awake. He was deeply troubled over his pending divorce with Della. He had hoped his son Richard would one day become a showman too, but Richard, still a teenager, lacked the discipline and drive that Alf and his brothers had. The driver drove on, the car occasionally sliding in the mud, all the while the wheels were packing with heavy mud. As light came up, the car came to a crest above a dip in the road, and the driver stopped. Down the hill, a small creek had overflowed its banks turning the bottomland to mud and water. Stuck in the mud below was a teamster, out of his wagon, crop in hand and whipping his horse furiously to get him to pull the loaded wagon through the mud and up the other side. All four brothers were awakening to the spectacle, but Alf was immediately out of the car. As he stepped off the running board his shoe sunk deep into the mud. Not stopping for his predicament, he headed straight for the man. The teamster was soaked and his hat soggy, but the horse was bleeding at the side of the neck where the man repeatedly thrashed at it. Without a word, Alf reached for the whip, and as the man drew back for another lashing, the whip was in Alf's hands. He began whipping the man furiously along his face and neck, "How do you like it? You shit!" He kept whipping over and over. Even in the rain, John could see blood running down the man's neck.

"Drive," John shouted to the driver who drove into the ditch and a car's length up the other side. Al jumped out the door and grabbed Alf who was whipping with a blank stare on his face, over and over.

"Alf! Stop!" Al shouted over the sound of the rain. The man fell to his knees, blood running down his coat, in the mud. All that Alf could see was Papa's face as he whipped the handler on the boat show, so many years ago. He dropped the whip. "Get in the car." Al pulled him and his legs moved puppet like, backwards as he fell into the car. They drove off. John and Charley looked back. The man was on his knees in the mud. No one spoke the rest of the drive. John called for newspapers from Woodbury and Williamstown, but there was never any mention of a man dying from a beating on the road. Still, they all were certain that the man must have bled to death. They never mentioned it to anyone, for years. In 1925, Charley told Edith. Her response was, "Some people are so cruel to animals. Animals are so giving to us."

Al's demeanor became haunted. He became withdrawn. He drank more heavily than ever before, often getting drunk at the end of the show. Lou became sick of it, and in a spat one night, asked him for a divorce. "That's it old man, I've had it with your shit. We shouldn't carry on with this charade any further. You've become a boring old drunk."

"Drunk is it, am I?" he responded in a stupor. "You don't know anything. You want a divorce. You got one."

"Oh go ahead you old drunk. You're going to kill yourself anyhow and you've left your whole shares in the show to your brothers. I'll be left to shovel shit in the God damn donnikers with the roustabouts!"

On May 15, 1914, Albert Charles Ringling filed for divorce against Eliza Louise Morris Ringling. After the Cleveland fire, Al was deeply weakened. The doctors said his heart was weak and perhaps he had suffered a mild heart attack. Lou was by his side night and day. He let off the drink, although the doctors allowed him one a day. He quit cigars, and within a couple weeks he was back in the show as Equestrian Director. No one but Louise noticed, but he was fast losing his eyesight. Like Otto, he was a diabetic, and also like Otto, he suffered from kidney disease. Later that season he dropped the divorce and made amends to Lou by giving her a hundred thousand dollars.

Al loved Baraboo. It had given him everything a showman could ever want, especially community. Early in 1914 he made plans to build a European style theater for Baraboo. They broke ground for the opera house in March of 1915. The pressure on Al was more than he could bare, as his illness was affecting his stamina, but he still tried to hide it. He felt that time was precious and wanted to leave something to the little town that gave him so much. The theater design had seventeen curved box seats, sat over eight hundred seventy people, and was a work of art, especially for a small town like Baraboo, Wisconsin. This was to be his gift to the town, his memorial and his expression of gratitude to those who had helped him get to the heights he attained.

On June 24th, while he was still healing from his heart attack, he returned to Baraboo, where the town proclaimed "Al Ringling Day of Tribute." Mayor Thurer gave a special speech and thousands attended. Al was already going blind, and when he looked out across the crowd, he saw only a sea of dark figures. But he heard their cheers. He returned to the show and acted as Assistant Equestrian Director.

The first performance at the Al Ringling Theater came on November 17th and was the comic opera, *Lady Luxury*. Louise was at his side, and some people would observe that she was describing the scenes to him, as he was mostly blind. He died on January 1, 1916, at home in his own bed in Baraboo. Louise was at his side. The future of the opera house was never concluded in his lifetime as he had not had time to finish the paperwork. The theater then was given to the control of Alf, John, and Charley. They tried to pass it to the town and follow their brother's dream, but there were gifting restrictions and taxes, so it was kept in the family until a solution could be found. It was around the same time that John came up with the derogatory description of the townsfolk as "The Baraboonians."

Is He Dead?

When there was banging on my door in the early hours, it was most often bad news. I opened the door, still in my robe, and a colored porter looked at me woefully and announced the dreaded words, "Telegram Mr. Ringling," followed by an apologetic, "sorry to wake you sir, but they tell me it's urgent materials." I took the letter without saying a word and closed the door. I walked to the window and pulled the drape aside so as to read it in the morning light. As I opened it, I could see the words, and my heart began pounding.

"fire... Al... dead..." I fell to the wing chair and looked out at the Detroit skyline, the smoke from factories against the hazy gray blue morning sky. Next to the chair was a candle stand and a phone. Picking it up, I flashed the hook until someone answered.

"Yes sir Mr. Ringling, what may we do for you?"

"Please send our breakfast to our room today. Coffee, juice, toast for two. Thank you." I hung the earpiece on the hook and set the phone back on the stand. I stared out the window and wondered. "What the fuck would the show be without Al?" As I looked out across the skyline from the Randall Hotel, I fumbled through the pages of my mind and fondly touched the recollections of Al: the days of our childhood, the early shows, the help he was to me and the boys. Shit, it was too soon for another brother to die! Mable came from her bedroom, wrapping herself in her robe.

"What's happened John?" she asked with complete concern, "you look like someone died." I handed her the telegram without saying a word, and she read it, spending quite a bit more time at it than I did.

"Sounds like you had better get to work, Darling."

"Work!" I practically jumped out of the chair, "for God's sake Mable, Al's dead!"

"Dead! Why, John Ringling wherever did you get that idea?"

"Says so," I insisted. Grabbing the telegram from her hand, I began to read the whole thing:

"mr john ringling   as I write this I feared that Al was dead however just dead tired   severe fire in Cleveland lumberyard burned most of train   four flat beds can be rebuilt   most of train not salvageable need help to make arrangements for renting cars   evening show on 25th cancelled   will make matinee and evening show tonight   al asleep now   worked tirelessly through the night   great inspiration to all   he and mrs Ringling will phone later   will let him sleep = tom milbank."

The War Horse

Alf was the War Horse. Shit, we should have named one of the advance cars after him. Ever since that day in 1884, when he went to retrieve the two Friesian nags. No one in our brotherhood loved animals more than Alf. By the close of the 1918 season, Alf was often in bed. His kidneys ailed him, and it just seemed like another one of my brothers, my best friends, was leaving, ill. Alf was dying, and now Charley and I were so used to it, and we neglected him. We knew he was dying, and now that we were experienced in having our brothers and best friends die, we just accepted it. Death comes, knocks at your door and takes somebody away. It's too sudden, and yet, it takes so long once it starts. The war was drawing to a close. Alf was our man. Alf T., never a more chipper guy. Like all of us, he was trying to say something at the end.

Troop trains ran up and down our states. The east and the central states were so often full of troop trains in 1918 that most people eventually figured that everyone was going to just get on the train and leave. Go to war. They did, but the trains came home empty and eerily moving like ghost transports throughout the east. On June 22nd, an engineer on an empty troop train fell asleep and ran the train into the back of a stopped Hagenbeck-Wallace circus train, outside of Hammond, Indiana. The performers were asleep. The shock knocked the kerosene lamps in the sleeper cars to the floor. Eighty six people burned to death. Over one hundred twenty who survived were seriously injured. Everyone knew Carl Hagenbeck. Carl had died in 1913, but his name and show lived on. Whether or not we were competition, circus people were family, a giant circus family. Carl had been the founder, and he was behind the vast majority of wild animal sales to shows in the U.S. As soon as Alf got the news, he rallied me and Charley. He had left the show to rest up at his place at Oak Ridge, New Jersey, and called Charley, who was in Baraboo. It was his last year at his Baraboo home. He suggested to Charley that we round up cars, acts, and animals and loan them to Hagenbeck-Wallace. Charley called me in New York. It took a lot of convincing, as we had had the worst year in a decade and probably the hardest, trying to get the government to allow us to stay on the rails, with crowds at just over half what they'd been, on account of the Spanish flu. It was a hard year to find help when every able bodied man was at war. But other shows joined in. I acquiesced. After all, I had more money than I had ever seen. But it was Alf who came to the aid of the greater circus family. That's the way he was.

Sometimes when people get to the end, they go really hard at trying to accomplish all the things they never got done before. Alf had talked for over ten years about the wrongdoing of having a menagerie full of wild animals.

"We're not a zoo!" he would say. "Animals deserve to be part of the family. What are we supposed to say when they die in our care?"

"Everyone expects wild animals in a circus," I argued. "It's our job to give 'em what they want."

Even after Alf was gone, Charley and I would continue the

discussion. During the winter of 1918 and 1919, as we were combining the two shows, he'd bring it up daily. It had been an odd year. Even before the war ended, we had to close both shows weeks early because so many people, including members of our show, were sick with the flu. Talk was that being in large crowds could spread the flu, so we couldn't even fill half the stands. We sent the Ringling show to Bridgeport at the Barnum winter quarters, to combine both shows. We left the people of Baraboo in shock. Just three weeks later, Henry died at his home in Baraboo from a heart attack. We were stricken with sudden grief, but the three of us had an urgent feeling that if we were ever to combine the two great shows, it would have to happen in 1919. The last season of running the shows separate had been a low point. We averaged a thousand dollars a day less than the year before, and wages were up because workers were scarce. Then, in November the war ended. We knew 1919 was going to be the right time.

Henry's wife Ida wanted no play in our partnership in the circus business and sold her shares to Charley, Alf, and me. She wanted to spend her time with her family in Wisconsin, and I bought the place in Eustis, Florida, and bought the Salome, their yacht named after Mama, which they had loaned to Mable who loved it like her own personal yacht. It was not a big yacht but a day cruiser, and she had kept it off Shell Beach, by the sea wall, where we had built an eighteen hundred foot pier so that Mable could have access to it. It was odd, how the war ended, Henry died, and we left Baraboo. Times were changing. We were changing. It felt like closing show: leaves swirling round, feeling of separation, going home. Baraboo would be silenced. The great winter quarters that people had dubbed Ringlingville was now a ghost town. There would be no homecoming of trains and animals, no roars of big cats on winter nights, no trumpeting of elephants heard from Water Street, no clanging of the blacksmith's shop. We let go almost everyone and left a crew of five to watch over the property. The Warren Inn could not look forward to the endless parade of acts arriving in March, and the townsfolk knew that we had ended a whole lot of employment. We had killed the future of Baraboo. Home was now Barnum's home, his barn, and everyone had a nervous feeling about them. Performers and roustabouts alike wondered, "Who's going on with the Big One? Who going to be left behind?" We left Baraboo behind, like someone died.

Six
Lightning Strikes

Ablaze

Sarasota was calm. The morning light came up in a cluster of orange marble clouds laid up against a backdrop of a larger darker cloud. The orange rising sun hiding over the land across the flatness of Florida illumined the thin green canopy. Sarasota's harbor was soft against a strange morning light.

By way of a charter, Mable's guests had come up from Havana two days prior. It had been a long and gentle journey, without incident, for the entire group. They had left New York by rail and traveled all the way south to Jacksonville, changing only in Washington, D.C. From Jacksonville by small cruisers to Miami then Havana and finally up the west coast to Sarasota. They traveled by private railcar, all arranged by Mrs. Ringling with help from her friends, Sam and Evie Gumpertz. Sam and John were becoming best friends, and Gumpertz was now Ringling's right hand man at procuring new acts for The Greatest Show On Earth. Sam however was aware that John, in his many business dealings, was spreading himself thin and neglecting details in managing domestic affairs as well as management of the show. John was in New York and was working on ideas for the show, reviewing acts, and also planning a visit with his crony and colleague Tex Rickard. Two of the guests were by John, the Honorable and Mrs. Ernest Heppenheimer. He was an appeals court judge from New Jersey and was part of this entourage because John Ringling insisted to Mable they needed all the help they could get, especially from an appellate judge. The Wallicks were there because L.C. Wallick was known for his ability to bring investors for hotels, and Mrs. Makeaver was surely Mable's best bet for New York social status. Mable had been ill and had finally revealed her diabetes to John. She suffered numerous problems, including weight loss, kidney pain, and fatigue. John could afford the finest doctors in New York and New Jersey, and Mable had seen most. This particular day in late February was good to Mable, and she was feeling her best.

Rumor had it that John had neglected the Salome. Sam Gumpertz had warned Evie that some of Ringling's crew had tried to tell John there was a strong smell of gasoline coming from below deck. John had little time for dealings in Sarasota that year. The two great shows had merged just two years earlier, and it was difficult for the two brothers to manage. John made for New York, leaving Mable to carry on with all the social happenings in Sarasota. The Salome, a day cruiser, was used primarily to ferry incoming guests around Sarasota to view John's real estate investments, known as the Ringling Isles. Mable had invited Evie to come along that day, but she found an excuse not to.

The small entourage boarded in Sarasota, accompanied by Captain Jarriott and his teenage son. The engagement would be a tour of Sarasota bay, followed by a lunch off Cortez. After a distant cruise by Bird Key, the party headed west northwest toward Cortez. Clouds mounted as they approached, and rather like summer they rolled across the gulf out of the west and south like sly silvery and orange upside down mushrooms, none seeming too large, but still threatening. The gulf water was calm. There were a number of small fishing boats off Cortez. Mable asked Captain Jarriot to cut the engines, which were unusually noisy and unsettling. The small party lunched, and Mable tried her best to keep it elegant. The bright and turquoise shoals off Cortez turned suddenly to silver grey and ominous black, as a mass of cumulous cloud approached and the waters swelled. Then, in an uncontrolled menacing instant, thunder and lightning erupted. The water was struck and dashed aglow. The three women were ushered into the cabin by gallant men, two of which had no apparent experience with the sea but stood by the captain and his son who repeatedly tried starting the engine. The starter whirred and then nothing, over and over.

"Well, try it again, man," the judge insisted.

"Yes, turn it over!" yelled Wallick in desperation.

Lightning struck the gulf waters turning them gold and red. The captain kept trying, the starter whirring over and over; then "Boom"! The engine roared a resounding backfiring blast and started, and as it did there was another resounding boom from below deck. A roaring flame blazed across the deck, flash burning the three men and the boy, and from inside the cabin came another rushing explosion of fire knocking the windows from the cabin. The entire cruiser was instantly ablaze. Mary Wallick's dress was a torch up the back, and as Mable tried to extinguish the fire, grabbing hold and pulling her tight, she was instantly ablaze from the front side. The judge dashed through the cabin door and pushed the three burning woman out. As fast as he was behind them and all six were at the side of the cockpit, the captain steered the boat seaward and the boat exploded again sending all eight persons into the water.

Three fishing vessels owned by Jack Hunter immediately picked up the eight. The judge and the captain and his son sustained only minor burns. Mr. and Mrs. Wallick, Mrs. Makeaver, and especially Mable had serious burns around their faces, necks and arms. They were taken ashore to Sarasota Hospital. All would recover, but Mable would now have something more to hide, along with her diabetes. As her burned arms and neck healed, the shocking loss of electrolytes had brought to focus a deeper condition, Addison's disease, a potentially fatal and incurable kidney dysfunction. She would, as she did with keeping the diabetes a secret, keep this from John, almost to the day she died.

The Thorn Garden

Bad things happened to John Ringling around Madison Square Garden. Some were life changing. In June of 1906 John and Mable had been married a year. John was soon to join the board of directors of the Garden, and joining the board was important to him at this time. Life had now given him everything he wanted, a beautiful wife, all the financial freedom to invest; the material things of the world were now his for the taking. Although he and Mable had their own apartment on Fifth Avenue, and another in Chicago, he did not yet own a real home. He could afford anything they wanted, but they would spend years living as if still newly wed. John, renowned as a flamboyant bachelor, remained faithful to Mable. Why not, she had everything he wanted in a woman. With no desire for children, they desired success, travel, culture, and while Mable often enjoyed opera and other very socially elite events, John enjoyed poker and a good whiskey with friends. Some of his friends were less than innocent.

As he joined the celebratory events around the Garden, it became apparent that John wanted to be of high rank in the club. The Garden had been built by such notables as J.P. Morgan, Mills, Astor, and P.T. Barnum, as well as other established millionaires. John wanted in, and he made his presence known. Further, John's friends, who associated with the events at the Garden, were eccentric, while John's willingness to associate with them was ostentatious. He occasionally brought Mable to the rooftop Garden Club at Madison Square Garden, as he did one night in late June of 1906. They shared a table with Tex Rickard and a young show girl who could not have been older than twenty. They sat four rows from the entertainment, which was a sloppy chorus girl attempt at "Mam'zelle Champagne." Tex was becoming one of John's best friends and best business allies. He had made his fortune in the Klondike during the gold rush and had traveled the world. He had once owned a ranch in Argentina with four million acres. The showplace was the largest restaurant in New York, and the celebrations there were gay and festive. It was the place where many a married fellow went without his wife in search of a chorus girl or a tart younger than his domestic mate. The vast open space stood in the shadow of a great tower; its design was inspired by The Doges Palace in Italy, and as the second tallest structure in New York, it held the offices of the Garden. The champagne flowed, hundreds of guests chattered, and the performance was scarcely audible through the sound of the crowd.

John felt a hand on his shoulder and noticed Tex was standing. As he turned, there was Stanny, Stanford White, who had designed the Garden and was the most noted architect in New York. He was also the most noted womanizer in New York; the gals nicknamed him "Stanny."

"John Ringling," Stanford shouted over the fray, "good to see you are keeping good company with your beautiful wife."

"Keep your eyes to yourself!" John shouted and stood greeting his friend with an extra handshake. "My wife happens to be the most beautiful woman here."

"You are a lucky bastard there, John," he shouted and then reached across and shook Mable's hand. "So good to see you again Mrs. Ringling." Mable had met Stanford White at the Player's Club on New Year's Eve 1903, the night that John proposed to her. Even though he had a reputation as a womanizer, John and Mable liked his style of architecture and interior design and had already talked about having a home designed by the great Stanford White.

"Good to see you again, Mr. White," she said, taking his hand. Then White reached out and shook hands with Tex. "Rickard," he started, "you never cease to amaze." He was looking at the young woman with Tex. Then Tex responded, "How do, Stanny?" He turned toward his guest, "This is Miss Darly Mart..."

"Hello Darly," White interrupted and shook her hand with great familiarity, to which she blushed and responded, "Stanny."

"Gentlemen," Stanford White interjected, "I have a date with a front row seat. It is a pleasure to see you all." Half of his farewell was inaudible, but Tex and John raised their glasses and toasted him as he strode to the front. They could see Stanny over the course of the next half hour, and he appeared to be getting totally drunk, all the while flirting with the dancers on stage. The outdoor venue was hot and humid that night, and at first John thought it odd to see Harry Thaw walking in an overcoat. But then Harry, one of the wealthiest men in the country, by means of inheriting the greatest long rail fortune in America, was eccentric himself. He had once tried to ride a horse into the New York Club and had also taken his clothes off in public and jumped into a fountain. Thaw's life was one of aplomb, with one exception, his marriage. He walked past Ringling's table without even stopping, and this was a bit unusual. Then he walked within one table of Stanford White, pulled a pistol from under his long overcoat, and fired three shots into White. One into his shoulder, and as White turned in shock and agony, Harry fired two shots into the side of White's head. As White fell to the floor, the crowd of hundreds went silent. Then an enormous roar of laughter went up, followed by cheers. John and Tex knew immediately that this was not a party gag, which so often could happen at such a venue but instead was an obvious assassination of the great Stanford White.

They were aware that Thaw had married Evelyn Nesbit who just two years earlier at the age of sixteen had been the romance of Stanny White. It was scandalous, and half of New York's elite knew of it, while others simply knew of White's character. Stanny White had a lavish apartment in the tower, wherein it was rumored that he took his young flower, Evelyn Nesbit, and pushed her to and fro on a velvet covered swing while she was naked. She had awakened after a champagne filled afternoon, only to find that White had taken her virginity. After her marriage to Thaw, she confessed that the only man to really give her pleasure was Stanford White. This added fuel to the fire that was already raging between the two men, as Stanny had made fun of Thaw in public, embarrassing him in front of the ladies.

From the table to the left of White's, a blood splattered man stood up and yelled, "He's killed him! He's really dead." Thaw produced the gun and held it up for all to see as he made for an exit. The crowd had stopped laughing, and there was an eerie silence. Then the silence broke into screaming and yelling and mass hysteria. John, Mable, Tex, and his escort made for the offices in the Garden and hid out of sight of the police and the ensuing investigation. It turned out to be an enormous mess. Thaw was found not guilty by reason of insanity. The greatest architect of the Beaux Arts era was dead. Evelyn Nesbit Thaw ended up divorced from Thaw with none of his estate but was content to become an artist and lived her remaining years in California, raising her only child, whom she claimed was Thaw's. John's Garden was a thorny place, and this was only the beginning of his troubles, which stemmed from wanting a world that did not belong to him.

In 1911, it was from the Garden that a telegram was dispatched to Chicago for John, Charles, and Alf to let them know that Otto had died. It didn't happen at the Garden, but it may as well have, as far as John was concerned, as Otto and Alf T. were opening The Greatest Show On Earth at the Garden when Otto took sick and his kidneys failed.

Then 1922 would bring about another incident at Madison Square Garden. Whether or not the incident was about or around the Garden, John thought it so. The evidence said so. The combined shows would open in the Garden that year, and John had decided to take his usual planning tasks to go to New York and make all the preparations. It was a massive undertaking, and because there were now only John and Charles to run the show, it was challenging to keep the behemoth show in operation. Ringling Bros. Barnum and Bailey Greatest Show On Earth had eighty eight railcars, over thirteen hundred personnel, forty elephants, five rings, and a stage. It was beyond any show ever seen in the world, whether in an arena or under canvas. Charley stayed in Sarasota until the show left for New York, fine tuning the entire logistics of the operation, while John would work from his office in New York, at the Garden, and prepare all of the season's routing, as he had always done. Mable loved New York but had revealed her diabetes to John that year. It was two years before the release of insulin, which would later help to extend her life, but her problems were mounting, from painful bouts with her kidneys to weight loss. They decided it was better if she stayed in Sarasota at the Palms Elysian.

John arrived in New York on the Jomar on Monday, February 13, 1922. He was met by his driver and picked up in his new Rolls Royce Silver Ghost, which had been built in Springfield, Massachusetts. After a brief visit to his apartment at Park Avenue, he made for the Garden and his office. The office was in the tower, the same tower where Stanny White had enjoyed his freedoms with Evelyn Nesbit, and the same place now where Tex had an apartment. John was greeted by his receptionist and secretary, Marjorie Williams, who informed him that Mr. Rickard was in and would like for John to call. He went to his office and went immediately to work, following up on the entire schedule that the great show would take, all the while studying every train and every connection, long rail, and short line. John knew them all by heart and was able to plan every run, almost to the minute. He was often teased about his ability to remember every train and every schedule in the United States. It was an ability possessed only by John, and no other circus man could duplicate it. The door to his office opened, and without introduction the tall and slender Tex Rickard walked in.

"Well I suppose you're up to no good."

"Probably more good than you," John answered without getting up, but reaching out and shaking Tex's hand. "What kind of trouble you been up to anyway, old man?" He asked Tex jokingly. Tex, almost always with a cigar in hand, stopped abruptly and puffed on the cigar which regained its smoke and power and came back to life, and then responded, while puffing, "Well, I hope it'll all blow over in a few days."

"What are you talking about?" Ringling asked. "It isn't whiskey, or some trouble over 'shine?"

"Well not exactly," he went on slowly, "there is a little whiskey involved."

"Yeah, go on," Ringling urged him.

"Well John," he puffed some more, as if he wanted to hold back, but began anyway, "there were these two girls..."

"Oh shit!" Ringling relit a cigar he had in the ashtray. "How old? What have you done, Tex?"

"Well they told me they were of age," Tex began the story, "you see I met this dancer girl, said she was eighteen. She said she had a friend and they would 'very much like to join me for a drink.'"

"Drink where, Tex?" John interrupted.

"Here, at the apartment." Tex sat down in the chair closest to John's desk. "Seems they were younger than they said."

"How much younger?"

"Well, one told the police she was eleven and the one I did it with was fifteen."

"What the fuck!" said John, obviously shaken. "Tex?"

"John, I swear they were older. That girl I fucked was no virgin either. Hell she practically swallowed my cock before I stuck it in her."

"So why are we even talking about this?"

"Well, a detective was here this morning; apparently this girl she blabbed it to her parents. I think it'll all blow over."

"Somebody got blow'd, that's for sure," Ringling joked, but he was quite irritated at his friend's blunder.

"They've been here asking questions, John, so I am glad you got into town later today."

"Pal," Ringling addressed his friend, "you will never find me with an underaged chorus girl. That's for sure." Ringling turned toward the mountain of books and papers on his desk and informed Tex that he had work to do. Actually he was so stunned he just wanted Tex to go.

"Let's talk about this later. Is that okay with you?" John snapped, not looking Tex in the eye. Tex left and there was an abyss between them. John had a load of friends who screwed around. John had not, although many a woman had cornered him at parties and poker games.

That night John decided to go out on his own. The town had changed greatly since the Volstead Act, which began Prohibition, and all the old favorite places had changed or closed, but actually there was more partying and drinking behind closed doors in New York than ever before. As he prepared to go out, he thought it would suit him to stay home and have his cook make him up a two pound steak. Away from Mable he enjoyed every bit of gluttony he could, from drink to steaks to being a foul mouthed fuckin' bastard who swore like a motherfucker every other God damn word! After a few glasses of whiskey, he called for his driver and went to the Red Head in the Village. It was a small place, a speakeasy, but was fun and filled with characters. Before he reached the place he had several glasses of scotch and was feeling quite warm and friendly. Few of his usual cohorts were there when he arrived, although there were many who pretended to know him well. In the onslaught of introductions, he repeatedly met eye to eye with a beautiful young woman. They were eyes onto each other. She was sitting at the bar, and some fellow on her right seemed to be pestering her. John feeling stronger than usual made for her spot at the bar.

"Can a fellow buy you a drink Miss?" he asked.

"A fellow can't, but Mr. John Ringling can." John signaled the bartender who poured them each a drink. The pestering fellow on her right slinked into the background.

"You seem to know who I am, but I haven't had a proper introduction," John said as he tipped his glass to toast her.

"Rebecca Daniels," she said as their glasses clinked. John thought to himself, "Here I am in the Red Head, the best speakeasy in The Village, run by my friends Kreindler and Berns, and what color hair does the gal have? Red!"

"You have beautiful hair, my dear," John complimented her, taking another drink, and he pondered a question that had plagued him since his youth, about "Where else is her hair so fair?"

"In fact," John went on, looking deep into her eyes, "I will just have to say, all out, that you are beautiful."

"You honor me, Mr. Ringling," she blushed.

"But Daniels, that's so English, and I would have to guess that you are most Irish," John surmised. She smiled and replied, "Irish I am, Daniels is my married name."

"Divorced?" John asked.

"No, my husband died in the war."

"I am sorry my dear," John responded awkwardly.

"No need, Mr. Ringling," she consoled him. "It's been four years and I am certainly over it now." The more John drank and pondered this fair skinned beauty, the more he admired her. He found himself realizing she was looking him up and down, and he was in no way concerned that this might take a wrong turn. Her clothes were revealing and her legs were showing. He was certain she wore a slip and something under and could see some edge of a brassiere, but clothes were fast becoming revealing. The Red Head speakeasy, quaint and compact, was able to sport a small band and there was dancing. The two of them danced more than one dance. He was amazed at how easy this was for him. He had not cheated on Mable and thought he would always be faithful, but holding this woman in his arms gave him a sense of renewal. It seemed out of the blue, even to himself, but finally the words just popped out of his mouth, "What if we continue this dance at my place over a bottle of champagne?"

In minutes they were in John's limo and heading uptown toward Fifth Avenue. There was little traffic after midnight, and when they arrived, the doorman pretended not to care that this was not Mrs. Ringling. The help was asleep and John quickly popped a champagne bottle and poured two glasses. They barely drank any wine but made love for what seemed like hours as if they were familiar lovers.

As he fell asleep, John was thinking about Mable, "Would she know?" He worried a bit. Would she see a lie in his face? When he woke in the morning she was finishing dressing. She noticed him lying there, eying her, and turned to speak, but he spoke first: "I can call for breakfast."

"Honey," she said, "it's been fun, really good." Then she reached for her coat. "But you are a married man. I don't think we are going to go anywhere together. Let's just leave it at this. I had a great night. Thanks." She headed for the door and John said nothing. She was gone. Later, as John was washing, he looked himself up and down in the mirror. He despised what he saw and felt sick. He had promised himself that he would never cheat on Mable and until last night had never broken that promise. He almost vomited. He thought, "Okay, I made a mistake. I know I'll never do it again." He believed he would be good. "Maybe I got it out of my system," he thought, trying to vindicate himself. "It'll never happen again."

He went to work as usual that afternoon. He had developed a habit of sleeping late and starting late. Tex did not show up at the Garden all day. The next morning John was awakened by his butler. "I am sorry Mr. Ringling," he said, knocking and opening the door. "Mr. Tex is on the phone and says it's urgent."

Saying nothing, John pulled himself up, put on his robe, and fumbled his way into the parlor to the phone. "Ringling here," he said into the mouthpiece, pressing the earpiece tight against his head.

"John, it's Tex,"

"No foolin'," John said, somewhat disturbed by the early hour of ten in the morning, "what's the matter?"

"John, I've been arrested. I need your help."

Within the next few hours John bailed Tex out, hired Max Steur, one of New York's best trial attorneys, and loaned his friend almost fifty thousand dollars, ten thousand to bail him out. While some of it was in cash, no questions were asked. Tex Rickard was charged with statutory rape. The New York Athletic Commission asked him to step down from his posts as president, promoter, and matchmaker for the Madison Square Garden Sporting Club, and his license was suspended. The story appeared in the New York Times on Thursday, February 16: "Rickard Gives up Control of Garden – Promoter resigns in Favor of Ringling, Circus Man." John picked up Rickard and drove him directly to Max Steur's office. They hardly spoke.

"You're an asshole," John told his friend, as they rode in the back of the Rolls, breaking a long silence.

"May might file for divorce," Rickard responded.

"You screwed up," John said raising his voice. "Fifteen fucking years old?"

"Look, John, this was almost like a set up," Tex defended himself, "one look and you would have thought she was older."

"Shit happens when you fuck around on your wife!" John raised his voice and then stopped talking and began reflecting on his actions two nights earlier. "Shit happens," he kept thinking to himself. Then he thought about how hard he'd worked to elevate himself to a new status. The people who had been on the board of the Garden, such as Stillman, Astor, Morgan, all following after Vanderbilt and the first P.T. Barnum Hippodrome. John had worked so hard to add his name to the impressive list. Tex had sullied John's name, not by cheating, but by getting caught, and with someone so young.

He dropped Tex off at Max Steur's, and before the driver closed the door and Tex was half out, John said loud enough to be heard over the street, but holding back the volume in secrecy, "It's better if we don't spend a lot of time together, for a while." Tex nodded and then went inside. John headed off to his office at the Garden. He kept repeating the line "Shit happens" in his head, and he felt sick, like he might vomit. As he entered the lobby of his office, he was greeted by Miss Williams, who stopped him abruptly.

"Mr. Ringling," she said, "you have been receiving an urgent call all afternoon from Sarasota." She reached down and picked up a message page, "It's Evie Gumpertz. She's been calling."

John took the note and went into his office. Looking down he saw that the number on the phone was at John and Mable's home,

Palms Elysian. He thought, "I hope Sam's okay." He picked up the phone and had the operator call the house. Evie answered, "Gumpertz residence, I mean Ringling residence."

"Evie, it's John."

"John, I've been calling all afternoon."

"Evie, is Sam okay?"

"John, it's Mable." John stood up abruptly and then sat, fearing the worst, "What is it, Evie? Is it her diabetes?"

"No... an accident..." she paused, "the Salome exploded this afternoon, several people were burned bad, especially Mable on the neck and arms, you'd better come home." It took John a few seconds to understand.

"I'll leave right away." John was trembling and so was his voice. "Is she in the hospital?"

"Yes John, Sarasota." Evie began the description, her voice also trembling, "They say she will recover, but her burns are serious. All three women were burned badly, but Mable's burns were the worst. Judge Hepenheimer, the captain, and his son were not burned. The women are all here, in the house, with nurses."

"I'll send a telegram along the way, but I'll leave as soon as I can hitch the Jomar." John hung up the phone and yelled, "Shit." Mrs. Williams opened the door, "Are you Okay Mr. Ringling?"

""No," he yelled. "I need the Jomar hitched. I have to go to Sarasota. Call my driver. Shit!"

By the time John had found a rail to hitch the Jomar, it was late night, and as he exited the New York area on into New Jersey, the New York Times press was at print. His name will have been in the paper two days in a row. This time the headline would read, "Six Injured In Fire On Ringling Yacht – Circus Man's Wife and Guests Leap from Craft off Florida, Are Rescued by Fisherman."

A Show Without Ringlings

A green and tan Rolls Royce stopped at the gates which were open. The driver got out to open the passenger door, but before he made his way around the car, the door opened and Charles Ringling was on Bayshore Road followed quickly by Edith. The late November morning was unusually cold for Sarasota, almost as cold as Evanston, where just days earlier they had packed away belongings, said farewell to Chicago, and headed south to the gulf. With the cold front across the gulf and western Florida came strikingly beautiful skies. Gold lit palms against deep blue skies gave a blessed homecoming to Charley and Deedee.

"I was going to open the door for you Mr. Charley," the driver said apologetically. His gray blue uniform was as fine as any Ringling costume, and his cap made of the finest spun wool outshone any driver in Chicago. At sixty four he was several years senior to Charles, but his dark skin was smooth and wrinkle free, and only a slight wedge of gray shone in his sideburns. Charles Ringling was aged. Even though his latter years had been in opulence, the hard life, the years traveling with the show, decisions which carried the weight of caring for the enormous circus family showed in the lines of his face and the gray white hair atop his balding head. Nineteen twenty four was difficult for Charles, and he had several times fought chronic bronchitis while traveling with the show. Doc Ewald, the family doctor, had suspected Charles had a minor stroke. Always a robust figure, he had lost weight, and some of the brightness had dimmed in his eyes.

"No need to worry, Ben," he responded in a kindly way, "Mrs. Ringling and I feel like children again. Besides, I think we're still pretty able to open an automobile door. How are those two grandchildren doing? Are they able to get the education they need?"

"Yes sir, Mr. Charley, Sarasota's schools have been more than adequate, sir. Thank you for asking sir." Charles and Edith always demanded that all the help and their families received at least a high school education. Charley had ended his education after ninth grade, and although extremely well self educated, he had always regretted it. Charles chuckled a bit as Edith took his arm. She was full and round and every bit as robust as when they were married thirty five years earlier. She wore a casual Florida hat, with a sprig of feathers to one side, but her dress was too light for the cold snap, and she pulled tight to Charles.

"It's beautiful," she whispered as they looked up at the great marble arch. Influenced by Stanford White's arch at Washington Square, with columns, lions, and subdued but grand expression, it was an entry that made those who would come have reverence for the great estate. In the distance was all the commotion of building: wagons, voices, machines, mixers. It was indistinguishable as to which site the sounds were coming from. She turned back to Ben, "We'll walk."

"You certain now? I mean I don't want Mr. Charley to be angry with me."

"You go on ahead, now. Don't worry about us," Charles spoke with a sense of assured confidence. A light came over him and he instantly seemed better, as if suddenly healed from a hidden predicament. Ben drove ahead, cautiously not accelerating too quickly so as not to spin the tires and send bits and pieces of the shell drive at his employers.

As they walked through the gates, amongst live oaks and pasture, they could see a truck parked down the drive. A crew of three, one on a ladder and two in the rack sided flat bed of the truck, were cutting Spanish moss from a huge oak. Off toward the left several cows grazed, and in the back was the huge presence of John and Mable's home, not yet named Ca' d'Zan. Charley and Deedee's home was more modest. At sixteen thousand square feet, it was modeled after English architecture, subdued and not boisterous like the gigantic and loud Italian architecture next door. As their home was progressing, they had already begun a second home for their daughter, Hester. The home, Mediterranean in style, was a simple architectural bridge between Charles' and John's homes. Although Robert, Hester's brother, was planning to live in Sarasota, he had asked his father to build him a modest home, which they did on the north side of the compound. The utopian family farm on the golden bay was finally coming about. So many years in the making, but now, the three homes, the farm that they had hoped would be self sufficient one day, and the plans for John and Mable's museum, already in discussion. As they walked Charles shuddered with joy and sadness. Except for Ida and John, everyone else was gone. "If only they could see it," he thought to himself, especially Al, who had visited Florida and decided that it was not his style. He loved Baraboo. And Alf. It was odd that he found his place in New Jersey because his utopian vision of a farm was some several hundred acres outside of Baraboo. Otto had no place, nor did he ever find a gal to be his life partner. He had Otto and the show. He enjoyed New York, if for nothing more than the easy access to the finest food, drink, and cigars. He was simple. But the sadness in Charles' chest was the disappearance of family. Still, John and Mable were here. Ida and her two boys and daughter were here. Deedee was here, and Hester and Robert were here, and he delighted in knowing there was a sense of family still clinging to each other. Family was what made Ringlings.

Although Papa had died in '98, he saw his boys rise to fame and compete for and take the number one spot in American circus. Mama had died just a short while before they closed the deal on The Greatest Show On Earth. Both Mama and Papa Ringling had instilled a great sense of family in the children, and although it was family life itself that had bound them all in unity, more bonding was demanded by Salome Marie Juliar Ringling on her children than any other singular person.

In December 1906 plans were made for all the family to gather in Baraboo and celebrate Christmas. It seemed that everyone but John and Mable had a home in Baraboo. John had already dubbed Baraboo "the home of the Baraboonians" between he and Charley. The other brothers wouldn't hear of such talk, and in fact John had his respect for the little town that gave them their start and held the magnificent winter quarters along the Wisconsin River. The family was gathered, absent Papa. Mama now lived in Charles and Edith's home at the corner of Ash and Eighth Street. There they would gather, all seven for Christmas, finally to be in the same place at the same time. Mable and John were in Europe assembling new acts for the 1907 season and expected to return on December 21st. On that day all gathered at Charley's house, at Mama's request, to celebrate the homecoming. Al and Louise, Gus' widow Anna, Otto, Alf T. and Della, Charles and Edith, Henry and Ida, and baby sister Ida and her Husband Henry Whitestone North. There were various grandchildren, and this pre-Christmas celebration was warm, festive, and made of all the charm that family should have. When a knock came at the door, and Charles' servant Benton answered, they were surprised to see only Mr. Hanson delivering a telegram. As Benton brought the telegram, emotions were mixed.

"I knew it!" snapped Alf, "they're not coming."

"Let's see what it says," Charley said defending against a barrage of brotherly upset, "before we jump to conclusions." With that he snatched the telegram and everyone moved in closer so as not to miss a word.

"charley and family   mable and i delayed   sorry will not make christmas we assure you we are making haste for new york and then baraboo will try for new years merry christmas = john and mable."

"Damn him!" Charley snapped. "Always about him isn't it?" Mama defended John, "Now Karl," she still called him by his given name, especially to let him know who was really in command, "he's your brother and I am certain he has his reasons for being delayed."

"Festivities in Paris, no doubt," Alf piped in.

"Stop it!" Mama yelled, "all of you shut your mouths. I'll not have Christmas spoiled by quibbling. Everyone is going to stay in Baraboo until John and Mable arrive and we can have a celebration."

That was the end of discussion and Mama Ringling made sure of it. New Year's celebration came and went with only another telegram. John and Mable promised a speedy return in January. On January 25th they arrived by rail in Baraboo. Plans were well underway for the

1907 show, and the brothers were soon due in New York and Bridgeport, Connecticut, to finalize the paperwork on the purchase of The Greatest Show On Earth. After meeting downtown with the brothers, John and Mable went to Charley's house and were welcomed by Mama.

"My baby boy!" she exclaimed at the door, throwing here arms around John. "And his lovely bride!" She hugged Mable and pulled them into the house. No time was wasted in planning for the festivities of dinner for the next night.

Dinner was like Thanksgiving, Christmas, and Mother's Day all rolled into one. Salome Marie Juliar Ringling was in the kitchen with the help at first light. Bethany Miller was head of the household and had two helpers working with her. As soon as Mama Ringling entered the kitchen, Bethany begged her not to help.

"You set yourself down at the table Mrs. Ringling, and Julia'll bring you some breakfast."

"Oh, I have little time to sit, Miss Bethany, I'm here to get started with the preparations for tonight's supper. After all, all my boys are in town."

"Well, at least let me pour you some coffee and over there's some cake." She pointed to the center cook's counter which had three kuglehopf cakes, one with dates, one with raisins, and one was plain, all with confectioner's sugar. Bethany had been taught by Mama Ringling to bake and cook every known Alsatian dish. The aroma of the yeasty soft cakes filled the kitchen.

"Coffee is just about fine," she reached for the cup that Bethany had poured her, "you know that I take it black." As she drank her coffee she slyly sliced off slivers of the delicious cakes and tried all three.

By the time Charles and Edith were up, Mama and the help had set a wonderful breakfast. The table had the three cakes, coffee, quiche, and Kassler, a thick cut bacon. It so delighted Mama that she could cook her native food for her children, as she often had neglected them when they were children. She had always done her best to make simple foods like dough and milk custard seem like Alsatian delights but was severely limited by deep financial constraints. Edith was first up and already dressed for the day. She ascended the stairs and could smell the warmth of holiday-like festivities.

"It certainly smells like Christmas all over, Mama."

"My darling Deedee, it is Christmas all over," Mama replied. "Sit. Enjoy." Ana was next up, and the breakfast was beginning to feel like a family get together. Alf and Al were busy at the elephant barn. There had been a chimney fire that morning, and they had to shut off the heat. This was a crisis, as the temperatures outside were in the teens and the wind was sharp. The elephants had to be kept warm. So the two Ringlings threw in with a team of local builders and several of the winter quarters crew to rip down the chimney and get a new one up and running as soon as possible. In the winter there was only one bullman, Tim Horne, and a helper. Al and Alf rounded up blankets to cover the animals, as the temperature in the elephant barn was plummeting. Still, Della and Lou wasted no time in joining the Ringling clan for breakfast and helping Mama with the preparations. Mable was up an hour before John. However, since Mable was obviously still exhausted from their travels, Della and Deedee made her sit.

"What can I do?" asked Mable.

"Sit, eat and rest," Deedee commanded. "After all, you've just sailed from Europe and traveled from New York; you must be tired."

"Nonsense! I've traveled with the show as hard as any."

"Please relax a while," Della begged, "let us serve you a bit, dear." Mable smiled in the Mable way, somewhat charming like a doll. She picked up her coffee and sipped it.

"Looks as if I'm no match for you two," she said as she cut herself a piece of Kassler and a very small piece of quiche.

"Mable, honey," Della said, "after you've plenty to eat, we'll work you silly."

John was last up and said little. He made his way to the table and made right for coffee and juice.

"Morning John," Deedee greeted him. He sipped his coffee and grunted. John was never much for socializing in the morning. He felt it was his duty to be aloof.

The day came and went with the brothers all meeting at various parts of Water Street and coming and going in the house, while Mama and the wives worked on the preparations. The girls were there helping as well; Hester, Charley and Edith's daughter, was sixteen. Already practicing for the stage, she was tall and elegant. Although Gus and Ana's daughter Lorene, now twenty-two, had just left for her final semester at Wisconsin State Teacher's College in Madison, her sisters Martha, now nineteen, and Alice, ten were helping. Alf's daughter Ruth was somewhere upstairs playing with her brothers Roland and Richard as well as Hester's brother Robert who was nine. The youngsters were given a day home from school for the family gathering. The home, this day, not far from winter quarters, nowadays dubbed "Ringlingville," was a Ringlingville of its own. By winter 1907 Ringlingville employed nearly one hundred off season workers, from blacksmiths to animal care and even ten people to run the boarding house. Every brother worked through the winter, even Henry who owned no stock in the show. During this day each and every one was present at some part of the lot, including John. By the time John had married Mable in 1905, he spent more time in other countries searching for acts, especially Europe. He and Mable so loved France and Italy.

The frenzied work on the elephant barn reached emergency levels, as they did not want the animals to get cold. By three in the afternoon, the stoves were working and the heat was back. They agreed to put off all other meetings until the next day and return to Charles' home for the festivities, if for no other reason but to celebrate Mama who was overwhelmed with the joy of having her boys in town all at the same time. She was seventy three. Her hips were ailing and she often needed help up from a chair, but once in motion she took no notice of her ailments and took every precaution to hide them from her family.

By 5:30 the sun was setting, and the Ringling men showed up almost all at once. The children were all downstairs, and the parlor was abuzz with activity. Deedee played piano, and most songs were upbeat and celebratory. Robert, only nine years old, accompanied her by singing. It wasn't long before Charley played the horn and the entire family was in unison. When dinner was served, everyone including Mama allowed the servants to bring all the food, as the family had played their role in all day preparation. This feast was the Thanksgiving of family, no matter what day of the year it was. Charles asked the blessing, "Heavenly Father, giver of all things great, we give thanks for all of us to be here together, and we give thanks for those who have been with us and cannot be here today, but are with you, and most of all we give thanks for Mama, who has brought us all together. Amen."

"Amen!" was answered by all in an uproarious and celebratory cadence. The meal consisted of soupe a la biere, a crème and beer soup, bebeleskas, a potato bacon crème on flat bread, cursalas, big round short fat sausages on salad, pallete a la diable with knepfle, a pork shoulder simmered in riesling, with a handmade pasta, and followed by a main course of jamon en croute, a pie crusted ham. Everything was enhanced by a table of the finest Alsatian wines. This of course was followed by the filling of every plate and the pouring of wine for all, including the nine year olds, Richard and Robert. Then Mama, after several attempts for her tiny but stoic voice to be heard, proposed a toast and stood to make it.

"This is the day I have been waiting for for so long. It seems like a lifetime – at last, all my boys are home together!"

"Here here!" arose from all. Mama still standing, sipped her wine. Her face flushed red, she wavered a bit, and Della, sitting closest, stepped up and grabbed her.

"Mama." She helped her be seated. A bit embarrassed Mama responded, "Just a little excited dear. So happy. My boys." Dinner resumed and everyone went on with feasting and merriment. Perhaps more than any Thanksgiving or any holiday, this feasting was insatiable, inexhaustible, especially for the children. The desserts arrived served with the tart grapey Gewurztraminer wine. Desserts included crème brulee tartes, vanilla custard, tartes aux fruits, tarte au fromage blanc – a cheese cake tart, souffle au Kirsch – liquor souffle, and for John, vanilla ice cream with cinnamon and maple syrup, which he joyfully shared with the children. This had been the feast Mama had always wanted to share with the family. This was the Alsace she had grown up in.

After supper everyone retired to the parlor. Unlike the fashion of the times, the women joined the men, and the children were present too. It was not like the Ringlings to separate family. However, the room quickly filled with cigar smoke. As musical instruments were being set up, John announced, "Mable and I have a belated Christmas gift for Mama."

"Oh come now you two, you have no need to give your old Mama anything but you." She tried to fend off the offering and was quickly turning red.

"It's just a little something, Mama." John pulled a long slender box from his suit coat pocket and handed it to his mother.

"Oh, my dear, I don't suspect it is something for the kitchen." She was blushing all the more.

"Well, go ahead, open it," Deedee jumped in attempting to break the suspense, "don't leave us all hanging here." Marie Salome Juliar opened the box and let out a gasp. It was a French styled silver necklace with diamonds surrounding an opal.

"Let me put it on you Mama," Mable asked, already taking it from her hands. It was striking in its simplicity, short, just above the high neckline of her dress.

"Oh my darlings," she said, "this is too much for an old woman." With that she was showered with compliments from the whole family. The music began with Alf at the piano, and the night became a Ringling gathering like no other. After only a few songs, Mama announced that so much fun, so much family, and such love had worn her to the bones and that she had to retire. After hugs and kisses from the grandchildren she disappeared up the stairs to her room. The merriment of Ringlings and music played on for hours. This night would not be forgotten.

Charley and Edith were having breakfast with Mable, Hester, and Robert when John came down the stairs. In his usual almost irritable manner he sat himself at the table. Mable reached for the coffee, but

Miss Sarah beat her too it.

"Please Mrs. John, let me." John already had the newspaper in his hands and didn't look up, didn't offer thanks. He immediately took the coffee in hand and sipped repeatedly. Finally, he looked at Charley and asked, "Where's Mama?" Before Charley could respond, Edith answered, "Still sleeping, I guess." John sipped again and then mumbled, "Hmmm." Breakfast continued to be served: ham, quiche, cakes. Conversation was light. After most of breakfast had been consumed, Edith called upon Hester to wake her grandmother, "Hester, sweetie, could you go upstairs and wake up Grandma?"

"Why, of course mother." Hester, all of sixteen, in her long gown ran for the stairs and hastily ran, skipping entire steps. Grandma was fond of Hester and the love was always returned. Sometimes she would lay in bed with her grandmother, and they would talk in the morning about important things, things that only a grandmother could talk to a granddaughter about. She was gone for only a minute when she came back down the stairs, quietly, and entered the dining room, stopping in the doorway and staring, saying nothing. She had an empty expression. She paused long enough until one by one everyone was staring at her.

Finally Edith confronted her daughter, "Hester, darling, what on earth are you staring at?" After a long pause she answered, "Grandma's dead." Although solemn, there was a matter of fact tone to her reply. The whole room was silent for what seemed like eternity. Then, both John and Charley pushed their chairs from the table in unison and hastily, almost running, hurried upstairs. Charley was in the room first. He went to check her pulse but brushing her face he noticed she was cold as ice. She was almost smiling, her little round head covered with a frilly sleeping cap on a beautiful lace pillow. John looked at Charley and at Mama.

"She is, isn't she?" he asked. Charley answered, "She looks so peaceful." They stared at her with adoration. She did look at peace. Then finally John broke the silence, "I guess she waited for me to come home."

"You stupid ass!" Charley snapped, "everything's always about you isn't it?"

"Well I didn't mean it like that, Charley."

"I believe you meant every word of it, just the way it sounded." With that Charley stormed out of the room almost knocking Mable over who was entering the bedroom door followed by Edith. It was January 27, 1907.

John and Charley were close as they always had been. There would be nineteen more years of great friendship between them. They would celebrate victories, build a new frontier of sorts in a town they had not yet ventured to, suffer the loss of all their brothers, and they would be the closest staff for each other that brothers could be. But that moment began a rift. Perhaps it was small, but like a tiny crack in a wall, against the hardship of time, mistakes, missteps, and the strain of being the last two leaders of an empire once led by five, the crack would grow.

So it was that cold Sarasota morning in November of 1925 when Edith and Charley walked up to the palatial manor they had waited so long for. There was a rift between John and Charley. Mable and Edith and Charley were all still close. But John had lost his way, it seemed to Charles Ringling. Moreover, Charley saw his brother become an egotistical monster, or so he thought. Charley had made a few conservative investments outside the circus – certainly he and John had both invested in real estate in Sarasota – but never lost track of where their hard earned success came from. It was always from the more than forty years they had invested in the circus. It was every penny they had saved from the Concert Company for the first canvas, the one step at a time, each piece built from their life's blood. Now as he arrived at the grand but tasteful entry known architecturally as a porte-cochere, in keeping with the subdued English theme of his and Deedee's dream, he looked to his left, south, past the smaller Mediterranean home they had built for Hester, where a wall was being erected between the two properties. Through the palms, palmetto, and the imported banyans, the great home of John and Mable pulled Charley and Deedee's attention from their dream home. His little brother had outdone everyone. It seemed a cruel trick. Charley called it "Johnny's Venetian Gothic nightmare." Still, this day was not to be spoiled by John's self importance.

This day was their day. As they were greeted by the help, the house was a flurry of activity, from the decorators to the finishing touches being made to the music room. They entered from the elegant porte-cochere directly into the great hall which was over thirty by fifty feet. Directly across the room a beautiful marble fireplace was receiving the last details. Building was still evident, but Charley and Deedee made hastily to the south for the music room. To them, music was opportunity, was family, was everything social. There, the grand room housed an organ with three story pipes which Charley had purchased at a cost of forty thousand dollars. The room was more than what they had pictured. The organ was still being installed, but the wood ceiling with tastefully painted scenes was complete. The room was designed to acoustic perfection. The carved travertine fireplace, nearly complete, brought tears to Edith's eyes.

"Oh Charles, this is like a dream come true."

"Dreams do come true Deedee." He began to cough. The cough

became deep and his face turned red, and the veins in his forehead swelled.

"Please, someone get Mr. Charley a seat," Edith called out, and a worker brought forth a paint stained chair. He sat, still coughing, but slowly it subsided.

"I'm alright dear." He coughed a bit more but tried to hold back. Outside they could hear voices. It was clearly John, talking to the workers. Edith went and opened the door to greet John Ringling.

"Hello John," she said, rather reserved, and reached out to hug him. John, with a cane in his right hand hugged with his left. He wore a white linen suit and a wide brimmed straw "boater" hat. This was a style he often favored in Sarasota.

"Deedee," he said as he backed away from the half hug, "you are elegant as ever."

"Spare me the formalities, John," she replied, "you always were a good liar anyhow." Looking past her into the dark music room, John began walking towards it and asked, "Where's my big brother?" And from inside came an answer. "I'm here, in my church," Charles called out, almost sarcastically, "where the hell'd you think I would be?" John stopped and offered his arm to Deedee and the two strolled into the great music room.

"There's my big brother," John called out. "Sitting in a worker's chair?"

"I have a cough and had to rest."

"Still ill, Charley?"

"It lingers a bit John, just a bit."

"Well, how'dya like Ca' d'Zan?" John asked. "It'll be finished any day now."

"You're in my house. For God's sake John, haven't you anything nice to say? Is it always about you?"

"I'm sorry Charley," he softened and apologized, "it's just that I am here almost every day, and I have been watching the progress. It's beautiful. It's a fine little place you two have built." Charles was well aware of the words "little place" and this angered him, but he hid it in a shrinking voice.

"John, I have to go and rest. Deedee and I will call tomorrow." Charley stood up. John could see that since he had left the show early that year in September, taken ill while in southern California, Charles had lost considerable weight. His face was reddened, and his eyes seemed pallid.

"Mable and I would be glad to have you both for lunch tomorrow at Palms Elysian." He put his hand on his brother's shoulder, "I hope you feel better."

"Thanks, little brother, I am better," he said looking down at the floor, which was covered with paint splattered rosin paper. "We'll see you then." John exited through the south door. There was a walkway between the Charles Ringling mansion and Hester's smaller home, where lines were being strung to create a portico. From there John walked along a path toward the newly constructed wall, where masons were laying the blocks. There was a makeshift set of stairs where he ascended and walked over the wall. Charley and Deedee watched him for a couple minutes, without saying a word. Finally when he was out of sight Charley remarked, "Why do you suppose there is no gate?" Edith said nothing. It was a rhetorical question. There was a gate, but John would have to walk all the way to the sea wall to pass through it. They assumed that he wanted to avoid getting too close to Hester's house.

There was always a healthy competition between John and Charley. In many ways it helped to push The Greatest Show On Earth to higher levels of excellence. But in Sarasota, trouble had been brewing for years. They both worked diligently toward the enterprise of building a future for Sarasota. But John always one upped his big brother.

When Charley and Edith arrived at Palms Elysian the next day, Tomlisen met them at the door. "I am sorry now Mr. Charley," he said as he opened the door, "but Mr. Ringling says you should lunch at Ca' d'Zan." As always, John was not "Mr. John" but "Mr. Ringling." This had been an annoyance to Charley for years but remained unspoken. Why they had to go all the way down to Palms Elysian to find out was somewhat annoying. They had walked down the road all the way to Palms Elysian. Ben had followed with their car, and they hopped in and drove the short distance back as Charley was tired. The entry to Ca' d'Zan was loud and influenced by Tuscany and far more over-stated than that of Charles and Edith's. The drive was more that of an entry to a Venetian or Florentine castle, with Putti statues as well as demi-gods in cast stone adorning the way, and like Charles and Edith's arrival entry there was a circular drive. Greeted by the butler at the door, they were wildly amazed at how near complete the home was. In fact, had it not been for distant construction sounds from upstairs, they would have thought the entire mansion was complete. The grand court entry felt almost like a museum, and as they were led toward a row of arches and a three story ceiling surrounded by gilded gold columns, there was Mable in light Florida attire, an off white dress, her hair short and curled and wearing pearls.

"Welcome my darlings," she said as she greeted and kissed them both. "You two are the first to lunch in our home, well, other than the builders and Mr. Burns and Mr. Baum." Baum had designed the palatial, thirty six thousand square foot home, and had worked closely with Mable who had spent years collecting scraps, postcards, drawings, and magazine photos, on their many trips to Italy. Owen Burns was the builder. "John will join us shortly; he's upstairs with a plasterer, going over some detail."   As they walked into the great room John stuck his head out from the balcony near the game room and called out, "I'll be down in a moment."   He leaned over the balcony, "Have a little refreshment while I finish up business." Not only was the enormous mansion almost a hundred percent finished, but it was nearly complete in its decoration. The rooms were filled with seventeenth and eighteenth century Italian antiques which John and Mable had bought while at art auctions in Italy, often in complete lots. Only the game room was still to be completed and several bedrooms. Within weeks the home would be ready for its first Christmas celebration. However, the official opening was a year off.

The three sat nervously downstairs and chatted only about trivia.

"Have you seen my rose garden lately?" Mable asked, breaking the silence. "I don't suppose that roses are your cup of tea, Edith."

"I have a rose garden Mable," Edith protested, "you know that. I am sure I'll have other little gardens, but Charles and I might be more interested in vegetables."   In fact they had an orange grove and did already have a vegetable garden, tended to by several caretakers. In 1913, not long after Charles and John purchased the Shell Beach properties, Mable had completed the rose garden. On the south side of the Ca' d'Zan property, it was a show piece on its own, and would divide or define the border between the museum and their home.

"You know Mable," Charley said, pausing to sip his mint julep, "Edith and I are more the fishing type."

"Charley bought me a small twenty eight foot fishing boat," Edith proclaimed. "I think I am going fishing next week."

"Sometimes we have guests fish off the Zalophus," Mable interjected.

"Isn't the Zalophus a bit large for fishing?" Edith questioned as the yacht was one hundred thirty feet and designed for entertaining. "I mean, surely a smaller boat..."

"Oh Deedee," she responded, "you know I have no knowledge of these things."

"What things?" John asked as he strolled into the room. The butler brought John a mint julep on a tray; without a word John took the drink and took a sip. "Oh, Andrew. This is much too sweet. Can you bring me a scotch – neat?" Andrew was filling in for Tomlinson, who was at the Palms, where John and Mable would reside until the perfect completion of their bedrooms.

"Yes sir Mr. Ringling, sir." He took back the mint julep and exited without further notice.

"I like my whiskey, whiskey flavored," John made a point of telling Charley, "if you know what I mean." John sat in a wing chair opposite his brother. Although he had always been larger than Charles, the two were vastly different now. Charles had lost significant weight during his illness, and John who had always sported a handsome full belly was a size larger than he'd ever been. Toward the end of the season they had seen less of each other, as Charley, no longer traveling advance, had taken ill with bronchitis. Charley had become a master at running the huge Ringling Bros. Barnum & Bailey Greatest Show On Earth, while John, still master of routing, spent more time in Europe than he did with the show. The place they saw each other the most was Sarasota – usually at the land offices at the John Ringling Corporation. Mable was still involved in the fishing boat question.

"When we had the Salome, I let guests fish off the back." She suddenly was nervous as the Salome, which had always been a sore subject, had exploded and burned Mable and her guests. Edith always blamed John. "I loved that boat!" she said.

"I see a lot of activity on the Symphonia," John said as he leaned toward his brother. "Are you fixing to go boating?"

"If I stay out of the breeze, the doctors say it's alright for me," Charley answered, "Deedee can take the fishing boat and see if she can catch a record tarpon."

The history of John's and Charley's boats and the competition between them was well known. John had first bought the Louise even before they landed in Sarasota. He sold it and bought an eighty foot steam yacht named the Withea. Around that time Charles bought his first boat, the Zumbrota, which he named after the little Minnesota town where Edith had grown up. Charley sold his first Zumbrota to the Navy as a coast guard boat during the war. The Zumbrota II at one hundred three feet was larger than the Withea, and before too long John had bought a boat from Palm Beach called the Vidoffner II at one hundred five feet. Charles and Edith commissioned their first custom yacht which was completed in 1922, The Symphonia. Its lines were elegant at one hundred twenty feet. It was fitted with fixtures fit for a showman, but tastefully done, stately just like their new, soon to be finished Sarasota home. Not to be outdone, that same year John and Mable had The Zalophus built. It would be one hundred twenty five feet. As it was being built, the Vidoffner II exploded while being worked on in Tampa, killing a young crew member and burning an engineer. Not wishing to be outdone by Charley, John leased a fair sized yacht named the Pastime.

Lunch was stressful, especially for Charles, as he felt that John could not stop talking about his acquisitions, the great stores of paintings he and Mable were collecting, and the museum they were to build on the very same grounds. Hardly a word was said about Charles and Edith's house, and certainly John almost never asked. Mable on the other hand was kinder and showed more interest. Her social skills were adept, and she knew how to take interest in others. She would take the time to ask questions.

"Deedee," she would interrupt John, "what made you decide to go with Marshall Fields to decorate your beautiful home?" And later, "I saw the drawings and paintings for the tapestry being made for your hall; it's beautiful. How did you come up with the design?" But all the while John spoke of John, of his dealings, his donations, his ideas and what he was doing for Sarasota. No mention of the land that Charles had donated for the new county magistrate courthouse, or the city bonds supported and sometimes bought in full by Charles. Everything they said was small talk, and it was as if they were always not saying something. But there was a conversation. One which would haunt John later in life and perhaps might be the ultimate price to pay for working with animals.

"John," Charley leaned forward breaking away from the art conversation the gals were having, "do you think we go too far with animals in the show?"

"What are you talking about Charley?"

"I mean wild animals," he paused to puff his cigar, "I mean pretty much everything but the horses and dogs, and maybe the elephants?"

"I hear that Charley," John changed his posture, and suddenly the last two Ringling brothers had engaged in a business conversation. "But I mean, how do we, I mean where can we go, how can we change the act?"

"Look, in the early days we did the whole show with horses and dogs."

"Yeah, sure Charley, but then we couldn't afford even a hyena." He lit himself a smoke and continued, "I mean we had to compete, you know, with Barnum and Sells, Adam Forepaugh, all the big guys."

"Yeah, John, we did," Charley responded. He exhaled a bit watching the smoke. "But now we are the big guys."

"Okay, but Hagenbeck is still a big animal show, and A.G. Barnes is based in wild animal acts." John leaned in closer to Charley and lowered his voice, "Are you suggesting, maybe, I mean, should we get rid of the menagerie?"

"I'm thinking that we should phase out everything that belongs in zoos."

"Zoos!" John raised his voice, "Then why would people want to come to the circus?"

"Lookit, brother, shows are going to change." Charley became authoritative and this often irritated John, but John listened, en-gaged, like the old days when they all sat down together and made decisions. "Those other shows you mentioned are all owned by the ACC, and they are the other guys – right? I think, one day there are going to be shows that just have people."

"What the fuck!" John exclaimed.

"John," Mable scolded him, "not in my house."

"Sorry Mable," he apologized, "it's just that, well, never mind." The gals returned to their conversation and John and Charley to theirs.

"Back around the time you and I were born, some fellow named Bergh started the ASPCA."

"Yes Charley, they have given us plenty of trouble over the years."

"I know, and sometimes we downright needed it. I think we have always tried to do good by our animals." Charley pointed with his index finger at John, "No one is kinder to animals than us. But once we bought the Sells show, it took a long time to get them to lighten up, and there weren't even enough bullmen that we could throw 'em off the lot for how they treated the elephants."

"Look, every showman in America knows that if you abuse an animal on the Ringling lot – you're out," John said. He leaned back in his big wing chair, definitive about that.

"But still, keeping a bull in a train, a four ton animal. Sometimes we ride a day and a half. It's not right," Charley said of the elephants.

"We have more veterinarians on staff than any show in the country," John argued, "our bullmen are trained by Punjabs and mahouts from Indonesia, to gentle the animals. You know how Al and Alf were about bull hooks and force." John puffed his cigar a bit, chewed the tip and then asked, "You're not suggesting we get rid of elephants?"

Charley just smiled and stared back at him. "Maybe I am, maybe I'm not," he said. Charley had a smug look and tilted his head at John.

"You forget Charles Ringling that elephants from Asia have been domesticated for thousands of years," John confronted his brother, "don't let us miss the fact that just like horses, they have been working along with people for centuries."

"The elephant bit is a tough one," Charley responded and then with cigar in hand pointed at John, "how 'bout we start by getting rid of all other wild animal acts?"

"You mean, like tigers, and lions?" John asked indignantly.

"I mean like limit all things that have to go in cages," Charles responded with that authoritative presence again, "like the hippo, like lions, birds. Add more equestrian acts, the dogs love to act, even pigs; hell they are happier acting than being dinner, right?" John rubbed his chin, scratched at his neck, and then said, "What do you propose we do with the animals we own, the ones that don't perform?"

"Well, just before Alf died he was trying to give animals to zoos," Charley continued, "he had this idea that if animals were disappearing from the wild, they should be given a happy life, a place where they can breed, and people can help bring the species back."

"Yeah, I remember," John responded, "like the way he was on the farm over by Portage."

"It was his way," Charley looked up to the right toward the three story ceiling, "of repaying those first two horses we bought." He looked back at John, "We should do this for him."

"What about the show, Charley," John asked, irritated. "I mean we got a huge nut, and if it doesn't pay at the right rate, we lose out. We could lose money."

"Okay, I'll give you that." Charley motioned with his cigar as if drawing a picture, "but suppose it worked for us?"

"It hadn't occurred to me." John rubbed his chin again, "Yeah, it could be a real boon."

"Look," Charley proposed, "let's make a pact. Over the next three to five years we begin slowly to cut back a few of the wild animal acts from the show. Maybe we could start a program for helping animals?" John just stared for a while mulling it over; then Charley asked, "What da ya say brother?"

"Not the monkeys!" John jumped in, "and we keep the elephants – at least for a while. And what about zebras?"

"Little by little, one step at a time," Charley answered, "we will keep pace because the world is changing, and we want to stay The Greatest Show On Earth." Charley leaned forward and reached out his hand. "Deal?" John reached out, "Deal!"

"What are you two taking about, anyhow?" Deedee asked.

"We are making a deal to make our show more respectable," Charley answered.

"That's the first time," Mable whispered, "I've seen those two shake hands like that in a long while."

"It's about time," Deedee responded.

Charles and Edith moved into their beautiful Sarasota dream home in May of 1926. Hester's house was finished by the end of summer. The Charles and Edith Ringling estate, modeled after English architecture and faced in pink, Georgia Etowah marble was every aspect of their dreams. The pipe organ, inspired by Alf's pipe organ in New Jersey, was one of the largest privately owned pipe organs in the United States. Even before the house was finished, Charley and Deedee spent evenings in the music room, playing everything possible, usually just for each other. This had always been their joy. The fountain in the circular driveway designed by George Isenberg was complete before May, and along with the sculpted lions in front, made an impressive greeting, yet still was an understatement of wealth and expression. But Deedee's favorite place was the courtyard on the bayside and the fountain, simply adorned with a winged cherub putti. Every room, completed in magnificent tasteful finishes was, compared to John and Mable's home, understated. The furnishings were almost all English antiques such as Hepplewhite.

Charles and Edith, along with Robert who celebrated his 29th birthday in Sarasota, now an accomplished young opera soprano and touring with the Chicago Civic Opera Company, decided to travel north to Evanston for Thanksgiving and their grandson Stuart Lancaster's 6th birthday, which also fell days before Charles' 62nd birthday on December 2nd. As much as they loved the new home in Sarasota, there was a sense of nostalgia for the little house in Evanston. Evanston was only a few hours' drive from Baraboo, and the entire family had such strong ties to it. Charles and Stuart, Hester's two boys, were born there, and even though Robert and Hester had grown up in Baraboo, it was Evanston, being a suburb of Chicago, that drew them for holidays. The modest brick home on Forrest Avenue was only a short walk from the lake. It had a large yard and a small barn. The barn being the favorite play arena for Stuart and Larly, as Stuart called his elder half brother. Charles Ringling Parks, Stuart's brother, was the son of David Parks, who was killed in action during the world war shortly after his wedding to Hester. Also along for the fun with the boys was Jimmy Ringling, a toddler, the son of Robert and his first wife Virginia. At age twenty nine, Robert Ringling was fast becoming one of the most celebrated voices in American opera, if not world opera. Meanwhile, his elder sister, Hester, nicknamed by the grandchildren as Dalma, also made her start in opera, although she did not have the vocal skills and dynamism of brother Robert. In fact when she performed Carmen the critics said, "Hester Ringling gave a mediocre performance and certainly lacks the great voice of her brother Robert." Although deterred from opera, she continued to work at it throughout her life while she pursued stage acting. Eventually Hester would win praise for her role on Broadway as Mama in *I Remember Mama*.

Leaving the new house in Sarasota for the holidays was an easy choice. It made sense in every fashion to Charles and Edith. The discussion over whether or not to be in Evanston for Thanksgiving, Charles' birthday, and Christmas lasted about two minutes. They were lunching on the back terrace, overlooking the bay, the fountain singing its endless water lullaby. It was November 15th, and they had lived in the new house for an entire six months.

"Deedee darling," Charles began, "haven't we had enough of my brother, his Ca' d'Zan, and self aggrandizing for a while?"

"Charley," she responded with a sarcastic smirk, "are you saying John thinks the world of himself?"

"Well," Charley paused a while, "yep."

"I have to agree." Deedee sipped her tea and then turned her heavy cast iron chair more toward Charley. "Are you by chance suggesting we take the family to Evanston for the holidays?"   A naughty smile that only Deedee could have overtook her anticipatory gaze at her husband.

"That's exactly what I was thinking, my dear," he answered, "after all, Hester and the boys are already there." Hester's home was still not complete, and Stuart and Larly were spending a last school year with their friends in Evanston. "And," he continued, "Robert is performing in Chicago. It seems to me that in January this place will still be here, and when we return, we can escape the coldest weather but before that be in Evanston, a place that's made for Christmas and family."

"It seems like the deal is signed and sealed!" Deedee exclaimed excitedly and reached out and held Charley's hand. The feeling they shared was as much of deep love as they had back in 1889 when they were married. Family, all together, was worth more than all the millions of dollars they now shared. In Charley's mind, he could give it all up just for the sake of family being together and sharing a future. Nothing could take from him the great feeling of sitting young Larly on the floor by his feet and playing his violin for him. Nothing could limit the joy of seeing the three young boys all stealing across the east side of the property, sneaking some "up to no good" game from the sight of parents, but within the scope of a loving grandfather. Even the day that young Stuart had attempted to make a sailboat out of Charley's Stradivarius violin and float it on the pool gave the old man great joy. He was glad, however, to snatch the instrument from the boy's clutches before it sailed a ruinous voyage.

They left for Evanston on November 20, 1926. They left behind the endless social gatherings, both at Mr. Charley's estate and those at John and Mable's. Sarasota could wait. The trip was normal, but some symptoms of Charley's respiratory ills came back while traveling. Charley had suffered a series of small blood clot incidents which showed most of all in his losing his huge presence and becoming a smaller figure of the man he had once been. Having completed the house in Sarasota, he felt somehow capable again and up to the task of traveling.

They arrived in Evanston on November 23rd, just two days before Thanksgiving. The house, grand by average standards, was just large enough for the three families. Hester and the boys were there to greet them. Hester's second marriage to Louis Gladstone Lancaster had been short lived. She had been seeing a younger man, Charles Sanford, but was single. She made the best of her motherhood and worked diligently with the boys to get the house ready for the festivities. She had a strange habit of having vegetables washed over and over; even sometimes the help was requested to use scrub brushes. She knew this annoyed her parents who embodied more Midwestern sensibilities, in fact farmers' ways, so she had as much prepared as possible before their arrival. Robert and Virginia were finishing performances in Chicago, and Jimmy stayed with Hester and her boys at the Evanston house. There was an unspoken credo amongst Hester and Robert, and throughout their lives they never wanted to admit it, but circus was somewhat plebeian and lacked the culture of stage and opera. Only in later years would they both come to understand how sophisticated Charles and Edith were, how dedicated they were to real art, to classical music, and that the circus itself was in its heyday an attempt to bring art and culture to the masses while giving them the thing they needed more than art itself - amusement: the ability to laugh and wonderment.

The house was alive with all the smells of warmth, harvest, sweetness, and turkey roasting in the oven when Robert and Virginia arrived Thanksgiving morning. The celebration would not be Alsatian like John so loved but very traditional American. There were hugs to go all around and even Charley hugged his son. He was reminded of the days back in Baraboo when Robert had hurt his back and hips in a high school football accident. It had changed Robert's life most of all, and Charley left the show early that autumn and spent day after day helping his son rehabilitate. He did the one thing he knew best, played music for his son day and night. Those were the last days in Baraboo. Ringlingville was soon to close. It was the end of the war, and the state of Wisconsin wanted its share of Ringling's revenues, along with those claimed by the IRS. Sarasota beckoned and Evanston offered a new opportunity, one where capitalists, industrialists, and self made men could come together in quiet neighborhoods by the side of Lake Michigan, a place they could call home.

Dressed in modern pirate pants and festive hat, Virginia arrived with Robert, not in costume, but sporting knickers and tweed. Jimmy ran and hugged his mother, "Mommy Mommy," throwing his hands around her waist.

"Oh darling," she responded, "you'd think we've been abroad."

"What no hug for Papa?" Robert asked his son and opened his arms. He was shorter than Charles and round and mostly bald. It seemed that the baldness came from the Conway side of the family.

Young Jimmy leapt into his father's arms. "That's more like it." The closeness of the family in its small group in a warm house just moments from the shores of the great lakes had a unique feeling that year. A chapter was coming to a close. Sarasota would soon dominate everyone's lives. There was more play than usual. It didn't take long for the boys to disappear up the stairs and the elders to find themselves in the parlor.

"You're looking stout and healthful, my son," Charles remarked. It was still considered a sign of wellbeing and good standing to sport a full figure for a man. Meanwhile, the image for women was changing rapidly: thinner, less clothing, and more skin were all the fashion.

"Why, thank you Papa," Robert responded softly. It had become a Ringling tradition to call father "Papa" and was a throwback to the days of August Ringling. "You've lost a bit of weight yourself." Robert, feeling that maybe he had insulted his father quickly corrected himself, "and it suits you well, I have to say."

"You always were the worst liar, my boy."

"No truly, you look well."

"It's this damn bronchitis thing," Charles explained, "it comes and goes."

"Your father has been getting severe headaches lately," Edith interrupted. "The doctor says it will clear when his lungs clear. We think as soon as Christmas ends, we'll go back to Sarasota. The weather in Sarasota is better for his lungs."

"Nothing a good stiff drink won't cure," Charley interjected, "I mean the headache thing." At that point he took a deep drink of his whiskey. It was the heart of prohibition, but money could afford the Ringlings the best of whiskey. The drink of choice in Chicago was Canadian whiskey. Robert and Edith watched closely as Charley seemed to drink a bit fast. There was an awkward silence. This was broken up by the sound of the coronet coming from upstairs.

Edith rose from her chair and walked to the front stairs and called to the boys, "Larly. Larly! Can you boys come down and play for us?" she shouted, with no response except footsteps. In moments they appeared, but only Charles (Larly) had a small coronet. Jimmy was too young to really play any instrument, but Stuart favored the bugle. "Alright then, it looks as if Larly is going to play for us," Edith said. Young Charles Lancaster was nine. He stood at attention and then played a short piece from Grandpa's music. He was already versed in circus music, Sousa marches, and military marches. But he wanted to play a piece he had studied by Grandpa Ringling. Charles Ringling's compositions were common not only in the Ringling shows but other circuses as well. He only played a part of it, and his short recital lasted less than a minute but was met with cheers and laughter by all.

Thanksgiving dinner was simple and traditional. The Evanston house had only two servants, so Hester, Virginia, and Edith all took part in the food preparation. Edith threw on the help's apron and did half the work. After the meal, Charles and Edith talked at length with Robert and Virginia about Robert's future with the Chicago Opera Company. Robert, a tenor, played a part time role in the opera, but there was talk for Robert of a full time position. Hester was still pursuing opera. She was a soprano. Her work with her voice coaches was ongoing, but her career was still less successful, indeed hardly noteworthy next to that of her brother. The night wore on, logs on the fire, and a warm and cozy, never-to-be-forgotten Thanksgiving was had by all. Evanston was so much home to Robert and Hester, as both had lived there beginning with Hester attending Northwestern University and later Robert being schooled there as well. Although Winter Quarters had lasted in Baraboo through the war and through Hester's first two marriages, Evanston had managed to be home to the family for years.

Because young Stuart would be turning six the following Tuesday, it was decided that Stuart and his grandfather Charles, whose birthday was two days later on the 2nd of December, would celebrate a joint party on Saturday the 27th. Stuart of course would have friends from school and an early dinner, followed by a steak dinner for Charles. The party was fun, with silly hats and noisemakers, and Stuart was most interested in two things. First of course like all boys, the cake, but second, Grandpa gave him something he would cherish for life, a bugle. Stuart, already able to make a few tunes, felt proud and thanking his grandfather remarked, "Maybe one day I'll play in the circus, Grandpa." With his most sincere six year old expression he added, "I could be like you." Nothing could have made Charley happier. By supper time, the boys were asleep on the parlor floor and the adults picking up paper and party favors from every corner. By the time supper was served, they were awake and ready for round two.

Eating however was not high on their priorities, and they insisted on the giving of gifts to Grandpa. Jimmy went first and sat on Grandpa's lap and presented him with a handkerchief that Virginia had purchased as well as a drawing of a boat. "That's the Phomoniuma," he said to his grandfather, as everyone laughed knowing full well that he meant the Symphonia. With Jimmy less than two years old, every word out of his mouth had been painstakingly coached by his parents. Next it was Stuart's turn, and he presented his grandfather with a conductor's baton, of course selected by Hester, and he too had a drawing. The image was that of a band leader and it said, "I love you Grandpa and one day I want to

grow up and be you." Finally, the eldest, Larly, also Charles Ringling's namesake Charles Ringling Lancaster, came forth and said, "I
don't have anything to give you Grandpa." He then picked up his
coronet and said. "I wrote this for you." He played a short, lyrical,
and circus-like composition. With tears in his eyes, Charles hugged
his grandson. Then he called all three of them.

During dinner Stuart and Jimmy fell asleep. However, with
efforts to move them before dessert, they both resisted and were
allowed to stay for parfait. One cake was enough for the day. After the
meal, Charles and Edith played piano and violin and on several
occasions were accompanied by Robert and Hester. This was the last
time they would all play and sing together.

The next morning Charles remained in bed with a raging
headache and asked Edith for medicine. His pain was so severe that
he was shaking. Edith summoned the doctor. By the time the doctor
arrived, Charles' bronchitis had returned with a vengeance. He was
coughing until his face turned red and veins rose from his temples.
The doctor gave Charles laudanum, an extract of opium, as well as a
syrup for the cough, also containing an opiate; it seemed to help calm
the cough but lulled Charles into a dream state. As he fell asleep, Dr.
Jarvin nudged Edith and summoned her from the bedroom for a chat.

"How soon can you get him to Sarasota?" After a long pause as
Edith searched her mind, she responded, "We can leave this
afternoon and be in Sarasota by the first."

"Perfect," he whispered, "I am going to leave you the laudanum
and the cough syrup. I'll have the pharmacist send over more right
away." Edith interrupted with grave concern, "It's that serious then?"
Dr. Jarvin looked her in the eye, leaned in, and whispered, "I'm afraid
that if he stays here, in this dry cold air, it could kill him. Further, all
the excitement of family has been too much for his fragile condition."
Edith looked down, paused, then held the doctor's hand, "Thank you,
doctor, we'll leave as soon as possible."

"I'm going to get you a nurse," Dr Jarvin said in very serious
manner, "one who will travel with you to Sarasota."

From downstairs could be heard the monotonous scales of
Robert's tenor vocals, scaling up, scaling down, up, down, from
behind the shuttered parlor doors. Edith walked the doctor down the
stairs and bid him goodbye, once again receiving the instructions to
keep Charles completely sedated. Then she quickly went to the parlor
to take control of the situation and quiet her son.

"Your father is seriously ill. We are leaving for Sarasota as soon as
I can get a reservations on the train."

"What?" he said frantically, moving away from the piano. Next to
his son Jimmy and even more than his wife Virginia, Robert loved

Charles more than anything in the world. "Mother, tell me, what is it?"

"His bronchitis has returned," she said quickly and then paused, "he's bringing up blood, considerably, and it may turn to pneumonia!" She pulled her handkerchief from her sleeve and wiped her brow, which was spotting with perspiration. She smeared her powder. Edith was short, stout, had once been a petite woman but now was round and full. She was prone to sweating when there was difficulty.

"We're coming along!" Robert announced, and I think maybe, Hester and the boys."

"Nonsense," Edith interrupted, "You have a show tonight."

"Mother, I'm an understudy," he interjected, "it's of no consequence." Without argument or pause, Edith continued, "We'll need a car where Hester and the boys' cabin is far enough from your father."

"Mother, why don't I call uncle John? He can arrange the whole business, schedule, car, and all."

With that the entire family went into action. Within three hours, John had them on a private car. By John's arrangement, being the owner of a railway, he could get free passage on any train in the U.S. and Canada. This was a gentleman's agreement amongst rail men. Charles was so heavily sedated that as they dressed him he thought they were going to dinner at John and Mable's. When the Rolls Royce pulled to the front of the home, it was followed by a taxi with the luggage for all. Hester and the boys rode in the taxi. The railcar was an average sleeper, but the entire car had been reserved for the eight Ringlings. John had spared nothing in his urgent attending to his brother's well being and called in all his cards in arranging the trip. There was one problem: the rail would have to travel east to New York and change at Grand Central and then again in Winston-Salem and on to Tampa. However, Charles would not be interrupted and would in fact be sedated for the entire journey. The timing was such that it would be quicker to meet the train by limo in Tampa rather than wait for the cars to be changed before going on to Sarasota. Dr. Jarvis had sent along nurse Eloise Hills, as an aide, who primarily kept Charles comfortable and sedated. There was nothing happy and celebratory about this journey. There was little talk, no operatic practice, and Stuart and Larl were kept busy by Hester reading and drawing. Stuart liked to draw clothing and had already convinced the family that he wanted to design costumes for the circus as well as "fashion for the fashionable." He did try from time to time to play his new bugle, while Charles played his coronet, but they were kept in the furthest cabin from Charles and music was kept to a minimum.

Arriving in Tampa, their driver was already waiting and a second driver waiting with John's Pierce Arrow. Once again, while being helped to the car, Charles remarked to Edith, "Are all these people joining us for lunch at John and Mable's?" Edith, placating, replied, "It will be a grand affair darling." The moving was hasty as no one in the family wanted the press to notice Charles' state. When they arrived at the home and pulled under the porte-cochere, Nurse Hills helped Charles from the car and was greeted at the stairs by Dr. Ewald.

"What the hell's Ewald doing here?" Charles shouted deliriously. "This isn't Ca' d'Zan!" He broke into a deep cough as the doctor and several servants helped him into the house.

"Let's get him to bed and cover his chest," Ewald ordered. Charles coughed so deeply he was bent over, and Edith and several others were holding him and walking toward the stairs.

"Take the elevator," Edith ordered, "it'll be easier on him." They were nearly carrying him. Robert, Virginia, baby Jimmy, Hester, and the two boys were all in the great room. Ben turned to Hester and the boys, "Happy birthday Master Lancaster." Ben reached out and shook young Stuart's hand. Stuart shook his hand without saying a word. "Let me drive you and the boys to the house, Mrs. Hester," Ben offered.

"Thank You Ben," she answered, "we'll walk. If you could just have our things brought over."

"Yes ma'am, I'll do that right as we speak, now." Robert and his family disappeared. Hester and her family went to the house next door, and the house fell silent. There was no sign of John and Mable. The rest of the day was quiet at the Ringling house. No calls, dinner at the big table was quiet. Robert, Virginia, and Edith ate without speaking. Hester and the boys stayed at their home, occasionally calling to see what mother had to say about father's condition. There was little change, with the exception that he complained of a worsening headache. He slept through the night, which Edith was well aware of, as she slept little.

December 2nd was Charles Ringling's sixty second birthday. The house was almost silent, and over breakfast there was little talk. During breakfast Hester arrived without the boys.

"How's Papa?" she asked as she entered the dining room, taking a seat and allowing Alma to pour her a coffee.

"Little change," Edith answered, looking up from her breakfast, her gaze concerned, her brow deep with worry. "His headache is worse and the doctor doesn't think he can take much more laudanum."

"Worse?" Hester asked, "How much?"

"He's rubbing his head. He complains of pounding and he's shaking."

"Have you spoken with Dr. Ewald?" Hester interrupted.

"Ewald's upstairs with him now," Edith responded.

"Has Uncle John called?" Hester asked.

"Not yet dear." The phone rang and a moment later Jerome the butler appeared. "It's Mr. John," he said, "calling to wish Mr. Charley a happy birthday!" He handed the phone to Edith, who held it for a while just eyeing the earpiece and finally, gripping the stem, put the earpiece to her ear, "Where the hell have you been John?" She spoke abruptly with a great deal of anger.

"I apologize Edith, but I thought my brother might need a day to rest and get used to being back in his home."

"Home!" She was shouting, and the family sat silently fixated on every word. "Do you have any idea how sick your brother is?"

"Deedee darling, relax, I'll be over in a little while."

"Well let's be sure you don't have any pressing business that might get in the way." She hung up the earpiece and gave the phone back to Jerome, with instructions, "If Mr. John calls back, tell him I can't take his call." Before Jerome had left the room, the phone rang again and Jerome, still exiting the room, answered, "Ringling residence, how may I serve you? Yes Mrs. John, please hold." He turned from the valet table where the phone was kept, "Mrs. Charley, it's..."

"I'll take it Jerome." Edith, who had already sat down, was up again and two steps behind Jerome, "Mable, dear?" She took the phone from Jerome and placed the earpiece to her head, as Mable apologized for John's behavior.

"Deedee, please forgive John, he's been under such pressure. In fact, since you left..."

Edith interrupted, "Charles is very ill, dear; it's not good, they may move him to the hospital if it doesn't clear up. We brought him home because the doctor thought the air in Sarasota might help his lungs. But they don't know why he is plagued by a debilitating headache."

"John's on his way over already," Mable interjected, "I'll be over as soon as I can be made up. Can I bring anything?"

"Thank you darling, your presence will be most comforting."

John arrived and offered to go see his brother, but the doctor insisted on quiet rest. The day was uneventful, with small talk downstairs and an occasional report from Nurse Hills. As night fell, everyone agreed to meet for breakfast at 9:00 a.m. Charles had little to say as Edith went to bed that night. He was heavily sedated and complained little, only that his head ached, and she kept him medicated. She kept a dim lamp on and watched her husband all night. She slept little as she worried throughout the night, lying on her side and watching Charles. She finally fell asleep just before dawn. At first light she heard her husband yell in his sleep, "Damn it John!" Then she went to his bed to comfort him. The life had already passed from his body. Charles Ringling died of an aneurism on December 3, 1926, one day after his sixty second birthday.

Me, Me, Me

For the last two years of Charley's life, we had been in what was mostly a friendly competition. We also were looking at a change, one that would not only begin to adapt circus to a changing future but one that would leave a legacy. It probably became apparent when in 1926 some of my projects had collapsed. Hell, Florida's great boom had burst, and Charley and I were in the middle of it. There had been a collapse in the Florida banks because the land that was being sold over and over was nothing more than paper. But, unlike other successful fellows of the day who relied on their bank interests, their timber or oil wells, Charley and I provided something that the common man wanted because it gave him something uncommon, the circus. No mistakes made in understanding, we - especially me - made money off real estate, timber, oil, cattle, and other investments, and folks seemed to think only Charles Ringling knew where his reserves came from, but I too never really lost sight of what the circus did for us.

I couldn't hold onto the Ritz-Carlton any longer. My cash reserves were tied up. In fact as cash goes, so went some of my ability to be on the go. Sure, I still made deals. When it became apparent that the Ritz-Carlton was on the rocks, I bought the El Verona from the Prudence Bond Company, after Owen Burns went bankrupt. Sarasotans blamed me for what happened. That's because my name was always on everything. I was a moving target. The El Verona was bigger than Charley's Sarasota Terrace. But it cost me. I had to move my cash around a bit. Like the wood for the John Ringling Causeway, which was supposed to be cypress. Instead I imported pine from North Carolina. Cypress would have lasted more than half a century, but the pine was already rotting before I finished the museum. Things started getting rotten between us in late '25, when we were most on the move. Not only were we building for us, and sales of real estate had dropped to near zero, but Sarasota was offering up bonds like a dying man pleading for help. Charley and I were buying up parts of bonds or all of them. Charley was humble about it. While I would get Gumpertz to publicize my every good deed, Charley would ignore publicity. However, it seemed Charley was getting all the acknowledgement. It never occurred to me, but I was racing Charley.

I finished Ca' d'Zan before he finished his home, at least un-officially. But you know what gets me? He made his opening day for the big house in Sarasota May 19, 1926. So what the fuck's the big deal?   May 19th! Is there any other day with more meaning to us Ringlings? It's the anniversary of our first circus! Once Deedee had the house ready, the music room done, the Pompeii Room complete, all of his God damn English furniture all laid out by Marshall Fields, Charles left the show after it played in Lancaster, Pennsylvania, on May 15th and arrived in time for the most tasteful of housewarming celebrations. Then, because he had to go back to Evanston, celebrate that little bastard grandson's birthday and I guess celebrate his love of Chicago, his attachment to that cold nasty place, he got sick. He died. He left me alone to run the show. It was enough that Charley and I could have the right folks to help produce a good show – hell the best show. We did it well enough that our brothers would have been proud. Charley was a genius. We had a mile and a half of train, canvas that could seat nearly fifteen thousand, more than forty elephants, every damn best act in the world, over one hundred baggage stock and two hundred ring stock. We were ready to turn our show, The Greatest Show On Earth, into the leader of all shows. We had decided that certain rare animals belonged in the wild and in zoos, and not enduring the hardships of travel and shows. Finally, Charley was ready for the big new winter quarters, somewhere in Florida. If we could negotiate it in the right place, it would be in Sarasota, our new home. Then he went and did the fucking ultimate "screw you John" – he died. I am alone. I love Mable. Edith is a circus lady. My nephews mean well, and I think maybe one day Henry will make a real showman. But everyone who knew anything died in the heart of Charley. What was left?   Mable and I have a dream. Sarasota was broken. The circus would go on. But it was hard to see the future of the show by myself.

Nineteen twenty seven was a broken year. For the first time ever, there was no Ringling traveling with the show. Sadness fell over the acts. I showed my face more than usual, and for the first time, when actors called me Mr. Ringling, I wanted them to call me Mr. John. It was odd. But, just for a moment, I thought, "If I could be Mr. John, maybe they'd accept us all back on the lot." Just Maybe it would be Ringling Brothers again. It was such a lonely feeling.

We opened Ca' d'Zan in December 1926 for the holidays. It was bittersweet. The festivities were grand, and everyone came out for the holidays. The unspoken was that we had just buried Charley. Mable and I dug deeper into the creation of the museum that year. It was no longer a dream. We chose the right place on the grounds for it. I was fully engaged in collecting art. In my mind I felt something I could no longer communicate with Mable. It wasn't just about the art, a direction, a focus, but rather, could we fill our dream enough to make an impact on Sarasota? What about the art world? Hell, the critics had already ripped me to shreds. They questioned my every move. It was a damn good thing I wasn't buying on my own. But I had other troubles, troubles at home. Sarasota. My two best friends, maybe my only real remaining friends in the world, Sam and Evie Gumpertz, especially Sam, were questioning my motives. Sam was aware of something that Charley had tried to warn me of. I had one reliable source of income – the circus. Everything else was fleeting. I knew it but was stuck on my dream for Sarasota. Since the land boom had already gone bust, no one was buying anything. No one could get rid of anything. There was an oil glut, and in due time the IRS would grab that source of revenue. Everyone I knew from Kentucky to Oklahoma was already a millionaire, and we all had more of the stuff than people were buying. Banks had already begun to have runs, especially the Florida banks. My investments were no different. I owned more businesses than I could sit on the boards of. It made my ass sore, so many board meetings. I couldn't even schedule them all. Meanwhile Mable and I made final plans for the museum. Not the kind that broke ground yet, but the kind that included what it meant. Like a college and the gift we could give, not just to Sarasota, but to Florida, and to the world. We had collected well over seven hundred books on art. We believed we could help foster a great school, like the Barbizon in France. It became bigger than us, and it made that part of our lives worthwhile. I mean, everything else was going to shit – land, hotels, oil, deals were falling to the wayside, but we were happy, we had our home. Deedee had her home. Hester and Robert were opera singers, the circus had big seasons, and although most circus parades were ending, our show really was The Greatest Show On Earth. It meant little to us that *The Jazz Singer* was a talkie. It was unnerving, and I didn't quite make sense of it at first. I mean, the new entertainment and amusements that would take over where circus left off. I should of seen it in sports, and in '29 I did, when boxing, which I enjoyed, pushed me over the edge. Yet, life was still golden and we were living the gold.

Sarasota was in need, like never before. I guess there were signs popping up all over the country, but we focused on our town. It was the county seat. Charley had donated a one hundred fifty thousand dollar property for the Judicial Complex. He stipulated that it had to be a courthouse and a bond was floated. We were right there buying as much of the bond as we could. If we could make Sarasota the dream we had all imagined, I knew it would pay off one day. Meanwhile Sarasota drank up our money while the circus paid, and we kept the money flowing.

We opened in the Garden as usual, and Family Nights were always a donation to a good cause, but when we played Chicago, 1927, I had to go to Evanston. The house was the same, but Robert, Virginia, and Jimmy were in Sarasota or at their apartment in Chicago, and it looked like Robert might soon become full time with the Chicago Opera. He was good. A tenor of world renown. The house was a beautiful place on Forrest Avenue. A street lined by tall oaks, just blocks from the lake. I was in Chicago two days ahead of the show. I had to go. After all, it was the last place my brother really spent his life. God I missed him so. I could picture him there playing music, singing with the boys, happy. I made my driver park on the street so that I could walk down the drive, under the trees. It was late May, but under the trees was cool. It made me feel at ease. I got to the front door. It really was an unassuming little brick home, I mean compared to what we had in Florida. As I reached for the door knocker, the door opened.

"Good day, Mr. Ringling." I was greeted by Hattie, the house-keeper. "I watched you come up the walk already, Mr. Ringling sir."

"Please call me Mr. John," I said, "I prefer it now, I mean, especially here in my brother's house."

"Yes sir, Mr. John, as you like sir." She opened the door and welcomed me in and offered to take my hat and coat.

"No Hattie, I won't be staying long. I just wanted to look around and maybe see my brother's study."

"Yes sir, as you please, Mr. Ringling, I mean Mr. John."

I noticed right off how the house smelled like Charley, his brand of cigars, his skin. I wanted to reach out and give him a big hug. His study was past the parlor, and as I walked by the parlor I saw the piano, imagined him playing, maybe Deedee too. Nothing had changed. Everything was left as if he would come right in at any moment. I wanted him to. No matter how hard I wished, I knew he wouldn't, and I wanted to cry, but I took a deep breath and fought back the tears. I went to his desk. I opened his cigar box and it was nearly full, a few missing, as if he had been enjoying them. Off to the left of the desk was a 1926 show poster, mounted on illustration board. It was stuck halfway between his brass globe mount and several boxes of what appeared to be children's toys. Charley would design the posters for the advance, even in the later days, just as he'd done for so many years. He had begun working with a new young fellow named Roland Butler. The print jockeys would paste a copy on illustration board for him to proof. It was always his direction, even if artists worked with him. I pulled it out. It was a great litho, highlighting Lillian Leitzel, her magnificent petite beauty and her great aerial feats. There was a logo of us brothers. It was odd because we had stopped using it after Al died. There was no P.T. Barnum, nor James A. Bailey. Then there was Charley's handwriting, next to my picture which was in the middle, our images from twenty years earlier. I sensed not only the emotion with which he wrote it, but I thought maybe he'd had a few drinks when scribbling next to my picture. I could feel him in the room. He spoke to me with the scribe of his pen, and there, next to my picture it said, "ME, ME, ME."

I left almost immediately. He was right, I thought. How could I have left my brother with such a feeling, with such thoughts? What had I done? Now, more than ever, I knew I had to make it up to him.

What I Borrowed

Fuck New York! The hell with the Garden. Why would they even suggest that The Greatest Show On Earth would not open the 1930 season. The nerve of those bastards. If it weren't for me and our show there might not even be a Garden. Oh for God's sake.

Sam Gumpertz had been my best friend over so many years. When I first met the man, he was running the craziest freak show in Coney Island. Dreamland. Sam was a bit of a freak himself. He had started with the circus and was a tumbler. After a jump from a pyramid act, he landed smack on his head, and a serious concussion ended his performing days. He had ridden with Buffalo Bill's show, but I think what told me the most about Sam was his ability to dream and see big, but he couldn't hold onto an act. Back in the early days he had helped a fella get started in his first revue called the Ziegfeld Follies. He figured it'd be short lived, so he sold his interests off cheap. He was a showman though, through and through. His most famous act was Harry Houdini. Houdini himself was the better showman. Sam played many circuses and in fact had worked with my competition, Jeremiah Mugivan, Bert Bowers, Ed Ballard, and the American Circus Corporation. At one time he was a butcher selling candy and running stands. He was best at procuring acts and especially the freaks. Coney Island had been alive and well since before the Civil War. But in 1904, just after I met Mable, I saw that the amusements were rivaling our show. I decided it was high time to see if a carnival amusement, a stand alone venue, so few actors, so many amusement stands, could give us trouble.

Upon my visit it became no secret that I was Mr. John Ringling, and I was presented with admiration bestowed a king. Management grabbed me as fast as I entered Dreamland. I knew the origins of Luna Park, but the newest attraction was Dreamland. It had just opened. Jesus God, couldn't I see the writing on the wall?   The principle actors were midgets and dwarves, and they were contrasted by lavishly dressed giants.   A fellow named Lewis C. Rosenthal introduced me to the managing director and founder, one Samuel L. Gumpertz. I don't know what it was, but I believe it was the circus in his blood. Whatever it was, we were instantly friends, which we remained until a short while after I had hired him to work full time in one of our shows. In fact Mable and Evie, his wife, became best of friends in New York, and they were frequent guests at our home in Alpine. They even once accompanied us on a trip across the country to our ranch in Montana. But it was after we put on the Big One that they were to move to Sarasota, and we would all become close as peas in a pod. In fact, even to this day, after all that's happened, I still appreciate Sam. Hell, I love the guy even though I hate his guts for what he just did to me. He had no choice and I had no choice. I guess it was just business. The problem being that this business was the life blood of my family. Now that I look back on what happened, it all becomes so clear. He was the little fellow, and had lined up and picked out the giants. I was a giant. Now I'm the little midget and he's the giant!

Sam has been working by my side for years as a contractor and not a full time employee of the show. But knowing his past helped me to pull my plan together and acquire more than The Greatest Show On Earth – I would become the Greatest Showman On Earth.

It was early February 1929, and I took the Jomar to New York. These days the Jomar was looking the less for wear, but it always gave me a thrill to ride in my own style. The show was wrapping up loose ends in Sarasota at the Barn, only its second year to home run in the new winter quarters. Acts were still coming, many had been picked by Sam. You might say that Sarasota was awash with acts arriving day by day. If there was any place that circus was born, it was always winter quarters just before opening day. It was the grand Spec of Specs. It was better than Baraboo. I wished Charley could have seen it. Nothing like it. Acts got off the cars and came in full dress ready to play. The circus welcomed them like long lost cousins. Sometimes they really were. It was also Sam's idea to create a circus community in Sarasota. It was a wise public relations move, and Sam was good at thinking on his feet and making press people jump. Sam and I would miss some of the big comings and goings in Sarasota, regretfully, because that's part of what gets the show all shined up – makes it ready for one grand entry on opening night.

We arrived in New York, and the telegram crumpled in my coat pocket was one that made my blood boil:

"john urgent meeting in new york board at garden wants boxing on friday nights april 1930 season circus can open saturday   board meeting thursday 14 february usual time expect your attendance = bill"

For a time I steamed over the whole bit. Why the hell didn't he just call? Was it that I kept missing board meetings? I wanted off anyhow – too many boards, too many companies, not enough time. Mable had helped me calm down. I took Sam along as he was my new Assistant Managing Director. Hell, someone had to calm my nerves. Mable had spent considerable time in the autumn of '28 with physicians, all of whom had recommended a restful winter in Sarasota. Her diabetes had damaged her kidneys, and she was occasionally prone to bouts of pain and fatigue. Three days on the Jomar would have caused her agony, so she stayed behind. Besides, New York in winter was not her favorite place, but entertaining and volunteering in Sarasota was. Anyway, she had come down with pneumonia the year prior, while we were in Europe. That was really our last art buying trip.

We arrived in New York on the twelfth of February, and I made my presence known to Bill Carey, my former friend and colleague who was now president elect of the board of Madison Square Garden. Calling from my apartment on 5th Avenue, I reached Bill.

"Bill, John Ringling. What's all this ab..."

"John, this meeting is one you can't miss." I took my time at getting to some of the meetings. In fact, I couldn't recall when last I'd been at a board meeting for the Garden. Hell, I figured they could wait for me.

"What the fuck is up Bill?" I demanded raising my voice. "You know Ringling always plays Friday nights in April. It's God damn *family night!* We have ever since the Big..."

"John, the board has other ideas and..."

"Other ideas! Who the fuck, what in hell's goin' on there?"

"Be at the meeting at 10:00 a.m. sharp John – okay pal?"

I felt sick. Sam was there. He took one look at me and poured me a whisky. Neat. I drank it all, and I saw that he could tell my hands were shaking. I didn't like letting on to Sam in any way that showed I wasn't the strong man that he'd come to know. In hindsight, I guess Sam had lost faith in me years back. And why not? I had made some blunders. My attention had been on other business and he knew it. Sam had been, in some ways, a part of our enterprise when Charley and me had struck it big, really big. I knew Sam even before we bought out Bailey. Even though Sam and I always worked our own shows, we were inseparable, like two fellas almost as close as me and Charley. The day that Otto died, Sam was the first person I telephoned. When Al died and when Alf died, it was Sam who wrote their obits. Shit, Sam Gumpertz was the best damn publicist I ever knew. Better than Alf and Charley. So here we were, me and Sam, in my apartment, and I had to tell Sam the truth.

"They want to run a boxing match on opening night next year." My hands were still shaking. I kept looking at that glass, and I swear I just wanted to throw it as at hard as I could against the wall.

"What d'ya mean 'they,' John, who?" Sam poured himself a drink. He drank a little, but he was the kind of guy who could nurse a glass all night. Before I could answer, half the glass went down in one swallow. I could see the concern on his face. I never saw him drink like that in the twenty some years I knew him.

"Well, you know Bill Carey," I explained, "he's the chair elect. Everyone knows Bill is as big a boxing fan as they come."

"John, there's no bigger fan of boxing than you," he paused and looked down, "well, maybe Tex was."

"Shit Sam, opening night for the circus," I was almost whining. "Friday is family night. It's a God damn tradition. If my brothers were alive this'd kill 'em." Sam put his hand on my shoulder. I was still shaking and didn't want him to know, so I turned and walked toward the other side of the room.

"We'll find a way to stop the board from..."

"Damn right we will Sam!" I was yelling and I could feel the blood rushing to my face. "Every damn one of 'em owes us Ringlings a debt of gratitude! Why we built the fuckin' Garden, every inch of it with our own family sweat and blood!" Of course, I was merely a player in Tex Rickard's Garden, but I always thought I was a major force. I realized I wasn't even talking to Sam any more. It was like all the boys were there, and I was talking to them, and they were hanging on my every word. But it was Sam Gumpertz there, and when I realized it, I was sort of embarrassed. I shut up and so did Sam. We stood there for a moment, speechless. I stood remembering, just three years earlier how Tex and I had finished the new Garden in just eight months. It was bigger and better than the old one. Without that ominous tower.

Sam paced around a while. We didn't say a word. I poured myself another drink. It went down like warm candy and I felt better. After about a minute Sam spoke, "It's like this, John," he began, pacing. He took a long drink from the glass and turned back, continuing, "You have to go in there like you have a counter plan. If they say no show, you have to have a way to take their show away." I had no idea what the fuck he was talking about. I didn't think he did either. I never felt so stuck.

"Sam, let's not talk about it any more tonight." I really meant it. I just wanted to be in New York. I loved the town. Nothing like it. "Let's get out and get a big fat juicy steak. Let's give it some time, kind of let it sink in a bit."

We agreed to relax and take in our town, go to the old haunts and let business play itself out. I figured time and a night on the town would have a way of fixing things. For the first time in a long while there was no other business on my mind. No real estate, no hotel deals, no oil wells, no trains, and especially no suits or creditors after their share. Hell, we were bound to run into something.

We went to the Lambs Club, only to be met by the doorman to say that most of the club was closed. Disappointed, we moved on. The rest of night went off without incident. Steak at the Ritz; then we went out for a few drinks. It was eerie. I didn't run into a single fellow that I knew, except porters and wait staff. It was like all the old business had left town. Me and Sam stayed out late, visiting the old places and having drinks. So many restaurants were closed. If they couldn't serve, they went dark. It was easy however to find a speakeasy and get a drink. I never saw anyone I knew – well. It was like I kept running into the old number two guys. I felt like a ghost.

Morning came and went, and when I arose I found Sam on the phone. He seemed like a fellow hot on the action, closing deals maybe, or making some sort of headway with opening avenues. It was two in the afternoon when my usual coffee, fruit, and rolls arrived. It was hard to eat citrus in New York. Just two days earlier I had eaten the best from our own plantation in Sarasota. Just the same, my staff always tried to do their best. Sam refused to eat and I could tell he had been up for hours. After a grapefruit and two coffees, I ate my usual. I had a plate of hash with a steak on top. I made my morning constitutional. Sam knew how to wait for me. It was three in the afternoon before we really spoke.

"It's like this, John." He glanced around nervously, almost as if he didn't want to tell me, "The whole thing is being spearheaded by Carey."

"Son of a bitch!" I exploded. "What a fuckin' traitor. He and I go way back, Sam, way back."

"I know John and I don't like being the one to have to..."

"Hell, what are we gonna do?"

"I got an idea." He proceeded to tell me what he thought was going to happen. "Most of the board is going to turn against you, no matter what you say. They already made up their minds. Hell, with the chair pushing the vote and money to back it, then you can see where this is going. They already did the math. Boxing is worth more to the Garden than the circus." I listened to Sam, because he spoke like a man who had figured something out. He had dug back into his past with the American Circus Corporation.

"Both Jerry Mugivan and Bert Bowers are in town. I know they might be willing to sell."

"Sell shit Sam, I don't have any money. What with the land deals gone south and all my holdings being in rail, oil, and timber, and there's been a glut of inventory of everything. All I got is the circus, and it ain't worth six million.

"The ACC isn't really worth six million. That was a fix. I have reason to believe it's all worth less than three."

"Why now? Why would I want to buy the ACC?"

"They're trying to shut you out John. These guys are greedy. They smell bottom dollar, and they want every last one of 'em."

I reached over and snipped the tip of a smoke and played with the cigar for a moment. I was sizing up what Sam was trying to tell me. I lit it and, turning it, passed my gaze back and forth between Sam and the smoke.

"Go on."

"This is the new way," he continued, these new corporations – they don't care about people any more. They are in business for that bottom line. Money for shareholders, John." Sam was up and pacing. He walked toward the wall and then turned sharply.

"Ringling Brothers and Barnum and Bailey doesn't need the Garden. You can play the Coliseum next year."

"Sam, for God's sake, that's Brooklyn!"

"Yeah, Brooklyn. It's open and they'll hold it for you." He explained it all, and I realize he had been scheming. "Meanwhile," Sam continued, "there's no other shows outside of ACC or us who can manage the Garden. They'll be screwed at their own game. They'll be left with boxing and nothing."

We developed a plan for business as usual. It had to run awful smooth. I had Friday with Mugivan and Saturday with the bankers. I would show up late for the board meeting and act like it was business as usual. I'd make my case and give 'em one more chance, but if they crossed me I'd just walk out. Yeah, we'd show those bastards.

That night we dined at Tucci's Delmonico. It wasn't the original Delmonico's I liked at 5th, but since prohibition, Tucci's opened a new Delmonico's on Beaver Street. This was no speakeasy, but it had private dining rooms, and since Jimmy Walker dined there with his girl Betty Compton, it was no problem to keep things under wraps. As we arrived and the driver opened the door, a limo pulled up behind ours, and there they were, Mayor Jimmy Walker and his mistress, Betty. God she was something. As she slipped out the door she spied me eyeing her gams, and they were beautiful enough that I could feel it below my gut. Jimmy was out before I could say a word, and we were face to face.

"John Ringling, this is a surprise. Didn't know you were in town."

"Business calls Jimmy, business."

"I heard rumblings about something at the Garden, too bad." This pissed me off, and I wanted to spill the story, but I held back.

"It's nothing Jimmy. Me and Sam will take care of it tomorrow."

"Hey there Gumpertz. Back in the old neighborhood – huh? Say, You know Miss Betty, don'tcha?"

"Why sure." I shook her hand. It was thin, small, and something pretty. I knew she could feel me.

"Why don't you two fellows join us?" Jimmy said, motioning toward the inside and looking about nervously. "We've a private party going in the back." He was flanked by a bodyguard and another behind. Times were dangerous, and the mayor of New York was involved with people in the shadows. We acquiesced and inside were escorted to a small room where two couples already sat at a table large enough for ten. I had never met the other two gentlemen. Me and Sam were introduced to Charley Stinton and another fellow I can't recall, but he seemed like one of those old cronies of Arnold Rothstein, the big fellow uptown. The girls only had first names, so I knew they weren't Mrs. The whiskey was the best in New York, no moonshine rye, but the good stuff. Jimmy, some called him "Beau James," only had the best. Tucci's steaks were never as good as the old Delmonicos, but they must have reserved the best for Jimmy and his guests. There were none better. About one bite into my steak I felt something warm against my leg. I knew in an instant. Betty was across from me and Jimmy at the head on my left. He was as much a gangster as his associates, like the former Rothstein or Jack "Legs" Diamond. Diamond had moved out of the city and gone up to Albany since Rothstein had been murdered. My money came from clean sources, but the drink was behind Jimmy's bank accounts, and so were the dark men that ran the trade. Betty, all of twenty three years old, wanted me. It felt good, but the last thing I wanted was for Mayor Jimmy Walker, the man connected to every gangster in New York, to know I had eyes for his gal or she for me. Just the same, me being sixty two and garnering the attention of a pretty young show girl made me feel good.

Jimmy, cigar in hand, turned to me out of the blue, "So you went ahead and started your museum in Florida." He was leaning in and didn't seem too pleased about it. "I told you we could have done something big here in New York."

"Jimmy," I responded, "next time you come to Sarasota, you will join Mable and I in our home, and I'll show you what we're up to – a personal tour." His tone lightened and he seemed less aggressive.

"I would like that," he said, "my last trip was only on the east coast, and I missed Sarasota. That opening party you threw in December 1926 was astounding." He referred to the opening of Ca' d'Zan, a bittersweet moment. Mable and I had forged ahead even though I was in shock after the sudden and unexpected death of Charley. Walker kept going on, talking about our home and the formal events of that weekend, but Betty kept pushing her shoeless foot into my thy. Suddenly, a fellow came through the door, I think it was one of those two bodyguards, and whispered in Jimmy's ear. His reaction was sudden and his posture changed abruptly.

"Friends, I have urgent business to attend to."   Dropping his napkin, he stood up and glanced at Betty.

"But Sweetie, the night is young," she pleaded with Jimmy to let her stay. Her beautiful gaze and dazzling costume overwhelmed me, and I guess it got the best of Jimmy.

"John, would you and Mr. Gumpertz do the honor of showing my gal a good night on the town?" His timing was fortuitous. I was most uncomfortable, but not wanting to let on to what had just transpired between me and Betty, I submitted. I was still dazed by Betty's actions, me being old enough to be her father. "Beau James" Jimmy Walker was forty and handsome, kind of mean, but handsome just the same.

"By all means, Jimmy. We'll take good care of her." I was nervous but concealed it, I hoped. "Thought we might go over to The Casino." Walker paused and gave me a good stare.

"Glad you're the man, Ringling," he said and reached out and shook my hand. At that moment I was not feeling myself but stood up and maintained some sense of civility. Jimmy left with a small entourage of men who had been waiting outside the private room. God knows what was coming, but I wanted no part of it. I had a feeling, but then again I'd seen too many things dark in the prohibition years in New York. I kept my dealings with Jimmy and his like in a manner that suited my business, not his. Being mayor of New York, he could get things done, especially for the show, and the Garden. The closest I ever got to his other business was a little purchase I made of some three hundred cases of fine whiskey, which were stored in my apartment and always gave me a feeling of security. Years later they would play a role in how I felt about my nephew, that little shit who bore my namesake. But then it would just be a part of how I felt about him; there would be other things, bad things he did to me.

At two in the morning at The Casino I noticed Sam was looking like a school child. He couldn't hold his liquor anyhow. Before I knew what was happening, I saw Sam with his coat on, hat and gloves in hand, go out the door. I had already danced half a dozen dances with Betty. I was well aware of the spectacle we were becoming and offered to take her home. It was in my limo where it happened. I don't think it started with me. We hit a pothole, and the car lunged in such a way that she was just in my arms. It was as if we had been waiting for it to happen. I don't know, maybe it was the drink, maybe her perfume. There was half the city to go to get to her home in Brooklyn, and before I knew it my hands were in her clothes and hers in mine. Her clothes were easy. It didn't take long before everything was loose. I had not felt the wet warm mound of another woman in years, since the redhead. I was faithful to Mable. At least I tried. This was exciting, wrong and alluring, and I went further. We necked and touched, and I tell you half our clothes were loosed by the time we were crossing the Brooklyn Bridge. The light and shadows of the bridge washed over her body again and again as her blouse was open and her brazier unpinned. The shadows made a play across her young breasts, and it took my breath away. Her nipples swelled and something rose up inside me. I had to go further. It wouldn't stop inside me. I was young again. Like the days me and Mable first had each other some twenty five years ago. I thought about Mable. Then, all at once I caught my senses. We never consummated anything; I mean it wasn't all the way, but by the time the limo stopped outside her place, we might as well have.

"I can't!" I proclaimed as I pulled myself upright in the seat. "I mean, my wife. I'm faithful, we never..." I whispered and held her shoulders. God I wanted to go at her again, but I didn't. I just looked into her eyes. I intended to convey a feeling of really caring – I actually did really care, and I think she felt it. I don't know, I was confused. She touched my lips then brought my fingers to her lips and kissed them and consoled me.

"Never, not a word, ever." The way she said it I realized it was also for my protection. God knows what would have happened if Jimmy Walker found out I almost screwed his mistress. As she left the limo, the driver seeing her to the door, me knowing I shouldn't, couldn't, I was overtaken by a sense of guilt. Mable. Shit what have I done? It's okay, we didn't, I mean I didn't... oh what difference did it make? My driver brought me home. I was silent. Sick to my stomach. Frozen. What had I done? Somehow I feared that Mable would know. I could never hide this from her. I knew she knew me, everything in my face, you know like she could read me, my thoughts, my actions. It'd always been that way between us. As we got older, we became more of one person. I felt sick.

Escorted to my apartment, I told the help to leave me be. This was unusual because I always let them take my things. Sam was asleep in his room, and the place was quiet. I walked to the washroom and drew a bath and looked in the mirror. I hated what I saw. There was an old man, fat, weak, a cheat. Was I a failure? My word was shit, and I couldn't hide it in my face. My eyes saw everything and concealed nothing. I vomited. I looked in the mirror and vomited again. I had gone so many years being faithful, and in one instant I screwed up. It had been seven years since the night with the redhead, and I'd promised I would never do it again.

Thursday was different than other mornings. For one thing, it was morning when Sam woke me.

"Sorry John, I know it's early, but we've got to give them the impression that you intended to be on time, even though you're going to be late. Your breakfast is waiting." Sam and I didn't really speak for almost an hour, until after breakfast and I finished my routine. As I returned to the parlor, Sam was sipping his coffee and eyeing me. I made believe I didn't notice and was busy looking at the library. Then I heard his cup on the saucer.

"You were good last night – weren't you John?" It was more than suspicious, damn it! He knew.

"I didn't screw Betty Compton, if that's what your asking."

"Well," he said, looking me up and down, studying me like he didn't trust me, "the two of you were dancing up a storm. I haven't seen you like that since Evie and I first visited you and Mable in Sarasota. I didn't know you had it."

"Shit Sam!" Blood rushed into my head and my voice was loud and angry, "I told you we didn't..."

"I believe you John. It's plain to see, you are faithful to your lovely bride." Sam was smiling, and I think he did believe me. After all, I told the truth. I didn't screw Betty Compton. I never claimed, however, that I had remained faithful to Mable. I felt it again. I might vomit. My coffee was still on the valet, mostly empty. I picked it up and drank what I could, sipping it. Tepid coffee. I felt better. Then I moved the conversation on to the business at hand.

"Alright Sam, let's get to work." We laid out our plan and went over it. I would enter the board meeting late. There was nothing strange about that. I would act like there was nothing wrong, just a little smug. Then they would inform me that they had already decided on boxing, and Ringling could show on Saturdays and the rest of the week but no Friday shows. That's when I would say little more than "Alright gentlemen, have it your way." I wouldn't let on that I have a deal in the works. I would just let 'em think they were in charge. They'd think they had the upper hand.

I entered the board meeting, as planned, over half an hour late. Everyone was there except for my vacant seat and my old friend Tex Rickard. Tex had died in Miami while promoting a boxing match in January. The cigar smoke was so thick it burned my eyes. I stared across at the absence of my friend and the league of men set against me, most of whom wouldn't look up at me or greet me. I looked away. In Tex's seat was William Carey, president elect; then there was Bernie Gimbel, and Jimmy Bush, who wouldn't even look up but had a smirk on his face as he rolled a cigar in his fingers. I wanted to smack that smirk off his head. And John, my old friend John Hammond, one of New York's most powerful financiers and an inventor of machines like radios and stuff that would one day take the world's eyes off our amusements. RCA they called his company. Bill Carey motioned me toward the seat, glancing up and not smiling.

"Take a seat John." I froze.

"What's the deal gentlemen?" I had forgotten the plan, and the blood was pushing through my veins so hard I could hear my own heart. "What ain't nobody saying here?" Everyone but Bill Carey looked away. I stood there, just to the left of Bill, my coat draped over my left arm, my cane under my right hand, actually using it to steady myself.

"You're late John." Bill looked back at some of the fellows whose eyes shifted nervously. He turned back toward me, "We already took a vote." Then I remembered the plan and felt a little at ease.

"The Greatest Show On Earth will open on Saturday in April 1930, and Friday nights will be reserved for fights." Carey looked away and pushed at his cigar. He seemed like he was waiting for me to explode. Maybe then he would have said something mean – cruel. But I never gave him the chance.

"I'm afraid you're mistaken Bill." There was muttering and rumbling and especially from Bush. He was a weasel anyhow.

"The Greatest Show On Earth can play Friday matinee," Carey went on to appease me, "but will have to be out by 7:00 p.m." This seemed to be their final offer.

"Ringling Brothers and Barnum and Bailey will not play the Garden in 1930!" I responded with anger in my voice. Bush muttered something more under his breath. I think he said something like they'd get some other show. But before I could decipher it, Bill Carey piped in, "Then, John, we've a back up plan. The American Circus Corporation has already agreed to supply us a show." I turned toward Bill and acted surprised, but this was the plan and I had expected it. I spoke the last words I would ever say to them fellas, "Okay then boys, have it your way. I hereby resign from the board of directors of Madison Square Garden." With that I turned, shaking, and walked out. Sam was waiting downstairs. Two managers of the Garden were talking to him, and I found it remotely suspicious. It seemed somehow that they were talking about me as I walked up.

"How'd it go John?"

"Let's get the fuck out of here Sam." I kept walking and he had to move quickly to catch up to me. We got into the limo, and I told the driver just to drive. Sam and I said nothing for five minutes, and I knew he was waiting for me to tell.

Over a couple drinks we covered everything. Including the next steps. It was all set for me to meet Jeremiah Mugivan. Bowers and Ballard would let Mugivan speak on their behalf. Sam thought the commonly acknowledged value of the American Circus Corporation was inflated – grossly. Just a year earlier *Billboard* had reported it had an estimated value close to six million. Less than a year ago I went to the Midwest and had a sit down with all three of them, and they told me that it was worth six million but would entertain an offer. A few years earlier Charley had talked to all three of them. They said they would sell us the entire lot for three and a half million, if Charley would allow the Ringling name to vanish when the last of us brothers died. They were out of their fucking minds. Charley walked out. There was a time when I could easily swing that kind of money deal over a glass of my private stock and a handshake. Times were different. I didn't have a million. I still had a handshake.

Friday night I met Mugivan at the Park Central. As I was greeted by the doorman and entered, I thought of another time I'd been in this same place: the whole scene came back to me.

It was November 4, 1928. Edward Ballard was in town. He invited me to a game in an apartment at the Park Central. Ballard, who had made his start with a casino in French Lick, Indiana, knew a good card game. In fact rumor had it he would set meetings up between Big Bill Thompson, the Mayor of Chicago, and Al Capone's people, in French Lick, at the casino. I arrived by myself and instructed my driver to wait outside and be ready in case I left early. I never knew how these things would play out, and being that the game was hosted by George McManus, a known cohort of Arnie Rothstein, I figured there might be some characters that I didn't want to associate with. I passed through the door and headed toward the elevator. From somewhere down the hall there were gunshots. The elevator door opened, and before I could step in, Jack "Legs" Diamond walked by from the direction of the gunshots. Without stopping he offered advice in that tinny weasel-like Pittsburgh voice, "I wouldn't stay here if I was you Mr. Ringling." He kept right on moving, and so did I, turning and following behind him toward the door. He was gone fast. When a gangster like that gives you advice to go – you go! My car pulled up and the driver opened my door. It all happened pretty fast. As we drove off I looked back, and coming out the door was Ed Ballard. He was moving fast too. He wasn't alone, either. I didn't recognize the other guy, at the time, but later figured out that he was George "Hump" McManus. No one ever knew who killed Arnie Rothstein. He was the king of New York. Even my own private stock came from Arnie. I didn't associate with him much. My old friend Tex Rickard and Arnie went back a ways. Hell, anyone who liked boxing and played big numbers knew Arnie. Jimmy Walker knew Arnie. Arnold Rothstein would die in a hospital the next day and never tell who shot him. He had played a high stakes game and lost three hundred thousand to Nigger Nate Raymond and a couple other fellows. Nigger Nate was not a nigger. He was a Jew. The whole syndicate was Jews. Hell, Gumpertz was a Jew. Fanny Brice was a Jew, so was Ziegfeld. It scared me for a moment that they were all Jews, but then I remembered how many Jews I liked, people of culture and education. Gumpertz was behind a whole lot of 'em. But I kept thinking about it, Ballard, Gumpertz, Rothstein, Joey Noe, Legs Diamond. The whole thing made my head spin.

So here I was back at the same place. This time I was meeting with Jerry Mugivan, Ed Ballard's partner. Sam was already in the room when I got there. We sat at a game table, and Mugivan's servant got me a drink.

"I guess Sam set everything up," I began the conversation, "and you know what we're talking about."

"John," Jerry said as he became very business like, "we are prepared to offer you the ACC for three million." Now that was way more than Sam had calculated, but I already knew it was within reach. I sipped at my whiskey saying nothing, and you could hear the ringing in the room silence. I puffed my cigar a bit, glanced out the window, and then looked back. Pointing my cigar just a little at Jerry and looking through his eyes I addressed him like I knew something, "You know Jerry, the last time I was here was the night that Arnie Rothstein was shot." Jerry looked stunned. I don't think he expected more than a little bartering.

"What are you saying John?" he asked nervously.

"I'm saying it's funny how what goes around comes around, don't you think?" He was clearly irritated, and nervous.

"What do ya... I mean," Jerry stammered, "what do ya want to pay me for the biggest circus corporation in the world, John?"

"Don't you think it's odd that I was here, at the invitation of your partner, the very night someone shot Arnie Rothstein?" He was stupefied, and I have to admit, I stunned myself because I was playing an odd hand, and I had no idea what I was talking about. "I'll go half what you just said."

"Half! Pfff," Jerry sneered, "this some kind of joke?"

"John," Sam interrupted, "don't you think..."

"Quiet Sam," I snapped at him, taking full control. "I said what I said and I think it's a fair deal. Besides, I think Jerry knows what I'm talking about." I don't know what the hell he knew, but then again I was flying by the seat of my pants. I don't even know why I said it. But I thought maybe, knowing how scandal could hurt the value of a show, especially a circus enterprise, family entertainment, maybe Jerry would get spooked. Jerry stood up from his seat and walked away and looked out the window. I couldn't see his arms as they were wrapped tight in front of him. I noticed from the back of his neck and down to his vest that he was sweating. He didn't have his suit coat on, like he was trying to play it loose and relaxed, and I could see the sweat under his arms. He spoke, but looking out the window.

"So John, what you are saying is that me and my partners might have been involved in the killing of Arnie Rothst..."

"Did you hear me say anything of the sort, Jeremiah?" I cut him off before he could pin me down.

"Well, no, but you inferred..."

"Inferred nothing, you asshole." I was angry as hell and I'm not sure why, but maybe it was because I believed there could be something there, and besides, the air was so thick you could smell the shit sweat running down Jerry's ass. "I'm just saying..." I paused because I didn't know what I was going to say next.

"You know John," Jerry said slowly, "rumor has it your old buddy Rickard was at that game."

"Now you're talking shit!" I spoke up for my friend, "Tex is dead and leave the dead lay." It was common knowledge that Arnie never made it upstairs. Sure Jerry was upset, but I could tell two things: he knew nothing, and he was spooked.

"Let's leave that night behind us, okay?" He went on, "Two million, that's as low as I'll go." Unexpectedly he blurted it out. I knew when a deal was good, and I knew when a man had been pushed all the way to the corner. I remember thinking I'd better grab it while I could.

"Fair deal, Jerry, let's shake on it." He turned around and shook my hand. His hands were clammy, warm. I didn't like the feeling much. Sometimes big money deals didn't feel so good. It always left me wondering. Did he know something I didn't about the murder of Arnie Rothstein? I had only used it as a ruse, to kind of shake things up. No one wants the publicity of circus mixed up with gangsters and murder. Whatever it was, it worked. Sam already had the letter of intent drawn up, and we signed off right there. It was melancholy. No celebration. I didn't even know where I'd come up with that much. I had about three hundred thousand cash, and that was gonna bust my bank. The one cash cow I had was the circus. Ownership and management was part owned by Deedee and part by Aubrey. I couldn't get their blessing on the deal, and besides, they were women. What did they know about running the circus me and my brothers made? I know, Edith had come back on the lot every day, only a year after Charley died, and everyone loved Mrs. Charley. But being the surviving brother it was my show to run. "Mine to nurture and mine to ruin," I thought. Shit, why'd I even think a thought like that?

The news would get out that I got the ACC on the cheap, and Sam and I concocted a story. One that would divert all eyes from the fact that we might have pushed Mugivan to cut a deal for reasons unbefitting The Greatest Show On Earth. Questionable reasons that could look shady. Sam would use his publicity savvy to get the word out that I was calling in an option, that Mugivan had offered it to me at two million a year earlier. Mugivan had let it out that he was prepared to sell in 1928 at a price that would make "Ringling happy." There had been no option on the table. Still, rumors develop over dinners and drinks. Folks talk. Stories grow.

The next day we met with Prudence Bond and Mortgage Company. Sam had arranged the whole thing. These weren't my guys. Hell, my guys had just screwed me over at the board meeting. I knew the Prudence Bond Company from the land office in Florida. They had helped finance a number of sales. In hindsight I recall that Sam had brought this company to Sarasota and got them involved in financing land deals. After the land boom went bust and Owen Burns went bankrupt, they called in his note on his hotel, the El Verona. That crushed Owen. It was the jewel of Sarasota, and he'd named it after his beloved wife. Later, after I bought the El Verona, everyone blamed me for ruining the great Owen Burns. It wasn't my fault. Sometimes we all have to do what we have to do. It's like we all have a role to play. I guess that's how Sam felt.

Although it was Saturday they opened their office for us. After disclosure of my holdings, the two bankers we met with said that the only thing that would be solvent to borrow against would be The Greatest Show On Earth.

"What about the new shows, Hagenbeck-Wallace, Sells-Floto, Buffalo Bill's, Howe's Great London, and the Barnes?" I argued. "These shows, all five of them, are more than double the worth of Ringling Brothers Barnum & Bailey Greatest Show on Earth." They argued that these show's books weren't clear, and the proceedings to account their worth could take months, maybe even a year. I wanted the shows now. I wanted to show Bill and the board who was boss. I mortgaged our show for one million seven hundred thousand dollars. Seems as president I had the authority. In hindsight I don't know if I did. But they sure made it all seem legit.

Sam and I lunched at Lindy's, on the west side, not far from the park. It was unusually quiet for a Saturday. I kept running through the whole thing. This had not been my best trip to The City. I screwed around on Mable. I just pulled our show from next year's opener at the Garden. I mortgaged the show, and I should have felt like the King Of All Circus, which I was. Then I started thinking about Hagenbeck-Wallace and eighty seven actors burned alive in that wreck. I hated that kind of stuff. Now I owned that show. I hoped I had done right. Was it bad luck to buy that show? Maybe I shouldn't of been so hasty. I had to ask Sam. I was feeling less than my strongest, and maybe he could console me.

"Did I make the right decision Sam?" I asked him almost like an insecure schoolboy. "I mean, Hagenbeck-Wallace. All those people burned!" I went on hoping Sam could make me feel better: "Some folks would say that the show's bad luck." Our food arrived and diverted Sam's reply. I could only stare at it. I wondered, given all that was going bad, what else could go wrong?

No sooner than I had that thought the host brought me a phone.

"Call for you Mr. Ringling." With my name being shouted the whole place went silent for a moment. It was a rotary phone and some folks stared. Two waiters held the long chord. Not everyone had rotary phones yet; a lot of 'em were sill two-piece. I held the receiver to my head and heard Deedee's voice, "John, it's Edith, John, can you hear me?"

"Yes Edith, I hear you." The first time she said it, I just stared into the room. People's mouths moved, waiters collected plates, but I could only hear the ringing in my ears.

"John, did you hear me? They want to move her from Sarasota to New York. You'd better come home. Evie is here. You and Sam get home. Come home now John."

"We'll leave right away," I said as I hung up and stared at Sam.

"What's the matter John? You don't look so..."

"It's Mable, Edith says she's dying of some disease called Addison's."

"I know about it. Evie told me, Mable didn't want you..."

"What the fuck Sam?" I shouted and the whole place went silent again. I lowered my voice, "Why didn't you tell me?"

"You know how wives are about secrets. I promised," Sam insisted. "I mean, there was apparently nothing you could do about it."

"You fucker!" I was yelling again.

"No John," Sam went on, "I only just found out about a month and a half ago. After she had pneumonia last fall, she told Evie she had this Addison's thing since the Salome blew up. Seven years. She kept it from you. Please, buddy, I wouldn't of kept a secret from you. I mean, Evie said Mable was going to tell you."

We left almost immediately. I would leave the Jomar in New York. It was quicker to catch the B&O and then change and head south from D.C. I went home, only to bring my dying wife to a New Jersey sanatorium.

Seven
In My Shadow

Sam

Sam and I were friends from about 1904. In fact I met Sam the same year I met Mable. An affable guy, more brains than looks. It was odd, but for much of my life I never had friendships with men except for my brothers. Sure, I worked close with men, and we had friendly business, but most men seemed to always want to one up me. Sam never seemed that way. It made me trust him. As I said earlier, I met him at Dreamland. It was just one year after the awful execution of Topsy the elephant at Luna Park. Sam never worked directly for Luna, but he brought them acts. He also connected them with circus shows like the Forepaugh which sold Topsy to Luna. He had a knack for finding acts. Harry Houdini, Florenz Ziegfeld, the Pinheads, freaks especially. When it came to finding acts in Africa, he went there, found a parade of peoples native to Africa, conned them into coming to New York, and sold the acts to Luna Park. Some folks thought it was like slavery. They built huts near the water front, and the papers wrote about slave camps. I knew better. He sold such acts to Ringling, and these people wanted to sleep on straw and sawdust, ride in the animal cars, and wash in streams. We never argued because they were performers like anyone else and deserved our respect. They were in the sideshow and got an average sideshow pay. Luna Park, however, paid them little respect and little money. Now that I think of it, this could have been Sam's doing. Cheap bastard!

The year after I met Sam, I married Mable. Sam went to jail that year. He had co-produced a play by George Bernard Shaw called *Mrs. Warren's Profession*. It was about an English gal who was only able to make it by becoming a whore – I think. I never read it but heard about it. She then went on to become one of England's great madams and run some famous brothels. Sam and a couple other fellows went to jail for producing the play. He was later acquitted of any wrongdoing. He used it all to his advantage. That side of Sam was like a Ringling, the fact that he could turn any publicity, even the bad kind, into a positive for himself. Alf had that ability.

We liked each other, especially in the friendly business way, right from the start. It was actually before I married Mable that Sam came to me for help. He had brought over a hundred twenty five Somali people who were captained by their warriors, but they were entire families. After the season was over at Dreamland, they didn't want to go home. Sam tried to send them back to Africa, but the U.S.

government ruled against him, and they could stay for a up to a year. They were here legally. A show promoter seized on the opportunity and brought them out to San Francisco for a show. The guy went bust and left these people on the streets of San Francisco to fend for themselves. When Sam got a hold of me, he said they were eating rats they'd catch in the streets. It was a mess. I stepped in. I helped get them on the rails back to New York, and we put them on a steamer to Africa. Sam ended up owing me four thousand for that. He was sloppy. I guess even today, that worries me more than anything about my show. I mean having it in his hands. I worried about what he might do to the show and the family name.

Sam and I didn't become close friends until the year we bought The Greatest Show On Earth. Even though the show's winter quarters were in Bridgeport, Bailey had always kept his offices in New York. After he died, his wife and his attorney tried to keep the show rolling. Bailey had run it ragged in the last years. He really screwed the whole thing up by taking it to Europe. It cost more money than it made, and everything went wrong. He ended up selling shares to London's wealthy elite just so he could pay his debts. Sure there were big stands that made big profits, but he was always playing catch up. By the time he returned to New York, Ringling Brothers' Worlds Greatest Shows was bigger, better, and more profitable. After we closed the deal and signed the paperwork that had taken over a year to process, me and my brothers and the wives went to Delmonico's to celebrate. We dressed for the occasion. Mable was so beautiful. I was proud to be married to a gal like that. She wore a white gown which seemed to light the room when I removed her cape. Her waist so slender I wanted to put my arms around her right on the spot, and her bustle was lacy and airy. Pinned above her breast was a small and unassuming ribbon, dark red, that matched the choker with a coral cherub in the front – a beauty I had given her for her birthday. An angel for an angel. Mable was the most beautiful woman in the room, and I'm certain that's not just my say so. All five of us were there, along with Mable, Edith, and Della. Lou had stayed in Baraboo to help get the new acts in for the 1907 season.

No sooner had we toasted the occasion than Sam Gumpertz and his wife Evie walked in the door. From our table we could look over the whole place.

"Sam!" I shouted across the room as if my words could roll over the tops of everyone's heads.

"John Ringling," he fired back as he pulled Evie across the floor. I could tell he was lowering his voice so as not to continue the attention I had so boldly commanded. Reaching across between Otto and Charley, he shook my hand. "How in the world are you, Ringling?"

There was a familiarity, like long lost pals. I stood to greet him and before you knew it, all of us Ringlings were standing.

"Sam Gumpertz, these are my brothers, the Ringling brothers," and I proceeded to introduce everyone and the three wives. It was a momentous night. The only person, with his wife, at our table who was not a Ringling would one day conspire to take from me everything that we honored that night. But there is one thing I will say for Sam: he paid us the highest of compliments that night when we told him we had just closed the deal on The Greatest Show On Earth. He raised his glass and toasted us.

"It is more than apparent that the Ringling show is already The Greatest Show On Earth." He was likely right too. We had bought our greatest competitor for just over four hundred thousand dollars. The acts were some of the best, but it needed polish and new canvas. The railcars were worn and tired. But we were about to make the best of it and keep it as Barnum and Bailey's Greatest Show On Earth for five or more years, or so we thought.

Evie and Mable had met and were already friends, but that night they were to begin a lifelong friendship. And me and Sam? Well I welcomed him into the bosom of my family. So did my brothers. We later would contract with Sam to find us some of our best acts. Was he already scheming? Or was it the real deal when Al said to him, "I feel like I've known you my whole life. It's like we have found a long lost brother!" Circus has many complexities. It is layer upon layer, kind of like family. It goes back a long way, and its reach can sprawl into tomorrow. That was 1907, almost thirty years ago.

He kept running Dreamland, with its freaks and magnificent sideshow attributes. I paid little attention as I overlooked his odd character. Had I seen more of what he was up to, I might have taken another course. That very next year, Sam brought Bontoc head hunters to his enterprise. One headhunter and his wife had a lovely young child, and they let Sam and Evie traipse all over New York and the boroughs with this four year old girl. It turned out that Sam and Evie wanted to adopt the girl. They offered the parents five thousand dollars for her. Can you imagine? What were they – slave traders? Of course the parents said no. I didn't hear about this until 1933. By then it was too late for me.

Signs popped up all over the place. In 1911 Dreamland burned to the ground, and I helped Sam out again. I loaned him money, and he later bought the contents of the Eden Musee, during the war. It was a wax museum, and while some of it was shocking, some was rather boring. He moved it, along with Ajeeb the automaton chess player, to Coney Island and reopened it. In hindsight I think Sam was playing a chess game. He was after me – The Circus King. Sam made the exhibits about the most horrifying crimes of all time. Crimes of passion, murder, awful things. That was the side of Sam I ignored, and that was the side of Sam I should have kept an eye on.

After 1911, when Mable and I bought the first house in Sarasota, Palms Elysian, Sam and Evie would come visit us every winter. We spent time on the yachts together, went to parties, and Sam and Evie took an interest in social gatherings. Oddly, he never told me they were going to build a house down there. It was late winter of 1919. The war was over. The Volstead Act was in. Mable and I bought the house in Alpine, New Jersey. It was grand, for us. It was a fieldstone, two stories, with sixteen rooms. It had an elevator, which we thought was fun and rode like a toy. It had a barn and servants quarters, and sometimes we would throw parties and have animals from the show in the barn. It was the year we opened the Big One. Sam was not my press agent, but he sure could shake the press. When the show opened in the Garden, some folks called it Big Bertha, but Alf, Charley, and me always called it the Big One. We had parties almost every other night, up in Alpine. The show was magnificent. With over ninety railcars, it was the greatest spectacle in amusement that ever happened. The parade however was a mess. It was over three miles long, snarled up the traffic, and they slapped us with thousands in fines.

When we bought the Alpine house, it had one thing that sold Mable on it – a rose garden! She had actually made her garden in Sarasota in 1913. That was her real rose garden. She loved that place. It gave her peace. But the Alpine house had a rose garden and that was that.

"You are going to buy it?" she said, as we walked over the grounds, "I mean after all, it has a rose garden." We had just walked down the edge of the ridge overlooking Yonkers, Hastings on Hudson, and Dobbs Ferry. It was the most magical view of the Hudson River, and it was all I ever wanted from the place, and all she could talk about was a rose garden. So I bought it. It was our second real home. We named it Gray Crag. That's what the overlook had been called by the realtor. Sam and Evie were there that first March, while the show opened at the Garden in March and April and then played in Brooklyn for the first week of May. Sam said nothing about the house they were building in Sarasota. It was like he was sneaking in. It wasn't until the show was in Albany in May that he told me. When in Albany I would stay at a small place called Keeler's Hotel. I liked it because it was downtown, close to the river on Maiden Lane. It had a great restaurant, Albany style, Dutch. The food was ordinary but good, although I think the management must of thought it extraordinary. I liked the bar. It was men only, and when in Albany I didn't want to be bothered by some gal who thought I was something special on account of the show. It was during the time period when congress was fighting about liquor and the Volstead Act. Sam came up to Albany to discuss working with the press guys. It seemed that they weren't getting the point across about the size of the show. That's what we were selling. The show was going to be back in the east and eventually Connecticut and back in Jersey in July, and we wanted to make a huge splash. It was June 6th, the day before the show opened in Albany. The parade was always easy because the show came over from Schenectady, but it tied up all kinds of traffic. After the show, we moved everything down Arbor Hill at night to Broadway and loaded in the yard at Union Station. This was dangerous, and we had to keep the wagons blocked, moving slowly down Arbor Hill. This was a massive operation, and I wanted to be in on it. Charley was with the show and had been since Utica. I was a step in front.

Sam went on about how the press agents like Ralph Clawson were missing the opportunity. "He just doesn't have the knack, John," Sam complained. "I mean, you have to have vision and get out in front of it, let the news guys feel it."

"Alf has always been the best at it," I said, taking a bite of my steak. "I mean, he always knew everyone." Sam lightly sipped a beer, in his usual light fashion.

"It's a new world," he commented. "I mean, the press is different. People are different, since the war. Business is different."

"So, I think you want the job?" I confronted him, as I didn't really think he did. "You want to be our press agent?"

"No, not really," Sam went on, "but I'd like to be a consultant."

"So Sam, you want to be free agent?" I said poking fun of him, "Shit Sam, you already are a consultant."

"Evie and I built a house in Sarasota," he blurted out, smiling.

"Why the hell didn't you let us know?" I questioned in anger. "Aren't Mable and I your best friends?"

"We wanted it to be a surprise." He quickly fended off my anger, "It's on the Gulfstream Avenue property. I thought you'd be happy about it."

"Well sure Sam," I said, kind of feeling sorry about him. He had this small defeated look, as if his feelings were hurt. I had sold him the property, but he told me he wanted it as an investment. "I'm just surprised, that's all."

"You sold me the property," he said defensively. "I thought you knew."

"Sam, you said you wanted it as an investment," I reminded him.

"Well," he continued, "it is." It was an odd lunch. Sam went back to New York and I stayed in Albany. I wanted to be sure that we could move such a massive parade down that hill in Albany and get it onto the rail. It was only ten days after the show played in Albany that Keeler's had a terrible fire. Then a couple weeks after the fire came the signing of the Volstead Act. Even though it wouldn't go into effect until October, it made for an odd summer. I don't ever recall going back to Albany.

That's how it was with Sam. Stuff came out of nowhere. He would tell me things after the fact. Worse still, my brother Alf, best talker ever in a Ringling show, was so sick he could barely get out of bed to see the show. He was inching toward his death bed, and Sam was inching into my business.

Sam was fast becoming my backseat driver, and I didn't even know it. In 1922 when Tex got in trouble and was accused of rape, it seemed that Sam was there awfully fast. In 1924 I picked up the news in Sarasota. There was an article: "Gumpertz and Ringling Urge New York Giants To Move Spring Training To Sarasota." I never did any such thing. Land sales were already beginning to slow, and it was a good idea, but I never put my name on it. The Giants' manager, a fellow named McGraw, lived next door to Sam and Evie. When I confronted Sam, the four of us were having dinner.

"What the hell is all this about the Giants?"

"It's a good idea, isn't it?" he responded, "I mean, Spring training camp, people like baseball."

"Yeah," I said, a bit annoyed, "but I didn't put my name on it."

"But you would have. Besides, when the opportunity came up, you and Mable were in Italy."

"Why are you being so hard on him?" Evie interrupted. "He did Sarasota a good deed." Then Mable jumped in, "Yeah, John, don't be so hard on Sam." So I was cornered. They all were right, but so was I. He hadn't consulted me. Sam was on my shirt tails. He was opportunistic.

Sam wasn't always so bad. He was often trying to do some good for the greater community of Sarasota. He loved the Boy Scouts. He was always giving them money, and when we opened Winter Quarters in Sarasota, it was Sam's idea to donate the twenty five cent gate to the John Ringling Community Chest. He was always right there in my shadow. It was Sam who suggested that the Prudence Bond Company open an office in Sarasota. He said it would help with land sales. It did, but it was covert. I didn't see it coming. He placed my future adversaries right in my own hometown.

There were many signs I should have seen coming from Sam and what he was up to. In February 1930 I was in New York, getting ready to open the show at the Coliseum. Things were different this year, as the Sells show would open at the Garden and close on Friday nights for boxing. Sure, I owned it, but the Garden had made the contract well before I closed on the American Circus Corporation. Now I had the headache of running two shows, and because Sam had been general manager of the Barnes Show, he had to stay in Sarasota and help get the new acts up and ready at Winter Quarters. My woes were already starting with the Prudence Bond Company, and considering we closed the '29 season early, on account of the stock market crash, we had to draw on cash reserves rather than surplus. Usually after good years, we built things up, made bigger shows, but now it was going to be – make do.

Here I was working my tail off, and Sam was holding lofty and lavish parties on the Zalophus, Mable's and my dream yacht. Sam had told me repeatedly that last year's dry dock didn't finish all that was needed and that the Zalophus needed more work. Being that it was 1929 when he told me all this, and he had helped me go almost two million dollars in debt, it wasn't like I had funds to throw around. Somehow I should have seen it, the way he just used everything that was mine, like he wanted my life. He was worse than my nephew John Ringling North, who seemed like he wanted to be me.

On February 4th, at night, Sam and Evie were holding a party on my yacht and headed south toward Usepa Island where the Collier Inn was located. The Collier, which you could only get to by boat, was the type of place where on any given night you could find the Vanderbilts or Gloria Swanson or any number of the most rich and famous. In route they ran into a stray boat which poked a ten foot gash in the hull and sunk my yacht in twelve feet of water. Besides Sam and Evie, there were a few people who shouldn't have been there. One was Jimmy Walker along with his girlfriend Betty Compton. Several others were some sordid folks in the liquor trade from Jersey City. I got a call from Sam, explaining what had happened and who was on board.

"Tell me good news Sam; it's like a blizzard here in New York."

"Sorry Pal, the news is grim." He paused a long time as if I was going to console him without even hearing the bad news.

"Well, how much worse can anything get?" I asked.

"John, the Zallophus went down."

"What the fuck are you talking about? Is it gone?"

"No, John, it was just off Usepa in twelve feet of water."

"Who was?" I asked, "Was anyone hurt?"

"No one's hurt, but it's bad company," he responded, "I mean they shouldn't have been..."

"Who was it Sam?" I asked angrily. "What are we going to have to cover up now?"

"John, Beau James and Betty were on board and a couple of their business associates from Jersey."

"Oh shit Sam!" I was more woeful than angry. "What the fuck have you done?" Then I switched into action. "You got to get everyone out of there. Get 'em to Tampa and then over to Palm Beach. Split Betty off from Jimmy so it doesn't hit the news that I was harboring the mayor of New York having an affair. Damn, right before we open two shows, in New York no less!"

Sam followed my directions and generally was a good manager. But after he put the seven folks on the train to Palm Beach, a reporter spotted him, Evie, and Betty at the Sarasota station. The news was out about the Zalophus, and the captain had already been interviewed mentioning that there had been ten guests on board including Sam Gumpertz. So this reporter went right after Sam and Evie, and somehow in the midst of the questioning, Evie told the reporter that the young dancer, Betty Compton, was my gal. It hit the news the next day that John Ringling's twenty four year old dancer girlfriend had been on board. It turned out to be a great cover for Jimmy Walker, who was going to be ousted one day anyhow and run off with Betty, but meanwhile it made me look like shit. The oddest thing was what had happened between me and Betty exactly a year ago. It just went round and round in my head; what was Gumpertz doing with these people, on my yacht?

The Bullman

Friday, September 28, 1928. The Al G. Barnes Circus train rolled into Kennedy, Texas, with two separate engines pulling twenty nine cars. It was a sizable enterprise with over one thousand personnel. Amongst the menagerie were numerous elephants, but the most renowned was Black Diamond, the largest Indian elephant bull in captivity. Black Diamond had been with ten different shows, including Gentry Bros, Hugo Bros, and even R.T. Richards, where it was rumored that he had killed a handler. At thirty years of age, he had spent most of his time with one trainer, whom he loved dearly, Homer D. Pritchett, otherwise known as Curley. Curley and his wife were both trainers, she an equestrian and Curley always a bullman. Although Curley was a man, actors often joked that the big old animal had a crush on Curley. Not only would he stomp and get unruly when Curley's wife Audrey was close by, but he was threatening and would not perform, if even her coat was left near the ring. Black Diamond had broken free in several shows and had once knocked over part of the grandstand at Barton and Bailey Combined Shows, injuring seventeen people. The largest and most beautiful Asian elephant in captivity, he was a showpiece. Some shows referred to him as The Traveling Elephant and others as The Runaway Elephant. Whatever they called him, he was well known amongst circus folks and the public.

As Curley and a handler marched Black Diamond down the ramp to chain him for the parade, Curley was aware that this would be their last show together. Audrey already had her bags set for pick up at the station by Eva Speed Donohoo, a Daughter of The Revolution and a member of The United Daughters Of The Confederacy and the Eastern Star. She was best known as the flamboyant society editor of the Houston Post. Eva had inherited her father's plantation in Kerens, Texas, and had hired Curley and Audrey to care for her animals, mostly horses, some cattle, and a few circus stock, including a zebra. Curley and Audrey were tired of traveling with shows and wanted to settle down and enjoy one place, for just enough time to find out if it suited them. Black Diamond was wearing a trunk hobble, a bar of steel across his shortened tusks, which made him less dangerous. It was customary for him to be chained between Tina and Royale, two docile females, which helped keep him under control. As they linked the three together, Curley pulled his hat off, leaned in, and rubbed Black Diamond's cheek, and placed his head against the elephant's.

"I'm gonna miss you more than anyone in this show," he whispered, as his eyes teared up. Sensing the sadness, the elephant, who had his trunk over Curley's shoulder, pulled up and looked at him with an expression of query. Curley reached up and patted Black Diamond and walked away. "Bye Baby," he said as he walked off. The elephant responded with a few sad trumpets and watched as Curley headed over the tracks and back toward the station. He watched closely as his old friend hopped into the rumble seat of a '28 Packard convertible. With the top down, Curley squeezed in next to their suitcases in the rumble seat. The two women were up front, and as they drove off, a cloud of dust raised from under the running boards made the curves of the back of the car look like great wings. Black Diamond watched, studying the driver, Eva Speed Donohoo, the woman who was taking Curley away.

The parade was near perfect with few exceptions. Black Diamond pulled a few times, especially when he spied cars that had no tops like the Packard. This only added to the spectacle, especially with his beautiful rhinestone studded costume which glittered in the pale light of the early fall day. His heart was broken, but his mixed emotions were full of rage.

Saturday, October 12, 1929. One year had passed since that day Black Diamond lost his best friend to a stranger in a convertible car. It was a beautiful day in Corsicana, Texas, as the Al G. Barnes Circus train rolled to a stop. The morning light was pale and the air crisp with hints of autumn. As the train slowly clanged past the station to the working lot, Curley Pritchett followed, walking slowly and knowing which car was his to greet. As it hissed to a stop and performers, handlers, and razorbacks appeared, you could hear the different shouts of "Curley!" Excited folks surrounded him, each wanting to be the one most close to the old "family member" and each seeming to be the very best of old friends. From inside the elephant car you could here it. It made all the other animals sing. Black Diamond was trumpeting, calling his old friend.

As the cars were opened and the animals appeared, the streets were bottlenecked full with passenger cars, trucks, and horse drawn wagons, and most of all, the hundreds of spectators, each wanting to see the parade before it becomes a parade. Bullman Mike Thompson, working with razorbacks and handlers, moved the first three elephants down the ramp and chained them in place. Then came Black Diamond. As he came down the bull ramp he all but forgot his handlers, nearly knocking them down, let out a short blast and headed straight for Curley. The huge bull, with tears in his eyes, placed his head near Curley who huggingly put his arm around the underside of Black Diamond's neck, and the two embraced. The unchained elephant, emotional, tears in his eyes, looked over the shoulder of his old friend, and there, honking, in the crowd of people and automobiles was the monster of a car and the awful woman who a year earlier had taken his friend away. Roof down, glistening gold tan, there it was and the sound, a trumpet of its own, calling. Black Diamond, now hugging Curley with his trunk, tightened his grip and made his focus on that woman. He threw Curley eighteen feet behind and over his head, where Curley landed atop the elephant car and bounced over the far side. The elephant bolted in a gallop. The crowds backed away and parted, opening a path for the charging beast, and Eva could see the ferocity bearing down on her. As her foot slipped from the clutch, the car stalled, and she went over the passenger side away from the beast. Black Diamond reached over the car, pulled her back with his trunk, and threw her to the ground. By this time there were over a dozen performers trying for the chains which were dangerously flailing in the air. Curley had pulled himself up and come across from the other side of the train, his arm fractured and bleeding; he ran toward the horror and was trying to get the elephant. Black Diamond head butted the car and pushed it sideways onto Eva. It rolled back and several roustabouts grabbed her, pulling her to safety, but again the elephant pulled her away and threw her to the ground and turned his hind quarters toward the circus men, kicking one and sending him flying. He pushed on another car and the driver jumped out running across the street. The car was a hard top and rolled over Eva and stayed on top of her. He pushed it away, and as she was still moving, several people again grabbed and pulled her, but the elephant grabbed hold and pushed her down on the ground. By the time Curley and two handlers chained Black Diamond to Tina, Eva Donohoo's skull had been crushed.

Black Clouds

I was in New York. I had come up in the last week of September after leaving the show in Beaumont, Texas. Texas was good to me, as I was still considered an oilman. I had dined with Governor Dan Moody in Austin on the 24th. Governor and Mrs. Moody had a dinner for me, and everyone was kind and consoling me over Mable's passing. It had been the hardest summer of my life. I visited the show in Beaumont on the 25th and then hitched the Jomar to the A,T& SF and headed east. I had to finish the paperwork on ownership of the new American Circus Corporation. On September 12th, I signed off on the final ownership, including the Al G. Barnes Circus. It was one month later that I received a call from Dan Moody.

"John, Dan Moody."

"Well Dan, what do I owe the..."

"Bad news John," he interrupted, "one of your elephants on your new circus killed someone." I knew immediately that it had to be Black Diamond, as the Barnes was the only show in Texas at that time and the Big One was in Columbia, South Carolina.

"Was it Black Diamond, Dan?"

"Yes John, and it's all over the newspapers. It was in front of hundreds of people. John, you have to destroy the animal." I didn't speak. Killing an animal was bad and killing an elephant was like shooting family. There was nothing sadder to me and my family. Now I had to take it all by myself. Moody was continuing to talk, and the words were rolling by like background noise.

"We can have our people do it, but..."

"God no, Dan, we have to take care of this ourselves. Shit! I just signed the final paperwork on the Al G. Barnes Circus. I've only owned it a month!"

"I'm sorry John."

"Who was it Dan?"

"A gal named Eva Speed Donohoo. She was high profile, the society editor of the Houston Post."

I assured Governor Moody we would take care of it. It was generally the law, if an animal killed someone, the animal had to be put down. In some states the owners could go to prison, and in many states the authorities could just come in and seize or kill the animal on the spot. As elephants were part of the larger family of circus, it had to be done humanely and had to be done by us. I couldn't help but wonder, why hadn't Sam called me? He was general manager of the show. I did what I had to do; sad as I felt, this was my responsibility. When I called Sam in Texas there was no answer. Finally he called me.

"John, Sam." He said abruptly as I answered the phone.

"Where the fuck have you been?"

"I was out," he defended himself, "meeting with officials."

"You should have called me right away."

"What do you mean?" He was again defensive, "Why are you..."

"The elephant, you should have told..."

"You know about it?" he questioned.

"Of course I know, Sam, I just got off the phone with Governor Moody."

"I'm sorry John," he apologized and went on, "I was trying to take care of stuff before I called you."

"Next time," I began to lecture him, "anytime anything big, or bad, happens on my show, I wanta hear about it from you first. You understand Sam?"

"Yes, John," he answered in retreat. "You'll be the first to know anything that's going on, I promise."

Sam and I talked with the veterinarian on the Barnes who came up with a plan and tried to feed the elephant cyanide in food, but the strange perfume-like smell of the stuff irritated the elephant's eyes and he wouldn't touch it. The show continued to travel, and we came up with another way. In Kennedy, the very town that the elephant had lost his trainer, the elephant was given a parade call. There, he was chained to three elephants and led into the woods. I was told that he was most obedient. About fifty circus folks went along. All along his march they bid him farewell. He raised his legs on command and allowed the handlers to chain him to a tree. Then, quickly, so as not to give him time to think about it, five hired marksmen appeared and opened fire, shooting him a hundred fifty five times. Every time I think about it, I get choked up.

It also makes me think of Sam, Dreamland, and Coney Island.

The year before it opened, Luna Park, next door, electrocuted the elephant Topsy. Topsy had been with the Forepaugh show for years but was sold to Luna Park. It had killed a trainer with the circus and had killed another in Luna Park. The two were said to be abusive. But the third trainer, well there's no excuse for a man like that, even if he was human, to even be with any show. The God damned son-of-a-bitch fed the elephant a lit cigarette! It went berserk and killed him. Rightfully so. If it happened on our show, he would of hit his head on the side of a fuckin' trestle as he was being red lighted. It became public that Topsy would be killed, and after ideas were tossed around, Thomas Edison came forth and built an electrocution machine. I'm told it died fast, in a blaze. Why the hell they had to do it in public, like a show, I can't figure. Killing any animal actor is sad. But doing it in front of over a thousand spectators - that's criminal! Sam said he had nothing to do with it, and I believed him. But nowadays I don't believe a word he ever told me. This is difficult to talk about and even harder for me to keep talking about Black Diamond. There were a lot of dark clouds rolling in that year. I could feel a storm coming.

Art School

Our desire for art and culture started early. For me it was one thing, for Mable something entirely different. But as time went on we had a meeting of hearts and minds, where we delighted in the beauty, the grandeur, and the sheer celebration of life through art. Life was a gay exploration for us in the early days of marriage. By the time of Stanford White's demise, Mable and I were already entering a new chapter in our lives. The very fact that Stanford White designed the Madison Square Garden tower after the Doges Palace in Italy was pure inspiration for us. Little did we foresee the effect White's architecture would have on us. As art and culture drove Mable and I, so did the Garden drive me. It wasn't all that long after Thaw shot Stanny that both William Vanderbilt and J.P. Morgan deserted the board of Madison Square Garden. It had never been profitable. That's when Tex and I saw our in. We jumped on it. It seemed that life was happening all at once for me and Mable. We had an apartment on 5th Avenue and one near the theater district in Chicago. We were plumb with funds. Between 1906 and 1910 my eyes were on the shows. I was smart enough to recognize what was filling my till. So much of life was educating us very quickly, and we hardly could catch our breath.

At the apartments, the Palms Elysian, and even the ranch in Montana, I was a good lad and held back my propensity for spending.

But where we appeared in our travels, France, Italy, New York, Boston, Kansas City, we played big. Mable liked it as much as me, and with her holding my reins I have to admit that I came off as downright respectable. We dressed in the finest clothes, were met by chauffeurs and footmen, dined on the finest food, and drank the best wines, champagne, and whiskey. If we didn't yet have our great home, we certainly appeared to have come from one. But there's more to the story than just my desire to show off and Mable's dream of a great rose garden.

We were both poor, as children. So poor that Mable ran away for fear that she'd end up a dairy farmer or pig farmer. Me, well, maybe I didn't make it clear earlier. There were eight kids total. By the time Al went off, seven of us were crammed into a couple little spaces. We had to wait in line to use an outhouse, and one time I crapped myself waiting for Otto. It wasn't much better by the time the family moved back to Baraboo, except the outhouse had a double. Some of the other kids in town had complete indoor plumbing. I had to shit alongside a brother, or worse yet Papa! By the time we had an indoor crapper, me and the boys were off for the winters in the Concert Company. Mable left home at fifteen. She married her first husband just to have a roof over her head. She said he was a plumber in Chicago, but I think he worked for the city, in the sewers. So if anyone ever asks why we got to be wanting – so bad – all the goods, the trappings, and the expression of prosperity, it's because we had lived the worst of it.

Mable and I admired what we saw in the culture and wealth of the world. Unspoken, we set out to learn as much of it as possible. We always treated life as an education. If we failed, wouldn't we be the better for it? We failed, flat on our faces sometimes. Sometimes I'd slip up in the company of the Vanderbilts, Palmers, or the Astors, and the likes, and some ill fated garbled shit would slip right off my tongue at the worst possible moment. The ruffian never left me. Around Mable I could be downright charming. When I got loose I swore like a motherfuckin' rogue that got the God damn clap from a two bit whore! But let me sit in the company of my beautiful wife, who could entertain those of the highest social grace, all the while discussing roses, antiques, Rubens and Titians, and I could be the perfect match, equally as eloquent and well versed in the arts.

I actually began my education in the arts before I met Mable. I don't know when it really started, but let me guess that back at age four I showed an interest in art when I wondered "Where is our Louvre in McGregor?" after seeing it in a French book that had circus in it, the night before we all saw that first Dan Rice show. You might say I got a bug for culture as soon as I got one for circus. Although people will argue that the two are separate, I have to disagree. If you

listen to my neighbor Hester, Charley's daughter, she and her brother
Robert are a couple of snobs. Sure – I love opera, although I had to
educate myself before I developed a taste for it. Hester and Robert
seem to think that circus is somehow beneath them. Now that their
mother Edith has pushed me aside, she has inserted little Mr. Opera
Boy into running the circus. He sees it as mere simple amusement,
which in some ways it is, but in other ways it is far more complex. He
and Sam Gumpertz are running it ragged. He is forgetting that
aspects of circus have their roots in dance, theater, comedy and
tragedy, and the finer arts. I'm sure Robert will come around. The
theater of the show will likely slap him awake. Why, we used to have
Shakespearean performances in our shows. We brought culture to
small towns where there was no more than a playhouse and a brothel.
Entertainment and amusement are important, but if you can elevate a
person at the same time, then maybe you've served your life's
purpose. Back in the '90s, after the Columbian Exposition, I really felt
like a whole fellow in Chicago. I began collecting catalogues from
auctions. Estates, art auctions, antique collections – I had my eyes on
them all. I'd get a catalogue, and then I would contact the auction
houses and pay for the catalogue that gave the prices and the
collectors. I figured if the Palmers collected it and paid good money,
then there must be something to it. Then again Bertha Palmer and
her husband collected all that modern art, like Monet and Renoir, and
that didn't appeal to me or Mable. We went in for art like the
Barbizon School or the art that inspired it, like the old masters.
Stanny White's design harkened back to a grander time, and that's
what we liked. In those early years, while Mable and I traveled to
Europe, mostly to garner acts for the shows, we explored auctions and
bought for our two apartments. After we bought the house in Florida,
we collected works for there as well, mostly antiques, jars, tiles, and
goods from estates that were disappearing as a new age seemed to be
shaping itself. A faster, less grandiose age when clothes were
changing, phones were in many homes, folks began buying
automobiles, and every other street corner had a guy making a faster
way to toast bread. By the time Mama died and we bought up The
Greatest Show On Earth, the whole world went like someone had
overwound a watch. We didn't want to lose the romance.

I bought art too, but it was not so good. I bought pieces because I
liked them, and that's always a good reason, but if you like a piece of
shit, it still stinks. It doesn't hurt a collector to educate himself. So we
did. Not only did we start collecting catalogues, but we began
collecting books on art. We immersed ourselves in culture even if we
did make fools of ourselves at times. If a man doesn't have sense
enough to pick himself up from a fall and get back on the horse, then

he never should have ridden in the first place. Mable and I decided to ride and we rode big. It was the year Al died. Mable and I attended an auction of the Davanzati Palace in New York in 1916. It was a Florentine collection which included paintings, ironwork, and antiques. We had marked our catalogue and knew what we wanted and where we wanted it to go. Some for New York and some for Sarasota. We actually did not get everything we wanted, and some of the best pieces were sold to the wealthiest families in the United States. The antiques were collected by the Davizzi family in the 14th century. A decade before the auction, Elia Volpi turned the palace into a museum. I think Mr. Volpi needed funds, and that was to our benefit. I understand the needing funds for a museum and having to sell pieces – even important pieces.

We were able to acquire some major art works, but I think it may have been more as a result of what we missed out on that pushed us to take collecting more seriously. The piece that always tugged on my heart was Raffaello Gualtierotti's Piazza Santa Croce, or more commonly called Football in Florence. Several people bid higher than what I thought it was worth, and it slipped away. Later, it was one of the last pieces I added to my collection in 1931. I had to have it, even then when I had stopped collecting and was thinking about what I could sell in order to get rid of Allied Owners, the corporation put in place by Prudence Bond Company, which put Sam in charge. I just had to have it. In fact it wasn't long after that I had my first stroke. I loved that painting. It was the sheer grandeur of Florence, the spectacle, knights on horseback, and the feeling of chivalry. It was about nobility and the celebration of a Medici wedding. The entire auction and the few pieces we were able to get our hands on all had that air about them. It was the real birth of our love affair with Florence. The war, already on in Europe and soon to drag the United States into it, slowed down many of our acquisitions.

After the Treaty of Versailles and then the Armistice on November 11, 1918, I was to acquire my first Rolls Royce. This was my third car, after the two Pierce Arrows. It was in New York at auction. Built in 1914 for the Czarina of Russia, it never made it to Russia as it was turned back to Great Britain at the border. Deep blue, almost artistic purple, it was a beautiful work of art. To me it was a collectable, and more than ever Mable and I began to see the life well lived as art. I had to have it. We were met by our driver after opening night in Madison Square Garden of the Big One, the first ever Ringling Bros. Barnum & Bailey Greatest Show on Earth. We drove to Alpine in style. There we entertained everyone of importance and some of the top performers from the show. Fashion was artistic and living was art. I remember, after breakfast, Mable and I walked to the edge of the Palisades, where we not only looked across at Yonkers and Hastings but surveyed our world all the way to Manhattan. There was a late winter mist across our faces, and the sun gilded the city from the east.

"There has never been anything so beautiful," Mable said softly. "It's like a dream, John."

"I told you dreams do come true," I said as my hand moved toward hers. I noticed, as I was looking across the magnificence of the Hudson, that even though we were not facing each other, our hands merged together, grasping in a familiar way, and then I said it again, "They do come true." I never felt such gratitude. I think it was then, at that moment, even unspoken, that the museum was born. We would give thanks for the magnificent gift of life itself. We spoke little of our motives for our collecting in those early years. In fact, I don't know if we really knew why we were doing it. At first it was for decorative and artistic enjoyment. Our offices, our two homes, Palms Elysian in Sarasota, and Gray Crag in Alpine, as well as the New York apartment and the Chicago apartment were adorned with odd, unfocussed art and antique collections. By 1922, the year the Salome exploded and Mable suffered such burns, we had storage buildings and warehouses full of uncatalogued collections. Very little, if any of it, would ever end up in the museum. It was after Mable was burned, when I rushed down to Sarasota from New York to be by her side, that we began talking about building our dream home in Sarasota.

That trip from New York to Sarasota was grueling. I took the Jomar but wished I hadn't. The entire east coast was in a blizzard, and by the time we passed through the blizzard, there were howling winds and miserable cold. Every time I had to change trains it took hours and then only to find out they were cancelled. The trip usually took a little more than two days, but I didn't make Sarasota until the evening of February 20th, the third night. Wilson met me and took me to the Palms. Mable was already out of the hospital and in her own bed. My heart was racing, and as we rode down the drive I had my hand on the door handle, which I opened before we stopped and ran in a most undignified manner to get to the door. Tomlinson opened the door and greeted me, "She's alright now Mr. John," he said as I raced by and ran for the stairs. "She's much better, sir."

"Thank you, Tomlinson," I said as I slowed, trying to catch my breath and compose myself. "Is she alone?"

"No sir, Mr. Ringling sir," he answered. "Dr. Ewald is with her presently." I walked the stairs trying to slow my heart and my breath. I didn't want Mable to see me like that. As I reached for the door, it opened before my hand was on it.

"I think we've seen a lot improvement Mrs. Ringling," came from

Ewald as he was exiting our bedroom. Then I heard Mable's voice and a calm came over me.

"Thank you doctor. I feel better even hearing your words."

"Well," Ewald exclaimed as he stepped into the doorway face to face with me, "look who's here."

"John!" Mable called, and her manner reminded me of when we were much younger, "John, is that you?"

"Wait for me," I commanded Ewald and entered the room, nervously, not knowing what I would see. I knew, whatever Mable's appearance, I would do my damnedest to comfort her and not let on. As I stepped in the room I was greatly relieved. Her neck was bandaged, but her face was untouched. Her arms were both heavily bandaged, and her hair was a bit unusual looking as some had been burned and one side was shorter than the other.

"Oh John," she said reaching up.

"Well," I started nervously, "how do I touch you? I mean you certainly need a good squeeze."   She smiled and made childlike fingers to thumbs as if demanding that I take her hands, which were unscathed. I did and smiled at her, so relieved, as it could have been worse. "My darling, I have been out of my mind with worry."

"I'm sorry, John," she began, "it was all my fault."

"Your fault, oh no Mable, it is all my fault. I should have had the boat checked over in December. Oh my God, my darling, you could have been killed!" I teared up. I was always an emotional guy around Mable. "Everyone else" I asked, "where are they?"

"The Wallicks have both departed for New York," Mable answered. "Mrs. Makeaver is still with a nurse, in the south bedroom. The Heppenheimers are here but are fine. She has a few burns."

It turned out that the others only had first and superficial second degree burns. Mable's burns were worse, especially on her arms, although she did not require skin grafts and they all healed well. There were strange discolorations and patches on her arms and sides which came and went over the years.

Over the next few days we made amends with everyone who consoled us as Mable had it the worst. Judge and Mrs. Heppenheimer stayed on a while and spent afternoons outside in the shade as Mrs. Heppenheimer rehabilitated and sat with Mable. Heppenheimer was an awkward fellow and tried to console me with an odd joke.

"Well, Ringling," he said with an edge to his voice, and then paused.

"Yes?"

"Who's your lawyer?" he asked.

"What?" I answered in an irritated fashion.

"Just joking," he chuckled, "just joking. You' re lucky John."

"How's that Ernie?"

"I don't think anyone who was on that boat is going to hire a lawyer." I didn't respond and was on edge that he would even bring it up, especially as he was an appeals court judge.

"There will come a day," he said, "when there will be a lawyer on practically every street corner chasing after every slip, fall, and automobile bump a person gets, and just waiting to make a fortune on the next law suit." It was untimely as there were already suits against me, the Garden, the circus, and now Tex was being charged for rape. I wanted Heppenheimer's friendship for the future, so I never continued the conversation.

After the whole of the event of the Salome burning was over, it was time that Charley and I got the 1922 show on the road and up to New York. Much of the spring was consumed by the work, and on top of it Mable was convalescing. Mable and I spent more time in Alpine that spring. It was the kind of place that could make one reflect on life, the future, and the sheer beauty of its gifts. After we opened in Albany, I came back to Alpine. Sam had triggered something uncomfortable in me when he informed me that he had built a house on the Gulfstream Avenue property. It wasn't that he did it all of a sudden, or that he hadn't told me until it was almost completed. It was just that he was building. I wasn't. Mable and I had the Palms Elysian. Unlike the first house that Charley built in Sarasota, we had worked to make ours artistic, added statuary, and moved the barn out of sight. We began to pursue an avenue of beauty inspired by our trips to Europe, especially those to Italy. But we had never built anything that was just ours. I felt life in the most urgent manner. Mable had nearly lost her life and we were mortal. All my brothers except Charley were gone now. I faced the truth. We would die – when – I did not know, but Mable and I would both – one day – be gone.

We continued on with collecting art, and it became more serious as we became more educated. In fact some of the early things we had in storage should remain there. It is an embarrassment to think that anyone would ever know how awful some of it is. We had sailed to Europe many times and even through Liverpool and traveled to London attending magnificent auctions. We bought little, but studied more. Mable was well again, and we found ourselves happy yet equally unfulfilled in 1923. That's when we began discussions of what we would like to build as a home at the Shell Beach property. We had owned the Palms since 1911 and felt it was really ours since 1913. Here it was ten years later, and Mable had long since fulfilled her dream of having a rose garden. It was larger than most homes in Sarasota. There was something about Mable that made beauty trail behind her and gaze out ahead of her. Maybe it was something in her name; after all, Mable means loveable. I had become consumed by my ideas for Sarasota, the development of planned communities all designed by one architect. I even got Charley involved, and he started a community development of his own. But it was the John Ringling Estates, Incorporated that had me so excited about Sarasota. I teamed up with Owen Burns, and Mable was part of the charter. Owen and I went hog wild, even though everyone tried to pin it all on me. Maybe it's because we put my name up front. Mable used some of our trappings we were buying up in Italy to decorate the real estate office. Boatloads. That's what we brought into Tampa and down to Sarasota, boatloads of antiques and statuary. We were getting better at our purchases, and not everything, it seemed, had to be purchased in Italy. The best art auctions were in London and Germany, and we were soon to figure it out. But without a goal, none of it mattered. In 1923 Mable was fully healed from her burns.

We went to Italy and invited the architect Dwight James Baum to view architecture with us. Ca' d'Zan, my own invented word which the house would be named later, was really Mable's dream. I wanted a grand home to show off in Sarasota which could help entice the wealthy and elite to buy and have winter homes there. My ideas were perhaps overstated and not yet defined. But when Baum met us in Tuscany, Mable, now with a very educated eye, began designing and envisioning something more grand than my imagining. For someone with no formal education, Mable had impeccable taste. Mable wanted several things that Baum could offer. She wanted a home designed for Florida in the winter. It had to appear like a palace and be both reminiscent of the country villas we had visited in Tuscany and also have the appearance and grand scale of Italian Gothic. It took several trips, and by early 1924 Owen Burns broke ground. I got Owen started before he had the blueprints. I had the general footprint of the place and Owen began the foundations. I don't think you are supposed to do it that way. I always say jump and then swim. It usually works out well, as long as you have basic knowledge of how to swim.

An unexpected series of events transpired that led us to Julius Bohler, the Munich based art dealer. We went up to New York in early 1924 to finalize the plans with Baum. Owen was angry that we still had not produced the plans. I had to be in New York for the show. We always opened in New York at the Garden. I had a permanent apartment at the Ritz-Carlton, and I frequently used this as an office and meeting place for things unrelated to the circus. I knew Albert Keller since about 1911. In fact we Ringlings all knew Albert. He was the founder of the Ritz-Carlton Finance Company. He had been the manager of the New York Ritz-Carlton since 1910. He had come over from Germany after managing a number of European hotels. His associations with the rich, famous, and important persons of the world were noteworthy. Mable and I were setting up for a meeting with Dwight Baum at the Ritz when Albert Keller phoned our suite.

"John," he greeted me, "Albert Keller." I had recognized his voice right off. Keller had a sharp voice, spoke English near perfectly, but having grown up with Papa trying to hide his German accent, I could always make out that sharp undertone.

"Albert," I answered, "this place would be lonely were you not in charge."

"Thank you, John Ringling, you always were a charming fellow."

"To what do I owe the pleasure of your call?" I asked.

"John, I would like you and Mable to visit with Clara and I at our suite." Clara was a wonderful gal. Albert and Clara had been married, like Mable and I, elegantly and quickly without a huge celebration. They had only invited a few family members as well as Mable and I. It was 1919 and the show was in the first year of the Big One. Charley and Deedee and Mable and I were in western Massachusetts with the show, and honored as we were, we could not leave the show for an informal wedding. We remained close, and we were already working on the Ritz-Carlton for Longboat Key.

"When would you have us?" I asked, always up for an intimate get together.

"How about this afternoon, say 5:00?"

"Sounds good," I responded, "we'll be there with bells!"

"Oh good, we have something we want to show you."

It was already 2:30, and Mable had been up since morning. I had just finished breakfast, and in our usual fashion we lived in two different parts of the day. However, the afternoon and early evening was a time we often shared in delight. Our meeting with Baum would be the next afternoon, and Mable wanted everything just so. It had been a while since Mable had seen Dwight and Katherine. This would be the only meeting of its type, outside of his firm, but Mable wanted us to review the plans in a more relaxed setting. This was really Mable's project, no matter what we were going to call the house.

At 5:00 we arrived at Alberts and Clara's apartment and were greeted by his butler. Upon entering I saw it immediately, on an easel, across the parlor.

"John and Mable," he reached out to greet us, Clara at his side. I walked right past him and straight up to the painting.

"Thomas Gainsborough," I said and then began to study the painting. It was about four feet by six feet, a river scene, the cool of the shade, some people on a boat and cows wandering to the water. It looked wet and dark, and in the background the world went on with something of people unidentifiable.

"Hello Mable," he shook her hand and Clara and Mable hugged gently.

"It's wonderful," I remarked, "is this what you wanted to show us?"

"Yes," he responded, "the first time I set eyes on a Gainsborough was at an auction in London. You were there. As I recall Mable was not with you."

"It was the autumn of '22," I reminded him. "Mable was recovering from an accident."

"Yes, I recall that she didn't travel with you that year," he said and went on, "Julius Bohler, the art dealer from Munich was there, and you met him for the first time." I searched through my mind putting together a picture of Bohler.

"Oh sure," I recalled, "the fellow with all the knowledge." Mable was now in front of the painting and admiring it.

"He and his wife Regina are in town," Albert explained, "and I have asked him to come over and see the painting and authenticate it."

"Is he credible?" I asked, "I mean can he lend authenticity to paintings." I was thinking about the few works I had bought in London and then had paid, immensely, to have the pieces authenticated, provenance or not. It didn't matter if they were the real thing, if you had enough money. The truth was that these paid certificates of authenticity were always suspect. I didn't like it but as yet had not really begun serious collecting. I was still so deeply involved in building Sarasota. The entire place was an explosion of opportunity that seemed as if, while overflowing, it would never stop. In the streets of Florence I remembered fellows selling gelato from carts. In order to keep it cool they had an endless flow of cold spring water pouring like a fountain over the entire cupboards of the delicious dessert. It seemed endless. That's how life felt. I loved gelato, and I loved ice cream. Life was my dessert.

"John," Albert went on, "Julius is one of the most respected art curators in Europe."

"Well," I said, "I'm going to have to meet him, I mean again. When can I..." at that very instant there was a knock at the door.

"I think," Albert smiled, "you'll be able to meet Julius and Regina now." Within minutes I was carrying on a conversation with the most elegant and eloquent of men, Julius Bohler. Regina and Mable were instant friends. It was as if it was meant to be, and in fact it was. We spent the evening talking art, antiques, collections, and places together, the six of us. We dined downstairs and later enjoyed after dinner drinks at our apartment. This was the beginning for Mable and me. We wouldn't get a direct idea about the museum until the house was well under way, later that year, and we really wouldn't begin discussing it with Julius, whom I later would come to call Lulu, until the following year.

After meeting with Baum the next day, it became apparent to me that this guy wasn't going to pull his punches when it came to spending my money. I had been through it before with him. I had even tried to get him to cut his commission from five percent to four percent. Maybe he didn't get the whole picture. Guys especially could see me coming. They saw the buildings, the projects, the size of the deal, and they smelled riches. Dwight was an alright guy; it was just that he didn't want to cut any corners. He wanted to build without limits. That was okay for Vanderbilt, but I was a fellow who had grown up in a shack. Mable wanted this, and so did I. In fact so did Dwight James Baum. We had all come so far. There was no turning back. This house was going to happen, albeit perhaps a bit of a compromise for everyone.

Mable went back to Sarasota and I stayed in New York. Baum went south as well to work through the project with Owen Burns. I had to get the show off and running, and that was still the heart of my business and Charley's business. Charley was building too. He was donating land for a Sarasota County Courthouse and making plans to build a hotel. There was so much activity in Sarasota it was like a boomtown. I admire Charley's taste. The courthouse was Mediterranean, Italian revival, like our home, designed by Baum. But Charley's house was inspired, in many ways, by Stanford White. It showed in the grand entry, which was reminiscent of White's arch in New York at Washington Square. The home was designed by Clas, Shepard, and Clas of Chicago. It was styled after fine English country manors. It is really quite something, and I regret that near the completion of it I insulted my brother by calling it a "nice little place." It is truly a work of art. Even Hester's house next door, which is more in keeping with the Mediterranean villa idea, is beautiful. I think as we Ringlings have come to our end days, we have made something that we ought to be remembered for.

Although Charley's house was finished before mine, I tried to outdo my brother that fall of 1925, when he came home to see the finish. None of his place was yet decorated by the Marshall Field Company, and Mable and I were still going full out at Ca' d'Zan. I invited Charley and Deedee to lunch, and we had finished the dining room. Very little else was complete, but I wanted to show off. I was always trying to show my big brother up. I'm sorry Charley. I'll always be in your debt. It was your last year, and I made life miserable for you. I think Charley blamed some of what happened to the land boom on me. It was my advertising, circus style, that made such a buying frenzy. When the '26 Florida bank collapse hit, sales in Sarasota slowed to zero. Mable's and my thoughts were already turning to the museum and the art school, and that's all I could talk about. We were off to Europe and back again and working with Julius, buying, buying, and buying. I never stopped to ask much about Charley's life, or his children, Hester and Robert. It seems that Robert was becoming a top voice in opera. Mable forced me to follow opera, and eventually I had developed a taste for it. I think what I really liked was the pomp. It was like circus sophisticate by the educated, the cultured, and the upper class. In 1926, when Charley's house was finished and we had not yet had the dedication for Ca' d'Zan, we had dinner with Charley and Deedee. I couldn't shut up about my acquisitions, the museum we were planning, and how we were talking about hosting opera at our home. It didn't occur to me to talk to Charley and Deedee about Robert and the opera in Chicago. I barely asked. It wasn't until I visited Charley's house in Evanston, after he died, that it all came back to me. He was sick, had lung problems, had a stroke, and what did I do? I kicked him when he was down. Charles Ringling was an artist. He was a classy guy. Not only was he a fine musician, he was the genius of a man who could manage the circus so well that our military studied it in the lead up to the war, and the Kaiser had sent spies to see how he did it. It was done with such flair. Eighty-eight railcars. A city of over one thousand people, with a school, a church which gave services to over a dozen religions, a blacksmith shop, menagerie, a cookhouse and dining tent, a post office, and a barber shop, and all of it unloaded, set up, with two performances, sometimes to as many as thirty thousand people a day, taken down, and moved. The moving was my job, and then it would happen again the next day. Charley was an artist.

By the time Charley died in 1926, Edith hated me. I could feel it. Well, maybe hate is awfully strong language. Maybe, it was just contempt. She knew I loved my brother and I was heartbroken. I was the only brother now – the last one on the lot. As we moved into the 1927 season, it was a monster of a job for me. Sam pushed me hard to move Winter Quarters to Sarasota, which we did in the close of the season. I couldn't be in New York, Bridgeport, and Sarasota. Those years were hard. It was bittersweet. Mable and I were at our stride. Construction of the museum was well underway in 1927, designed by John Phillips who had designed the exterior of the Metropolitan Museum of Art. Much of it was Mable's doing. Mable was elected the first president of the Sarasota Garden Club's Founders Circle that same year. Where I fumbled, my beautiful wife picked up the pieces. She helped work to beautify Sarasota's commons. Everyone loved her.

Me, well where they glorified Mable, they crucified me. Oh, I pretended not to notice. Hell I was going broke faster than ever. I wanted to save Sarasota. I still believed in what it could be. By 1928 we had a circus community, the coming of an art museum, a wreck of a land boom, and promise. That's where they'll get you every time. Promise. Maybe it's all about your word, but promise is all about dreams. I still believed that if you worked hard for a great dream, threw everything you could into it, and never gave up, it could happen. I do believe it will happen – one day. Maybe we can't always control the end.

Mable was named to a Chamber of Commerce panel in late 1927. We hosted celebrities at Ca' d'Zan, such as Ottocar Battik, Ballet Master of the Metropolitan Opera. It was a special time at Mable's house, brief as it was. We held musical celebrations at Ca' d'Zan for her Garden Club membership and the Woman's Club to which she was named director in 1928. We even held public radio programs from Ca' d'Zan, featuring musical performances of the Aeolian Organ in the central court. We wanted to bring the finest of classical music to Sarasota. Mable and I continued working with Julius, or Lulu, as I called him. The museum design was moving along however with great changes. Every day we had to cut something out of it. By 1928 Julius and I were buying some of the last of the collection I wanted for the museum. I never let on how bad things were getting. The art critics were cutting and lashing at me half the time, but I swear I know more than most of those sly bastards. Lulu, Regina, Mable, and I were now best of friends, and somehow Sam and Evie seemed to be moving in their own direction, even though we still enjoyed each other's company. Sarasota felt the depression before the crash of 1929. I remember thinking, "It can't get any worse, and maybe in a few years it'll all pass. Then we'll get the town back on track and we can have our dream and share it with everyone here – like we promised." Meanwhile, Mable was able to keep pace and give so much to the children of Sarasota and Bradenton, especially the Boy Scouts. She held special luncheons and gave out prizes and candy. Even then, Sam was honing in on the Scouts. Once again I hadn't seen it coming and didn't know it had happened until it was over. That's how life is.

By 1929, in February, I was through with most of my collecting. I had collected some of the finest Rubens in the world, Titian, Van Dyck, El Greco, Gainsborough, to name a few. We had over six hundred of the finest Baroque pieces, an indisputably important collection of antiques, the Italian statuary, including the reproduction of Michelangelo's David. Mable and I had read over six hundred books on art and collecting, and we now had amassed a library on art. We were ready to finish the museum and share our dream. But then it was time to get the show off and running, and that's when the board at the Garden threw me a curve ball. They had no interest in the show itself. They were going to put their profits ahead of Ringling Brothers and Family Night. I headed to New York in February with Sam to see if we could head this thing off. Then Mable's kidneys collapsed. By the time I got back to Florida, Mable could hardly speak. She had been one of the lucky few to get insulin in the early years, but she had kept this Addison's disease a secret from me. I contacted doctors in New York through Doc Ewald. It seemed that all the best were there, and even though I knew a trip on the Jomar would be hard on her, I had to take a chance. I got Mable up to New York by late April. Julius had wired me as we kept trying for a trip to Europe. The four of us had talked about it through the winter. We had cut our last trip short as Mable had contracted pneumonia while we were in Italy. On May 18th, I had to send Julius a telegram and tell him I couldn't make it as I had pressing matters to attend to. I had taken Mable out of the hospital and to a sanatorium in New Jersey. I didn't know how to tell my dearest friends that my wife was dying. On June 7th, I cabled them and said that Mable was seriously ill. I didn't want to spoil their plans. On June 8, 1929, Mable died. I didn't know who to tell. I was so alone. I cabled Lulu and Regina. My heart broke into a million little pieces. I was sure I would never smile again. I gave away almost all of my festive clothes, my linen suits and other clothes that reminded me of our fun times.

I couldn't bring myself to carry Mable back to Sarasota. We had always talked about a crypt at the museum, under the David sculpture. We had considerations that it would be odd to have people walking on top of us. The museum was still unfinished. I resolved that this would be a memorial to my beloved wife. After Mable died I was all alone. I mean, my friends consoled me, folks invited me to the usual social gatherings, dinners and such, but it was a lonely time. A time when I had made too many blunders and was hiding a vast array of them from Edith and Aubrey, from Sam and Evie, from the public at large and the social blabbermouths of Sarasota, but never could I hide them from myself. While Sam and Evie wouldn't forgive me for what happened to Mable, Sam was mounting a campaign behind my back, that shit, to take control of what was rightfully mine. Edith and Aubrey were setting the play in motion. Every step I took was to be countered by Edith at the reins, ready to crush my moves without mercy. So, when Dr.Ludd M. Spivey, president of Southern College, approached me about lending the Ringling name to an art school, Edith got word and pounced on it. This was the fifth time in two years he had approached me about it.

Her response to Spivey was direct and obviously pointed at the pained relationship between us: "No Ringling name should be at the forefront of any art school, unless it is otherwise separated by the family to singularly have the name John Ringling, or John and Mable, but do not place the rest of us in his plight to ruin our family heritage." Once again I was being blamed for what was happening to the circus, Sarasota, and the family. They had such strong feelings against me, the museum, and the idea of an art school. For me this was all about Mable. It was cruel of Deedee to say what she had said, but I understand why she would be so angry at me. After all, I had mortgaged the circus and put the whole family on the line. Then I saw my opening and offered Spivey our names, "John and Mable," and they were to choose the name School of Fine and Applied Art of the John and Mable Ringling Art Museum. Spivey and I had talked about this for a long time. In fact it had been a pursuit, like a hunter tracking and stalking wild game. He wanted money, but I didn't let on that I had no money to spare. Mable and I had so wanted this. Funds were tight, but I came up with something to get a little school started at the site of the old Bayhaven Hotel. My position on the founding board of directors was short lived, for as soon as they took my circus and placed Sam in charge, the board decided to rename and charter the school as The Ringling School of Art. It seemed there was a legal right to shorten the name. God, this really pissed Edith off. Before they did, I was invited to speak at the opening. I didn't like making speeches, but things were bad enough, and I had to make right my personage by Sarasota standards. I spoke about Mable, the museum, our years collecting, and our dream of the museum. I mentioned that it would be my hope to one day donate some land at the museum to house part of the college. It all seems like a blur. Then again so did the final years of completing the museum, cutting costs, cutting the dormitories out, and the money, running through my fingers. Where'd it all go? Still I went on. When I spoke, there were some hundred or so benefactors and a terribly small body of students, but plenty of the gimme gimme Sarasota socialites and business people. It made it seem so much bigger. I do remember my closing statements some:

"If any educational institution is to progress, it must be administered intelligently... I know of no other school in America equipped as this one to educate in art... Here I hope a famous school of artists will rise, for though life is short, art is long."

Yes, art is long. Long after the artist, long after the act, if in performance, a memory and a feeling, if a painting, the art itself remains. So it was with this school. My bitter feud with Edith and Aubrey, just beginning, my friendship with Sam ending, and alone, my judgement was without focus. My foothold in the family enterprise was slipping away. In the spring of 1932 when I felt a change coming over me, I had already had a stroke. Sam was now in charge of my show. Deedee and Aubrey had sided with Allied Owners, a Delaware Corporation put in place by the Prudence Bond Company to remove me from any activity in the circus. I was still president, but it was in title only. When the train pulled out for New York, I stood at a distance and watched. There, Deedee, Robert, Aubrey, Sam, and Evie all waved from the back deck of the railcar. I felt so lonely I could have vomited. They rumored, like circus talkers do, that it was because I was ill. The museum was officially opened. I was happy for that. I was able to collect a little extra money from the parking fees. My circus income had been reduced from fifty thousand a year to five thousand. The change that was coming about, in me, was something I couldn't control. From the year after Mable died, the suits started big. Mable's sister Alma sued me. Her sister Darcey and her husband sued and tried to take the home in Alpine. The IRS shafted me, and they haven't stopped hounding me. Creditors came from every direction, and few people seemed to give a shit. Ida was kind to me, and after my Alsatian cook Sophie quit, Ida would cook the Alsatian food I loved. Ida's son Henry, I called him Buddy, was kind to me. His brother Johnny, who reminded me of myself, was a little shyster. But maybe that was good. He was going to need something to get through the pending storm. I had two more strokes and suffered some problems from diabetes myself. Ina Sanders, my nurse, became closer to me than almost anyone.

Salome and the Secret Garden
Excerpts from
The Later Diary of Mable Burton Ringling
1922 -1929

Thursday – March 9 – 1922 – I thought I'd never write a diary again. I feel alone. John went back to New York. He has to be there to be ready to open at the Garden. My burns are healing faster than Doctor Ewald thought they would. The Salome was mine. I ruled the waters off Sarasota from her decks. When she sunk something in me went down with it. Little by little the Ringling Family has gone. Time is so small.

Saturday May 6 – Started Secret Garden today. It is to the North of my Rose Garden. I want a place that no one else will go unless I take them there.

Monday May 15 – John wants me to come up to Alpine. He telephoned from Washington. The doctor says I can go – there is only one burn left unhealed. He says I should be fine. I will leave for Alpine on Wednesday and be there by May 19. John will arrive the morning of May 22 when the show will be in Newark.

Saturday September 23 – John is in Albuquerque. While so far away, this week was a good time to see Doctor Lindsey. Test results came yesterday. He explained the rash and strange colors on my stomach and neck he said it was something called Addison's. He also explained that is what causes me to almost faint when I stand. I am taking some kind of hormone pills – I am not going to tell John.

Tuesday – October 31 – John in Charlotte – home in a few days – end of season. I am glad to be back in Sarasota. The secret garden is coming along beautifully. Have bromides growing.

Monday – December 11 – convinced John can not go to Europe as the convalescing still ongoing. Dizzy spells. See new doctor when John leaves. We talked more about building a house.

Thursday – July 5 – 1923 – John leaving Albany tonight after show and will be here in Alpine. Tomorrow we meet with Thomas and Frank Martin in New York to draw up plans for the new Florida house. I am so excited!

Monday – July 16 – I don't think Martins can be counted on. John thinks he can get a deal – Owen Burns mum about their quality. John in Chicago with show. Doctor changing my medication.

Wednesday – October 10 – John leaving Corsicana, Texas and we will meet in Pensacola on the 12th. Then off to New York and then Europe. New architect – DJ Baum will join us in Italy. This is so exciting.

Monday February 18 – Had dinner last night with Albert and Clara at the RC. Met Julius and Regina Bohler. Talked all night. Much too late for me. John stayed up. Today we are going over plans at RC with Baum. Owen already building at Shell Beach. So excited. Must get back to Florida soon.

Thursday – April 3 – 1924 – Show in Garden – John and I in Alpine. Sailing to Europe next week. Will meet with Baum in Tuscany. More villas and gothic castles to see and consider design.

Thursday – June 19 – I have been with show for over 2 weeks since Bridgeport. Arrived in beautiful Niagara Falls last night. John and I will travel a few days by car and rejoin show at Erie. John angry at razorback who scratched the Rolls. John worked with Tomlinson to rub out scratch.

Friday – June 20 – Buffalo – saw an amazing building today with tile work outside. It's on St Bonaventure Monastery. I saw the same in Italy. John called Dwight and he is coming out here by train to look it over. I am learning so much from my husband on how he gets his hands in everything. He wants the exact price – the size – to know how it's made. We found the tiles were made in Pennsylvania and I will ask Dwight to accompany me to the factory. These will go so well for the house. John wants me to have them make Ca' d'Zan in tile for the name of the house. It's some Venetian dialect of House of John.

Monday September 8 – Lulu and Regina left yesterday. I showed them the secret garden. We had such fun. They have become good friends. It seems like John mentioned our idea of a museum. I thought it was our secret. John called today from Kansas City where the show is. He had bought some bar that closed – says it's a favorite place. He had it in storage. I guess it was one of those places where he was all night while I was sleeping on the Jomar.

Sunday December 21 – Gifts – children in Sarasota. It took two weeks to buy everything. Their faces – so happy!

Friday October 16 – 1925 – House going faster than we thought. Charley and Deedee coming home soon from Evanston

Tuesday February 23 – 1926 – Architect John Phillips building for Ralph Caples. Good design. I want him to design the guest house.

Saturday – May 1 – Lulu and Regina here. John Phillips came back and had wonderful model of museum. John is so excited. It is like the carousel – the golden ring – we all pulled it at once. John should spend more time with Charley and talk about Charley and his endeavors. He is so engrossed in learning about art and makes

Julius tutor him   When he gets going about something you can't make him stop.

Wednesday May 19 – 1926 – Charley and Deedee have celebration at home today. Beautiful music. Such a splendid affair.

Sunday – November 28 – Robert called from Evanston – Charley very sick! John got them a private train car to come home to Sarasota. John worried but tries to hide it.

Friday December 3 – Charley died. Businesses closed – flags at half mast. John heartbroken – but tries to conceal.

Saturday December 4 – John locked himself in bathroom. I put my head to the door. He sobbed for hours. He is crushed. Deedee – angry with John. Charley's death so sudden.

Wednesday December 22 – Julius and Regina arrived – so Did Jimmy Walker, his wife and an entourage. The festivities start tonight. John said he wished Charley could be here and then he got choked up.

Sunday – May 15 – 1927 – I held a tea today. It was a first meeting for a garden club for Sarasota. I want to show everyone how we can make the world more beautiful with flowers. There were thirty four in attendance and several people talked about having garden circles and beautifying store windows. Flowers tell the world – thank you – because we grow them and it gives back something for the eyes and hearts of others. Oh I wish I could say it with words!

Monday – August 9 – Construction starts again on museum. This time John has our Alpine neighbor – Lyman Chase as the builder. I think finally we will get to give something really important to Sarasota. People here are angry with John. They don't understand him. I know his heart is with this place.

Sunday – May 20 – 1928 – Over three hundred people for the afternoon festivities   2 bands – Merly played orchestral and marches. Sam Gumpertz had Boy Scouts parking cars. Ever since John had the affair for Calvin Coolidge we have had non stop parties! I am so tired. I love the people here just the same. Deedee has parties all the time too. Are we running a social circus as Ringlings of Sarasota? Deedee and John have other joint business ventures now. There is tension between them.

Sunday – August 19 –   Sailing for New York tomorrow. I am much better now. Pneumonia is gone from my lungs. St. Moritz was very restful after the Czech spas – they were too much work. Can't hardly wait to see John.

Sunday – October 28 – John scheduled two extra performances right here in Sarasota! He said he did it for the town. I know he did it for me. He was so worried when I got sick in Europe. He worries too much – about me. The show was so beautiful. Five Rings! Lilian Leitzel just wonderful and Codona!! We had dinner with them after the show. The love. It's like John and me. He adores me. I can hardly breathe without him. Yet we spend so much time apart. John is up every night until dawn. I wake up just after dawn. I am glad we have dinner together. We grow more fond of each other as we age.

Wednesday February 6 – 1929 – John and Sam left several days ago for New York. It seems there is some kind of trouble with the Garden. I fell last night. No one knew. I guess I got up too quickly. Going to see the doctor.

Thursday February 14 – I am so tired I can barely write. I wish John was here. Evie wants me to stay at Deedee's. The doctor told me the truth today. I want John to come home.

Wednesday March 20 – everyone is all excited. I don't remember the last three weeks. They say I was very ill, but now I am sitting up and I feel quite well. There are flowers and cards. I read one today from the Boy Scouts. It made me feel even better. The doctor said I could walk around tomorrow with help from the nurse. I don't even know how I got to New Jersey! I don't know who brought my diary – was it John? I hope he didn't read it. John is talking about taking me back to Sarasota.

Sunday May 19 – Great day to arrive back in Alpine. John left NY after the show closed in Brooklyn and brought me up north. I am stronger and am back on my feet. Maybe it is because I am home in Alpine. The nurse helped me walk out to the edge and look out over the Hudson. I was thinking I should have a secret garden here – next to the rose garden. I could spend so much time there.

Sunday June 2 – The pace of life is too much. We are back on Fifth Avenue. I am so tired. My back hurts and I can hardly breath. I am

*going to have to tell John and then he will want to call the doctor –
again. I can't seem to focus on the page – will try again tomorrow.*

JUNE 9 – MRS JOHN DIED YESTERDAY – I AM TAKING THE
DIARY – MR JOHN WANTS TO THROW IT OUT – I HEARD HIM
IN THE BATHROOM FOR TWO HOURS CRYING – F.T.

The Donniker Man

On October 2, 1931, John Ringling dedicated the *School* of Fine
and *Applied* Art of the John and Mable *Ringling* Art Museum. It was
not the realization of his or Mable's dream. The original concept was
to house the school and its dormitories at the museum. It couldn't be
done. The Depression whittled away at the school, his funds, and his
dreams for Sarasota. John donated forty five thousand dollars so that
the school could open at the former Bayhaven Hotel and some vacant
nearby structures. Funds were hard to come by for John as he was
squeezed for his payments to the Prudence Bond Company, which
threatened every step of the way to take the show from him. There
were few things remaining in John Ringling's life which he loved. He
loved and honored Mable, his memory of her and the dreams they
held. Unbeknownst to Sarasota, he not only loved the place and the
people but lived on for its future. He loved Ida, his sister, and her son
Buddy, and even loved his nephew, John, if for different reasons
which reminded him of himself. Finally, he loved the circus. It held a
deep sense of family, the legacy of the brothers, and the satisfaction it
gave him to make people happy. He was always in love with Mable
and had fought hard to keep creditors and others away from any
attachment to the museum. It was the embodiment of their love for
each other.

On October 3, 1931, John opened the John and Mable Museum of
Art for a second viewing for the public, especially for Sarasota. He
needed to prove that it was real. He wanted Sarasotans to know that
although he had his shortcomings, his partnership with Owen Burns
that brought Burns to bankruptcy was not ill intended. He had done it
all for them, for the place itself. Sam Gumpertz had always prided
himself at working with the Boy Scouts and in particular had been a

big booster of the Sunny Land Boy Scouts of America, which were based in both Sarasota and Manatee Counties. When John and Mable hosted members of the Metropolitan Opera at Ca' d'Zan in 1928, Sam had arranged for Boy Scouts to help with parking cars and to serve refreshments. The opera was broadcast from the grand home by radio to thousands in the Sarasota area. In fact the Boy Scouts had been there to help out at many social gatherings at the Ringling mansion while Mable was alive. It had been a more upbeat time for John. John did his best to make this day special. He had tried for over a year to get Julius Bohler to publish an official catalog of the collection, but Julius had been weighed down by the financial crisis in Europe and was unable to create a full catalog for either of John's first two unofficial openings of the museum. However, Julius had done his best to create a written description of the more than three hundred forty paintings and sculptures that would be on display along with the acquisition information of each piece. John was able, through volunteerism and some paid staff, to open the museum for a short time in October.

The weekend event was well attended but lacked anyone of notoriety inside the museum walls to greet and escort the visitors. John, feeling he had made enough of an appearance at the previous day's dedication, preferred to remain outside, on the grounds, greeting and helping to park cars. He worked with a small team of Scouts and paired off with one boy in particular, fifteen year old Frank Williams. Frank was of medium height, had very slender shoulders, thick dark brown hair, and wore heavy, thick lenses on his glasses. He was not athletic looking but carried himself well with good posture. His uniform was perfect and his chest pinned with awards and merit badges. He had an extremely deep voice for such a slight figure, and because of this his friends called him Frog. After Scout Master Kendall delivered the boys and instructed them on what they should do, he paired Frank with John Ringling.

"Frank," Kendall instructed, "you'll be over here working with Mr. Ringling. After Mr. Ringling greets the guests, you'll be directing the cars over to the right, where the other boys will get them parked." Kendall then introduced the boy to John, "This is Frank Williams."

"I remember," John remarked, and with his keen mind and memory it is highly likely that he did. "Hello Frank," he went on, extending his hand to Frank, "you were at the house for the opera. A pleasure to see you again." Frank, not saying a word at first, shook John's large slender hand.

"Hello Mr. Ringling, it is good to see you again." John smiled, towering over the boy, both in height and stature. John was well dressed, wearing a brown suit, no tie, and a straw boater cap.

"We'll do fine," John reassured the boy, "this will be all about making the people feel welcome."

"Yes sir," he answered, "I'll do my best." They stood about fifteen feet apart so that John had room to welcome the visitors and Frank could point and motion which direction they should go.

It was almost 10:00 in the morning and the visitors had not yet arrived. Saturdays in Sarasota were often a slow start. The circus had not yet returned to Winter Quarters, and the town had more of an early autumn feel than the frenzied arrival time of circus folk. For the winters of 1928 – 1930 John had been the largest employer in Sarasota, using Winter Quarters personnel to help finish the museum. The depression had ravaged Sarasota, and almost one third of all working people in town were looking for work. John stood smiling, taking in the sun, the slightly cooler October morning, and the momentary feeling of not being hounded by creditors, or the Prudence Bond Company, or having to manage the circus without Charley. He marveled in thinking he was so much closer to manifesting the dream that he and Mable had begun. He was not really present to the moment but staring into the deep cerulean Florida sky when Frank slowly walked up to him.

"Mr. Ringling," he asked, waking John from his daydream.

"Yes, Frank," John answered smiling at the boy and admiring his civility, "what is it?"

"Can I ask you a question, sir?"

"Yes," John answered suspiciously.

"Well, sir," Frank slowly worked his way up to the question, "well, sir, I mean, well, why are you out here parking cars?" John looked puzzled and then asked, "Why do you ask, son?" John really had not understood the nature of the question.

"Well, sir," he fumbled around a moment, "well, I mean, you are a famous person." John smiled as the boy searched to explain the question more fully. "I mean that, why is someone who is important like you out here with us kids doing this kind of job?" John looked at the boy with great sincerity and let him continue. "Shouldn't you be doing something more important?" John paused, looking not only very thoughtful but seemed to be searching deep inside for an answer. Finally after what seemed to Frank like eternity, John spoke, "Frank," John began slowly, "do you know what a donniker is?"

"Nnno sir,"

"Frank, when I was just your age, me and my brothers set out to put on little shows in Wisconsin."

"Yes sir, I've heard about it."

"Well, we learned early on that if we were going to be successful, we had to do everything. After we started our first little circus show in

1884, it only took about ten years before we were giving the biggest shows in the country a run for their money." Frank moved in close hanging on every word. "One day, when I was on the lot, and let me say as managers me and my brothers weren't always on the lot because we often had to travel in advance of the show, and... well, this one day there were huge thunderstorms while the roustabouts and riggers were putting up the big top. Lightning struck, and two fellas holding the king pole were killed, right there on the spot."

"Oh!" Frank took a deep breath and then John went on.

"Twenty other riggers were knocked unconscious," John continued," it was awful, and the dead guys smelled like burnt meat!" Frank looked alarmed by the statement. "That was bad," John continued, "but we had to put on the show. A half hour later, after we took care of the dead and injured, me and my brother Charley replaced the two fellows that had died. Roustabouts who had never done the job had to replace the riggers, and as they continued putting up the tent, Charley and I noticed, because we were short about twenty men, that we were going to have to jump in and double in brass."

"What's that?" Frank interrupted.

"Double in brass means we had to do other jobs than just being managers. Do you know what a donniker is?" He stopped himself and then said, "right – I asked you that already. Have you ever dug a slit trench or anything for when you boys are at camp?"

"You mean a latrine?" Frank asked.

"Yeah, that's it," John responded, "a latrine."

"Yes sir," Frank answered and went on, "usually if you dig it you have to bury it and clean up the mess."

"Precisely young man," John said and continued with the lesson, "a donniker is a latrine and in my world, the circus world, no person is better off if the job doesn't get done. I mean we double in brass. We are willing to do anything to make sure that everything is done just right. So my brother and I dug the donnikers. Do you understand?"

"Yes sir, just like the Scouts. We are ready and willing."

"Now you've got it!" John exclaimed, "That's my boy!" At that moment the first car was driving down the drive, and Frank wandered back to his position. Behind it was a procession of cars. John Ringling went to work parking cars.

High Stakes Marriage

I'll admit it. I've made plenty of mistakes. But the biggest mistake of my life was Emily Haag Buck. After we closed the 1929 season, after the crash, and after I would heretofore always blame myself for the awful death of Black Diamond, I went to Europe. My soul hurt so bad after Mable's death, I could feel it in my bones. Times were bad, but I had reserves. Shit, I needed reserves; as the season closed, we couldn't fill the seats in Atlanta. We had nearly thirteen thousand seats, and when we could fill a show to the ring banks we could seat fifteen thousand shoulder to shoulder. Hell, the kids could smell the elephants fart we'd be so full! But at closing of the '29 season, we filled only six hundred seventy three seats. It was hard to get a clown to make anyone laugh. If anyone had any money, they weren't gonna let go of it. If they bought a ticket, they were sneaking in their own food instead of buying from the candy butchers. So I was drawing on my reserves. No one would ever go without pay at a Ringling show. It was awful everywhere, but still, most of us with money thought this was not going to last.

Sam Gumpertz was acting less like a friend and more like a businessman. He was now my full time employee. I had made him General Manager of the Barnes Show. I was getting old. I felt old and without Mable, I thought I'd never feel young again. It wasn't more than a good week after she died that women began giving me the up and down. Now, at sixty three I was no dummy. Sure, I was still a pretty handsome sort of fellow, but what made the gals wet between the thighs was the size of my bank accounts, or the accounts they thought I had. Oh for God's sake, other than the fifty thousand a year I got from the show there was nothing paying out. In fact most of my business endeavors were sucking me dry faster than a three dollar whore. The IRS had put a lean on the money from the oil wells. Charley had been smart with his money. Deedee could manage well on what the circus had placed in her bank accounts. But now it was coming down hard on me. God, had I screwed up. Why, if Otto was still around he would have had me put it all aside. Otto knew that a million dollars was nothing more than a hundred million pennies, and he valued every one of them – pennies.

Okay, so Charley was dead now three years. Mable was dead, and everyone said it was cause of the Addison's disease, but no matter what the doctors said, I knew different. The Addison's had started after she was burned. My two best friends Sam and Evie blamed me. I started my first formal weeks of being the greatest King Of All Circus by also being labeled an elephant killer, and the fucking world economy just got flushed down the toilet. Along with the market crash, all my options disappeared as my debts mounted because of the stupid mistake I had made by putting up The Greatest Show On Earth to borrow the money needed to be Mr. Dumbass Circus King of Kings! So, what was it I should do now? It seemed obvious. Get the hell out Sarasota, leave the country and go to Monaco. Gamble. That'd take my mind off my troubles. Like life wasn't already enough of a gamble? So off I went to Monte Carlo. I had been before, but it was with Mable. When we went, we were everyone's feast to the eye. Mable was scarcely beyond her thirties last time we were there, and she was the most beautiful gal in the casino. By the end of the world war, women, especially those with money, flaunted their goods, tastefully so, but still, everything showed and Mable was no exception. Here I was in Monte Carlo, practically broke, by my standards, and practically the richest American in town. You could tell as I made my entry into the casino that my presence and my reputation were known, and some of the more attractive and unaccompanied gals shifted their attention to me. I played small but tried to make it look big. I asked the maitre 'd for a credit line, and he replied, "With us, Mr. Ringling, your credit has no limits." So as I slowly watched my monies disappear, I spied a beautiful woman; maybe she was aged thirty eight, maybe older. I wasn't good at guessing a gal's age, especially a wealthy gal. She wore a stone studded cap, an elegant long gown, and long diamond studded pendant earrings with pear shaped pearls. Her necklace matched, with an enormous pearl surrounded by diamonds delicately looming toward her cleavage. From that moment on I wanted to be seated with that gal and her glowing blonde hair.

I was playing baccarat, and the English fellow next to me named George seemed to be forming a bond with me, as we were both losing equally. I gently nudged his elbow to get his attention, "Tell me George, who is that beautiful blonde who seems to be winning all the money, over at that table ?"

"Well Mr. Ringling, good sir, that is the infamous Emily Haag Buck." He responded a little too loudly, and so I whispered even more lightly, hoping to quiet him down, "Tell me, George, why is she so famous?"

"Well sir, she has no fear of losing and taking high stakes risks." We went on betting and the two of us lost again.

"Tell me George," I was asking a bit more boldly, "is there a chance in hell that I might be able to get an introduction?"

"Why, you are 'The' Mr. John Ringling, and it seems to me that any woman here would be happy to make your acquaintance. But first, allow me the honor of either winning or losing enough that I reach my limit." I barely heard another word, and although I kept playing (and losing) I kept my focus on Emily Haag Buck, who now was betting such high stakes that she had an audience. In the following ten minutes she lost thirty two thousand dollars. Losing was never an attribute, but she did it with style and grace. What a gal! So when we'd had enough, George brought me to the table as she was standing and saying, "I do believe that I have contributed enough money to the Monaco economy for one night." Then she turned toward me and George and said, "Well George, are you going to stand there like an idiot, or are you going to introduce me to Mr. Ringling?" I gave my great stamp-like smile of approval, and all I could say was, "Miss Buck, the pleasure is all mine. Let me buy you a drink, my dear." It took little more than that for the two of us to begin what was for each the biggest pile of bullshit marriage ever created. She wanted a rich man and I wanted a rich gal. What I got was a damn good lay and a woman who had no assets and a modest heap of cash. She got an aging dreamer who had a heap of assets and a dwindling pool of cash. But that was the good part.

I don't know if it was the times, my age, or were things just happening faster? We returned to the states, and we were married all in little more than a week's time. The affair itself was less eventful than the marriage. Once back in New York, we went to Jersey City, and my buddy Mayor Frank Hague married us. No family, only a few familiar witnesses, my attorney John M. Kelly and Tommy McCarter who was head of the Jersey PSC, and a confidant of Emily's. On route to the wedding I had Kelly draw up an agreement. It was a prenuptial contract and protected the paintings from Em, who I think had it in for them anyhow. During the week before our marriage, I borrowed fifty thousand dollars from her, convincing her that I was "just a bit short" that week. I had offered her three paintings as collateral, although I tried to make the fifty thousand loan a dowry. Truth is I had John write up the prenuptial contract quickly and had Em sign it in the limo on the way to the wedding. At the wedding she showed it to that bastard McCarter, who told her she shouldn't have done it. I was a fool to have just had the one copy. After the wedding, we went back to my Fifth Avenue apartment, and I got drunk. Some honeymoon. Emily took the God damn prenuptial contract, tore it up, and flushed it down the crapper. Great start to a shitass marriage.

No sooner had we arrived in Sarasota than she somehow befriended Edith – almost right off. Makes sense now that I think about it as Deedee and I were on the verge of becoming enemies. She began filling the house up with friends. Well, she called them friends. To me they were blood sucking leeches. They wanted my whiskey, my wine collection, and my stores of dry aged beef. Okay, I clearly asked for a lot in return. Em could see I was a man of great wealth and very tight on cash. I must admit, it was unusual to borrow the fifty grand. In my mind it was a dowry, but she made me put up the three paintings. It should have been a big deal, but money flowed through my hands like water slipping through the spaces in your fingers when you're trying to get a drink in your hands. Besides, the paintings I gave her were suspect. They had been some of those early pieces where I'd bought the provenance.

I guess I was no prize either. I gave Em her own room. It was lavish, hell all the rooms were lavish, but it was a guest room. No one was going to take Mable's room. That just was a fact of life. Mable and I had our own rooms, one for a king and one for a queen. Mable was dead, but she was not gone. Being 1930, there were a few big things still occupying my mind. First was the museum. This drove Emily nuts. She would ask more than once a day, "Why don't you just call it the John Ringling Museum of Art?" I knew what she really wanted; she wanted her name in there.

"Em," I would answer, as I had repeatedly answered the same answer, "because this was the dream that we put together. It was Mable's and my idea and that's how it's gonna be."

The next thing on my mind wasn't the show. For some odd reason I believed it could just go on by itself. Not so. It was bigger and more complex. Every lawyer from Sarasota to Palm Beach had my face in his cross hairs. I couldn't even take a piss without some joker knocking at the door and serving another God damn summons. And, if it wasn't a private suit for some unfinished business, then it was the IRS with their bloodthirsty hands out. We were still trying to settle the debt from 1917 to 1919 when two superintendents from the Barnum Show stole and pocketed our tax money. As if all that wasn't enough, the interest payment on the 1.7 million I owed on the debt for the show was more than I could hold. My first decision was to sell two of the five shows from the American Circus Corporation Holdings. All the while there was something going on behind my back and I could feel it. You know how it is when you get a hunch, suspicion, and it's so far out of your beliefs. The things in life you trust so deeply can't be wrong; you won't entertain it. It just can't be true. But my mind kept rolling back to New York, the week that Sam and I were there making the deal to buy the ACC. Some things didn't add up. Like why was Sam talking to the managerial folks at the Garden while I was at the board meeting? How had Sam managed to get the Prudence Bond guys to have everything all laid out? And how come they couldn't muster up the paperwork on five circuses, especially when the Hagenbeck-Wallace was considered the second biggest show in the country, maybe the world? They sure seemed to be dancing to the tune of Sam Gumpertz.

So my life was full up, like my house, over thirty six rooms and fifteen baths, half of 'em full of Emily's cohorts, lovers or whatever these Palm Beach sons o' bitches were, and then to top it off I was pushing Mable's sisters out of the house because they were suing me. It wasn't like they just blamed me for Mable's death and all. They now believed I owed them some of the estate. Problem was we had spent most everything we had. What was I thinking? Just buy stuff and it'll manage itself? Meanwhile, the last three years of her life, Mable had to suffer through the daily whittling away of our dream, the museum. The whole time she had held back from telling me how much pain she was in. She was experiencing a debilitating disease and keeping it a secret from me. At one point our museum had a college in it, and then later it had a dormitory, and eventually the attic would be sort of a dormitory. All we ever really wanted was to give something back. So much had been given to us. So much money, culture, and wealth was just placed in our hands. We thought, "Let's see what we can leave for Sarasota." Hell, we thought it could be the "other" center of culture in the east, I mean outside New York. Circus was great, but wasn't there something more to give? To leave behind?   Maybe that was it. If Charley was here he'd want to kick my ass! I am sure he knew that his success, hell all our success, came from the show. Maybe it just slipped my mind.

It was December 1930 when we were married and arrived in Sarasota. It's clear to me now that Emily had wanted a homecoming at Ca' d'Zan, like, "Welcome Mrs. Queen Em to your castle." And in a way it was. But the dark mist that settled over what should have been her celebration was the wedding of my niece, in the grand courtyard. Here we had a small but spectacular wedding for them, and Em and I had just had a ceremony at city hall, in Jersey City, followed up by her flushing the prenuptial contract down the toilet. I didn't feel so grand, not about this. It left me empty, and I have no doubt it left a gaping hole in our marriage.

I was developing a bad taste for Februaries. It seemed like bad things kept happening to me just before opening at the Garden. I had married a woman who hated all the things I loved, the circus, our museum, Sarasota; hell she hated Florida. The depression had not softened or begun to turn to better fortune, but it was getting worse. Even the rich in Sarasota were suffering. We even held parties with themes like "How to have fun when you're going broke!" Schools were closing, and the properties at the center of the land boom, which was long since over, were now beginning to look like a war had happened. Only 30% of Sarasota's taxes were paid, and teachers were accepting half pay. By January it was decided that public schools would close in April.

It was February and I was in New York. Emily hated Sarasota, and even when the climate was so inviting, she would rather be in New York. She wanted to be where the "action was" and left her sister and a few friends in Ca' d'Zan, where they could eat up and drink up my goods. We went to the Ritz-Carlton, avoiding my apartment because I was several months in arrears in my rent. That's when I got the news. It was the evening of February 17 when I got a call from Gumpertz.

"Sam, please don't tell me you have bad news," I said sarcastically as it was only a year after I had received a call from Deedee and Mable was dying.

"I'm sorry John, it's really bad." Then Emily interrupted, "Do we really have to have business calls at nine at night?" She was drinking a martini, a drink I detested, and waving it in my face.

"Shut up Em," I raised my voice, "this is important."

"You and the fucking show always take over the night," she scoured.

"Quiet!" I shouted.

"John," Sam continued, "Lillian died!"

"I'm sorry Sam, say again."

"Lillian Leitzel died, she died today in Copenhagen."

"Holy fuck Sam, are you sure?" I got choked up. "Does Alfredo know?" Emily had calmed down, realizing that something serious had happened.

"Yes, I got a telegram from him today. She fell two days ago and broke her neck and had internal injuries."

"I gotta go Sam. I can't talk anymore about this. We'll talk tomorrow." I hung up. I had a newly poured full glass of whiskey. I drank the whole thing.

"What happened sweetie?" Emily asked.

"Lillian Leitzel died." Lillian was our star act. She was the greatest aerialist in circus history, beloved by all. Five feet tall, she was adored and adorable. She had the ability to spin on the hoops in such a way that her arms would dislocate and reassemble repeatedly over and over. She had a saying about the danger of her career: "I'd rather be a racehorse, and last a minute, than be a plow horse and last forever." She thrilled circus goers everywhere. She was married to Alfredo Codona, of the Flying Codonas, who were the greatest flyers we ever had. The triple somersault had been performed since the late 1800s, but Alfredo was the only one who did it in every performance. Their love was a circus love like no other. She was a goddess to him. Even in his loss I was envious. Maybe it was because my marriage to Emily was already rotten to the core, even though we had been together less than a year.

It was January 1934. I needed to raise fifty five thousand dollars to satisfy the interest on the debt to Allied Owners and the Prudence Bond Company. There was no way in hell I was going to let Sam Gumpertz take any more of my show. It was reminding me of when I had to have my toe amputated and stayed in his place in Coney Island, the Half Moon Hotel. They were going to carve me up piece by piece until there was no Ringling brother left on the lot. For God's sake, I *was* the last one on the lot. I had remained close to Henry Ringling North, and continued to call him Buddy, as he had really been a help to me when I was sick. But John had to have my name stuck in there with his Whitestone North name. I couldn't stand it. He kept trying to be – like me. I don't think he ever understood that. I was not just about wearing finely tailored clothes, smoking the best cigars, and drinking my own private label whiskey. Sure, I lived like that, but that's just what I did to celebrate my success. Kids these days have all kinds of illusions. I told them, "You can have anything you want in life." But did they listen to the whole story? There's a catch. You can have anything you want in life. First, figure out what you want. Then, work your ass off to get it, and don't stop until you have it. They seem to forget the "work" part.

I had gone back to Sarasota in late 1933 to recoup. I had another thrombosis – blood clots; I guess they call it a stroke. I hate that word. Doc Ewald kept trying to blame it on the cigars and whiskey, rich foods and such, and Nurse Sanders, she would pull cigars right out of my mouth every time I lit one up. Damn it, I had to hide cigars in my own house. But I think what was making me sick was the more than thirty law suits against me, the IRS breathing down my back, and Emily and her sister trying to rob me blind.

I began to recover pretty good in early '35. Johnny was quitting some job he had in New York at a brokerage firm and moving to "help" with my affairs. Frankly I didn't want that kind of help. He had referred me to new lawyers as it now seemed that our circus lawyer, John Kelly, had sided with Edith and Aubrey. But my nephew's guys actually wanted up front money – from me – John Ringling! So that about made my hair stand on end. New York Investors and Allied Owners were now threatening to put Ca' d'Zan up for auction if I missed my next payment, so I had to come up with a way to raise the fifty five thousand – fast. I revealed it to Buddy, a big mistake, and before I knew it, Johnny was on the phone with me talking about my three hundred cases of whiskey I had in the New York apartment, where he had now set up shop. These were from 1886, and even at wholesale, worth a fortune. He told me we could get fifty bucks a case on the sly from a distributor in New York. With a license, the stuff would have brought nearly thirty bucks or more a bottle. I said go ahead and see if you can sell 'em. That would handle a large chunk of the debt, and somehow I knew we could swing the rest. A week later I got a phone call. No one was by the phone except Nurse Sanders, so I answered it myself.

"Is this John?" a fellow asked.

"It certainly is," I answered, "and to whom am I speaking?"

"It's me, John, Ed Wingate," he replied, "you remember, the liquor wholesaler."

"Oh," I answered, and played dumb. "To what do I owe the pleasure?"

"Well, Mr. North..." he went on – God did that feel queer to be called Mr. North – "...I sold all the cases of whiskey already and wondered if you had more?" I decided to play along, and besides I had little trust for the fact that Johnny North was up to anything other than working with New York Investors and the Allied owners. He was trying to get my show.

"Tell me Ed, what did you pay me for that first batch?"

"Why one hundred a case, dontcha remember?" I reached for a cigar I had hidden under my cap on the valet, put it my mouth and began to chew it a bit. Then I regained my composure, "Why sure, Ed, I remember."

"Well, you got any more?" he asked, as I thought quickly and schemed up a plan. I'd catch that little fucker of a nephew in the act.

"Ed," I talked slowly putting it all together as I went along. "You know you reached me at my Sarasota number?"

"Why yes," he replied, "your valet gave me this number when I called in New York."

"Well Ed, I am headed to New York tomorrow. I'll be in town in three days. I'll tally up what I got and I'll call you from there." I had to make sure Johnny knew nothing of this, so I said, "Give me your number again and I'll call you when I get in." Which he did and then I requested, "Don't call me about this in the meantime. I don't want the help to know a thing about it."

"Why yes sir. You can count on me."

Lucky for me Buddy was away. He had gone ahead to New York to help his brother and Gumpertz open the show at the Garden which was going to open on March 30. I convinced Nurse Sanders that I was well enough to travel, and even Ewald said I was okay if I didn't overexert myself. So we hitched the Jomar and headed to New York, without fanfare, and in fact I left at night so as not to get it in the papers or have my nephews know I was coming. I had to leave the traveling limo home as I couldn't get a flat car that would accommodate it. It was easy when we brought it with the show, but when I was unable to travel with the show it became a big luxury. When we arrived in New York, I was mad as hell when I couldn't get

my other limo to pick us up, as I was told, "Mr. North is using it on business, Mr. Ringling." So Nurse Sanders and I got a taxi and headed to my apartment. I asked her to wait downstairs while I took the elevator up, but she insisted on wheeling me around in that damn contraption. As we exited the elevator and she reached for the door, we both were aware of what we could hear.
She paused from opening the door.

"Go ahead, damn it – open it," I demanded. She did so, reluctantly. From inside was coming some of the loudest screaming I'd ever heard from a gal getting laid. It was Emily, and it was pretty obvious to both of us. Sitting on the valet were a pair of man's gloves, a black fedora, and what appeared to be my nephew's cigarette holder. "Damn," I thought to myself, "she never fucked me like that!" I looked at Nurse Sanders, who was pale and ghostlike as if she was going to get sick.

"I think we've heard and seen enough," I said, "let's go."

"But Mr. John," she said, "Aren't you going..."

"Let's go," I said again, "just don't forget what you saw and heard here tonight."

"How am I supposed to forget that?"

"You're not."

"I can't, I mean..." she was stammering and maybe a bit aroused, "oh my.."

"Ina," I smiled at her and although she was rather homely, at that instance she displayed a rather complicated and attractive glow, "Ina, forget about it."

"But you told me to remember."

"Yes Ina, remember, but for now – forget about it."

Emily was supposed to be in Jersey, and I am sure she never had any idea I was there. I had dropped the divorce the first time. This time I decided she was gonna get screwed. It was my turn to do the screwing, and it wasn't gonna happen in a fucking bed! Maybe I would have a way of keeping her mitts off my last dough and art collection. That bitch! I filed for divorce on April 4th. In the first divorce she was served in Woolworth's, and this became a contentious matter as her attorney told the court I had humiliated her. Now, I didn't give a shit if they served it to her on her dinner plate at Delmonicos!

The first divorce was dropped as it had served to make the collateral of the paintings official. The second time around, I did get my divorce from Emily. It was because of her cruel behavior, and the judge allowed that I treated her like shit too. Hell, she was such a fuss budget, scurrying around, always hopping from person to person. I tried to have the bit about what we heard in New York allowed, but they dismissed it as it was just hearsay, literally. Tomlinson, my butler, also falsified some entries in Doc Ewald's journal about my pulse rising when Em verbally assaulted me, and that didn't help. All that Emily really got were the three paintings from my collection that she had retained with the post nuptial contract after the first divorce. She had wanted to get her mitts on my art collection, the pinnacle of Mable's life and my life. I made sure she got three of the most worthless paintings in the whole collection. I screwed her and she deserved it.

Eight
What Goes Around

The Last Laugh

Some people think John Ringling made a terrible mistake when he wrote a codicil on Ritz-Carlton stationary and wrote his nephews, John and Henry North, and his sister Ida North out of the vast majority of his will. It seemed, if one linked together all of the incidents and placed them in a timeline, that his anger had gotten the best of him. His last will and testament was dated May 19, 1934, exactly fifty years after the launch of the first Ringling circus in Baraboo. On November 2, 1935, John Ringling summoned Eugene Garey to his room at the Ritz-Carlton in New York. John was behind again by several months on payments for the Park Avenue apartment, so he had checked into the Ritz-Carlton in order to avoid being confronted regarding his rent payment. Eugene was not John's usual attorney, although they had worked together over matters of John's oil dealings, and for Madison Square Garden, of which Eugene was the official attorney. There was nothing usual about John's life anymore. John M. Kelley had been John's attorney, in fact the circus' attorney, since about 1905 after a boy had broken his wrist at the show and his parents sued. Charley had hired him, and he had remained steadfast loyal to John and the brothers. The family was now fractured, and John had been moved to president in title only, a motion made by Allied Owners, who held a ten percent share, and seconded by Edith, only to be followed by Aubrey, Richard's widow, making it seventy percent to John's thirty percent. John was merely a figurehead. His salary of fifty thousand dollars a year was reduced to five thousand. He had ceased all contact with John Ringling North since his nephew had gone to work for the show, and his closeness with Henry was waning. But for Nurse Ina Sanders and a few old cohorts such as Frank Hennesy, John was alone, dazed, and seemingly confused. John telephoned Garey, "Gene," he greeted him as if they had just been talking.

"Hello, yes," Garey answered,

"John Ringling here."

"Oh, yes," Eugene Garey responded, not really wanting to engage in any matters with Ringling as he heard that John's mind was slowly fading into obscurity.

"I have an urgent matter to discuss with you. I have worked out the basis for a document that I would like to make official."

"That's fine, John. Can you bring it by my office and we'll look it over?" After a silence Ringling spoke, "Actually, I'd like you to come here, to the Ritz-Carlton." John cleared his throat, "Today, this afternoon."

"I am free this afternoon," Garey continued, "but say, what's this all about?"

"It's a codicil," John went on and waited for a response, "to my will, of course."

"These matters are best addressed in an office, where we can have witnesses and make it official," Garey responded.

"No, I want it done here," John insisted. "I have two witnesses who can be here. This is important," he paused, "to me."

"All right John, I can be there," Garey conceded, "at two o'clock." Ringling hung up the phone and turned to Nurse Sanders, "Then it's done!" he proclaimed.

"I don't understand your motives," she said, "is this because you're angry?" Nurse Sanders had seen every twist and turn John had taken in his relations with his nephews, especially with Johnny. First, the scotch, then the alleged affair with John's now ex-second wife Emily, and finally, watching his nephew join forces with Sam Gumpertz and Allied Owners.

"I have a plan," John snapped. "No one but me can understand it, but I know what I am doing." Nurse Sanders frowned and made a deep sigh. John disliked it when she did that, and it seemed as time went on, she did it more often, as he would reveal his schemes to her. She was more than just a nurse to John; she had become his confidant. She was even closer than Frank Hennessy, one of John's last remaining friends and noted road show promoter. "Frank's in town. We need to call him up and get him over here, as a witness," he paused, as if waiting for Sanders to leap into action, "this afternoon."

"What d'you mean? You don't need to bring..."

"Let's call him," John interrupted insisting, "we need another witness."

"I have to be a witness to this?"

"My dear," John said somewhat sarcastically, "you already are!"

Just after 2:00 there was a knock at the door. Nurse Sanders greeted Eugene Garey and took his coat. Against Sanders' wishes, John had a decanter of whiskey and a tray of glasses on the table. The table was laid out with the codicil and next to it a box of cigars, and to the side of the box, three pens. The two men shook hands, and John turned toward the table.

"Have a seat," John invited. "Everything is already on the table." The codicil, a small handwritten document, was placed less prominently than the whisky and cigars. "Drink?" John asked.

"Not now, perhaps later," Garey responded. "I thought you said there would be two witnesses," Garey probed as he took a seat.

"The other will be here." John took a cigar from the box and left it open, "Cigar?"

"No thanks. Don't smoke." Garey took his reading glasses from his suit pocket and put them on and immediately picked up the document. The codicil was more of a tangle of notes, in John's handwriting. The original date was May 19, 1934. It was written right after the second time John had filed for divorce from Emily. Without a word, Garey picked up one of the pens and began making corrections. John sat, fumbling with the cigar, and finally, after snipping the end, looked up at Nurse Sanders who quietly returned a gaze of disapproval. John lit the cigar and puffed. A satisfied and relaxed appearance came over him. It didn't take long for Garey to get to the end of it and finish his notes. He put it on the table and took off his glasses and looked at John.

"Well?" John asked, waiting for some sort of congratulatory remark.

"Well," Gene responded, "why are you doing this?"

"I have very good reasons," John answered and then puffing, focused on the cigar.

"Let's hope you do, but not having seen the will, I can't advise you very well." There was a knock at the door, and Sanders quickly arose, getting away from the tension between the two men, and answered the door. "Hello Mr. Hennessy," she greeted Frank, somewhat formally. They were not strangers, as Sanders had known Hennessy for years, in Sarasota.

"Ina," he answered stepping in and taking off his hat. John began to push up from the table. "Don't get up old man," Frank commanded Ringling, "you and I are already too close."

"This is Gene Garey," John introduced the two men, "Gene, my good friend Frank Hennessy."   Garey, barely deterred by the introduction, did not rise but shook Frank's hand and asked him to take a seat. Then he spoke, "My advice, Mr. Ringling, is to take more time and not make a hasty decision. However, if this is what you want we can do it, here, today." Ringling drew a deep and raspy breath, "Let's do it – now!" he said and pushed on the neatly stacked stationary which had been under his notes. "You can hand write it, can't you?"

"If I have to." Begrudgingly, he looked down taking a couple pages of the stationary with the letterhead "Ritz-Carlton." As Eugene Garey prepared to write, he looked over to John and again tried to advise him: "This really should be done in Sarasota, I mean, along with the will." John snapped at him, "I have my reasons for doing it in New York. I want it done now, today. Let's get this behind us!"

Eugene Garey went through the exercise in less than twenty minutes. No one spoke. Ina Sanders and Frank Hennesy witnessed the document, followed by John pouring a drink for the two men and one for himself. Sanders would never drink whisky and glared at John with contempt as he poured it. Hennessy, one of John's oldest friends, had long since given up on trying to stifle John's habits. He was John Ringling, after all, still the large and imposing figure who got what he wanted. After the three men raised their glasses and toasted, Garey rose from the table, not finishing his glass and placing it on the table, and then addressed Ringling, "This has been most unusual John."

"I am certain of that," Ringling responded. "Thank you for your patience, Gene."   The men shook hands, and Garey asked if John would have further business in New York. However, John would have little more dealings with Eugene Garey. After he left, Frank asked John, "Why are you doing this?" He went on as if it had been a rhetorical question, "It's your flesh and blood we're talking about here!"

"Frank, trust me. I have my reasons," he tried to assure his friend. "One day the whole world will understand." Frank and Ina looked at John Ringling with empathy and pity. Here was the great Circus King, now a beaten man. Not making any sense, at least not to them. Yet they both knew him all too well to not respect and love him, just as he was. Within a day, John and Nurse Sanders were on the Jomar bound for Sarasota. His entire visit to New York had been for the codicil.

Days of Golden Memories

It was early spring 1936. I had come to hate Ca' d'Zan, as it was empty without Mable. I thought some rooms were occupied by Darcy Shuller, Mable's sister, and her family on occasion, and I thought I could hear their voices. Then I remembered that Darcey and her husband had sued me, and I had not seen or heard from them in years. Sometimes I'd swear there were other strangers in my home. There was a sound of memories, the radio programs, the garden parties, opera, and emptiness. In much of the late winter I had been dining every night with George Thiebedoux, the IRS auditor, a man whom I considered was a two faced bastard and was trying to get at my very soul and rip away what was left and feed it to the U.S. Government. Something frightened me about his kind manner, which gave me the feeling that if I could take away his mask I would reveal the face of an ominous monster that would devour me. I had only a few of my servants left. They never wanted to leave, but most had become tired of waiting for pay, which I would occasionally find somewhere and settle accounts. Frank Tomlinson never left. He was devoted. He would stay by my side without pay. Nurse Sanders never left. She was my last companion. I guess I even chased Henry away. He had been kind to me, but I had to do it. I knew I was close to my last days, and I didn't want to let on that I would leave nothing to the Norths. They would have to figure it out, but just the IRS debt alone would crush them. So Ca' d'Zan, Mable's dream, a ghost castle with distant voices and strange smells of cooking from Hester's house next door, made me feel so alone.

I had been dreaming of a way I could regain the stage and resurrect a real Ringling Show. Gumpertz had ruined the show, and he was either suckering my nephews into it, or they were smart enough to position themselves ahead of what was coming, by working with him. He had even allowed graft into our show, including that sideshow talker Harry Lewiston. I never had it in for Jews. In fact most of the Jews in and around my business, the arts, and The Greatest Show On Earth, were educated fellows who had the ability to make things happen. But hell, Lewiston, actually he was Israel Harry Jaffe, was a talented Jew but a grafter. Because of what was going on between me and Sam, I became suspicious of a lot of Jews. Meanwhile I could see that Sam and Allied Owners were sucking the show dry. My sources told me that wagons were falling apart: paint peeling, cracked, splitting. The canvas was the same one I had bought in '29, and the wardrobes hadn't been renewed in years. It was a terrible mess of an economic crisis, yet Gumpertz was riding high. Allied Owners was making money, and every exact date that my loan payment was due they were right in my face with their God Damn claws out! If it had been me and my brothers, we might have foregone taking any money out and put back everything we could into the show. That's how we made it so big. Something else annoyed me. Rumor had it that Gumpertz allowed abuse of animals. That was unacceptable.

I reached back into my past and came up with a theme. One that would exemplify what we had founded the whole thing on. Primarily equestrian feats, the historic clowns, beautiful women, maybe some dogs, goats, and old time acts. But big, with a spectacle of wonder and marvel that harkened back to "Days of Golden Memory." Of course every show has to have elephants. That'd be the ticket. All this modern stuff, talking pictures, radio, fast cars, and planes had become a distraction. People needed the past, and I was going to give it to them. I had one show left that they used to let me coordinate when I was well enough, and rumor had it that Allied Owners was trying to stop it. Every year we put on shows for sick kids in hospitals. We would set up right outside Belleview in New York, with ring banks, and we would get some elephants. Kids love elephants, clowns, and other acts, and equestrians. The hospital staff and some parents would bring the kids outside to watch. Clowns would get right in there with the children, and the show would last an hour. This was the best medicine kids could get. We had done this as Ringling shows in many towns as far back as the 1890s. But ever since that letter in 1934, when Gumpertz tried to keep me from talking to my own performers, they ruled me out of setting it up. I feared the worst, that when I'm gone they won't do it any more. Circus is about kids. Me and the boys always tried to do good for people. If we could just make 'em laugh.

I had started in February writing to some of the old timers: Merle Evans, Fred Bradna, and Pat Valdo. I let them know I was going to come to New York in late March or early April, and knowing that the show would open on April 8th, I wanted to be there. I told them we could get the whole thing back, and Allied Owners would be out. I wanted to meet with them and plan a new show, for 1937. I called it Days of Golden Memory. It was going to be like the old days. When circus was chivalry, when we had great themes, and everything reawakened people to another age. I had worked it out, in my mind, with a great spec, shining surreys and buggy races. It would be new, from the ground up. I couldn't wait to see the old gang. I wouldn't let on that I didn't have the rights, but I'd make everyone think I had nearly paid off the debt. I still owed about nine hundred thousand. But if I got the whole show fired up, I believed I could borrow the funds necessary. I had sold some more stuff that winter and kept coming up with cash. I had almost paid my loan current, paid up most of my apartment, and paid the livery to date for my limo fees. John Ringling was back, I tell you!

Everything took longer than expected. First Doc Ewald wanted to check me over for a couple days before I left for New York. Then there were lists of medicines for Nurse Sanders to get. I had to have some gook to make me spit as my lungs were so congested. My clothes had to be cleaned and pressed and everything ready. Ina made sure she brought that cockamamie contraption, that settee with wheels on it, to make me feel like an invalid. There was no real staff at the New York apartment, so nurse Sanders and Tomlinson would do it all for me, take calls, cook, clean. Everything takes longer when you're old. Sometimes, when I dress right and feel good, some gal will still give me the eye, but I'm old. The Jomar is still grand, and because I still own a few rail lines, we get to hitch all the way into Manhattan. I thought that things were looking up for me. I had been planning this all summer. I now had stacks of old articles and current ads from *Greater Show World*, of which it was rumored they were going to feature a salute to Sam Gumpertz. I had old issues of *Billboard* and other ads from the past, and my notes and contacts from acts going back almost twenty years. Everyone was there. On April 1st, I dashed off a couple of telegrams, one to Pat Valdo and another to Karl Wallenda, and informed them of my 1937 show idea, Days of Golden Memories. Valdo was the best director of performance we'd ever had. We left on April 2nd.

I was really coming back. Yes, I'd show 'em! A Ringling was going to be back on the lot. We arrived late in the evening of April 4th. Nurse Sanders and a porter had to wheel me to my car, and I avoided eye contact with people in the terminal because I didn't want anyone I knew to see me looking like an invalid. I could walk plenty fine. I was saving my strength for opening night. The first night in New York was without calls or event. In fact I fell asleep early and have little memory of it. It was not like me, being a Saturday night, but then, little of me was left from the day when I'd make business deals at four in the morning having drunk the other guy into submission. I hadn't been in the apartment for quite some time, and the air was stale.

It was one of those days in New York when you finally were aware that spring was really going to stick around, the trees leafing out, people without overcoats, and everyone walking with a bounce in their step. Nurse Sanders opened the windows, and the fresh air flowed through. There were the obnoxious sounds of cars everywhere, while the sounds of wagons and horses on the streets were now just distant ideas, and assholes who thought they owned the place were honking horns right and left. Still, spring was in me as well, and I drank up its aroma and its giving generosity, and set my sights on Wednesday night, when the show would open in the Garden. Sunday was a day when people would be out and about and especially in such fine weather, so I stayed in and read *The Rubber Band*, by Rex Stout, which had appeared in serial form in several *Saturday Evening Post* issues. It was a mystery, and I fell asleep reading much of it, but I remember the feeling of getting more and more suspicious about Gumpertz and the conspiracy they were all leading against me.

A small breakfast from Nurse Sanders, soup for lunch, and no steaks was making me angry. After all, this was New York! What's a fellow to eat, if you don't have steaks in New York? Clams Casino, maybe pork chops, but vegetable soup? I was angry as shit, and I let Sanders know. She was stubborn and always won. Finally, I convinced her that an afternoon whiskey would be good. She saw that it would likely calm me down, so she gave in. Night time was better, and she cooked us some pork chops. But damn it if she didn't trim all the fat off! I had an evening drink and a glass of wine, and when she went to the lavatory, I poured a second wine and took an extra nip out of the whiskey bottle.

By Monday noon, I had eaten breakfast and I couldn't stand the confinement anymore. As I finished dressing I yelled at Sanders, "God damn it Sanders" – I almost always called her by her last name – "I can't take another day of light soup and being pent up in this place."

"What would you have me do, Mr. John? Do you think that I should just let you die by eating a giant steak and drinking in the afternoon?" I just stared, raising my left eyebrow, and we said nothing for a long while. Then finally I answered, "I don't really give a shit; we are going to lunch – out."

New York was vastly different than John remembered it. It had only been six months since he was last in town. He had left quickly after making the codicil a legal document removing his sister and his nephews from any inheritance from his estate. He had hoped that Johnny would grow up and get the message. After all, John and Henry had never been heirs, only executors. Some things had been meant to remain the same. The New York of 1936 seemed faster, more dangerous, and less caring than the New York John had hoped to shape. John, although from another world, felt that he was up to the task. It was opening night at the Garden, April 8th, the moment he had been preparing for all winter. John had stayed put in his apartment as long as he could. He had a terrible fight with Nurse Sanders, and they had barely spoken for a couple days. Even when they first went out to lunch, at Lindy's, she and John sat in silence, as she watched him devour a plate of food and thought, "Surely this will be the end of him," and he, not looking up at her, knowing full well that she was judging him for every swallow of beer he drank. He drank a new beer, modern in name but was like the old style lagers made by Germans. It was called National Premium. "Odd name," he thought to himself, "America is pulling together for some great national event."   He thought about Europe, the coming Olympic

Games, Hitler, and Roosevelt. The world was changing and he thought himself left behind. His thoughts plummeted, and he saw himself as older, out of date, and his mind simultaneously raced through images of yesteryear's circus shows, Mike Rooney, Delevan, Jake Posey, and the forty horse hitch. "God what a show!" he thought to himself, as he remembered when a six or eight horse hitch, with Al at the reins, was a plenty big show in the early days, and remembered the whole thing growing until Jake, a man of insurmountable stature, could drive that bell wagon with a forty horse hitch. His heart raced and he was excited.

"I can get it back," he thought as he pictured his brothers' faces. He had a hard time seeing them as they were, only as they gazed out from those last posters of the five of them, and then he'd see his own face and recognized that his eyes were gazing at something else. "Shit, I fucked it all to hell," he thought, "I missed the boat. Even Charley, dreaming big for Sarasota, never forgot the source."

"Eat the beans," Nurse Sanders interrupted. "For God's sake, if you're going to gobble all that meat and fat, eat something green." He smiled at Sanders, and for a moment he was back in Ca' d'Zan where he imagined she was Mable, and they were eating Alsatian wonders, prepared by Sophie, who had brought forth delightful cooking like Mama. John stared at Sanders' mouth, remembering Mable. Sometimes she would talk, and John would just watch her lips as if heaven's music was brushing up against his heart.

"Eat your beans," she repeated, "you have to eat something healthy." John shook himself from the dream and drank some beer. "You're trying to fuckin' kill me," he shot back.

"Oh for God's sake," she defended herself, "why do you even have me here if you're not going to listen?" John's mind fell back into the Golden Memories, the idea of great races, posing statuary high over head, Lillian Leitzel, Katie Sandwina the strong woman, and he kept seeing Jake Posey and that forty horse hitch.

"Nothing like it," he responded.

"Like what?" Nurse Sanders asked, a bit puzzled by his response.

"Like beans," John answered, as he stabbed a forkful, shoved it in his mouth, and talked with his mouth full of beans, "I can't get enough, see?"

On opening night John was nervous and pacing. He had dressed in a darker suit. It was not black, he despised black suits, but dark gray. He searched his hats for the appropriate one. There was a knock at his door, and he went, leaving the hat business behind, and opened the door knowing full well it was Sanders.

"Yes," he said as he left it one quarter open, looking down at her and noticing she was dressed to accompany him.

"Should I call for your car," she asked. "I know you wanted to be early."

"I'm going alone," he answered, noticing immediately that her expression became somber. "Don't try to change my mind. I have to do this by myself."

"But John..."

"Ina, this is my show, my night." He paused and became softer as he addressed her, "Ina, I know you are here to help me, but this time it is my decision, my night, and you have nothing to say about it. Yes, call for my car." He closed the door and went back to the hats.

John arrived at Madison Square Garden later than he had planned. Wet snow was falling, and the traffic was barely moving. It was less than half an hour to show time and the crowds were immense. He had his driver stop at 8th and 49th, instead of right in front. He didn't want to draw attention to his Rolls but rather thought he should just walk in like he belonged there, which he felt he did. His driver opened the door, and John used both canes as he slid his feet to the curb and pulled himself up and looked at the Garden.

"Watch for me," John commanded, "I don't know how long I'll be."

"Yes sir, Mr. Ringling," the driver answered and did not try to help John, as he knew it annoyed him.

John stepped to the curb, largely unnoticed by the crowds in the massive line, children pushing, parents corralling. Some eyed him, an elegant man in tailored clothes, his overcoat over one arm, two canes and a stylish Homburg hat, not as modern as many hats of 1936. He stood admiring the Garden. "Tex and I did a splendid job," he thought to himself, remembering the construction, which had taken only about eight months to build. He kept outside the fray, walking toward a door controlled by an usher. They held it open for him, knowing full well who he was, having been given orders not to confront him but merely to alert management that Mr. Ringling was on the lot. As he entered, he was warmed by the smells and sounds, the yeasty funnel cakes, the popcorn, the children with twirly toys and bullwhips, and the overwhelming roar of anticipation. He felt himself heading for his seat, wanting to see the show but turned and made for the back lot. As he walked through the halls he eyed the circus lithos, designed by Roland Butler, who John had brought to the show in '28. Although beautifully executed, they were not the style John would have wanted. "I'd better have a talk with Roland," he thought, "and why the fuck does the show have pygmy elephants in it? People like elephants because of the huge size. Must be Gumpertz's doing."

John's eyes were searching. "Who should I start with?" he thought, knowing that many performers were not permitted to talk to circus execs, and John was still president. As he walked down the hall past performers and handlers, people stared, and as he looked up to meet their eyes he noticed they nervously and quickly looked away. Then he saw Harry Lewiston, who spied John and walked quickly up to Frank Cook, whose back was to John as he was talking to someone; it looked like Jenny Rooney. Cook and Lewiston turned and looked back at John, and then they walked off quickly. "Lewiston, God damn prick," John thought as he recalled that Lewiston was a grafter, "hell of an orator, but what is a grafter doing on my lot?" Jenny walked up and greeted John.

"Well, this is a surprise, Mr. Ringling," she said, reached out and shook his hand. Jenny Rooney was an aerialist, beautiful, and she was strong and could command the scene. "We haven't seen you on the lot for a few years."

"Hello Jenny," John replied with a kind and soft John Ringling voice. Although most performers were not permitted to speak to the execs, the stars were, and John had originally brought the Rooneys to the show. "Tell me Jenny, is that grafter Harry Lewiston part of our show now?" She reacted nervously.

"The show is about to start," she said quickly, her eyes darting about. "I'm not, I can't, I have to go, sorry Mr. Ringling." She retracted her hand quickly and walked off. John continued walking as performers, handlers, and management walked by. He continued down toward the lower level. Then he made out Karl Wallenda who passed John hurriedly.

"Karl," he called out, "Karl!" Wallenda stopped, looking ahead, not wanting to turn and look at John. After a moment, he turned and smiled. "John," he greeted him stepping forward, both hands out and shaking John's hand and gripping his upper arm toward his shoulder. Karl Wallenda, head of the family and troupe of actors the Great Wallendas, was one of the only performers allowed to greet John Ringling solely by his first name.

"Karl," John continued shaking his hand nervously, "after the show, I have a plan, a new show, it'll be..."

"John, I'm not supposed to talk to you," said Karl, pulling back. "I could get fired!" John stood, coat in hand, speechless. He watched as an endless stream of circus family walked by. Some would look at him, and then quickly their eyes darted away. Karl walked off, fading into the crowd. John continued on and headed down the hall away from the back door, the place where every act entered the show, and into the menagerie. There he was, in with the sawdust and the shit. For the first time he really loved the smell. All those years he had merely put up with that smell; now he wanted it, he wanted to bask in it, fill his every breath with it.

I stood there for a while in the menagerie. I looked around and realized I was completely by myself. The public was leaving as the whistle was about to blow. The show was about to start. It was strangely quiet. I could hear elephants rumble and camels chewing. There was a line up of Sam's pygmy elephants. Handlers gave the signals and elephant shit was falling. I always admired how they could get the elephants to do that before the performance. Then I saw George Henderson. His eyes met mine, and he made no effort to look away. His head tilted, and we both smiled at each other. I wanted to run up and hug the guy. Then his eyes looked over my shoulder and behind me. His expression changed.

"John!" came a call from behind. It was Sam. As I stared ahead looking for solace in George's gaze, he said it again, "John!" I hated him for that. It was like he was snapping a bullwhip at a big cat, like Frank Buck and the exotic animal acts. As I drew a deep breath and turned, all the way around, people, actors, handlers, roustabouts, and twenty or so from the public had stopped, made their focus on me and encircled me. It reminded me of when I was a kid in school and a bunch of boys gathered round me and Kendall Baird. We had a fisticuffs and he bloodied my nose. Kids laughed at me. The kind of laughing that made me sick. There he was, Sam Gumpertz and an entourage. Some of them were my guys, Pat Valdo, Frank Cook, Ralph Clawson, and back of Sam, like a timid little mouse, my nephew Johnny, all dressed up like he wanted to be a showman. I leaned on my cane on my left side, and my overcoat slid off into the sawdust. I pretended not to notice. I raised the cane on my right and pointed it in Sam's face. He was only about fifteen feet away.

"You're a cheap fuckin' son of a bitch thief Sam."

"I've only taken what was mine to take, John," he replied in an arrogant voice, "you blundered pretty bad."

"I blundered what was mine to blunder," I yelled shaking the cane at him. My heart was pounding. "You conspired, the whole fuckin' time."

"Watch your language, John, this is a family establishment."

"Family," I inched closer still holding the cane, every bit of my blood surging. "Family, what would you know about family, you weasel?"

"John," he went on, "I can have you removed." That made my

blood boil. That was enough, but he went on, "Why don't you just walk out the door like a good little fellow and spare us all the drama?" He turned his back on me and began walking away.

"Don't you turn your back on me you little kike!" I don't know where the word came from, but he stopped, and turned, looking back at me.

"That's right, you're a fuckin' thieving Jew, just like that little grafter over there." I pointed at Lewiston who was behind Gumpertz, shaking his head. I don't know why I said those words, kike and thieving Jew, but I wanted to hurt the man, like he'd hurt me.

"I'm gonna make you eat your words," he fired back, "you tried to kill the show, little by little, just like you killed Mable." I can't even remember how the rest of it got the way it did. I just know the cane was in my hands, and I swung it around with all my might, screaming at the top of my lungs, and fell forward toward Sam with the cane going straight at his head. "You fuckin' son of a bitch. I started this circus with my own flesh and my own blood." The cane came down in mid-air making no connection with Sam, and I went with it, smack down on my knees and my belly. I could hear the circus folks let out a moan of despair. I heard some fat people with kids laughing, and then one of them actually whispered to another, "He thinks this is his circus."

Sam turned to a roustabout and said, "Show Mr. Ringling out." Then Sam and his entourage turned and walked off. I felt like a stupid school kid. Right in front of everybody. George Henderson ran up and helped me to my feet. "I'm sorry, John," George said softly, so as not to be heard by Sam and the others. "Help Mr. Ringling to the door would ya, Bernie."

"Yes sir, Mr. George," said the roustabout as he helped me up. We headed toward the door. My knees hurt something awful, but I didn't want anyone to see, and I could feel the cool air on my butt and knew I'd split the seam of my pants. As we went down the hall, the roustabout went on, "I'm sorry Mr. John." That made me feel good, to be called Mr. John. "I'm sorry sir," he repeated. He held the door open for me, "Good night Mr. Ringling." I walked out.

That's it boys. That's all there is to tell.

Luchow's had long since closed, and the night light was turning to dawn. John Ringling took a large swallow of whiskey, not finishing his glass. He stood up, putting his coat over his arm, and headed for the door.

"Aren't you gonna try to get your show back?" Ed called out.

"Nope." John turned and looked at Jimmy and Ed, "The show's got its own life now. But, Ed and Jimmy, I do appreciate your willingness to hear my story."

"What about Gumpertz?" Ed said, "I mean, he did you wrong."

"Boys," John replied, "it's a circus. What goes around comes around." John opened the door, and Ed urgently asked, "What about your nephew, Johnny North?" John chuckled.

"Oh, he'll figure it out," John looked up and pondered his last words, "that is, if he's going to become a real showman." Laughing lightly and thoughtfully, John Ringling closed the door. The two men watched in silence as he climbed into his Rolls Royce, and it drove off.

The Long Ticket Line

John had enough of Florida. The show would come home in a couple weeks, closing in Tampa on November 11th. He didn't want to be in Sarasota one more time at closing. The thought of it made him sad. At the end of October, he hitched the Jomar and headed for New York. He brought with him several things, the new show ideas he wanted to create and the July issue of *Greater Show World*, honoring Sam Gumpertz in his Golden Anniversary as a showman. His notes were kept in a pigskin portfolio that Mable had used to collect her images and scraps for the design of Ca' d'Zan. It was worn, and when he held it he gripped it hard. Occasionally he would smell it, when no one was looking, and he thought he could smell her, her neck, that smell, like a rose garden, the memories. The issue of *Greater Show World* had devoted the cover to Sam, with a huge photo portrait of him, his round glasses, his humble face, a forward glance with that expression, quietly emitting what appeared to John Ringling as the "I own it all now" look. John did not like the cover, so he usually left it rolled up as he had carried it that way for months. He brought Nurse Sanders too. His health was failing, but he made believe he was getting stronger and even said so, every day. The train made from Tampa to Jacksonville and then on up the east coast. He stopped on November 1st in Charlotte, North Carolina. There he stayed that night and dined in the Jomar with Nurse Sanders. His meal annoyed him, as she had him eating chicken and green beans. There was no potato, no steak, no second helpings, and only one scotch. She allowed him a glass of wine with dinner. He had a bottle of scotch hidden under the seat cushion of his large wicker chair in the sitting room, but he feared she would catch him taking a nip, so he waited for her to go to sleep before he tried for it.

"Why are we stopped in Charlotte?" she asked him after dinner began. He waited a long time to respond and took the time to take a bite of chicken and chew it. He chewed slowly and on the right side because his left side teeth, both top and bottom, had bothered him for several months.

"I have business, here in town tomorrow afternoon." He didn't look up at her, and she suspected he was hiding something but didn't pry.

"I can go with you?" she asked, sipping her wine. Sanders never drank more than half a glass of wine, and this pissed John off. "The waste of it all," he would say to himself.

"No, I'll get a driver." He looked up, and her eyes were questioning, so he looked away. "I have to do this by myself. I'll be fine."

"Are you sure?" She wiped her face and put her napkin on the table, in the same fashion a fellow does when he takes off his glasses and wants to look sincere.

"I'll be fine." He was a bit annoyed, so she dropped it.

After the meal they both read, she a dime novel, and John the dreaded *Greater Show World*. He stared blankly at the pages and the names of his old pals, acts, some of whom he had given a start to, and the pages and advertisements, all of them sucking up to Gumpertz. Fred Bradna, Pat Valdo, The Concellos, Ed and Jenny Rooney, the Wallendas, and it went on and on. He thought to himself, "Have they all lost their minds? Maybe he put something in the water." He thought back to that March night, when Jenny Rooney simply walked away seeing John entering the menagerie and Karl Wallenda said, "John, I am sorry, I can't be seen with you now." It was like a nightmare. "The freak Gumpertz had put a spell on them," he thought. Nurse Sanders retired to her room, and John reached behind the pillow for the bottle, where he had hidden it in Tampa. It was gone! Then he felt and there was a flask, not full. He pulled it out, and it had a bow on it. "Shit," he swore to himself, "she took it." Nurse Sanders had taken the bottle leaving John's flask half full. "It's half empty," he thought. "How does she expect I'm gonna have any pleasure anyway?" He opened it and took a big swig, finishing most of it, trying to save some for a second nip. He pawed through the notes for Golden Memories, making believe he was going to do something with it. After he had spread the whole thing over the sofa, he slowly organized it again and eventually put it back in the portfolio. He closed it and brought it to his lips, and under his nose, he inhaled. He swore he could smell her but knew he was smelling only the sweat and oils from his hands. He tried to conjure up her face, her beautiful smile. It was blank. His chest heaved and he tried to stop it. His eyes welled up. Then he looked down at the rolled up magazine. He stopped just before he would have collapsed into an uncontrollable breakdown, as he had done so many times. He used to sit in the bathroom at Ca' d'Zan and sob. Sometimes for a half hour or more. He kept it a secret. He picked up the flask and drank the rest.

The next day he was up at eleven and had his usual breakfast. Nurse Sanders had already eaten and drunk tea with John. They talked little. She had gone for a dawn walk and figured out John's "business." Down the tracks she had seen the huge entourage off loading before the show moved from the tracks to the fairgrounds. There were no more parades for The Greatest Show On Earth. Still, hordes of school children and eager onlookers watched a parade without music. It was eerily quiet.

John had watched his last parade at another show, the autumn of 1935. John had remained close to Buddy, Henry Ringling North. He had let on about the codicil; however, he had never disclosed to his nephew the full contents of it, nor his own intention in having made a codicil. John, having suffered more than one stroke, knew his end was in sight. Buddy took him everywhere that he wanted to go that year, touring western Florida in the top down Rolls. The car, expressing a great need for maintenance and repair, was still grand, and Ringling enjoyed the open air journeys. They made for Pensacola and the arrival of the Cole Brothers Circus. John wanted the opportunity to see one more circus parade, and this would have to be it. Since the arrival of the Big One, The Greatest Show On Earth, when the two great shows finally combined in 1919, the Ringlings could not maintain a circus parade. God knows they tried. The huge parade was almost three miles long and not only tied up traffic and left the show with countless and expensive fines, but the public became bored of it.

After a time, people could not maintain an interest in something so grand that went on for hours. Even Jake Posey with forty horses at the Bell Wagon did not garner enough excitement. Sure, the kids loved it, but they too became anxious after a while, fired slingshots at horses or wild animal cages. Ringling Bros. ended their magnificent parades.

John and Buddy arrived in Pensacola and had arranged a room in the Hotel San Carlos on Palafox Street. When Buddy went to register at the front desk, they were surprised to find that they had been given a room in the back overlooking an empty lot.

"We requested a room with a balcony, where we could watch the parade tomorrow," Buddy insisted.

"I'm sorry Mr. North," the young clerk responded with a whiny voice. "There are no balcony rooms left." At that moment John Ringling walked in. He was still an imposing figure, in his tailored suit, and although somewhat hunched over his cane, he still was taller than six feet.

"Am I hearing correctly," Ringling began raising his voice, "you have no balcony room for us?" At that moment an older gentleman appeared from a room behind the counter. "What seems to be the problem here?" he asked with authority and acted as the manager, which he was.

"We reserved a balcony room," Henry responded, and although he was angry, his young voice lacked command. "We want to be able to see the circus parade tomorrow."

"I see," the manager answered, half looking down at the counter beneath and glancing occasionally at Ringling. "I am afraid, young man, that we do not..."

"Do you know who this is?" Buddy asked, as if the fellow had no idea.

"Well, I..." the manager hesitated and Buddy leaned in, as John was eyeing the ceiling of the grand old hotel. He remembered staying there in 1910, when it was new and elegant.

"The man is Mr. John Ringling," he said quietly as if John could not hear him, and John pretended to not be listening.

"I see," the manager responded equally softly, and then in a louder more audible voice, "let me see what I can do." He turned and went into the office, partially closing the door. The young clerk looked around nervously, and then as a young couple strolled to the desk he asked, "May I help you" and began to accommodate their reservation. The manager returned with some paperwork in hand.

"Now, it seems we had a mix up," he began, "I found your reservation, and indeed there is a balcony." John turned from his reviewing of the lobby and looked over, admiring young Buddy. The man smiled at Ringling, but John pretended not to notice. It turned out they had the best view from the whole place.

The next morning, as they sat on their balcony, they heard first the drums, then an air calliope. Slowly the parade made its way up the street. Henry was shocked at the condition of the show, the deteriorated wagons, the uniforms from another time, and the overall condition of what was once a great show. John paid little attention, and in fact at times did not even look. His heart was racing, and his memory hearkened back to the Ringling Brothers' World's Greatest Shows. He remembered another time. It sparked an idea in him about recreating another age. His memories were Golden, a time when it all meant something. His eyes welled up, but he did his best not to let on. He never liked the boy to see him cry. That October day in Pensacola was the last circus parade John Ringling ever watched.

In Charlotte at 1:00 p.m. Tomlinson told John that his car was ready, and John, now dressed in his best linen suit, made for the limo. It was not his Rolls Royce or Pierce Arrow but a rented Lincoln. As they held the door open, John, with a cane to walk on and a second held sideways, stepped in, totally in command. They arrived up front, and there was no fanfare and the crowds did not part. Those attending the matinee were eager to get under the canvas as a light rain was falling and the day was cool. John had to wait in line like the rest. Children pushed and people talked loudly, and no one paid respect to Mr. Ringling. He wondered, "How would they act if they knew who I was?" It felt like a dream.

As he approached the ticket office, he saw Frank Cook, assistant manager, who pretended not to notice John and quickly disappeared. A mother and two boys were in front, and as they got their tickets, the boys were fighting and pushing, and one boy turning to run smacked right into John's crotch, stepped on his large shoes, and almost knocked him over. The mother grabbed the boys. "I'm so sorry sir," she said to John and began scolding the two boys. "If you don't act your age, we won't be going to the circus, do you hear me?" She had one by the wrist and one by the back of his collar. John leaned forward using both canes and got right down at eye level to the boys.

"You boys should be excited. You're gonna have fun today. Don't you ever forget it." They looked at John, slowly nodding, a bit perplexed that an old man and a stranger would talk to them. The mother said again, "Sorry." Ringling, struggling to get upright, tilted his head, smiled and said, "You needn't worry about them, ma'am. That's how boys should be." She walked off and scolded the boys again, leaving John at the ticket office, now under cover. The rain began falling harder. The ticket seller looked at John and greeted him anonymously, "Yes sir, how many tickets?"

"I'd like a hundred please," John said and stared back as the ticket taker bunched his lips together, looked down and then back up at John.

"A hundred tickets sir?" He looked at John, knowing full well who Mr. Ringling was, but pretending not to.

"A hundred dollars," John answered. The man stood in silence, breathing heavily.

"I'm sorry Mr. Ringling," he began and then tilted his head empathetically, "but Mr. Gumpertz said we ain't sposed to give you no money – no more." The ticket man took his eyes off John and looked at the crowd behind him. Then as he looked back, John had already turned and had begun walking away. As the rain fell harder, John Ringling walked past his car and headed towards the rail yard. In the pouring rain he noticed the lines of children, the smiles on their faces; wet or not they were happy and curious faces. He had lived for that.

As the Jomar made for New York, a notice appeared in the Sarasota Herald that Ca' d'Zan, its furnishings, John's art collection, one hundred thirty six acres on Longboat Key, and the remainder of John Ringling's holdings in the Sarasota Ritz-Carlton would be placed in auction on December 7th. As John arrived in Manhattan he received notice. He swore it would never happen.

On a rainy day in December, in his apartment in New York, John's doctor, Nurse Sanders, and Frank Hennesey sat by his side. He coughed wildly, bringing up blood. Pneumonia had penetrated deep into his lungs. He did not seem to know where he was. John called out for Ida, "Ida, Ida, it hurts, it, Ida..." Nurse Sanders moved close to the bed and sat in the chair next to it, and then leaned in, making believe she was Ida.

"I'm here."

"Ida," John said in a soft, almost whisper.

"I'm here John," she said, leaning in close.

John whispered, "Boy figure – Boy." John's breath changed and a smile came upon his face. He said, "Charley?" He died on December 2nd, 1936. It was Charley's birthday.

Requiem for a Showman

When John Ringling died, he had three hundred eleven dollars in his bank account. His estate was then valued at over twenty million dollars. In 2010 dollars that would be over $325 million. As John Ringling passed, the longest estate battle in U.S. history began. Those filing for pieces of what was left of Ringling were piling on to the more than one hundred law suits already pending against him in his last days. Estate lawyers say that it lasted ten years, the time that it was in probate. Family battles over the circus lasted almost thirty years, until the show was sold out of the family. There were many battles, and more people won than lost. In the end, whether it was 1966, or 2007, John Ringling was the ultimate winner. From the grave he got everything he wanted.

Ida Ringling North, John's sister, and her son John Ringling North remained as executors of the estate. The now famous codicil, written on Ritz-Carlton stationary, removed Ida from inheriting John's residual estate. By adding the codicil, written in New York, a new complexity was added to the already lengthy probate process, making it more drawn out. John Ringling North and his mother Ida gained more time and were able to further control the estate. As executors, they were well paid and able to manage the long affair. John Ringling North was able to pay off Allied Owners. It seems he really did become a showman. The show had been grossly neglected, and Sam Gumpertz was replaced by John Ringling North. John North and his brother Henry gained control of the show, and after lengthy battles with Edith Conway Ringling and Aubrey Ringling, took the show out of tents and ran it as an indoor circus. The term "under canvas" would no longer apply to The Greatest Show On Earth. The show was sold out of the family in the end of 1966. The deal was signed by John Ringling North and the new owner, Irving Feld, with partners, in the Coliseum in Rome, Italy. Today, "Ringling" is synonymous with "circus" worldwide. Henry Ringling North remained active in management of The Greatest Show On Earth through much of his life. He died in 1993. Although they died seven years apart, both John and Mable died in New York, and their bodies were put in a New Jersey mausoleum. It had been their wishes to be interred in Sarasota, on the grounds of the John and Mable Ringling Museum of Art. Henry Ringling North persevered to see this happen, and in the 1990s they finally got their wish. Their bodies now rest near Mable's rose garden, which thrives today and is honored amongst Mable's fans and supporters. That final resting place is adjacent to Mable's secret garden. Ida Ringling North is buried alongside of John and Mable. Henry Ringling North's son, John Ringling North II is a revered showman and owns the Kelly Miller Circus.

In 2007 the museum celebrated the completion of a seventy six million dollar expansion and renovation. One of America's largest museum complexes, it is designated the Official State Art Museum of Florida. It houses the John and Mable Ringling Museum of Art, Ca' d'Zan Mansion, the Asolo Theater, the Ringling Museum of the American Circus, several other galleries, a learning center, the Mable Burton Ringling Rose Garden, and the Wisconsin, John and Mable's first private train car. Had John Ringling died six days later, all of these properties would have been auctioned off to private owners. The Jomar, their second train car, is also in Sarasota being restored by private owner and enthusiast, Bob Horne. The Ringling College of Art & Design is a thriving institution and the top animation school in the United States.

If one is to look at Sarasota today, one might see the very vision that John Ringling held for the place: planned communities, resorts, and even an elegantly appointed Ritz-Carlton with a boardroom called the John Ringling Meeting Room. John and Mable Ringling's Greatest Show lives on, in Sarasota and in the hearts and minds of children of all ages.

Glossary of Circus terms
also called "Cirky Lingo"

24-hour Man - An employee who travels the route twenty four hours before the rest of the circus, putting up roadside arrows to direct travel and making sure the lot is ready.

Aba-daba - Any dessert served in the cookhouse.

Ace Note - A dollar bill.

Advance - Teams of employees who traveled ahead of the circus route to put up posters and arrange for advertising, usually arriving in each town four weeks, two weeks, and one week before the show. They often traveled on dedicated "advance cars" or "bill cars," railcars carried on freight trains, and had just one day to carry out their assignments. The team and its ad campaign were simply called "the advance." "Bill Posters" pasted multi-sheet posters on the outsides of buildings and fences with buckets of flour-and-water paste, long-handled paste brushes, and ladders. "Lithographers" bartered with local merchants, trading passes for the right to place one-sheets, half-sheets, and panels in store windows. Any of them might hire local youths to distribute heralds door-to-door. Certain advance men also ordered goods, such as food, feed, sawdust, and reserved services such as hotels.

Advise - The official schedule, posted on the outside of the backdoor and elsewhere, listing the current revision of the time and sequence of the acts.

Aerialist - Circus artist who performs suspended above the ground on a trapeze or similar equipment.

AGVA - The American Guild of Variety Artists, a union representing performers in the variety entertainment field, including circuses, Las Vegas showrooms and cabarets, musical variety shows, comedy showcases, dance revues, magic shows, amusement park shows, and arena and auditorium productions on tour.

Alfalfa - Paper money.

All Out and Over, All Out, All Over - The entire performance is concluded, the audience has vacated the big top and workers can begin re-setting or tearing down.

Annie Oakley - A complimentary ticket or free pass, also "ducat." The hole customarily punched in such a free pass recalled the bullet holes that Oakley, a wild west show sharpshooter, fired into small playing cards during her performances.

Arena - The large cage in which big cat acts are performed.

Arena Show - An indoor show, not under canvas.

Arrow - A paper sign, consisting simply of a large (usually red) printed arrow, used to mark the route between towns. Taped to the posts of road signs by the 24-hour man the day before the show arrives. Can be placed in any orientation: straight up arrows every few miles to let you know you're on the right road, a single tilted arrow to warn of an upcoming turn, and two or three tilted arrows in a group to indicate where to turn.

Artist - Preferred term for a circus performer.

Back Door - Performers' entrance to the big top.

Back Lot - The area outside the Big Top, especially where equipment, the wardrobe tents, and other non-performing areas are. The Cook Top (dining tent and dining shack) is located in the **back lot**. The back lot is also called the back yard.

Backyard - Name of a circus trade publication, also used to describe the back lot.

Baggage Stock - Horses used for hauling, as opposed to performing horses called "ring stock." On some small mud shows horses also "doubled in brass," meaning they could be working baggage stock and ring stock.

Bale Ring - In a large tent, the canvas is perforated by holes where the support poles will be, and each hole is fitted with a sturdy metal ring. The poles are placed in the rings as the canvas lies on the ground, and the rings are raised up the poles by ropes using blocks and tackle.

Ballet Girls - Dancers who appeared in multiple acts. Oftentimes they were actual ballet dancers. Circus could be more lucrative than ballet for many or at least provided steady employment.

Bally Broads, Bally Girls - Woman and girls who sang and danced in the circus spectacles. On the latter day shows, these girls also worked in the Aerial Ballet, rode menage horses, and appeared in multiple acts throughout the entire performance. Use of this term probably came from the employment of real ballet girls and dancers in the great circus spectacles of 1880 to 1910.

Ballyhoo - A clamorous attempt to win over customers. An orator calls out Ballyhoo, which not only describes acts but also sensationalizes them to bring the customers to the tent, i.e. the sideshow.

Banjo Light - A large, round pan-shaped metal reflector containing a gasoline or kerosene flame, used to light tent interiors before electricity.

Barn - Winter quarters. "Back to the barn," after the closing stand means going home.

Benefit - A contractual arrangement under which the entire profit from one or more entire performances would go to a star performer. The idea was that this part of the performer's pay would, in fairness, depend on the performer's drawing power as well as the chance factors that affect the business. Benefits went out of use early in the 20th century.

Bibles - Souvenir programs. Also, boards placed under the reserved seat chairs, so called because they folded closed like a bible. *amusement Business*, the trade magazine, was sometimes also called "the Bible."

Big Bertha or The Big One - Ringling Bros. and Barnum & Bailey Circus. The Big One was first used by the last three brothers to describe the show when the two great circuses were finally combined in 1919.

Big Cats - Performing lions and tigers.

Big Top - The main tent used for the performance. (A tent is a top plus some walls, so the "big top" would be the largest tent on the lot.)

Bill - An advertising poster.

Blowdown - When the tents are blown down by a storm. Some shows were totally lost to a blowdown, and they could be deadly to people and animals.

Blow Off - The end of the show when the concessionaires come out. Also, the visual "punchline" of a clown gag.

Blues or Stringers - The general admission seats, usually painted blue. In engineering, "stringers" are long supporting members.

Boat Show - In the 19th century Boat Shows traveled the Mississippi River, with circus and wild west shows. They only played to towns on the river.

Boss Hostler - The man who traveled ahead of the mud shows to mark the way for the caravan, sometimes used to denote the one in charge of all horses in a show, also acted as a foreman. In the early days, he may have been the general manager.

Brodie - An accidental fall but one which has an element of stupidity or clumsiness, rather than disaster. From the name of Steve Brodie, who in 1886 claimed to have survived a jump off the Brooklyn Bridge.

Bugs - Chameleons or green anole lizards sold as novelties by butchers.

Bullhook or Ankus - The dull hook on a stick used by elephant trainers to "get the elephant's attention" and guide the animals to their tasks. If used properly, it is a good training tool. If misused, it can hurt the animals, just as a whip is used gently on a horse for training but if misused can hurt the animal. Mahouts have trained elephants for thousands of years and have learned to gentle these animals with respect.

Bullhand or Bull Handler or Bullman - Employee working with the elephants.

Bulls - Elephants, whether male or female. Also (mostly with affection) "rubber cows." Females are often referred to as "cows'" even though the entire group may be called "bulls."

Bull Tub - Heavy, round metal pedestal upon which an elephant sits or stands.

"Bump a Nose" - Some people cite this as the "good luck" phrase clowns used with each other before a performance, rather like actors' "break a leg." In reality, it's amateur clown jargon. A circus clown would be much more likely to say something like "go f**k yourself" as a good saying.

Bunce - Profits, perhaps derived from "bounce."

Butcher - Vendors, whether strolling or stationary, selling refreshments or souvenirs. Circus food is usually sold in an order, i.e. very salty food first, followed by drinks, then the last and slowest food, chewy candy or caramel apples at or near the end of the show.

Calliope - A musical instrument consisting of a series of steam whistles played like an organ. From "Calliope," the Greek muse of music. Later calliopes were driven by compressed air. Circus people pronounce it "cowley-ope."

Caring Clown - Not a traditional circus term. Used by amateurs (and Ringling publicity) to refer to clowns who specialize in hospital visits. Ringlings began sending clowns and other actors to children's hospitals in the mid 1890's.

Carpet Clown - A clown who works either among the audience or on the arena floor.

Catcher - The member of a trapeze act who catches the flyer after he has released himself from the bar in a flying return act.

Cats - Lions, tigers, leopards, panthers.

Cattle Guard - A set of low seats placed in front of the general admission seats to accommodate overflow audiences.

Center Pole or King Pole - The first pole of the tent to be raised. It is about sixty feet high and holds the peak of the tent. The techniques used to raise and hold it are said to have been first used by the early Egyptian stone masons.

Character Clown - A clown who dresses in a character costume, often a tramp, but sometimes a policeman, fireman, etc.

Charivari - A noisy whirlwind entrance of clowns, musical performers, etc., an alternate spelling of the word "shivaree."

Charley (v.) - To ditch a poster or group of posters or handbills instead of posting or distributing them as assigned.

Charley (n.) - "To pull a Charley" referred to getting rid of bad actors, with full pay for services performed. It came from Charles Ringling's idea to ditch the performers who refused to "double in brass," in the early Concert and Comedy days.

Cherry Pie - Extra jobs done by circus personnel for extra pay.

Chinese - Extra jobs done by circus personnel without additional pay. Circus contracts often call for employees, in addition to the job they signed on for, to make themselves "generally useful," the meaning of which is often stretched to include all sorts of labor at all hours, until employees often feel that they are being abused by management as badly as Chinese laborers were while building the railroads.

Circus Candy - Very cheap confections with deceptively impressive packaging. Often sold in a special intermission pitch, with prize premiums as an incentive to buy.

Circus Fans Association of America - Fan organization established in 1926. Its local clubs are called "tents" and "tops." Publishes the members' magazine *The White Tops*. The loyalty of the fans is sincerely appreciated by circus performers and is seen as indispensable to the survival of small shows. Many a mud show performer has gotten a ride to the laundromat from a fan. However, fans can at times (like fans in any field) be both obsessive and intrusive, feeling entitled to enter the performers' private areas uninvited or meddle with the animals, entirely unappreciative of the danger.

Circus Headache - A real ailment, named because prolonged exposure to the ammonia fumes generated by animal waste can cause splitting headaches.

Circus Pole - Very early, mass produced candy hawked by candy butchers inside the tent. Stick candy, with a hard, brown, brittle outer layer and a soft coconut center.

Circus Report - Name of a weekly circus trade magazine.

Circus Tape - Adhesive cloth tape used to wrap trapeze bars and other circus equipment.

Cirky - Circus counterpart to the word "carny;" a circus employee.

Clem - A fight.

Cloud Swing - A swing without a bar used in an aerial act, really just a "u" of rope. Most performers using the cloud swing never used safety features.

Clown Alley - The clowns' dressing and prop area.

Clown Stop - A short clown gag (as opposed to a lengthy routine).

Come In - The period an hour before showtime when the public is entering the arena before the circus begins. Elephant and camel rides are offered for a fee during Come In. Butchers are selling their wares and clowns are on the floor. Some clowns specialized and only performed during Come In.

Concert or Aftershow - A second show as a concert sometimes following the main show, generally costing extra. Ringling Bros. World's Greatest Shows offered a pre-show concert beginning in 1895. It was free and was more classically oriented.

Contortionist - One who contorts his or her body, especially an acrobat capable of twisting into extraordinary positions.

Coochie Dancers - Burlesque dancers.

Cookhouse or Cookshack - The show dining area, sometimes separate from the dining tent. The dining tent would provide one sit down meal a day; the cookshack was a stand up operation.

Crier - Often used to describe sideshow talkers. With the advent of the big daily, free street parades, the talkers walked the parade route ahead of the "March" warning the towners to "Hold your hosses, the elephants are coming." Others followed the parade exhorting the on-lookers to "Follow the parade to the show grounds. Big free exhibitions on the show grounds immediately after the parade." This talk was also called Ballyhoo.

Day and Date - Two shows simultaneously in the same town.

Donkey Kick - The bareback rider's flip from a standing position to the hands.

Donniker - A restroom or toilet. Derived from "dunnekin," in common use among lower class Britons in the 1700s meaning "outhouse." Probably derived from "dung" and "kin." In the workingman's car there were donniker buckets instead of toilets. Some shows made the roustabouts and razorbacks pay to have the do niker buckets emptied.

Doors - Call meaning the house is open to the public.

Downtown Wagon - A circus wagon featuring a simple exhibit, parked prominently on a downtown street as advertising on circus day. Sometimes a ticket wagon would be located downtown to increase sales.

Dressage - An act by horses trained in dancelike stylized movements; the animals' paces are guided by subtle movements of the rider's body.

Dressing the House - To sell reserved seat tickets in a pattern so that all sections appear at least moderately filled with no obviously empty areas.

Ducat (sometimes "Ducket") - Free ticket to the show, also knows as an "Annie Oakley," or "comp," a term shared with theater. Sometimes also used to refer to money.

Ducat Grabber - Door tender or ticket collector.

Dukie or Dukey bag - A bag lunch provided for workers on the go.

Dukie tickets - Tickets to buy food from the cookhouse. This was used in place of money so that workers, especially riggers and roustabouts, would not take their food money and spend it on alcohol.

Dukie Run - Any circus run longer than an overnight haul. When Ringling's Sunday School Circus would leave a Saturday stand, they might have a Dukie run and get in late Sunday. They did not play any Sundays until 1895. Even then they often continued to skip Sundays. If they arrived early in town on Sunday, they would often play baseball with the locals or go fishing.

(the) Educator - Slang for *amusement Business*, a weekly publication for the outdoor entertainment industry.

Equestrian Director - The stage manager of the show, in formal riding wear (top hat, red jacket, etc.) who decided and signaled the pacing of the acts. His costume, functions, and whistle were later adopted by Ringmasters when they became chief announcers instead of livestock handlers.

Excursion Car - An advance railroad car with the larger circuses. The team on these cars made arrangements for special railroad excursion trains from various points to the show and were able to bring patrons to the circus. These trains were run to unprofitable towns and often brought in hundreds of show goers.

Exotic Animal Act - An animal act involving mixed species, i.e. lions and tigers in the same act.

Feet Jump-In - The leap of a bareback rider in equestrian acts, standing with the feet together, from the ground or teeterboard onto the back of a running horse.

Fink - Anything broken. Also "larry."

First of May - A novice performer or worker in his first season. Shows usually play the season's opening spot on the first of May, and you'll always find new help hired on the first of May who have never worked shows before.

Flag, or Flag's Up - The cookhouse is open.

Flare - Kerosene torches placed along the route from the railroad loading spur to the circus lot, to light the way during a night haul.

Flip-Flaps - Backward handsprings done on the ground.

Flukum - Refreshment butchers' term for no-brand grape or orange drink to be sold in the stands, usually made from cheap powdered flavorings.

Fly Bar - Aerialists' swing with a bar instead of a flat seat.

Flyers - Aerialists in flying acts, which involve "flying" through the air, from one high swing to another, the aerialist being propelled by the swing's momentum. The flyer's partner is the "catcher."

Flying Squadron - The first trucks or wagons to reach the lot.

Forty Miler - A newcomer who perhaps never traveled more than forty miles from home, similar to First of May.

Frog Pond - A lot that is under water, or pure mud.

Funambulist - Rope walker, from the Latin "funis" (rope) and "ambulare" (to walk).

Funny Ropes - Extra ropes added to regular ones, usually at angles, to give extra stability and spread to a canvas tent.

G-Top - A private tent where staff drink or gamble.

Gaffer - Circus manager.

Gag - A short clown trick that is over too quickly to be an act of its own.

Gallery - General seating area (the cheap seats), consisting of backless bleachers in the old days.

Garbage Joint - The souvenir or novelty stand.

Gaucho - Someone not born into circus life who takes a circus job. Possibly a corruption of the gypsy word "gadjo" (sometimes "gadje"), meaning a non-Gypsy. It is not related to the Spanish word "gaucho."

Geronimo - A "death dive" act, jumping from a great height onto a big air bag (as movie stunt men do today) or as a "sponge plunge" into an impossibly small amount of water. Most of the time it would be a man; he would climb to the top of the building out onto the beams, yell "Geronimo," and dive off hitting a big air bag on the floor. For dramatic effect a big bang would go off.

Gilly - Anyone not connected with the circus, an outsider or towner.

Gilly Wagon - Small utility wagon or cart.

Giraffe - A unicycle with seat and pedals atop a long pole, putting the rider high above the ground.

Graft - A piece of work, whether easy or hard.

Grafters - Different types of individuals who follow or work in the show and scheme the public out of funds. Also refers to gamblers who often trail a show.

Grand Entry - The opening parade, also called the "Spec" (for "spectacle"), in which all the artists enter.

Grandstand - The seating area facing the center ring of a three-ring circus, flanked by the less favorable viewing area called the "stalls."

Grease Joint - The hot dog or grill concession trailer. Hamburgers may have been invented in Chicago at the circus when sausage stuffers, or tubes, ran out, and sausage meat was first cooked as patties.

Grinder - A person who has a certain set sales pitch or sequence of words that he delivers on the front of a show as long as the doors are open. This pitch, given between ballyhoos, is called the grind. A good ticket seller "grinds" as he passes out the tickets.

Grouch Bag - A small bag or purse worn under the clothing, carrying the performer's valuables (which are likely to be stolen from an unattended dressing room).

(to) Guy Out - To check and tension the guy wires.

Guy Wires - Ropes that give horizontal support to rigging. Most things in the air use guy wires: flying acts, cloud swing, high wire, single traps, double traps, cradle, pretty much anything with a crane bar uses them.

Hair Hang - An aerial act in which a woman performer was suspended by her hair. More of an act was possible by this method than by the "iron jaw" method, because performers could hang longer by their hair than by their teeth.

Hammock Act - An aerialist is suspended entwined in one or two long cloths, alternately sliding down them, swinging from them, and wrapping them around the body. There is no rope or loop hidden in the cloths; the body suspended by friction. Similar to the **Strap Act**.

Harmonica - Considered a bad luck instrument.

Haul Route - Directions through the city from the rail yard to the lot or arena.

Hay Burners - Any of the hay or grain eating animals, i.e. horses, elephants, giraffes, etc.

Heat Merchant - An unscrupulous, advance sale, phone room ticket seller.

Heralds - Circus advertisements of black and white type, approximately 9 x 20 inches, sometimes pasted down but usually handed out.

"Hey Rube!" - Traditional battle cry of circus people in fights with townspeople. In modern times more likely to be "It's a clem!" or just "fight!"

High School Horse - A horse who has been taught fancy steps in special riding academies (see **Dressage**). Also refers to a horse being ridden, or one in a Lunge Line.

High Wire - A tightly stretched wire far above the floor on which a wire walker performs.

Hippodrome Track - The oval area between the rings and audience.

Hits - Good places to paste posters, like the walls of grain elevators, barns, buildings, or fences.

Home Run - The trip from Home Sweet Home (see below) back to winter quarters.

Home Sweet Home - The last stand of the season. Bill posters sometimes pasted one pack of posters upside down for the last stand.

Horse - One thousand dollars.

Horse Feed - Poor returns from poor business.

Horse Opry - Any circus (jokingly).

House - Theatre term for the audience seating area. As in "a full house" to indicate every seat taken. "Full to the ring banks" was often used also.

Howdah - Indian term for the seat on the back of an elephant or camel. Elephant and camel rides would be sold for an extra fee during "Come In."

Icarian Act - See **Risley Act**.

Iron-Jaw Trick - An aerial stunt using a metal bit and apparatus which fits into the performer's mouth, and from which he or she hangs suspended. Most of the time used as an opening number; someone dressed as a butterfly for example was raised to the top of the arena, waved a round a bit then lowered.

Jackpots - Tall tales about one's exploits in the circus ("war stories").

Jill - A girl.

Joey - Derived from Joseph Grimaldi, a famous clown in 18th century England. Some sources say it only refers to an auguste type clown; others say it is an amateur term not used on the lot.

John Robinson - A signal to cut or shorten an act, or to give a very short show altogether. Performers headed out to the ring might hear a manager say "John Robinson" to call for an abbreviated performance. In the middle of an act, if the ringmaster announced: "John Robinson please come to the rear entrance," the performer knew to go right into his last trick. Rarely used, but valuable in case of emergency or sometimes just a very long haul to the next lot.

Jonah - From the Biblical story of Jonah, a person who brings bad luck to everyone in his vicinity. This term was never exclusively a circus term but was in much wider general use in the past. A mother watching her child perform in the ring is almost certain to be a Jonah.

Jonah's Luck - Unusually bad weather or mud.

Jumbo -The popular use of the word "jumbo" to mean anything large comes from the name of a famous large elephant first exhibited in London, then sold to P.T. Barnum in 1882. London zookeepers named the elephant, probably drawing on "jambo," the traditional Swahili word of greeting. The elephant's popularity drove the word "jumbo" into general use. After Jumbo's death, Barnum stuffed the body and continued to show it, then donated him to Tufts University. Although the remains of Jumbo were destroyed in a fire, Jumbo is still the official Tufts mascot.   Other shows often referred to the Barnum show as "the old elephant bones" because of Barnum's exhibition of the elephant's body.

Jump - The distance between performances in different towns. "On the jump" might refer to having to work quickly, e.g. "Roustabouts were given dukie bags, from which they ate quickly as they were on the jump."

Jump Stand - An additional ticket booth near the front door used to sell extra tickets during a rush by spectators.

Keister - Sometimes used to refer to a circus wardrobe trunk, or any luggage. Also 19th century slang to mean buttocks, e.g. "I kicked 'im out on his keister." It also was used to mean a jail.

Kick Out - A date or ticket selling campaign that falls through.

Kicking Sawdust - Following the circus or being a part of it. Also "on the sawdust trail."

Kid Pusher - Employee, usually on a mud show, assigned to the job of recruiting and directing local youths in setting up the tops in return for free passes.

Kid Show - A sideshow. Also **Kid Worker**.

King Pole - The main support pole or mast for the tent, one, two, four, or more in number. A king pole sticks out through a hole in the canvas, and the canvas is pulled up around it with ropes. Very old canvas tents were rather fragile and had one king pole in the center with four, eight, or more queen poles around it. Queen poles also passed through holes and had pull up ropes, but were around the edges of the tent. Quarter poles were between the walls at the same distance from the king pole as the queen poles.

Kinker - Any circus performer, originally specific to acrobats.

Knockabout Act - Comedy act involving physical humor and exaggerated mock violence.

L.Q. - Living quarters on the lot, a trailer, an eighteen wheeler, or the sleeper car.

Lacing - The system of eyelets and rope loops that holds together the panels of a tent's walls.

Larry - "Something's wrong with it." Might describe damaged merchandise, something worn out beyond any usefulness, or even a person, however affable, who's a loser. Not a name and not capitalized: "He's just a larry."

Layout Man, Lot Man - The lot superintendent who decides the location of the various tents.

Left Hand Side - Most people move to the right. Right hand ticket boxes sell more tickets, right hand gates handle more traffic. A show that caters to children and early patrons is spotted on the right hand side. An attraction appealing to the late coming, "sporting element" are put on the back end or on the left hand side. Attractions with plenty of noise, like the motor drome, are laid out for the left side so that the noise will pull attention there.

Liberty Act - Liberty horses are trained horses performing without riders or tethers. It was said that horses "danced at liberty."

Lift - The natural bounce with which a bareback rider jumps from the ground to the back of a running horse.

Little People - Midgets or dwarfs. It is important to note that most people in circus sideshows are highly respected by all of the circus personnel. People were not judged for their differences but regarded as part of the "family."

Long Haul Town - A spot where the lot was a long way from the railroad loading spur.

Long Mount -When several elephants stand in line, each on hind legs, placing front legs on the back of the elephant in front of him.

Lot - The show grounds. Also **back lot** refers to the non public areas of the show, but in an indoor show might refer to every place other than the main show.

Lot Lice - Local townspeople who arrive early to watch the unloading of the circus and stay late. They are often called this derogatory term because they get in the way.

Lunge Line - A long tether allowing horses to run and do stunts around the periphery of the ring while the trainer stands in the center holding the line.

Mahout - Elephant trainer, bullman, usually from India, Thailand, Cambodia, or other far eastern countries where elephant training is a multi-generational tradition. Also slang "Mahut."

Main Guy - Guy rope to hold up the center pole in the Big Top.

The March - The street parade.

Marquee - The small entrance tent on most tented circuses.

Mechanic - A safety harness used in practice sessions by flyers, trampoline, bareback riders, high wire, perch acts, and tumblers. The practicing performer wears a harness attached to a rope that hangs above the middle of the ring. Called a "lunge" when the rope is fixed to the center of the ring and keeps the performer from falling outward.

Menage - Although in general horse terms it refers to an arena and dressage area, in circus it refers to a less sophisticated horse act occasionally called "high school." However, it gave both horses and trainers a chance to grow. Large shows would have very large menage acts.

Mud Shoe - A metal fitting to help slide center poles up when raising the Big Top.

Mud Show - A small tent show playing rural areas. Between 1884 and 1889 the Ringling shows were all mud shows. In that time it meant that it traveled by wagon and not by rail. These shows were often mired in mud.   Today Ringling Bros. Barnum and Bailey

Greatest Show on Earth is the only show that travels by rail.

Mule - A tractor used to move wagons. Most often it refers to rubber tired tractors although early versions sometimes had metal wheels.

Night Riders - Bill posters for competing circuses, who posted paper for their employers in a gentlemanly fashion by day, and tore down or covered up the bills for their competition by night.

Nut - The cost of the operation, overhead. "A big nut" was an expensive show.

OABA - Outdoor amusement Business Association, a lobby group for the rights, regulation, and protections of outdoor amusements. Mission: *"To encourage the growth and preservation of the outdoor amusement industry through leadership, legislation, education and membership services."*

On the Show- Describes performers and all others connected to the circus.

Opposition Paper - Advertising posters put up by competing circuses.

Pad Room - Room near the animals for pads and tack and harness, especially for elephants and horses. Many of the animal show handlers might keep their wardrobe there.

Paid Off, or Paid Off in the Dark - When someone is paid "off the books" in cash. Also "handled in the dark."

Paper - Posters, handbills, or advertisements for a carnival. Paper used to be mostly in the form of posters of various sizes pasted on walls, or handbills distributed door to door. Now, with laws against posting on the public right-of-way, and with flier distribution often called littering, paper mostly consists of coupons distributed in stores. Since local charities often "sponsor" the circus or carnival, posters put up by the charity are often officially overlooked by law enforcement. Beginning in the 1950s, there was a union for bill crews: the International Alliance of Billers, Billposters and Distributors. When a show played towns with a billposters' local, union member crews were required, and the paper would be rubber stamped with a small union logo indicating that the posters were put up by union members. This practice was often ignored in towns where there was no billposters' local or where there was not a strong pro-union sentiment.

Paper the House - Giving away free tickets. It served two purposes. First it helped give the sense of a packed house, and second, it helped increase sales. If the mayor and his family were going and each alderman had a ticket, the aldermen would buy tickets for their entire families. The Ringlings were all Masons and would give a bunch of tickets to lodge brothers. It served to get all the rest of the lodge brothers to buy more tickets for their families.

Patch or Patches - Those who walked the lot spotting trouble when grafters or pickpocketers riled customers. Their job was to smooth out the relationships with locals and keep fights from breaking out.

Pedestal - The platform that aerial fliers perch on while waiting to catch the swing (the "fly bar").

Perch Act - A balancing act involving use of apparatus upon which one person performs while being balanced by another.

Performance Director - The person in charge of the overall look of the show and all artists, very much like a theatrical director.

Performer's Trick - Something the performer does with great pride but which only other performers would appreciate, like a magician who learns sleights so skillful they awe other magicians but seem to the public no different than what their Uncle Bill can do.

Picture Gallery - A tattooed man or woman. Also **Paint Gallery**.

Pie Car - The railroad dining car. After the shows stopped traveling by rail, someone opened a "pie car" on every show. Opening after the cookhouse closed, it was probably the first convenience store. You could buy beer, cigarettes, sodas, chips, sandwiches, and sundries like socks, razors, and cards. If it was a little show, you would get fewer items such as soda, coffee, tube steak (a hot dog).

Pie Car Jr. - On the modern Ringling show, a trailer or wagon that provides meals on the back lot of the arena. What movie companies call "craft services" and rock concerts call "catering." Earlier versions were called **cook shacks**.

Pitchman - Generally a person making a pitch (sales talk) over the loudspeaker during a break in the show. Balloons, peanuts, souvenirs, toys, and more might be pitched. "While we are setting up for the next act, for the next two minutes Jim our balloon man will be selling balloons right in center ring for only a dollar. This will be the only time that this offer will be good! On the bottom of some of the balloons you will find a gold dot. When you find that gold dot, make sure you take that right out to our toy store and get your free prize. So hurry down and see Jim; you have only one minute left!" The people who sold the goods would tip the pitchman because the better the pitch the more you sold.

Plange - Aerialist's body swing-overs in which one hand and wrist hold a padded rope loop.

Pole Direction - The direction the wagons face on the railroad cars. For efficient unloading, they all needed to be positioned uniformly.

Ponger - An acrobat.

Possum Belly - Storage box built into the underside of a work wagon to carry cable, stakes, rigging, etc. At times a place for a quick nap by a worker, and at times the temporary home of an unauthorized traveling girlfriend (a "possum belly queen"). This was often a way for girls to escape their small town lives. During the first Ringling Concert Company, John Ringling may have hidden in the possum belly of the old Democrat wagon.

Privilege - The fee paid to the circus for the right to place a concession on the midway. In many shows a large privilege was paid by unscrupulous butchers and vendors who would short the customers and make very large sums. When Otto Ringling managed the show, he never allowed such grafting. This only furthered the circus perception of Ringlings' Sunday School Circus. It also improved public perception and increased family attendance.

Prop Hand - Crew member responsible for setting and placing props for the next act.

Punk Pusher - Supervisor of the work crew.

Quarter Poles - Poles which help support the weight of the canvas and take up the slack between center and side poles. A quarter pole does not pass through the canvas but usually has a mushroom shaped cap with two small holes. Ropes are sewn to the canvas on each side of a leather pad, and they pass through the holes to pull up the pole and secure it.

Rag Out - To tighten the tent poles.

Rag Tag, also **Rag bag** or **Stick and Rag Show** - A sloppy small show.

Rat Sheet - Advance posters or handbills with negative claims about the opposition.

Razorbacks - The men who loaded and unloaded railroad cars.

Red Lighted - A method of getting rid of unwanted cirkies: the owner departs and abandons the unwanted employee without paying.

By the time the abandoned employee realizes what's happened, all he sees is red lights disappearing down the road. An owner might tell a razorback to meet the circus somewhere, but the circus goes somewhere else. Some sources even use this word to mean that an unpopular person is thrown from the back of a moving vehicle or off a train. Also **Oil Spotted**, the moment when there's just you and the oily stains where the bus used to be. The Ringling Show never Red Lighted anyone during the years the original brothers were alive, with one possible exception: it was said that several people who seriously abused animals may have been thrown from the train.

Red Tent - Cooch tent or burlesque tent. The Ringling shows never had one.

Red Wagon - The main office wagon, also Red Car, the main office railcar.

Rigger - Worker specializing in assembling and managing the rigging.

Rigging - The apparatus used in high wire or aerial acts.

Ring - The circle in which circus acts are presented. Center ring was about forty two feet in diameter; it was also bigger and heavier made because that is where most of the animal acts worked. It was made strong enough that horses could walk on it. The side or end rings were about thirty six feet and not made as heavy.

Ring Banks or Curbs -Wooden curbing around the ring. "The show was full to the ring banks."

Ring Barn - A permanently roofed, full size circus ring for rehearsal at winter quarters. Occasionally used to describe a permanent or non-traveling show.

Ring Doors - The canvas panels artists push aside as they enter the performance area of the big top. Behind the ring doors is a small vestibule artists can stand in inside the "back door" but out of sight of the audience.

Ring Horse - A horse which performs in the center ring, trained to maintain timing despite distractions.

Ring Stock - Animals which perform in the show.

Ringmaster - The show's Master of Ceremonies and main announcer. Originally, he stood in the center of the ring and paced the horses for the riding acts, keeping the horses running smoothly while performers did their tricks on the horses' backs. Originally he was called the Equestrian Director; however, the Equestrian Director managed the entire cadence of the show. A good ringmaster could raise a small or poor show to a higher level.

Risley Act - Acrobatic act in which one or more performers support other performers on their feet. When the performers support props instead of people the act is often called "foot juggling."

Rola Bola - A board placed flat on top of a cylindrical roller. A performer stands on the board and balances while performing various feats.

Roll-Ups - Tame American aerial planges.

Roman Riding - A rider standing with one foot on the back of each of two horses.

Roper - A cowboy.

Rosin - Powdered dried plant gum used to prevent slipping.

Rosinback - Horse used for bareback riding. Horses' backs were sprinkled with rosin to prevent the rider from slipping. Percherons and other broadback horses are the most popular rosinbacks. Also called **Resinback.**

Roustabout - A circus workman, laborer.

Route - The annual itinerary, the schedule of towns to be played.

Route Book - Like the "captain's log" of a ship, the route book contains notes about each stand: where, when, conditions, attendance, anything noteworthy about the performance or anything else that happened.

Route Card - A bare bones schedule published for wide distribution, listing the season's stands by date. Circus route cards are valuable information for performers and valuable souvenirs for collectors.

Rubber Cows - Affectionate term for elephants.

Rubbermen - Strolling balloon vendors. Balloons were blown up with air and attached to sticks. Helium-filled balloons were expensive and unsold ones don't last long.

Run - A show that lasts for more than a day. The Ringling show at Tattersals in Chicago in 1895 lasted four weeks. It was a four week run.

Runs - Ramps to load and unload wagons at the railroad cars.

Safety Loop - The loop part of a web rope into which a performer places her wrist in aerial ballet numbers.

School Show - A show promoted for classroom field trips to the circus.

Screamers - Standard circus march tunes, so called because they are usually played with great vigor.

(to) See the Elephant - The circus origin of this phrase is obvious. It passed into general popular usage about 1835 meaning "to have seen everything there is to see in the world."

Seventeen Wagon - The wagon where paychecks are distributed.

Shanty or Chandelier - The man who works the lights.

Shill - One who pretends to play a game, or to buy a ticket to an attraction, in order to entice others to join or follow him. Shills lead the way and "break the ice" or tension in a crowd. Once the shill spends the money, others will follow.

Showman's Rest - Two sites share this name. A section of Mt. Olivet Cemetery in Hugo, Oklahoma, is the final resting place of many proud circus and carnival veterans. There is a similar section of the Woodlawn Cemetery in Chicago, overseen by the Showmen's League of America, created when eighty six performers and workers of the Hagenbeck-Wallace Circus were killed in a 1918 train wreck. Fifty six of the victims are buried there. Many of them remained unidentified because they were known only by their "handles."

Showmen's League of America - Founded in 1913 by a group of outdoor showmen meeting at the Saratoga Hotel in Chicago. The League promotes the image of the circus and carnival and performs charitable work. Buffalo Bill Cody was the club's first president.

Side Poles - Short poles at the outer edge of the top canvas.

Sixteen Wagon - The show office wagon.

Sky Boards - The decorative boards, sometimes detachable, around the tops of wagons used in parades.

Slack Wire - A wirewalker's wire that is set up slightly slack, creating a much less firm footing than a tight wire.

Slanger - Trainer of cats.

Sledge Gang - Crew of men who pounded in tent stakes.

Slide For Life - Usually performed by a woman who would climb to the top of the building, hook a hand loop or a foot loop to a cable connected to the top beam and the floor, and slide down the cable. An acrobat named Herbie Webber would do such a slide standing on the cable, even sliding down backwards, adding a fake fall during his wire act. Later, taking a fake fall became known as "Taking a Herbie." The purpose of the fake fall is to remind the audience of how dangerous the act really is. It keeps the audience on edge. It is not used as often in modern circus. Some say that the fake fall took more skill than not doing it.

Slop Shoes - Wooden clogs with leather uppers, easy to slip on and off hands-free. Worn by performers over their performing footwear, to keep costumes clean while walking to and from the big top.

Snubber - A pulley and cable on the side of a railroad flatcar, used to slow a wagon coming down the runs (ramps) to the ground.

Soft Lot - A wet or muddy lot, also called a **Frog Pond.**

Spanish Web - A long fabric covered rope suspended vertically from far above, which may be used to climb to an aerialist's apparatus, or on which an aerialist might perform.

Spec - Short for "spectacle." A colorful pageant which is a featured part of the show; formerly used as the opening numbers, now presented just before intermission. Sometimes called the "Production Number."

Spec Girls - Showgirls who appear in the spec.

Splash Boards - Decorated boards, sometimes detachable, around the bottom edge of wagons used in parades.

Spool Truck, Spool Wagon - Truck which carries the tent canvas.

Stake Bites - The ankle wounds caused by the sharp metal tent stakes. These were often caused by walking into them at night. As the stakes get older the repeated sledge hits bent the edges and left them razor sharp.

Stalls - The medium cost seats in the auditorium. A less favorable viewing position to the left and the right of the grandstand. Also, horse stalls in the railcars, which were padded and allowed little room for the horses to fall if the train ride became rough.

Stand - Any town where the show plays just one day, usually a matinee and an evening performance. It is the origin of "one night stand."

Star Backs - More expensive seats, usually indicated by painted stars on the seat backs.

Stars and Stripes Forever - The band reserved this Sousa march as a signal that an emergency had come up, calling for the clowns to come running out, directing public attention away from the emergency, or for the audience to be evacuated. It was first used c. 1898 for the circus. Before that, each show had different "emergency" musical scores.

St. Louis - Doubles or seconds of food, named because the St. Louis engagement was played in two sections.

Strap Act - A variation of the "Spanish Web" popularized in Cirque du Soleil, the strap act features acrobatics performed with the use of "aerial straps," long straps hanging from the top of the tent, reaching almost to the floor. The act often includes dance moves on the floor away from the straps, as well as having the straps pulled partway up and let down during the act.

Straw House - A sold out house. Straw was spread on ground for spectators to sit on in front of the general admission seats.

Stringers or Blues - The general admission seats.

Suitcase Act - A performer who has no costumes or equipment of his own (and so shows up with just a suitcase).

Swag - Midway game prizes, or souvenirs and toys bought from vendors.

Sway Pole - An act in which the performer perches atop an extremely tall pole, then sways and rocks the pole giddily from side to side. Often played for laughs, it is very dangerous to perform.

Tableau Wagons - Ornamental parade wagons on which colorfully dressed performers ride.

Tack Spitter - Banner man or bill poster.

Tail Up - Command to an elephant to follow in line.

Tanbark - Shredded tree bark, more durable and manageable than sawdust, used to cover the greater circus arena ground.

Taps - Businesses that have bought groups of tickets in the past, e.g. "Maybe we can tap them again this year."

Teeterboard - A board like a playground teeter-totter, usually about six feet long, used in an acrobatic act. The performer stands on the lowered end of the board and his partners jump onto the upper end, vaulting him into the air.

Title - The name under which a circus presents itself, regardless of the name of the actual owner of the show, e.g. Feld Entertainment owns Ringling Bros. Barnum & Bailey Greatest Show on Earth and as such has the "Title."

Toby News - Gossip found only on the lot.

Top - Technically refers to the canvas on the top of the tent; however, tents are often referred to as "tops": Big Top, Round Top, Dressing Top, etc.

Train Master - The person responsible for the various aspects of the train, such as the razorbacks, the animal cars, sleepers, etc.

Trouper - A veteran performer. Spends a full season with a show and takes responsibility for the circus family.

Trunk Up - Command to an elephant to raise his trunk in a salute.

Turn - Any act in the show; you do your turn.

Turnaway - A sold out show.

Twenty-four-hour Man - An advance man who travels one day ahead of circus. Usually puts up "arrows" to guide trucks on the jump.

Under Canvas - Term used to describe shows that operate in Big Tops – tented shows.

Under the Stars - To show outside without a tent. The entire show set up with seating, rings, etc. without a tent over them. Also "showed or played with sides only." Sometimes it was just too windy, while other times the Big Top had been damaged by a blowdown.

Walls - Canvas side walls of a tent, as distinguished from the roof or "top." Also called side sheets.

Walkaround - A clown feature in which they stroll through the crowd and perform comic bits interacting with audience members.

Water Wagon - The water wagon circulated around the lot dispensing water for numerous uses: filling water buckets for performers to wash in, watering the animals, spraying the ground to keep the dust down, filling the drinking water barrels placed around the lot (they had blocks of ice in them and a tin cup on a chain), and hosing down the elephants.

Weather - Bad weather.

Web - Dangling, canvas covered rope suspended from swivels from the top of the tent.

Web Girl - Female who performs on the "Spanish Web."

Web Sitter - Ground man who holds or controls the web for aerialists.

(to) Wildcat - To change the announced route on short notice due to problems on the planned route, abandoning the benefit of already-placed advance advertising and possibly conflicting with the usual territories played by competing shows. Major droughts or layoffs might mean that nobody would have the price of a ticket, or a animal disease epidemic might make it inadvisable to take valuable livestock into an area.

Windjammer - A member of a circus band.

Windy Van Hootens - An imaginary term for the perfect circus. It is often used in slang, "Yep – real Windy Van Hooten!" Could be a description of a show that paid performers and employees everything they deserved while every show was a straw show (sold out).

Wood - Phony ticket sales slips submitted by boiler room agents to inflate their commissions just before they leave.

Zanies or Zanni - Clowns.

About The Fifty One Rules

The Ringlings began their first shows with rules of conduct for themselves as far back as the Concert Company. When they noticed other shows had problems stemming from pickpocketers to grafters, they realized that being clean and moral was the best way to success. After a murder on their own lot when two drinking roustabouts got into a fight, they began the "Fifty One Rules." The rules were added to over the years. It earned them the nickname "The Sunday School Circus," as other show people made fun of them. It helped them to climb to unimaginable heights of success. Many rules were also for dress codes and safety. Circus life was dangerous, and workers were sometimes sliced in half or lost limbs in train accidents. The Ringlings never had a Red Tent, also called a Cooch Tent. These were burlesque shows, and the girls who danced there were often called Coochie Girls. Their concept was family and family values. This list was made after the Ringlings owned both The Barnum & Bailey Greatest Show on Earth and The Ringling Brothers Worlds Greatest Shows.

The Fifty One Rules

Suggestions and Rules Employees Ringling Brothers Circus Circa 1910

The object of these rules and suggestions is not to limit the employees in the enjoyment of their rights, but rather to promote harmony and goodwill, and co-operate with our employees in conducting our institution in a business-like, high-standard manner.

The personal appearance and behavior of each individual is important, not only in so far as the relations of employee with employee are concerned, but equally as much for the impression we make on the public. We should want the "town folks" to feel that the "show folks" are real men and women and ladies and gentlemen as well.

Undoubtedly few of us would adopt a course opposite to some of the rules given; however, the rules are made to protect the majority against imposition by the few who might thoughtlessly annoy and disturb:

1. Be cleanly and neat in dress and avoid loud display.

2. Absence from work will not be permitted without making arrangement with your department head. If this is not possible and you are unavoidably absent, you must send information at the earliest possible moment in order that your place may be filled; and on your return, immediately give explanation of cause of absence. In case you should be ill and not able to leave the cars, you must immediately notify the head porter, who will send a message to the show grounds.

3. No employees will be permitted to loan money to other employees and receive any profit from the transaction.

4. Gambling, especially in the cars or near the cars, on or near the show ground, is strictly prohibited.

IN THE CARS

5. No pet animals, revolvers, intoxicants or inflammables allowed in the sleeping cars. Candles must not be used in the cars; if an individual light is wanted, supply a "flash light" type electric. No others will be allowed.

6. No smoking in cars at any time.

7. Loud talking, singing, playing upon musical instruments, or disturbing noises in or near the cars must stop at 11 P.M.

8. Do not clean teeth at wash-bowls.

9. Cooking is prohibited in the cars.

10. Be considerate in using toilet rooms.

CAUTION - Look both ways; be careful in crossing railroad tracks or in walking upon same.

AT THE DINING TENT

11. No dogs allowed in the dining room during meal time.

12. Coats must be worn in the dining room at meal time.

13. When the "HOTEL" flag is up the meal is ready; when the blue flag is up the meal is over.

14. No food nor dishes can be taken from the dining room without permission.

15. Drinking glasses are thoroughly washed and rinsed. Do not waste water washing them at the drinking tank.

16. People bringing friends into dining room to eat will purchase meal tickets at the commissary wagon.

17. MEAL HOURS: Breakfast will be over at 9:15, excepting on late arrival of show. Lunch will be over at 12:45 noon.

18. People will remain outside the guard rope until the flag is raised.

TO PERFORMERS

19. Take the same care of company wardrobe as you do your own; do not sit on dirty boxes, pedestals, wagons, on the ground, etc., while wearing spectacle costumes.

20. Ladies must return bundled wardrobe to wardrobe mistress as soon as possible.

21. Gentlemen must fold costumes and place in proper location.

22. Do not bring liquors or intoxicants into the dressing rooms.

23. Remain outside of Big Tent until time for your act or assistance.

24. Do not take strangers or friends into dressing rooms without permission.

25. Cooking, making coffee will not be allowed in dressing rooms.

26. In going from dressing tents to dining tents do not pass through the menagerie or circus tents, and never pass through the main entrance.

27. Do not chew gum while taking part in spectacle.

28. Male performers are not to visit with the ballet girls. The excuse of "accidental" meetings on Sunday, in parks, at picture shows, etc., will not be accepted.

29. The use of alcohol or gasoline irons for pressing is strictly prohibited on show grounds or in the cars.

30. Do not lounge in wardrobe department of dressing rooms.

31. Do not practice or rehearse in main tent after 6:30 P.M.

32. Do not change position of trunks as placed in the dressing room.

33. Do not play ball in the main tent or "back yard."

34. Employees listed for Street Parade must be dressed and ready to "mount" at 10 o'clock am, unless notified to report earlier.

35. Do not run horses to "catch up" in parade - be on hand in time.

36. Do not sit "crossed legged" on floats or tableaux wagons.

37. Button up coats, etc.

38. Absolutely, do not chew (gum or tobacco) or smoke in parade.

40. Report to the management at once any accident you may observe which may have been caused by the parade.

41. Do not loiter about the "front" of the show grounds.

42. Do not nod to friends or acquaintances who may be in the audience.

43. Avoid arguments with other employees. Be agreeable and promote harmony.

Since you have chosen to travel with the circus, it is evident that your success depends upon the success of circuses in general, and the one by which you are employed in particular. Therefore, the greater the success of the circus, and especially the part of that success to which you contribute, the better it is for you and the more valuable you will be in your profession. - Don't overlook this point - do your best - it is for you first and the company second.

BALLET GIRLS

All the foregoing rules and suggestions will also apply for the government of the Ballet Girls. In addition thereto the following especial rules are given for their guidance:

1. Do not dress in a flashy, loud style; be neat and modest in appearance.

2. You are required to be in the sleeping car and register your name not later than 11 P.M. and not to leave car after registering.

3. Girls must not stop at Hotels at any time.

4. You are not permitted to talk or visit with male members of the Show Company, excepting the management, and under no circumstances with residents of the cities visited.

6. The excuse of "accidental" meetings will not be accepted.

7. You must be in the ballet dressing room at 1 o'clock for matinee and at 7 o'clock P.M. for night performance.

8. You must not go into the big dressing room.

NOTE - If some of the rules seem harsh and exacting, please remember - experience has taught the management that they are necessary. It is intended to protect the girls in every possible way. Good order and good behavior are necessary, if you are to be comfortable and happy. The management urges each girl to live up to the spirit of the rules as well as to the letter.

Acknowledgements

I hope no one finds me at fault for omitting anyone in my acknowledgements. So many people have come forward to support this project. I will do my best. First I wish to thank the five original Ringling brothers for living their dreams and sending forth a legacy of vision and hard work. They have truly inspired me. I must thank and acknowledge my wife Barbara and my daughter Amrit for listening to me talk about this for so long. Barbara has listened to my "Ringling speak" for over thirty years and Amrit for her entire life. I honor the memory of my mother, Betty Warren, and her wonderment, for walking on Bayshore Road in 1948, looking at the great Ringling properties, and wondering, "Who are these people?" I must acknowledge the family members who have shared the stories directly with me: my father, Stuart Gage Lancaster, the grandson of Charles Ringling; Aunt Knobby, Alice Lancaster *nee* Alice Knobloch, who wanted so badly for me to tell the story her way; Kirk Ringling and John Ringling North II, both of whom I have never met in person but have willingly opened doors for me; and my older brother John Lancaster, aka Guruatma Khalsa, who expressed to me a sense and familiarity with Sarasota that I was too young to experience, and who as a youngster jumped in front of a lion cub to save me as it bit his stomach! Special thanks to Lori Musil Levacy for her coaching on equestrian understanding and terminology. I would also like to thank Peter Shrake of The Robert L Parkinson Library and Research Center at Circus World, and Stephen Freese, executive director of Circus World. In Sarasota I owe a special thank you to Ron McCarty, curator at the Ca' d'Zan Mansion; Larry Kelleher of Sarasota History Alive; the curatorial department at The Witte Museum in San Antonio, TX, and Mr. Bob Horne, whose mere presence is the very mirth of circus, for his willingness to share countless stories from those who were there. And finally I must thank Ivan Henry, fourth generation showman who, even as I am finishing my work is breathing the life breath of circus into my life and thus into my stories.

    I cannot express enough thanks to my editor, Steven Davis, who has both demonstrated the need for discipline and pushed me to be more disciplined. Both Judy Nelson-Moore and Jennifer Drumm have been my digital pals all the while listening to my stories while they helped design the web site and the book cover. Finally, I thank my mother who in her wisdom and teaching to her students said, "There comes a time when a painter must put down the brush and walk away from the easel." The following authors have contributed, even if they can't always agree: David Weeks, Jerry Apps, Gene Plowden, Chappy Fox, Henry Ringling North and Alden Hatch, and Alf T. Ringling. To everyone, who has been there for me, I say, "May all your days be circus days!"

Michael Lancaster